# S'postu

To Ted.
Don't stop writing!
Best Regards,

# S'postu

Lee E. Foster

Writers Club Press
San Jose New York Lincoln Shanghai

S'postu

Writers Club Press
an imprint of iUniverse.com, Inc.

For information address:
iUniverse.com, Inc.
620 North 48th Street, Suite 201
Lincoln, NE 68504-3467
www.iuniverse.com

ISBN: 0-595-13241-3

Printed in the United States of America

To Patty, my absolute inspiration and timeless love.

# CONTENTS

# ACKNOWLEDGEMENTS

Immeasurable thanks to Kathy Shepard, Kevin and Cindy Batey, Kendra Lassiter and Eric Williams without whose constant support and encouragment this story would have never made it to paper.

# PART ONE

# CHAPTER 1

The windshield wipers slapped at the light rain as Alicia Freed turned her 1974 Pontiac into the Oakwood subdivision. She pulled the car over to the curb, "Think girl, is this really necessary?" she asked aloud. Her hands were cramped from their white-knuckled grip they had on the steering wheel. Closing her hazel eyes, she rested her forehead on them as if it would make her think better. Her long, greying brown hair fell in ringlets. Alicia drew a deep breath and opened her eyes. She reached down out of habit for another sip of coffee, but found the cup empty. It was just as well; she was jittery from the caffeine already.

"S'postu," she asked aloud, "do I really hafta do this?"

"Yes," said the voice in her head, "you know you do."

Coffee or not, she fought sleep. It had been forty years since she pulled an all-nighter and at fifty-eight, she could barely cope. Alicia exhaled and raised her head from the steering wheel.

"Ok, S'postu, you know I'm scared!" she pleaded, hoping maybe, knowing how she felt, S'postu might let her forget the whole thing.

The voice in her head commanded, "Be still, my child, everything will be fine if you will just listen to me and do what I say." It was obvious to her he would make her go through with it despite how she felt. "Yes, child, I've waited for you for a long time. Your forebearers couldn't hear me. You are the first. Now do what you said you would do and remember what I suffered at the hands of his kin."

Alicia felt a sharp pain at the back of her skull, as if someone had struck her. She cupped the back of her head knowing this was only a small taste of what would come if she refused.

"Ok, ok, S'postu, I'm goin'!" she yelled. The pain stopped instantly. After hesitating, to gather courage, she reached down and picked up a small notepad. In the cold, grey early morning light, the address was barely visible: 1842 Palm Road. She placed the note pad back on the seat, and picked up a Knoxville City map to remind her of the directions. The highlighted streets and roads made it easy to find the home of Charles Westchester. She tossed the map back on the seat and began to drive slowly, her thoughts in violent conflict.

The light rain stopped as she turned right on Palm Road and parked across the street from 1842. From the driver's door window, Alicia studied the house. It was finished with red multishaded brick. A gable roof connected the front porch to the attic, supported by white Greek-style columns. Black shutters on each side window added a charming touch. This modern Colonial style house appealed to her since it was a nice change from her own, a 200-year-old large wood frame house on 400 acres of partially wooded land in the country.

Rain droplets glistened on the neatly trimmed lawn. A sidewalk ran from the street to the porch, with a flower garden on each side. Sprouts of plants she could not identify sat in neat rows leading up to the porch. She had a clear view of the front door.

Alicia reached into her large handbag, and pulled out a ten-inch carving knife. Anxiety approaching nausea swelled in her stomach like butterflies on steroids. She forced herself to calm down enough to glance at the fuel gauge. It read half full. There was enough gas to sit and run the engine for a while, not knowing when Westchester would leave for work. Alicia gripped the knife so hard her knuckles turned white. She waited, barely breathing, her eyes fixed on the front door.

"S'postu?" Alicia asked aloud.

"Yes, my child."

"I don't think I can go through with this. You know I've never hurt anyone before, and I'm scared."

"I'll help you. Just let your feelings go. Trust yourself to me and I'll do the rest."

"O-Okay," Alicia shook with fear. S'postu had never done anything or spoken to her like this before. "H-how'll you do that?"

"Clear your mind and let me in."

"But I can hear you, ain't you already in?"

"It's not the same. Right now I can only speak to you. Relax as if you were falling asleep, and I will do what I must do."

"Why, S'postu? What're we doin' here?" She was almost afraid of the answer.

"I must avenge myself against the kin of my betrayer."

She trembled, eyes glued to Westchester's front door. Nausea crept through her and her ears began to ring.

Charles Westchester finished in the bathroom and headed into the kitchen where Nadine, his wife, was busy at the sink with the breakfast dishes. He stopped for a moment in the dining room to watch her staring out the window, her mind a million miles away. He knew she was traveling the same road in her mind she had gone down too many times these past few weeks. He wanted to talk to her about it but didn't want to throw salt in an open wound. *It wouldn't matter anyway, the conversation would come up all by itself.* He approached her. She extended her left cheek toward him. *The mechanism of 34 years of marriage.* He kissed her quickly without breaking stride on his way to the calendar hanging on the wall, then pulled out a ballpoint pen from his shirt pocket. *Maybe this vacation will be enough to take her mind off the situation—maybe it would be enough to take my mind off it, too.*

"You know, my love," Charles said as he took the calendar off the wall, "I never really looked at this picture before."

"It's beautiful," Nadine replied somberly, her eyes still fixed on the window.

The picture on the calendar showed palm trees silhouetted against a beautiful ocean sunset. The pomegranate red of the sun shimmered on the water, reflecting off the blue and white crashing waves. He could almost hear the ocean in his ears. Charles angled the calendar to cut the glare from the fluorescent kitchen light, and read the words under the picture.

"Lahaina Beach, Maui. Sure wish we were there right now."

Nadine smiled at him. "We will be soon enough. How long do you have left?"

*Were there tears in her eyes?* Charles placed the calendar on the counter, and drew an X in the box marking out May 9, 1978. "Thirty-one days and counting. But you already know that. You've been counting too." *This whole conversation feels like such a facade. I sound hollow, just like I feel. If we could go on as if nothing happened, maybe that would comfort her. No, that would just be a lie. This whole thing started with a lie. Lies beget lies, and would only make things worse.*

"Well," Nadine said, "we've waited all our lives for this trip and I don't want anything to spoil it."

He looked lovingly at his wife. They had planned to go to Hawaii for their honeymoon, but the war made it impossible when they were first married. After that, it had been lack of money, and they never went. He knew she always held that against him, although she never said anything. Now the trip was threatened by the death of their son. Not merely his death alone, but the added almost unbearable pain of suicide. Even worse, after he died they found out about Charles Jr.'s four year affair and illegitimate child. He turned and hung the calendar back on the wall, then held his wife tenderly.

"Sweetheart," he said, squeezing her comfortably, "I'd better not be late or they'll fire me before I can retire." His words were measured and deliberate. *Another facade.*

"Oh Charles," Nadine sobbed, "how could this have happened? I thought we raised Charles Jr. better than that. Where did we fail?" She buried her face in his shoulder.

"We didn't fail honey, he was a grown man." *How many times have I told myself this? Maybe one more time and I can start to believe it myself.* "There comes a point when you have to let your kids go out on their own and trust them to do the right thing. Charles Jr. was an adult. We couldn't be with him every moment and tell him what to do—you know, we couldn't live his life for him. Every parent has to let their kids go, you know that."

"Yes, but Charles, he put a gun in his mouth and pulled the trigger. A GUN! Right in front of his wife! How could he do that to us?"

"To us? To us? Nadine, he didn't do that to us. It wasn't about us. It wasn't about us at all. It was about him. It was a decision he made when Nancy found out about his affair with that whore in his office. It was about guilt that he couldn't live with. It was about his cowardice."

"Are you calling our son a coward?" Nadine almost sneered.

"Yes. What else would you call it? We raised him right, Nadine. We raised him to be a man. And a man doesn't run from his problems. Especially ones that he created."

Nadine knew he was right. Yet she felt betrayed by her son for taking the easy way out and leaving them, *leaving her,* with this awful self-guilt and overwhelming sense of loss. Lashing out at Charles was just a way to relieve some of her pain and grief. She looked up at him. *Now here is a man who has stood by my side faithfully for over three decades. Through thick and thin. Through good times and bad. This is most certainly the bad. He will be here for me like he always has and we'll get through this.* She forced a smile and pecked him on the lips. It was time to change the subject. "Ok, I'll see you when you get home."

"I love you."

*I know you do, honey.*

Charles turned toward the door and grasped the knob. The latch released and the door cracked open.

"Wait Charles," Nadine called. "You forgot your briefcase."

Charles stood with the door half open as Nadine approached him with the briefcase. He grasped it with his left hand, but she would not release it.

"Sorry," she said, "I didn't mean to get into this right before you have to leave for work and ruin your whole day. You know I love you even though I sometimes don't show it too well."

"Darlin', there's nothing you can do to ruin my day. It's okay. I'll be fine. I'll call you a bit later this morning, okay?"

"Okay."

He smiled and bent to kiss her. Nadine released the briefcase and Charles stepped out the door. *Maybe the worst was over. After all, the rain had stopped and the sun was coming out. Besides, what else could happen?*

Alicia saw the front door open and immediately swung open the car door. As her feet touched the ground, S'postu overwhelmed her, and she felt suddenly powerful and free. The last of her will dissipated as cool jolts of electricity coursed through her, filling her with an extra corporeal energy. She watched herself move like a young woman. She was frightened and struggled to regain control of her body, but S'postu was too strong for her fatigued state.

Leaving the car door open, she felt herself walk briskly across the street, step onto the curb, and cross the sidewalk. She saw a man standing in the doorway, and assumed he must be Charles Westchester, kissing a woman, evidently his wife. She ran toward the porch, as the woman disappeared behind the closed door. Alicia's forearm ached from gripping the knife. Charles spun around and Alicia leapt onto the porch. Their eyes met. She hesitated as two forces fought for control inside her. Then she saw Charles' eyes widen, and felt her arm draw, wielding the knife.

"Your blood for his! S'postu—this to avenge S'postu!" Alicia shrieked.

The knife plunged into his left shoulder, cutting through the fabric of his suit jacket and into his flesh. Each second seemed an eternity. Charles screamed as his shoulder recoiled, fear overcame the pain as he felt his blood soak through his shirt. Her sweet perfume mixed with the odor of his salty-metallic blood, assaulting his nostrils.

Alicia drew the dripping knife back and began a second relentless attack. Charles instinctively swung his briefcase around, slamming it into her left shoulder. He didn't want to hurt this woman, he just wanted her to stop. As the briefcase swung around, the knife missed his chest and caught him in the left arm, slicing into his flesh and glancing off the bone. Again, Charles cried out in pain. The briefcase sent Alicia sprawling as the knife flew from her hand and landed on the grass.

Nadine heard the commotion and ran to the door. She opened it just in time to see Alicia careen off the porch. The weight of the briefcase sent Charles off balance, and she caught him as he slumped down. She staggered under his weight and could only let him down slowly.

Charles groaned in agony. The memory of Alicia's sickeningly-sweet perfume made him vomit.

Bewildered and terrified, Nadine knelt behind him, her arms under his and across his chest. She felt a warm liquid flow over her left hand and looked down to see blood gushing out of his arm and shoulder. Nadine began to shake uncontrollably as Charles looked agonizingly at her.

"Call…for help…" his words trailed off as he lost consciousness.

Nadine carefully laid him down in a pool of blood and vomit and stumbled frantically to the phone.

The blow from the briefcase brought her back to her senses and Alicia resumed control of her body. Waves of fear washed over her as she instinctively ran toward her car.

"S'postu, S'postu, what have I done? What have you made me do?" Alicia yelled as she leapt behind the steering wheel, slammed the door, threw it into drive, and stomped the accelerator. The right rear tire spun wildy on the wet street, sending huge swirls of smoke billowing as the car hurtled forward.

"S'postu, I'm real scared. I can't believe you made me hurt that man," she screamed to the thin air. The voice in her head remained silent.

As Nadine dialed the phone, she looked out the kitchen window just in time to see a woman running for a large blue car, jump in and speed down the street. She got a glimpse of the license plate.

"Operator," said the voice at the other end of the line.

"Help me," Nadine screamed. "My husband's just been stabbed!"

"Calm down," the voice said. "I'll call the paramedics."

Nadine yelled, "Oh, I can see her tags, S-T-D-2-0…oh!…I can't see the last number. It's a big blue car…I need an ambulance…NOW!"

# CHAPTER 2

Alicia turned the Pontiac into her driveway and parked next to the kitchen door. The adrenalin was beginning to wear off, leaving her utterly drained. As she walked up the back porch steps, she found each one harder to climb than the last. She fumbled with her keys and stumbled into her kitchen.

"S'postu, talk to me. S'postu? S'postu–?" Alicia hollered to the empty house. He remained silent. Rage filled her. She felt abandoned and used.

"Fine!" she yelled. "You want to be silent, I'll make you silent!"

"I'm sorry I hurt you, my child," S'postu replied cautiously. "I never intended to hurt you."

"Why didn't you talk to me? I thought you left me."

"I was only thinking of my revenge. Now, that the passion has left me, my spirit weeps for your destiny."

"What d'ya mean? All that was for nothin'?" Alicia was more enraged than ever. "You made me hurt that man for no reason? I'm sick of you. I want my own life." She threw her things onto the kitchen counter and looked around desperately. All she wanted to do was find something to hurt S'postu. Her eyes settled on the electric can opener. She grabbed it from the counter and quickly walked out of the kitchen, too angry to see that it was still plugged in. When the cord reached its length, the can opener ripped from her grip and fell to the floor. Alicia spun around and looked down.

"Tore it out of my hand, did you?" she yelled as she bent down and grabbed it off the floor. "Well, take this!" She stepped into the dining room and hurled it through a pane of glass in the French doors leading into the sunroom. The can opener slammed against the far wall and came to rest as shards of glass scattered across the hardwood floor, glinting in the mid-morning light.

Suddenly, the kitchen sink faucet came on. Alicia ran to the sink and turned it off, then yanked open a drawer and grabbed a flat-blade screwdriver.

"Go ahead, S'postu," she snarled, "turn on all the water you want," and walked to the French doors. "I'll get even with you. I know what you love, and I know what will keep you out of my life." She opened the French doors and bent down to remove their screws. But they would not give up their century-old grip easily. Alicia turned the screwdriver with all her strength. A loud crack broke the morning silence as each screw broke loose. When she finished removing the lower hinge, she grabbed a chair from the dining room table and began to attack the screws that held the top hinge.

Suddenly, the light above the dining table came on. Alicia looked at the switch on the wall, still in the off position. She smiled wickedly.

"What are you doing, S'postu? You're not gonna change my mind. These doors are coming off."

"Please stop, my child." His voice thundered in her head. Alicia continued her work, and the door came loose from its frame. She jumped off the chair and carried it to the wall. Then she went to the next door and began to remove it the same way.

"Please stop, my child," S'postu pleaded. "My voice to you is fading, if you keep going, I won't be able to talk to you."

His voice was indeed softer, and for a moment Alicia almost reconsidered when she thought of the times, as a little girl, S'postu relieved her loneliness, while at the same time, his presence was the brunt of jokes from her childhood playmates. At least until she realized she had to keep him a secret. Even then, she was known to the other children as "Wacky Alicia"; the name even stuck through her adolescence. How bitter it was to be an outcast. Now she was not only an outcast, but a fugitive as well.

The light from the dining room chandelier became brighter. She looked up and shaded her eyes. White light washed through the room as she felt heat radiating from the bulbs.

"You don't have the strength to talk, but you have the strength to play these games? I don't think so. These doors are coming off, and I will be rid of you!" Alicia was now more determined than ever and returned to her work. The light got brighter and brighter, and the heat from the bulbs was so intense that beads of sweat appeared on her forehead. One by one, the five light bulbs in the chandelier burst. Each explosion sent hot shards of glass flying through the room. Searing pain slashed her brow. Alicia touched her forehead and a line of blood dripped from her fingertips.

"And now you've hurt me?" she cried out in disbelief. The second French door came loose. She carried it over and leaned it against the first one. After dragging the chair into the next room, she began to remove a second set of French doors in the living room.

"You see, S'postu," Alicia said, "I will probably go to jail for what you made me do, and if I'm gonna be in prison, then so are you!"

She carried the third door into the dining room, and leaned it against the second. As she came back into the room, the television flared to life.

"Look," she said sternly, "enough of these distractions." She slid it back a bit from the wall, and pulled the plug. The television immediately went off.

Alicia went to the final French door. The very instant the screwdriver touched the screw, the television came on again. Alicia quickened her pace, her arm ached from twisting out the ancient screws.

"S'postu," Alicia yelled, "stop it! Stop it now or I'll break every pane of glass in these doors. I know these doors are your favorite thing about this house, I doubt you'll want them broken." Alicia finished with the bottom hinge and stood on top of the chair to remove the last three screws.

The television volume rose with each turn of the screwdriver. The glass panes on the doors began to vibrate to the music of some game show—an obvious, desperate act to get her to stop. It would not work in spite of the fact that Alicia's arm hurt, and was almost too painful to continue. One screw remained. The volume was now so loud, the distorted sound pierced her ears. With the last screw almost out, the noise became unbearable, and the panes vibrated so violently she thought they might shatter at any second. The moment the screw cleared the hole and the hinge fell away from the door jamb, the television fell silent. The house rumbled as if with a small earthquake: S'postu's final desperate act. She knew he was asleep when an empty feeling hung over her, and for the first time since she could remember, she felt completely alone. It was clear to her that they were connected somehow. For all the good he was to her, he had caused her just as much pain, and this Westchester incident was the last straw.

She rummaged about the house, gathering four old blankets, eight large plastic trash bags, and a roll of masking tape. She wrapped each door in a blanket, covered them with the trash bags, and secured each package with tape. Because she was so tired, she considered moving them later, but decided if she didn't do it now, she might lose the nerve, and hauled them out to the loft in the barn. She would decide later what to do with them.

Completely exhausted, Alicia stumbled back into the house. She was famished but too tired to eat.

She suddenly had the urge to go into the sunroom and look out the window. Why was she going in there? Could S'postu still be controlling her? Since she still felt empty, and didn't feel those cool jolts of electricity, she was sure it wasn't him. Certainly, S'postu was asleep. Pushing the thought aside, she headed into the sunroom, too tired to question or fight.

As she crossed the threshold of the now absent French doors, she stopped to look at the holes in the door jamb that the hinge screws left behind, and reached up to touch them.

"Sleep, S'postu, sleep," she said aloud. Her voice echoed as if she were in an empty house. She peered out the window to look across the yard. In the distance were the great Smokey Mountains. The earlier rainstorm had left scattered, low-lying clouds in the hollows, which looked like smoke hanging in the heavy air, a trait the region was famous for.

"What a beautiful morning," she said to herself, trying to push the morning's events away.

The clouds had broken up and beams of sunlight cascaded down on the new spring leaves. They glistened from the clinging raindrops. Alicia yawned, turned and headed for bed.

The house had three bedrooms, two upstairs which were used as guest rooms, while she used the lower one. As she crossed the threshold of her bedroom, she felt a severe drop in temperature. It was much colder than the rest of the house. *S'postu is asleep, and now my bedroom is cold?* Even though this was something new, she was simply too tired to care.

She laid down on her bed and tried to sleep. But sleep was elusive. The image of Charles Westchester with his eyes wide open, pain slashed across his face, would not leave her. Tears formed in her closed eyes. *What have I done? How could S'postu have ever talked me into hurting that man?* She'd never met Westchester before. His name came to her one day and S'postu would not let her rest until she finally looked him up in the city phone book. S'postu had haunted Alicia all her life, and she felt immense relief knowing that he would not bother her again. Yet aching in the back of her mind, she knew she would miss him. The thought left her as cold as her room.

Fragile sleep finally came, but only from pure exhaustion.

# CHAPTER 3

Nadine Westchester was sitting quietly next to her husband's hospital bed, thumbing through a magazine, wrestling her thoughts between Charles and their son. Her mind was consumed with nothing except Charles Jr. since his suicide four months earlier, and now this attack on her husband had left her on the brink of a nervous breakdown. The lone streak of silver lining was that her attention was becoming more focused on her husband instead of her son. Somehow, seeing Charles lying on that bed in front of her made her see her own self pity. *Charles was right, we didn't kill Charles Jr. We didn't make him have that affair. We didn't lie to Nancy for four years. We didn't make him father an illegitimate child with that damn hussy at his office. He did that all by himself. We didn't know anything about it until the very end. My God! Who do I have to thank for this revelation? That murderous bitch.*

Detective Milton Salter walked into the room. She looked up and pressed her finger against her lips.

"Shh," she whispered, "he just got off to sleep." Her voice was barely audible above the beeps of the bedside cardiac monitor.

Salter reached around to his hip pocket, pulled out his wallet and displayed his police badge. Nadine stood and put the magazine in the chair when Salter motioned for her to follow him from the room. He quietly shut the door behind her.

"Nadine Westchester?" Salter asked, extending his hand.

"Yes," she answered, taking his hand.

"I'm Detective Milton Salter. Can I have a word with you?"

"Yes. Yes, of course."

"Now, as I understand it," Salter began, pulling a small notebook from his suit pocket, "you gave a partial license plate to the operator?" He thumbed through the pages.

"Yes, I think it was S-T-D or B, 2-0 something. I couldn't see the last number,"

Salter took notes as she spoke.

"Can you describe the woman that attacked your husband?"

Nadine exhaled slowly. "I only saw her from behind. She had on blue jeans and a brown, no, a light brown top." She went on to describe everything she had seen concerning her husband's attacker.

A man, whom Nadine assumed to be another detective, came up and spoke quietly into Salter's ear. Salter nodded.

"Mrs. Westchester, this is Detective Miller. He's helping me with this case."

Miller smiled briefly at her. Nadine returned the gesture.

Salter said to her, "Thank you, Ma'am. If I need anything else, I'll get in touch with you."

"Wait!" Nadine said quickly. "What about my husband? He was stabbed! What are you doing to find that witch?"

"Yes ma'am," he attempted to soothe her. "We're working on it now. Don't worry, we'll find her."

"But, did you get the knife?"

"Yes ma'am, we're running a fingerprint search on it now, but sometimes these things take time to sort out."

Nadine turned to go back into Charles' room. She was still in shock from the whole ordeal, and disappointed. It seemed to her that the police were really kind of impotent. All they seemed to do was ask the same questions over and over again. The uniformed police officer back at the house had just asked her the same questions. She couldn't see how they could come up with any answers from this repetitive questioning. *You people are useless.* Charles had done nothing to provoke such an act, and burning in the back of her mind were thoughts of Nancy and her grandchildren and, lastly, of how their retirement would be ruined. *If I ever find that woman, I'll strangle her with my bare hands for robbing us of what Charles and I have worked for all our lives.*

"Just one more thing, Mrs. Westchester," Salter broke her thoughts. "I know you were asked this before, but…"

"Yes?"

"Do you know of any reason why this woman would attack your husband?"

*Do you want me to do your job for you, too?* "No. I don't even know who she is. And I don't think Charles had ever laid eyes on her before, either."

"Thank you. I'll be in touch with you if I have any more questions." Salter handed her his business card. "If you think of anything later, here's my number." Nadine took the card and nodded, then went back to her husband.

Salter faced his partner. "What did you come up with on those plates?"

"Well," Miller replied, "there are two possibilities. One, a Norman Trelaine Hutchinson, here in Knoxville, and two, an Alicia Beatrice Freed with a Knox County address, we're checking that one out. It shows more promise since Mrs. Hutchinson died two years ago and Hutchinson never remarried. Neither car has been reported stolen."

"Where does this Freed woman live?"

"Uh," Miller began, looking at a notepad, "oh, here it is, Box 543, Rural Route 2."

"Where the hell is that?"

"It's on Highway 61, somewhere outside of Corryton. That's north of here."

"I know where Corryton is," Salter barked.

"I meant that Rural Route 2 is north of here."

"Well, Tom," Salter commanded, "don't just stand there holding down the tiles, check with the Post Office and find out how far north you're talkin' about so we can have a little chitchat. Go on, get to it!"

"Yes, Lieutenant," Miller replied, with a mock salute. "My ass has already left, the rest of me's gotta catch up with it."

Milton Salter smiled as he watched his subordinate and friend walk down the hallway laughing. He stuck his head in the door. "By the way," he whispered, "how is he doing?"

Nadine looked up from her magazine. "His shoulder will be sore for a while and the doctor doesn't know yet if the tendons in his arm will heal on their own, or if he'll need surgery," she said softly, frowning. Charles stirred slightly. "The doctor wants to keep him overnight for observation. Find that woman who did this to my husband."

Salter nodded and backed out of the doorway quietly.

Tom Miller was leaning against Salter's Plymouth Fury in the hospital parking lot.

"What are you still doing here?" Salter asked.

"I got directions to the Freed woman's house," Miller answered, holding up a piece of paper. "I thought you might like to come along."

Salter looked at his watch. "Sounds good, but I get to drive."

"I do." Miller retorted, pointing to his chest.

"All right, fine, but you get to buy lunch. You know I don't arrest well on an empty stomach."

"Deal," Miller laughed.

They discussed the case after lunch, as they drove north toward Corryton. After nearly an hour, they neared Alicia Freed's house. From the direction they were heading, the house was on the right side of the road. Miller slowed his unmarked police cruiser to a crawl to survey the situation before entering the driveway. The house was a large white Victorian-style farmhouse. All the curtains were drawn closed and from their vantage point, they could see no signs of life. They could see the gravel driveway as they passed slowly in front of the house. At the end of the driveway was a light blue Pontiac. Behind it, was an old barn with a large sliding door mounted on a track outside the building. The barn was a two-story building and looked large enough to house three or four horses below and a good sized loft for storing hay. Miller pulled the car into the driveway behind the Pontiac.

"When do you think this house was built?" Miller asked, bending to look at the structure through the passenger side window.

"I'd say maybe mid-1800's, give or take a decade," Salter answered, eyeing the structure. He shifted his attention to the car in front of them. "Check the plates."

"Got um," Miller answered, "S-T-D-2-0-8."

"Let's check it out," Salter said, leaving the car and walking over to the Pontiac.

Miller peered in the driver's side window and saw a notepad with Westchester's address and a highlighted map. Salter had his back to the car, looking for any sign of movement in the house.

"I'm thinking probable cause," Miller blurted out.

Salter spun around and looked into the car. "Oooh, nice," he said, smiling, "and we don't even need a warrant."

"Nothin' like leaving evidence in plain sight for us to see, is there?" Miller said as he opened the car door to retrieve the map.

Salter turned and headed for the back door of the house. "Let's see what's going on."  Miller followed.

Alicia stirred in her sleep. She was cold, and sometime in the last few hours had kicked off her shoes and pulled the covers up. Her sleep was not restful and she fidgeted often in a surreal dream world.

There were explosions all around her. In the distance, she could hear the sound of guns being fired, single shots fired one at a time. Men screamed as they were hit by bullets. Alicia crouched in the woods and stared into a clearing. The surrounding trees partially obstructed her view. She jumped at the sound of someone stepping on a twig. Alicia's stomach tightened as she moved a branch to get a better view. She looked down at her hands and saw that they were thick like a man's hands. The sleeves above them were the grey sleeves of a Confederate army uniform.

Not far away, she saw two men in blue uniforms through the trees. She recognized them as a two-man Union army reconnaissance team. How could she know who they were? Yet, she seemed to know things that she could not possibly have known. She knew the lay of the land, and that two other Confederate soldiers she trusted were not far away. There was someone, not too far south, whom she needed to get back to.

"RAT-TAT-TAT, RAT-TAT-TAT." More gunshots sounded in the distance. It had to be shots from different guns. Alicia was no historian, but she knew that there were no machine guns in the Civil War.

The reconnaissance team was watching something she couldn't see. As they started to move off, she leaned a bit to the right to keep them in sight, shifting her weight. A loud snap ripped through the air. The two men spun around, spotting her. One of them pointed his finger.

"There…!" he yelled.

The other man raised his rifle. She turned and as she began to run, a shot rang out. She felt a burning pain in her lower back and fell to the ground.

"RAT-TAT-TAT." More gunfire. Alicia jerked into consciousness.

"RAT-TAT-TAT." It was the sound of someone knocking on the glass mounted in the back door. *Now, who could that be?*

"RAT-TAT-TAT."

She threw the covers off and swung her legs over the side of the bed, and sat trying to wake up. She shivered. *Why is this room so cold now? And it feels so empty. Like S'postu has left me—with the cold feeling of death.* She stood up and stumbled out of her bedroom.

Her lower back hurt. Warm air hit her like a blast furnace as she crossed the threshold into the living room.

"RAT-TAT-TAT."

"I'm coming!" She tried to wipe the sleep from her eyes as she passed through the dining room, and almost ran into the wall that separated the dining room from the kitchen.

"RAT-TAT-TAT." *Whoever they were, they surely were impatient.*

"Don't get your panties in a wad!" Alicia yelled as she entered the kitchen. When she arrived at the back door, she hesitated for a second to draw a deep breath. Her hand trembled with fear when she moved the curtain aside to see who was at the door, and gasped at the sight of two men in business suits standing on the porch. *Oh my God, it's the cops.*

"Alicia Freed?" asked the man on the right. His voice was muffled by the glass that separated them.

"Yes."

"Police. We need to have a word with you. May we come in?"

Silently, Alicia opened the door, left it halfway open, and went into the living room. The two men entered and followed her.

Salter noticed the broken glass from the chandelier bulbs on the dining room table and crunching underfoot, and wondered what had happened. He wasn't sure if this was relevant to the task at hand, but made a mental note in case it was.

Alicia's mind was racing. She thought about making up some alibi as to her whereabouts that morning, but couldn't come up with a plausible lie. Her head hurt. Her lower back hurt. She was still shaken from her dream and now here were these two men. She simply could not take it. All she could do was sink into the armchair across from the sofa and wait. The two men sat. The one who had done the talking at the door spoke.

"I'm Lieutenant Milton Salter, and this is Detective Tom Miller." Alicia, shaking, nodded a greeting. Salter continued, "Let's get down to business. Where were you this morning between six-thirty and seven o'clock?"

Tears welled up in Alicia's eyes. Miller, who was still holding the map, laid it on the coffee table in front of him. She glanced down and locked her eyes on it.

"Looks like you already know where I was," she said slowly, wiping the tears from her eyes. The two men looked at each other. Miller reached over, picked up the map and stuffed it in his coat pocket. Alicia continued to stare at the spot on the coffee table where the map had been.

Salter stood up and reached around to his hip pocket, and produced a small card. He began to read: "You have the right to remain silent. Anything you say, can and will be used against you in a court of law."

Miller stood up and reached around to a clip on his belt and exhibited a pair of handcuffs.

"You have the right to an attorney." She caught a glimpse of metal in Miller's hand as it glinted in the sun. Handcuffs.

"If you cannot afford an attorney, one will be appointed to you by the court." Salters' voice droned on. Miller reached over and put a handcuff on Alicia's right hand, grabbed her left shoulder, and firmly, but gently turned her so that her back was to him. He secured her left hand with the other handcuff, and turned her to face him. Salter continued, "Do you understand these rights as I have read them?" Alicia looked up at the ceiling as reality dawned on her.

"Ma'am, do you understand?"

Alicia trembled violently. "SSSPPOOOSSTUUUU!" she screamed, "I hate you!"

"Miss Freed," Salter raised his voice, "do you understand?"

Alicia turned to face him. "Yes," she breathed.

Miller took hold of her left arm and began to lead her out of the room.

"Wait," she said abruptly, "my shoes, I need my shoes."

Miller looked down at her feet, then looked over at Salter. Salter cocked his head quickly toward his left shoulder, motioning for him to retrieve them.

"They're in my bedroom," Alicia instructed.

Miller led Alicia back to the armchair. She sat, back upright, the handcuffs digging into her wrists. Miller walked into her bedroom. As he crossed the threshold, he felt the sudden drop in temperature. He found her shoes, and brought them to her.

"Damn, sure is cold in there!" he said. Salter added this comment to his mental notes. Miller bent to put on her shoes, then gently took her left arm and lifted slightly, signaling for her to rise. Alicia stared ahead. Again, they were walking to exit the house. As they walked through the kitchen, Alicia spotted her purse.

"My purse," she pleaded. "Get my purse."

"I got it," Salter said.

Miller led her out of the house and helped her into the car saying, "Watch your head." Alicia bent over and slid into the back seat. Miller sat beside her and closed the door. Alicia cried. She had never so much as received a parking ticket before, let alone been arrested. Putting S'postu to sleep hardly seemed like justice, and to add to her frustration, she couldn't even wipe her tears. Miller only stared straight ahead.

Salter locked the house, slid in behind the wheel, started the engine and backed out of the driveway. As they drove off, Alicia watched her house grow smaller in the distance. Silent tears rolled down her face and she thought she would never see home again.

# CHAPTER 4

The wooden chair behind the defendant's desk in the Knox County Criminal Courtroom creaked as Alicia tried to get comfortable. Max Bailey, her attorney, was seated next to her shuffling papers. She looked around the courtroom. At the prosecution's desk Henry Walton, Deputy District Attorney, sat stiffly, looking eager to get started.

Beyond the prosecution's desk sat the jury, twelve people. A jury of her peers. *What a joke! How could any of these people understand my situation with S'postu?* No one in the room could possibly understand the attack on Charles, including Alicia. It was a small bit of comfort knowing S'postu was asleep, and could not get her to say anything stupid to make things worse. She was truly sorry for what had happened to Westchester, and only hoped her attorney would express this adequately enough to clear her. The whole court procedure frightened her terribly, for she was completely ignorant of anything having to do with the justice system, and knew only what she saw on TV and she was sure that was wrong.

Behind Henry Walton, Alicia saw Charles and Nadine Westchester sitting in the seats behind the wooden railing. Charles' left arm was in a cloth sling. Nadine stared coldly at her, scowling, making her even more uncomfortable, but she could not blame her, nor for the anger she was sure they felt.

Alicia let her eyes wander about in an attempt to distract her from Nadine, and was amazed at the amount of money that must have been spent in building the courtroom. It was finished in cherry paneling and expensive-looking molding. The bench was dark stained oak. The floor was terrazzo tile.

The court reporter passed through the little gate and began to set up her stenography machine. It was now 8:45. In the time left before things would begin, Alicia reflected on what had taken place in the seven weeks since May 9. She remembered sitting in this very courtroom, only four days after her arrest, for the preliminary hearing, where the State was able to show probable cause for a trial. Next came a competency hearing. She was interviewed by a court-appointed psychiatrist who testified, based on his examination, that she was indeed competent enough to understand the trial process and converse intelligently with her counsel. She couldn't understand why she had to go through the hearing, because of course she was competent. Bailey said it was just the way the law is. A grand jury indictment was next, followed by the arraignment hearing where the formal charges were read against her.

The judge's voice thundered in her ears when he said, "Alicia Freed, you have been charged with attempted murder. How do you plead?"

Her attorney stood up. "Max Bailey, counsel for the defense, Your Honor. My client pleads not guilty." The sound of Nadine Westchester's gasp was burned into her memory. Alicia knew that Bailey had tried to get the charges reduced from attempted murder to assault with a deadly weapon, but the D.A. wouldn't budge. The District Attorney was not a young man, and it seemed unlikely to Alicia that he would be trying to make a name for himself. When she asked Bailey about the D.A., he informed her that Henry Walton was one of the most difficult District Attorneys he had ever gone up against. Alicia secretly felt that Bailey simply didn't try hard enough, and was using Walton's attitude as an excuse. But she didn't have the money to fire him and hire someone else, so she had no choice but to follow his recommendations.

Bailey had her see an independent psychiatrist and said that the interview would be vital to her case, so she agreed. The psychiatrist was an acquaintance he had used once before to aid him in another trial. A meeting was arranged, and during the interview, the doctor tried to qualify himself by informing her of all the cases for which he had been a witness. He attempted to reassure her on the basis that he would give the correct answers on the stand to insure the outcome she wanted in the trial. After that statement, she realized that he was a professional witness which made her feel slimy and cheap. He only asked two questions, both regarding her financial status. Alicia wasn't about to divulge any information. After that, the doctor lost interest. This was just as well, as she did not want to depend on this quack for her future. She informed Bailey and he agreed. Besides, his fee was far too expensive for her anyway.

Alicia remembered the judge saying, "Very well, jury selection will take place in two weeks." The gavel crashed down—another sound she would never forget. Her mind drifted to the many times the judge called the two attorneys to the bench when they got into an argument about the qualifications of some juror. It took three weeks for the two lawyers to agree on twelve people. Finally, a trial date was set, and here they were.

She had used her house as collateral with the bail bondsman. With no living relatives, she was on her own regarding financial responsibilities. All she had left was the house and land, and a small savings account. The bondsman was eager to take her house as collateral. She was glad that the judge saw fit to release her from jail after the preliminary hearing. She hated jail almost as much as she grew to hate S'postu for what he had put her through.

At 8:55, the bailiff walked into the courtroom. He carried a stack of papers, which he placed on his desk to the right of the bench. The bailiff sat and began to sort through them. About a minute later, the phone on the bailiff's desk rang. He quickly picked it up and spoke quietly into the receiver. The bailiff hung up the phone and stood up. In a loud clear voice, he said, "All rise." As everyone in the courtroom stood, the sound of chairs being pushed back echoed throughout the room. The door behind the bailiff's desk opened and the judge walked in. "The State of Tennessee, Knox County Criminal Court is now in session; the Honorable Judge J. Thomas Finney, presiding."

Judge Finney took his seat behind the bench. "Please be seated," he said, looking down at the docket.

Everyone sat except the bailiff, who remained standing and said, "Case number P.V.A.F. 3345-286, people versus Alicia Freed."

Judge Finney said, "Let the record show that the defendant has pleaded not guilty."

The court reporter typed away.

The judge turned to the jury. "Jurors, this is a case involving an attempted murder. You are hereby instructed to pay attention only to the facts as they are presented. You will no doubt be subjected to some graphic details, but do not get caught up in emotion. Your job is to listen only to the facts as they are presented to you, then deliberate, and return your decision to the court."

He turned to face the D.A. "Counselor, state your name for the record."

The D.A. stood. "Henry Walton, counsel for the people of Knox County," he said, then sat.

Judge Finney turned to Alicia's desk. "Counselor."

Alicia's attorney stood. "Maximillian Franklin Bailey, counsel for the defense," he said, then resumed his seat.

Judge Finney said, "Gentlemen, your opening statements, please."

Henry Walton stood, moved his chair back with his legs, glanced at a yellow legal pad, and walked in front of the jury.

"Ladies and gentlemen of the jury, the State will prove beyond a reasonable doubt that Alicia Freed, the woman you see in the defense chair, did willfully, and with malice of forethought, attempt to murder Charles Westchester. She not only viciously attacked him once, but came after him a second, brutal time. The State will prove premeditation. The State will further show, by a preponderance of the evidence, that this woman is a menace to society, and therefore, the State seeks the maximum allowable sentence: twenty years in the County Correctional Facility for Women. I thank you, good people of Knox County." Walton sat and gazed smugly at Max Bailey.

"Counsel for the defense," Judge Finney commanded, "you may proceed."

Bailey only sat in his chair, resting his chin on his hand.

"Mr. Bailey," Judge Finney said sternly, "your opening statement please. And, Mr. Bailey, no theatrics."

Bailey stood. "Of course, Your Honor." He walked over to the prosecution's desk and leaned against it, almost sitting. "Well," Bailey said, crossing his arms, "that was quite a speech. Yes, quite a speech." Bailey stood up from the prosecution's desk and walked over near the jury. He looked down slightly at the floor and, with a faint laugh said, "Menace to society, ha! My illustrious colleague has been watching too much Perry Mason! Ladies and gentlemen, my dear friends, look at this woman. Why, she's no more a menace to society than my mother!"

Muffled laughter broke out.

"Move to strike," Walton piped up. "The counselor's mother is not in question, your Honor."

The Judge banged his gavel, "Mr. Bailey, this is a court of law, not some circus act. If you don't want to have any problems in my courtroom, then I suggest you act appropriately, or I will have you spending the night in jail for contempt. Do I make myself clear?"

"Yes, Your Honor," Bailey said, shrinking a bit. "Clear as a bell."

"Strike any comments about Mr. Bailey's mother from the record," Finney commanded. "Get on with it, Mr. Bailey."

Bailey turned his attention to the jury once again. "Let's see, oh yes. As I was saying, the prosecution would have you believe that my client is an unholy monster. Alicia Freed is no monster. Now, it is true that she did impale Mr. Westchester with a knife, there's no denying that." Bailey paced back and forth in front of the jury, allowing his words to be digested. "But, I'm sure that you'll find, when all the facts in this case are made clear, you will have no choice but to find my client not guilty, due to temporary insanity. With that verdict, you should mandate that the State provide my client with the care necessary to enable her to return to society as a productive member."

Bailey sat. Alicia looked, horrified, at her lawyer. She knew what he was going to say, but when the words were spoken, it sounded so ridiculous and contrived. Alicia thought that she would be convicted now for sure. Why, all she did was explain to him the truth about S'postu, and now he's made her out to be some Freudian reject.

"Mr. Walton," Judge Finney said in a commanding tone, "you may proceed with your case."

Walton stood. "For my first witness, I call Charles Westchester."

Charles came forward, was sworn in, and took his place at the witness stand. He sat, nervous but excited. He had never been to court except for an occasional traffic ticket, but never as a witness. Intrigued with the judicial system, he secretly wanted to do something in connection with the court system. But this was only a pipe dream, for he ended up spending his life as a mechanical engineer designing struts and supports for the structural steel in buildings. The whole thought of a trial sort of brought out the child in Charles, and even though he was sixty-four, he felt as giddy as a child of eight. His arm was still sore and every time he moved, the pain reminded him of his age and the reason he was here.

Nadine was not as impressed. She knew that this trial had upset their lives and would not have happened if it hadn't been for Alicia Freed. She would have much rather been basking in the sun in Hawaii, enjoying their retirement. Even though Nadine knew that Charles was having fun playing witness, she deeply resented Alicia for the whole affair. Every time she got the chance, she narrowed her eyes and scowled at her.

The prosecuting attorney watched as Charles sat. Henry took a deep breath. "Mr. Westchester, please state your name for the record."

"Charles Allen Westchester."

"And your place of residence?"

"1842 Palm Road, Knoxville, Tennessee."

"Please describe, for the court, the events of May 9 of this year."

"Well," Charles began, "I was just about to leave the house for work when I was attacked," Charles paused, looking over at Alicia, "with a knife."

"And?" Henry said, gesturing for Charles to continue.

"She stabbed me in the shoulder and arm." Charles pointed to his sling with his right hand. "But I managed to knock her off the porch with my briefcase before she did any more damage."

"Did you feel, Mr. Westchester, that you were ever in any mortal danger?"

"Yes," Charles' eyes narrowed at Alicia. "I saw her eyes. I felt like I could see right into her soul. I thought I was a dead man. I knew she was trying to kill me. I only felt fear like that one time before, and that was in World War II. It shook me down to my core."

"I see," Henry said, raising his hand to his chin. "And do you see your attacker in this room?"

Alicia felt Charles' piercing stare. She cringed and braced herself.

"Yes," Charles stated, pointing. "She's sitting right there."

Judge Finney said, "Let the record show that Mr. Westchester has indicated the defendant, Alicia Freed."

The court reporter continued to type away.

"Do you know of any reason why the defendant would try to kill you?"

"No."

"Do you know Alicia Freed?"

"No, sir."

"Thank you, Mr. Westchester. That will be all for now." Henry Walton took his seat at the prosecution's desk. Charles began to stand.

"Just one moment, Mr. Westchester," Judge Finney commanded. Charles sat back down. "Mr. Bailey, do you wish to cross examine?"

"Yes Your Honor," Bailey stated as he rose.

"Mr. Westchester, how's the arm?" Bailey asked.

"It's getting better."

"I'm glad to hear that. Now I know that it was very confusing, because everything happened so quickly, but I would like you to think back very carefully to the day that my client attacked you."

"I'm not likely to forget it for a long time."

"Really? So, would it be fair to say that you have a clear recollection of that morning?"

"Yes, I would say so."

"Did my client say anything to you either before or as she attacked you?"

"Yes, as a matter of fact she did."

"Would you tell the court what she said to you?"

"She said, 'Your blood for his. This is to avenge S'postu.'"

"Did you understand what she meant?"

"No, I can't say that I did."

"Would you say that is a normal thing to say when attacking someone?"

"Objection!" Henry Walton cut in. "Counsel is asking the witness to draw a conclusion."

"Sustained." Judge Finney said, "Defense will withdraw the question."

"Very well, Your Honor," Bailey retorted.

"The jury will disregard Mr. Bailey's question."

"Thank you, Mr. Westchester." Bailey said. "That is all I have for now."

"Very well," the judge said, "Mr. Westchester, you may step down." Charles nodded and rose to rejoin his wife.

The prosecutor called the E.R. doctor who had testified about Charles' condition right after the stabbing, then called the policeman who had arrived to Westchester's house first. The Officer testified how he had found Alicia's knife.

"Your Honor, I would like to submit this knife as State's Exhibit B."

"So accepted, State's Exhibit B."

"It's now eleven-thirty, court is now adjourned for lunch."

*Where had all the time gone?* This was fine with Alicia, she was hungry anyway.

"Court will resume at 1:30." The crack of the gavel echoed off the walls like a shot through an empty house.

# CHAPTER 5

Everyone shuffled out of the courtroom. Alicia hurried to keep up with Bailey, followed him into the elevator, then waited for the doors to close. They were now alone.

"What the hell are you trying to do to me?" Alicia asked sternly, placing her hands on her hips. "You made me sound like I'm crazy." She raised her voice slightly.

"You knew what we were going to plead. That's all we've been talking about. Besides, if you really believe all that stuff you told me about your, uh, what's his name?"

"It's the truth." Alicia's face flushed with anger. "And his name is S'postu."

"Well then," Bailey consoled her, "all I have to do is tell the court what you told me and you'll get what I pleaded for you."

The elevator doors opened at the ground level, where the cafeteria was. The room was buzzing with muffled conversations and clattering dishware. The two of them exited the elevator silently, bought their lunches, and sat down and ate together wordlessly.

When Bailey was through with his lunch, he announced that he had to leave the courthouse for a few minutes to take care of some other business. He assured her he would be back in time to return to court. She looked up at him anxiously as he got up from the table and left. As she finished her lunch she wondered what exactly motivated a man like him, for his body language eluded her.

Alicia returned to the courtroom well ahead of the required return time and found it empty. She sat in her seat and thought of S'postu. Now that he was asleep, the only reminder of his existence seemed to be that recurring dream about the Civil War. Each time she dreamed it she received a little more information, or remembered more, she couldn't tell which. Something about the surreal quality of that dream reminded her of the attack of Charles Westchester. She had the same feeling when S'postu took over her body and totally suppressed her will. The dream was eerie and left her feeling uneasy when she woke. The more she thought about it, the more she realized that the dreams were S'postu's memories, leaving her to wonder who he was. What connection did he have with her? Alicia was beginning to fear sleep, yet at the same time wanted to experience more. Intrigued with the thought of gaining more understanding, she considered reinstalling the French doors, but thought better of it.

One by one, people began to filter back into the courtroom. As the time slowly ticked toward 1:30, more and more people returned from lunch. Max Bailey had not returned yet, and Alicia felt her anxiety increase as the minutes ticked by. She felt terribly alone in the courtroom by herself, and with each passing moment longed for Bailey. He was her comfort, her shield against the scathing words of the prosecuting attorney.

The bailiff had returned by now, along with Henry Walton, who gave her an eerie toothy grin as if to say, "I have you now." At three minutes to go, Alicia became alarmed. Each time she heard the door open, she spun around to see who came through. Each time it was not Bailey, she turned around to face the bench, anticipation turing to disappointment, disappointment turning to horror. From the corner of her eye, she could see Henry Walton looking, too. Each time they glanced at each other, Walton gave her that sardonic smile. Alicia didn't know whether he was smirking at her or trying to soothe her. Then decided he was probably smirking, which made her even more nervous. Trying not to appear intimidated, she looked at her watch. It was now 1:30 and still no Bailey.

Alicia's stomach tightened, and she was filled with terror when the bailiff stood up to announce that the courtroom proceedings were starting again. After the judge was seated, he looked up and noticed that Bailey was not present.

"Miss Freed," he began, clearing his throat, "where is your counsel?"

Alicia sat horrified. She opened her mouth to speak, but no words came out. He intimidated her so much. Just then, the courtroom door burst open. Bailey trotted to the defense desk.

"Sorry, Your Honor," he began, apologetically, "I was unavoidably detained."

"Mr. Bailey," the judge commanded, "I will not tolerate tardiness. If you are late again to my courtroom, I will cite you for contempt. Is that understood?"

"Perfectly clear, Your Honor, it won't happen again."

"See that it doesn't." The judge exhaled loudly, "Sit down, Mr. Bailey." He turned to the prosecutor, "You may proceed, Mr. Walton."

"I call to the stand Detective Tom Miller," Walton announced. Miller was sworn in, and proceeded to explain to the court in great detail the events leading to Alicia's arrest. Then Detective Salter was called to the stand. He described how she was arrested. The testimony lasted for hours. Finally, Walton was done.

"Mr. Bailey," the judge began, "do you have anything for this witness?"

"Yes, Your Honor," Bailey said, standing. "Lieutenant Salter, did my client say anything else while being arrested?"

"As I recall," Salter said, remembering, "your client yelled, 'Post you,' or something like that, and 'I hate you,' very loudly."

"Did you or your partner understand what she meant?"

"No sir, I can't say that we did."

"Could she have said, S'postu?"

"Yes, yes, that's what she said."

"Is the statement, yelled by my client, a common response to being arrested?"

"No, sir."

"Do you have any explanation for her outburst?"

"No, sir."

"Thank you, Lieutenant Salter." Bailey turned toward the judge, "Your Honor, I would like to retain this witness for questioning at another time."

"So granted, the witness shall be expected to return for later testimony." Judge Finney turned to Salter, "Do you have any problem with that, Lieutenant?"

"Of course not, Your Honor," he replied.

"Very well, you may step down." The Judge turned to the prosecutor, "You may proceed, Mr. Walton."

"Your Honor," Walton said proudly, "the state rests its case."

"Very well, Mr. Walton. Due to the lateness of the hour, court will be adjourned until 9 a.m. tomorrow." Judge Finney banged his gavel, rose to his feet, and left the courtroom.

"Well," Bailey began, speaking to Alicia, "the ball's in our court come morning"

Alicia nodded her head.

"Go home and get some rest," Bailey said firmly. "You look tired." She smiled feebly. Without saying a word, she left the courtroom. She was tired, in fact she was downright spent. It amazed her how exhausting it was to just sit in a courtroom all day. All she wanted to do was get some sleep, hoping she would be too tired to dream.

# CHAPTER 6

The house felt strangely still and quiet. Alicia walked into the living room and slumped into her armchair. The screw holes left from the French doors were clearly visible, and attracted her attention every time she looked in that direction. The house looked and felt incomplete without them. She tried to relax and not think of S'postu or the French doors, as she looked out the sunroom windows. Her eyelids became heavy and she soon dozed off.

Alicia woke with a start. Something woke her. Stalking in the shadows of the back of her mind was the memory of a dream, but she couldn't remember what. She looked around for anything that would jog her memory, but it was dark. She rose and fumbled sleepily for the light switch, then stumbled into the kitchen for some dinner. After eating and cleaning the dishes, she headed off to bed.

She crossed the threshold into her room, closed her eyes and gritted her teeth in anticipation of the severe temperature drop. The icy air washed over her as she expected, amplified by the torrid late June night. The temperature never seemed to change much in the room. At first, the temperature difference was not as noticeable because of an unusually late cold snap that had gripped East Tennessee. Alicia had always kept the house a bit cold anyway in an effort to save on utility expenses. But now the temperature drop was extreme. Her body shivered as she stepped into her bed clothes. After reaching over to set the alarm clock on the bedside table, she slid into bed and pulled the blankets and quilt over her. She almost liked the cold because she enjoyed the heavy blankets weighing on her body. That was the one thing she liked about winter. It made her want to snuggle under them, ensconced in their safety.

She played back the events of the day in her mind. Max Bailey had said that things were going as he expected, and for her not to worry. But how could she not worry? Her life, her very future was at stake. These thoughts fought each other until she finally drifted off to sleep.

Her body swam with pain. Her face had been plowed into the hard ground; she tried to raise her head to spit out a mouthful of dirt and leaves, but could barely move. She was sure her nose was broken. The sound of footsteps and snapping twigs as the reconnaissance team ran away could barely be heard above the ringing in her ears. She could not move her legs. Each time she tried, agony gripped her lower back.

"Look, the Sergeant's down!" a voice rang out. Somehow she recognized it as the platoon leader named Dunlop. Explosions burst in the distance. Gunfire rang out all around her. Suddenly she felt the touch of a hand on her shoulder. "Sarge, we'll get you fixed up," Dunlop said. "Reese, get over here, the Sarge needs help, let's…" His voice trailed off. All the sounds around her faded to silence.

Alicia found herself sitting in a wooden chair in her living room. The sun was streaming in through the open windows. The aroma of a stew cooking filled the air. She looked around the room. The television was gone. The phone was gone. In fact all the furniture was different. It seemed Victorian. Some were handmade pieces, some very old. She looked over at the French doors. They were hanging there as if she had never removed them, and felt even more strongly about them as her eyes locked on them. She had always liked the doors, but never quite like this.

Alicia looked down. There was a large wheel on each side of her legs, which felt strangely numb. Below her legs, she could see a hardwood floor. She wondered what had happened to the carpet.

"Supper's ready," a woman's voice called out from the kitchen, startling her. She knew it was Daphne's voice and her heart sang with delight, yet somehow she knew these feelings belonged to someone else.

"Come in here and eat," Daphne continued. Somehow Alicia knew by the tone of her voice that something was wrong. As she grasped the top edge of the wheels, she looked down at her hands. They were the thick and strong hands like the man's she had seen in the Confederate uniform. Strangely, she was not disturbed by this, and felt comfortable with the revelation. She spun the wheelchair around and began to push herself in the direction of the dining room.

As she passed through the door leading into the dining room, her eye caught some movement. As she began to turn her head to see what moved, she felt a tremendous blow to the back of her head and a cracking sound ripped through her ears. Pain washed over the back of her head. The force of the blow sent her sailing out of the wheel chair. Suddenly, everything went black.

The alarm clock jerked Alicia into consciousness and she sat up quickly. Her back hurt, her head hurt, and she trembled from the memory of the dream. She threw off the covers, slid out of bed and went into the living room. Everything was as it should be. At least that was a relief. The dream was so real. She needed the reassurance of familiar surroundings to soothe her. But it was of little comfort as she remembered the trial.

She went into the kitchen and got her breakfast. After eating, she showered and dressed. As she began her one hour trip to the courthouse, it began to rain. Looking at the storm, she thought that perhaps it did not look too serious, but still hated to be out in the rain. The last time she had been out in the rain she had stabbed a man, which she was sure she would pay for somehow for the rest of her life. Thunder rumbled in the distance. Lightning lit up the grey morning. In all the books that Alicia read, whenever a storm was brewing, it always meant something bad was about to happen. The thought sent shivers up her spine. As she drove slowly to the courthouse, she tried to put the thought out of her mind, forcing herself to wonder what the day held in store for her. Butterflies filled her stomach anyway.

# CHAPTER 7

Alicia sat on a bench in the hall outside the courtroom. The elevator doors opened, and Max Bailey stepped into view, smiling.

"How are you this morning?" he asked.

"I'm okay today." The interaction from a living, breathing human being was comforting even if it was a lawyer.

Bailey sat beside her. "Are you ready?" he asked softly.

"I…I think so."

"You'll be fine Alicia," Bailey comforted. "Just answer the questions truthfully, and I think you'll come out of this okay." Alicia smiled.

"Excuse me," Bailey said suddenly, "but I've got to make a phone call." He stood.

"Wait, Max," Alicia called. "Please don't be late for court. You scared the dickens out of me yesterday."

Bailey smiled, "Oh, yeah. I meant to apologize to you about that. I just got tied up with a phone call, and lost track of time. Lawyers live on the phone almost as much as a teenager does."

"That's okay, I guess there was no harm done."

She watched Bailey disappear down the hallway. Under her breath, she hummed the tune S'postu had taught her when she was just a child. It seemed to quell her growing anxiety as she waited alone.

One by one, people began to get off the elevator. First the court reporter, then the prosecuting attorney, then one witness after another.

Alicia felt eyes upon her. The feeling was sickening, yet she resisted the urge to cringe, and maintained her posture. The offending eyes belonged to the prosecuting attorney, Henry Walton. She returned his glance, and in spite of what was going on, found it hard to harbor any animosity toward him. After all, he was only doing his job.

The elevator doors slid open. Charles and Nadine Westchester stepped into the hall. Alicia suddenly felt naked without Bailey. She swung her head away from the Westchesters to avoid their stares, and felt extremely awkward. She desperately longed for Bailey's protection. Damn his phone call, anyway! She needed him now, and was frustrated with him for not running interference from the hateful glare she knew Nadine was giving her.

Finally, Alicia could take the pressure no longer. She was just about to walk over to Charles and apologize, when the bailiff stepped off the elevator and unlocked the courtroom doors. People began to shuffle in.

Charles and Nadine moved slowly toward the door. Alicia looked around quickly for Bailey, but he was nowhere in sight. Sitting stiffly on the bench, she watched the crowd disappear into the courtroom. An almost uncontrollable urge to talk to Charles swept over her. She wanted to apologize for the pain she had caused him. They were in front of her now, moving toward the door. Alicia stood and walked over to them. Charles drew back with a wary expression. Nadine held him by his uninjured arm.

"What the hell do you want?" Nadine hissed.

"I…I just wanted to say…" Alicia tried to justify with tears welling in her eyes, "I'm sorry for th…"

"We don't need your apologies, you murderous bitch! Just leave us alone!" Nadine cut her off.

Alicia recoiled.

"Come on, Charles." Charles protested weakly as Nadine pulled gently on his arm.

Alicia's mind raced with thoughts of running away and hiding with an overwhelming sense of futility, but, she went back to the bench and cried. Finally, she went into the courtroom herself. As she passed Charles and Nadine, she tried to wipe the tears from her eyes.

Nadine, glaring at Alicia, noticed her red eyes and tears as she walked past them, and suddenly felt a twinge of pity toward her and softened her expression. Alicia noticed the change on Nadine's face and almost paused. Maybe there was hope yet that Nadine might forgive her. This suddenly became important to Alicia. Nadine turned to say something to Charles.

Henry Walton sat at the prosecutor's desk, shuffling papers in his briefcase. Alicia felt awkward sitting alone at the defense desk. A man in a business suit walked up to Henry and whispered something in his ear. Henry nodded in acknowledgment and followed the man out of the courtroom.

At twenty minutes before court was to reconvene, Alicia became increasingly nervous. Bailey was nowhere in sight and now she was alone, and sure everyone was watching her. Where was he? Every few minutes, she would turn to see if the person walking through the door was Bailey. Anxiety surged through her each time it was someone else.

A familiar odor wafted to Charles. A sweet, floral scent—that perfume! Suddenly he was nauseous. It took all of his concentration to keep himself from vomiting. He jumped when Nadine squeezed his hand gently.

"Do you think she's really crazy?" Nadine asked in a soft whisper.

"Nadine," Charles spoke slowly to maintain himself, "we've been over this a thousand times, I have no idea why that woman attacked me. I've never seen her before she stuck me with that damn knife, so why would she try to kill me if she isn't crazy?"

"I don't know, honey," Nadine soothed, "but that's not what I meant."

"Well, what did you mean?"

"I mean, well, she really seems sorry that she hurt you. For weeks now I've tried to hate her. But I can't keep it up."

Charles turned to his wife. "What?"

"I mean, in the hall, when she tried to apologize, I've never seen that side of her. I know we've never talked. So, I made her out to be a monster. You know, a complete, murderous, psychopathic bitch."

Charles laughed softly. "Well, we can't just go up to the judge and say, 'sorry Your Honor, but my wife and I have had a sudden change of heart, and we don't really want to press charges after all.'"

Nadine listened to him go on, with her mouth open a bit.

"Besides," Charles continued, "when she was about to stab me, I saw the look in her eyes. She wanted to do me in. If I hadn't knocked her off the porch, we wouldn't be having this little chat right now."

"I know, honey," Nadine consoled, "but maybe she was temporarily insane. What else would explain why she did it? And you know, we certainly had other things going on in our lives."

"I've hashed that out time and time again, and there ain't no reasonable explanation for what she did except that. Besides, it's a little too late to stop everything right now."

"Charles," Nadine said, rearing back, "I never said anything about stopping this trial. That woman needs to pay for what she did to you. I just don't think she needs to spend the rest of her life in jail, that's all."

"So, what do you have in mind?"

"I don't know," Nadine sighed, "but twenty years just seems a bit harsh."

Alicia was staring straight ahead when the chair next to her moved suddenly. She jumped and turned to see Max Bailey sitting down beside her.

"Max," Alicia said crossly, "you scared me."

"Sorry," Bailey replied, "but I think I've got a surprise for you."

"What?" Alicia asked, suddenly hopeful.

"Shh. Shh," Bailey answered, placing his index finger to his lips, "it's starting."

The bailiff stood. "All rise," he commanded. Everyone in the courtroom stood. "The State of Tennessee, Knox County Supreme Court, is now in session. The Honorable Judge Thomas J. Finney presiding."

Judge Finney banged his gavel. "Please be seated."

Everyone sat except Bailey. "If it pleases the Court," Bailey began. Alicia stared up at him in astonishment, "may counsel approach the bench?" The judge looked at Bailey, puzzled.

"Come." He motioned for him to approach the bench.

Both attorneys advanced. Judge Finney covered the microphone with his hand and leaned forward.

"What's going on, Mr. Bailey?"

"Well, sir," Bailey whispered, "the District Attorney and I have reached a propitious agreement…" Bailey explained the phone calls that made him late the day before, as well as the one he made earlier that morning.

"Very good, Mr. Bailey," Judge Finney began, "I like the idea of saving the taxpayers a little money." He turned to Henry Walton. "Do you concur, Mr. Walton?"

"Absolutely, Your Honor."

"Fine, gentlemen. Now, Mr. Bailey, I suggest you run this by your client. Now then, Mr. Walton, I want you to please explain to me why you rested your case without establishing a motive for this crime."

"Well, Your Honor, I don't think there is any motive."

"What do you mean, there is no motive? How could there not be a motive?"

"Your Honor," Bailey cut in, "it is my opinion that this woman is insane."

"YOUR opinion?" His eyes narrowed at Bailey. "Did you suddenly change your career to the mental health profession?"

"No sir."

"Then what makes you think I will accept your opinion regarding your client's mental health?"

Bailey felt a knot forming in the pit of his stomach. He swallowed. "I...I don't..."

"Look," the judge cut him off, "I see by your witness list that you have a psychiatrist scheduled. And as I recall, this was the same individual who tried to make a mockery of the justice system in my courtroom a few years back, wasn't he?"

Bailey grimaced. He had forgotten that Judge Finney presided over a case that he threw together while in the midst of a nasty divorce. He hardly prepared for the case and in the confusion, got his witnesses from different cases confused.

"Yes, Your Honor, I believe he was," Bailey responded.

"Well, nevertheless, I want the court to have Miss Freed evaluated independently. So, in order that justice is served, I want you to have your client evaluated by a professional. Only then, will I entertain the notion of insanity. Have I made myself clear, Mr. Bailey?"

"Completely, Your Honor."

"Very well. Now the two of you fight it out between yourselves as to who is suitable for that evaluation."

"I think that can be arranged, Your Honor," Bailey responded.

Judge Finney paused for a minute, thinking. "All right, you two, I will grant you a recess so that you may handle this...development," he sighed. "Please take your seats."

The two men returned to their seats. Confused, Alicia looked at Bailey.

The judge said in a commanding tone, "There will be a twenty minute recess." He looked at Bailey. "Is that sufficient, Mr. Bailey?"

Bailey nodded his head and the gavel crashed.

Bailey was smiling as he led Alicia out of the courtroom and into a small room down the hall. She sat silently in a chair while Bailey shut the door.

"Alicia," he began, "I have been talking to the D.A. and I think I have been able to come up with an equitable solution that we all can live with." She listened intently. "Now, I haven't been able to get the charges reduced, but I managed to reach an agreement about the sentence. Look, this is a political year and the D.A. wants to be reelected. Therefore, he will recommend that you be sentenced to Rhinewood Mental Institution in Union County, and you won't see any jail time."

"What are you saying," Alicia breathed, "that I live in a loony bin?"

"Would you rather spend the next twenty years in a jail cell?" Bailey paused long enough to let her digest his words. "If we allow this trial to run its course, pleading temporary insanity—which is very hard to prove—I fear you'll be convicted, and the Judge will sentence you to jail. And Alicia, you don't want to go to jail." Bailey sighed. "Look, you're a nice lady, those bitches in prison will tear you up."

"Yeah but," Alicia pleaded, "I don't know if I can spend the rest of my life with a bunch of certified crazies."

"Who said anything about the rest of your life?"

"But, I assumed..."

"That's the problem, you assumed. Don't ever assume. That's only reserved for lawyers and crooked politicians. Here's how it works: If you are found not guilty the judge will sentence you to the mental facility in Union County."

"Wait a minute, Max, if I'm found not guilty, then why would I be sentenced?"

"You would be found not guilty by reason of insanity. Temporary or otherwise. That would absolve you of the crime, but Tennessee law states that something has to be done with the insanity part."

"Even with a not guilty verdict, I still don't get to walk free?"

"No. Remember this is a conditional not guilty."

"Well then what will happen to me next?"

"You will be institutionalized at Rhinewood. Henry and I will recommend it, then you will be evaluated every six months. That's pretty much standard. When you pass the evaluations, you'll be out."

Alicia thought for a moment. "Okay, Max. Do it."

Bailey smiled. "There's one more thing, Alicia."

"What?"

"You will need to be evaluated by a court-appointed psychiatrist now. Is that acceptable?"

"Do I have a choice?"

"Not really."

"Then what's the point of the question?"

"Ah, well…"

"Relax Max, I'll agree."

"All right, go back and sit in the courtroom. I will be there shortly. I've got to talk to Henry and tell him what we've decided."

Alicia nodded and left the little room, sat in her chair at the defense desk and patiently waited. After several minutes, the two attorneys came through the door and took their seats.

Alicia leaned over to Bailey. "What's happening?"

"No problem, we've got it all worked out. Now the only thing we have to do is tell the judge and he'll make it official."

Bailey straightened in his chair. He lifted his briefcase from the floor and placed it on the desk. "Hang on a minute." He opened his briefcase and removed some papers. "We've got to ask for a continuance."

Alicia looked on silently.

The bailiff stood. "All rise." Everyone stood. The judge walked into the courtroom and seated himself.

"Well, Mr. Bailey?" The judge spoke up.

"Your Honor," Bailey stood, "after conferring with my client, I would like to ask the court to grant my client a continuance."

"On what grounds?"

Alicia's stomach tightened with every word.

"If it pleases the court," Bailey cleared his throat, "I would like my client to have a psychiatric evaluation."

"For the record, Mr. Bailey," the judge retorted, "I want it understood that this is a procedure that you should have done before this trial even began. You have practiced law in my courtroom for many years, and I want you to know that I am disappointed with your lack of professionalism."

"Your Honor?"

"I will not see this lack of foresight again without serious repercussions. Have I made myself clear, Mr. Bailey?"

Bailey's jaw dropped. He swallowed hard. "Yes, Your Honor," he squeaked.

Alicia's butterflies were doing back flips. It was getting more difficult to deal with this constant emotional roller-coaster. If this kept up, she would snap any second. Then they really would have to commit her.

The gavel crashed. "Court will reconvene Monday following the psychiatric evaluation."

Alicia hugged Bailey and let out a quiet squeal of delight. She was thrilled with the idea, just accepting it as the lesser of two evils.

Bailey let her hug him for a moment, then gently pushed her back. "Hold on Alicia," he said softly, "we're not out of the woods yet. You still have to see the doctor."

"I realize that, but I don't have the foggiest notion as to whom to see."

"Don't worry about that. Let me make the arrangements."

"Do you know someone?"

"Yep, I know just the man for the job. You just sit back and I'll set it all up. I'm sure he will see you this afternoon, or first thing tomorrow."

"He's not like that turkey you sent me to the first time, is he?"

"No," Bailey laughed softly. "He's not like that at all."

"Well okay, but can you make it tomorrow? I'd like to rest this afternoon. I'm exhausted. This whole thing is taking everything I have just to cope."

"I understand. Now you go home and get some rest. I'll call you later today, after I talk to the doctor."

"Okay Max, my life is in your hands." Alicia turned and left the courtroom.

Max Bailey watched silently as she walked away. He was taken aback by her words. Making a deal with the D.A. was part of the American justice system, and there was nothing wrong with it at all. But that wasn't what he was about to do. There was no way to shake this dirty, sleazy feeling. Wheels had already been set into motion, solidified by Judge Finney, and there was no way to stop it. He had to finish what he had started, but it still made him feel beneath contempt.

He rode the elevator down to the first floor and went to a row of pay phones mounted on the wall. He dropped a dime in the slot and dialed the number.

"Rhinewood Mental Institute," a female voice on the other end said, "where may I direct your call?"

"Director's office," Bailey said, barely above a whisper.

"May I say who's calling?"

"Look lady," Bailey said, raising his voice a little, "don't give me any static. Just connect me with Freeman." He hated to be questioned by people who couldn't care less about the answer, especially when it wasn't their business in the first place. After what just happened with Judge Finney, he was in no mood to be interrogated.

"Right away, sir," she said, obviously annoyed.

There was a round of clicks, then suddenly, "Director's office, Freeman here," a man's voice said.

"Pat, it's Bailey. We need a meeting."

"Ok, what time?"

Bailey looked at his watch. "It's 9:45 now, how about noon?"

"That'll work. Where?"

"Lyon's."

"Ok. I'll call Walty."

"He already knows." Bailey informed him.

"Fine, see ya there."

Bailey hung up without saying goodbye. He gathered up his briefcase, and walked out of the courthouse, got into his car, and drove to his office.

# CHAPTER 8

Max Bailey stepped out of his car and onto the parking lot at Lyon's Steak House, angry with himself for being late. He prided himself on being punctual, although the events that had transpired in the last few days would not illustrate that particular character trait. Normally, he was a fanatic where time was concerned.

The sun was bright and the humidity high as usual from the morning rain storm, leaving the late June air heavy. He walked across the parking lot toward the door of the restaurant. Lyon's Steak House was not an eatery that Bailey frequented. In fact, he had only been here twice before. Both times, he had met the same two men. This particular location was selected for its isolation from Bailey's downtown world. It was at the edge of an industrial area of town, and was frequented by the managers and administrators from the local manufacturing plants. The patrons were usually dressed in business suits, allowing Bailey and his party to blend inconspicuously into the background. Anonymity was imperative.

The restaurant was decorated in a rustic style. Vertical cedar planks with red barn stain covered the exterior, and half-buried wagon wheels flanked the walkway leading to the entrance. Bailey stepped through the door and removed his sunglasses. He stood in front of the hostess station, waiting for his eyes to adjust to the dim lighting.

"One for lunch sir?" asked a pleasant voice.

Bailey, who was concentrating on looking for his cohorts, was startled by the hostess. He peered at her. She was a short woman with a small frame, perhaps five feet, one inch or so, with brunette hair. The woman's most redeeming quality, in Bailey's opinion, was her bustline, which he immediately noticed. Her full breasts pushed her flimsy white top to the limit. As in most restaurants, the air conditioner was working overtime and the cool air was a sharp contrast to the heat outside. He had worked at a restaurant during law school, and the owner had told him that people always ate more if the air was chilly. It had something to do with metabolism trying to keep the body warm—he wasn't sure of the exact medical reason—he just knew business was better when the thermostat was kept around sixty-eight degrees.

"Uh, no thanks," Bailey began, staring at the woman's chest. "I'm part of a party that's already seated." Bailey surmised this, since he didn't see his buddies waiting in the lobby and remembered seeing their cars outside.

"Go ahead and look," the hostess said, feeling self-conscious because Bailey would not look her in the eyes, a common practice of most men with whom she came in contact.

"Thanks," Bailey muttered, walking to look for his buddies. As he entered the dining area, he could hear the tinkle of silverware hitting stoneware, and the sound of muffled conversation. In the dim light, he could see Henry Walton and Pat Freeman in a dark corner. He strode over to the table. The two men looked up at him.

"Well, this is a first," Henry chuckled, "the forever punctual Max Bailey, late!"

Bailey slid into the booth beside Freeman. "Did you see that incredible babe at the hostess station?" Bailey asked, pointing his thumb toward the front of the restaurant.

Freeman smiled. "Oh yeah?" setting down his glass after taking a drink of water, "what color were her eyes?"

"Nipple brown," Bailey clowned.

"That's what I thought," Freeman snapped playfully. "You probably never even saw her face."

"Max is an insufferable tit man," Walton spoke up, laughing softly. Bailey blushed. The three men laughed quietly.

A pretty blonde woman came over to their table.

"Hi," she said with a thick southern accent. "Muh name's Rita, and I'll be servin' ya today." As she pulled a pad out of the pocket in her short skirt, she said, "What can I gitch ya?"

Bailey's eyebrows shot up. *A reservation for an hour or so at a nearby motel.*

Freeman saw the look on his face, and grinned.

Rita noticed his expression and knew at once what he was thinking based on the countless men she had waited on in the past. Shrouding her anger with professionalism, she forced a smile.

"Well, Rita," Bailey said, picking the menu off the table in front of him, "I just got here, can you give me a minute?"

"Sure," Rita replied. "I'll be back in a minute with your water."

"Ok," Bailey said.

Rita went off to the waitress station, leaving the three men to look over their menus in silence. When she was out of visual range of Bailey's party, she shook her head in disgust. Why is it that when some men get together, no matter how old they are, they always seem to act as if they were still in high school? After several minutes she returned to the table, gave Bailey his glass of ice water, and took their orders.

The three men engaged in small talk until Rita left. The tension at the table increased as the conversation became more serious.

"What's the all-fired emergency on this deal?" Walton asked.

"If we don't act now, we'll miss a golden opportunity," Bailey said quietly, leaning across the table. "My present client, in whom we both have a vested interest, has no living relatives, no ties, and best of all, a house on 400 acres that is completely paid for."

"Sounds interesting," Walton acknowledged.

"What do you need from me?" Freeman had a pretty good idea what Bailey was about to say, but wanted him to say it anyway.

"Does the name Jake Streator ring a bell?" Bailey said, leaning back in his seat.

The three men sat in silence as Rita set their lunches before them.

Four and a half years ago, a fairly well-to-do black man had sought the legal assistance of Max Bailey. Jake Streator had come to Knoxville from Detroit some years before. He brought his wife with him, a beautiful, light-skinned black woman named Dora. The two of them opened a dry-cleaning business and successfully operated it for years.

Matt Cole was a local barber who had a shop across the street. Cole, a white man, had a secret fetish for black women. For months he would watch Dora from his barber shop as she waited on customers. One night, while Dora was locking the door at closing time, Cole forced his way inside. Jake was in the little office in the back, counting the day's receipts. Cole forced Dora behind the counter and began to rape her. Jake heard the commotion and went to investigate. When he saw Matt Cole raping his wife, he lost control and grabbed a baseball bat, and beat Matt Cole to death. In the struggle, he accidentally hit his wife on the head, killing her as well.

After calling the police, he became despondent over the accidental death of his wife, and attempted suicide. The police arrested Jake. The D.A. charged him with murder. Jake hired Max Bailey to defend him. He signed over the dry-cleaning business to him in order to pay his exorbitant legal fees. Because of the suicide attempt, it was easy to cop an insanity plea.

At this point, Bailey was going through a very messy and costly divorce, leaving him in serious debt. In the original deal, Jake was to sign over his business, providing that Bailey got Jake acquitted of all charges, until Jake paid off the fees. But Bailey needed more money than was due him from Jake Streator. He called on two of his high school buddies: Pat Freeman, who had just been promoted to the director's position at Rhinewood Mental Institute, and deputy D.A. Henry Walton. The three of them conspired to have Jake Streator found not guilty due to temporary insanity. Walton recommended that Jake go to Rhinewood Mental Institute. After listening to the testimony of Pat Freeman, the judge sentenced Streator to the institute for a psychological evaluation. After the thirty-day evaluation, Pat Freeman testified, in a closed hearing, that Jake Streator should be kept for six months for treatment. By manipulation of the justice system, the three of them managed to keep Jake in for two years.

In the meantime, Max Bailey immediately sold Jake Streator's drycleaning business, splitting the proceeds among himself, Henry Walton, and Pat Freeman.

Rhinewood received twenty-five thousand dollars per year from the federal government. Through creative bookkeeping, Freeman managed to siphon off several thousand dollars of the money the institute received on Jake Streator's behalf, which he promptly distributed among the three of them. Freeman kept Streator pumped full of Thorazine and testified against his release each time an evaluation hearing was ordered.

One morning, a new nurse did not administer the Thorazine as ordered by Freeman. With his mind clear for the first time in two years, Streator realized that he had lost all he had, and hanged himself. The morning orderly found him. He had punched a hole in the drywall above the bathroom door and used several wraps of a telephone cord to hang himself. It was a gruesome sight and had quite a stint with the local press. No one suspected any wrongdoing and no questions were asked.

Each man silently remembered his involvement in the Streator case. Pushing the thought from his mind, Bailey turned back to the business at hand.

Bailey said to Walton, "Her house alone is worth at least 50 K."

"Look Max," Walton began, "the trial has already begun, so I think the best plan of action would be to go ahead with your defense."

"I figured that much," Bailey started, "but you'll need to recommend to the judge that she be committed. You know, in light of the testimony that Pat will give." Walton nodded his head in agreement.

"Pat, can you do a psychiatric evaluation tomorrow morning?"

"Let me think," Freeman began. "I, I think I've got staff evaluations in the morning, but I can bump them."

"Good. That's good," Bailey said, finishing his water.

"I suppose," Walton suddenly blurted out, "that I could botch the summation. Or maybe I could just say something like, in light of the new evidence and testimony by Mr. Freeman, I change my recommendation from the maximum penalty to institutionalization at Rhinewood, or something like that."

"That's good, Henry," Bailey said, thoughtfully, "but I wouldn't botch your summation. Judge Finney knows that you're not capable of that kind of incompetence and he might think something is up."

"That's reasonable," he agreed.

"Well Max," Freeman said, "tell me about my patient."

"She's a real live one, says that a voice in her head told her to kill this guy. And get this, the voice's name is S'postu, or something like that. She says that this, this S'postu made her head hurt and threatened her with more pain if she didn't track this guy down and kill him."

"How did she know where to find him?" Freeman asked.

"She says that the voice told her his name, so she looked him up in the phone book and then drove to Knoxville and found his house."

"Sounds like I don't even have to commit perjury this time." Freeman said, remembering Jake Streator. "Have your client at my facility at 9:30 a.m., ok?"

"She'll be there," Bailey assured.

"Max," Walton said, "since you're winning this case, you can buy." He motioned that he wanted to leave.

Bailey nodded his head in agreement. He slid out of the way so that Freeman could get out. Walton headed to the men's room. Bailey finished his lunch, paid for the meal and left the restaurant.

As he drove across town to his office, he felt bad for what he was about to do to Alicia Freed, so he began to justify the conspiracy to himself. *After all, I didn't make Alicia stab Westchester, she did it to herself. With that story she told me, maybe she really should be committed.* Bailey was a lawyer and deserved to be compensated for his work. He was, after all, a damn good lawyer. So taking her house in return for services rendered was perfectly fine. Still, he felt bad. That was strange to him, since he had never felt remorse before for anything he did for profit, except when Jake Streator took his own life. He never intended to see the man die, he just wanted the money. *What was it about this woman? Could she commit suicide too?* When Streator died, he told himself that he had nothing to do with it. That it was all fate. He buried any guilt deep in his mind. *Besides, there are two other people involved. What would they think of me if I suddenly decided to back out now?*

When Bailey arrived at his office, he told his secretary not to put through any calls, and closed the door to his office. He thumbed through his Rolodex and found Alicia Freed's phone number. Her phone rang several times before she picked up.

"Alicia?"

"Yes? Oh, hi Max."

*Why does she have to sound so pleasant?* "Bailey here. I just talked to the doctor. I set up an appointment for you to see him at 9:30 tomorrow morning. Can you be there?"

"Yes, of course I'll be there tomorrow. What else have I got to do?"

He ignored her question then proceeded to give her directions to the Rhinewood Mental Institute, then ended their conversation.

Bailey turned his chair around and didn't do anything else for the rest of the day except think of Jake Streator and Alicia. Hearing her voice only reminded him that his actions would once again affect the life of a living, breathing person, not merely changing the outcome at the bottom of some obscure profit report. *How can such a nice person be mixed up in such a tangled mess? She seems to be more of a victim in this case, instead of a murderer. Even before she hired me.* Guilt and remorse swept over him. He looked out the window and silently wept.

# CHAPTER 9

Alicia pulled into the parking lot of the Rhinewood Mental Institute at 9:15. The institute was a large, one-story building finished in red brick. After driving under the large porte cochere and finding a parking space close to the front door, she checked her make-up. Finding it satisfactory, she shut off the engine and opened the door. She stood beside her car for a moment, wondering what the doctor would say, then smoothed her skirt and walked toward the front door.

As she stepped through the vestibule and into the lobby, the faint scent of isopropyl alcohol reminded her that she was definitely in a hospital. She looked around for a receptionist, but only found a square window in the wall, opposite the door. She walked over to it and saw that it was a reception area. A small counter formed its lower ledge. The window was actually one sliding glass pane and one stationary pane that separated the receptionist from the lobby. It had been pushed all the way to the right. She looked past the window into the room beyond. There was a desk under the window with a phone and stacks of papers. The trouble was, it seemed to be deserted.

Alicia rang the little bell. Seconds later, a heavyset black woman rounded a corner. She was dressed in a white nurse's uniform, and the first thing Alicia noticed about the woman were her horned-rimmed glasses, translucent pink and attached to a tether that encircled her neck. The glasses swung to and fro as she walked toward her, like some gaudy necklace. The woman sat in the chair behind the desk, her face expressionless.

"I have an appointment with Doctor Freeman," Alicia announced. The woman looked up, stone-faced, lips pursed together. She silently pulled a book from in front of her, glanced at the contents, then returned it.

"Have a seat," she said to Alicia, picking up the phone receiver. "I'll tell him you're here."

Alicia sat down on an orange vinyl chair. Behind the grey metal door to her right, she could hear muffled screams and shrieks coming from somewhere. The whooping and hollering of the patients was a sound she loathed. How sad it was as people succumbed to Alzheimer's or Parkinson's disease, the once noble reduced to nothing more than infants. This institute reminded her of the convalescent hospital where her mother had spent the last three years of her life. The smell, the layout, and most of all, the sounds reminded Alicia of one of the saddest times in her life.

She thought about her mother and how she had gone from a viable, independent, strong woman to a blathering, incoherent wretch. Alicia was on the verge of tears, angry at the callous treatment she felt her mother had received.

The metal door opened without warning and Alicia jumped. The receptionist stuck her head through the door. "The doctor will see you now," she stated, then retreated, leaving the door ajar.

It was strange that the woman seemed to know who she was, since Alicia hadn't announced her name. She dismissed the thought, assuming that Dr. Freeman expected her and had informed the staff. When she reached the door, the woman was nowhere in sight. She entered a long hallway.

"Two doors down, on the left," the woman's voice boomed out of an open doorway. Alicia walked toward the sound of the woman's voice and stuck her head in the room. "Thank you."

The woman completely ignored Alicia, so she proceeded down the hall. The floor was shiny linoleum and her footsteps echoed off the walls. As she looked for Dr. Freeman's office, she could see two huge metal doors at the end of the hall. Through the security-glass windows, Alicia could see people in wheelchairs. Then she saw a young man, his blonde hair unkempt and sticking out in all directions, walking around. He looked as if he were picking leaves or fruit out of thin air and storing them in an imaginary basket. The whooping and hollering was a little louder than before, but still muffled. The audio barrage sent shivers down her spine. The smell of isopropyl alcohol was much stronger. Alicia arrived at the third door on the left. There was a small plaque on the door. Patrick L. Freeman, Director. She opened the door, and stepped inside the Director's office.

"Come in. Come in," said the man behind the desk, rising.

Patrick Freeman was in his early to mid forties, Alicia guessed. He was dressed in a light blue dress shirt and striped tie. He wore dark blue polyester slacks. His white overcoat seemed to flow as he stood. Patrick Freeman's hairline had receded all the way to the top of his head, and his large ears appeared to protrude from his head even further than they actually did, reminding her of two radar dishes searching the stars for distant voices. He had one chestnut brown eye on the left and a light blue eye on the right. His overall appearance seemed comical to Alicia and she had to restrain herself to keep from laughing. Freeman was extending his hand to greet her.

There were two high-backed chairs in front of the desk. Alicia could see the top of someone's head in the chair to the right, but could not tell who it was. As she approached the desk, Alicia leaned over to shake Patrick Freeman's hand and saw Max Bailey sitting in the chair.

"Patrick Freeman," said the doctor, squeezing her hand softly. "It's a pleasure to meet you, Miss Freed."

"Thank you."

"Good morning, Alicia," said Bailey.

"Mornin' Max," Alicia said, turning to him, "I didn't expect to see you here today."

"Oh yeah, I wouldn't miss this."

Alicia wasn't sure whether his comment was derogatory or not, but she was sure she didn't like it.

"Have a seat, Miss Freed." Freeman said, gesturing to the seat to the left. Alicia sat. "May I call you Alicia?"

"Please do," Alicia answered, nodding.

Freeman looked over at Bailey. "Max, I'm going to have to ask you to wait in the lobby. While you're at it, why not give Clara a hard time? She could stand a little humility."

Bailey grinned, and left the room.

"Well, Alicia, let's cut to the chase, shall we?" Freeman began. Alicia exhaled, then nodded her head in agreement.

"Now then. Why did you try to kill Charles Westchester?" Freeman asked.

"Boy, you sure ain't waistin' no time, are you? Well, no matter, here goes. S'postu told me to do it. Actually, and I know this is going to sound crazy, but S'postu was really the one who did it."

"Who is S'postu?"

"I'm not really sure. He could be forgotten kin. Well, anyway, I know he's more than a figment of my imagination. He has, uh, done things."

"What kind of things?"

"Sometimes, if I argue or don't do what he says, he hurts me."

"Hurts you? How?"

"I really can't say how. All I know is that my head hurts, here." Alicia bent forward and pointed to the back of her head.

"Please explain to me how S'postu is the one who hurt Mr. Westchester?" Freeman leaned toward her, getting interested.

"Well, he sort of took over my body."

"How did he do that?"

"I kinda, uh, let him." Freeman wrinkled his forehead as Alicia continued, "He'd never done anything like that before, it was kinda scary. I'm not sure, I, uh…"

"Ok Alicia," Freeman questioned, "what else has he done?"

"It's not all bad. One time, when I was twelve, I lost my locket. It was a really old one, it had a picture of my grandmother in it. I searched for days and couldn't find it anywhere. I guess I lost it in the grass in the front yard. I liked to play out there when I was a little girl. Anyway, I was so upset. I cried to S'postu. He was the only one who would listen. My mom was always so busy and my dad died when I was nine. So S'postu told me he couldn't stand to see me cry anymore, and said he would find the locket for me. I remember telling my mother that S'postu would find it. She just told me that I was too old for imaginary friends." Alicia paused for a moment.

"Please continue," Freeman encouraged.

"Well, I went to bed that night, trusting S'postu. My mother said I was being silly. When I woke up the next morning, the locket was in my hand."

"Are you sure you didn't have it hidden somewhere? Maybe, retrieving it in the middle of the night?"

"Positive."

"That's a very interesting story, Alicia." Freeman picked up a yellow pad and began to write. As he wrote, the sound of pencil lead on paper filled the air, no one spoke.

Alicia could not stand the silence any longer, she was nervous knowing that this interview may be the key to her freedom. The whole prospect scared her to death.

"Lately," she began. Freeman looked up at her without lifting his head, "I've been having dreams."

"Oh?" Freeman lifted his head, more interested.

"Yeah," Alicia explained, "about the Civil War, I think."

Alicia explained to Freeman about her dreams. She described the grey-sleeved uniform, Dunlop, and the shooting in the back. She told of the pain when she awoke, and added that she could not account for it, which disturbed her. She also recalled the wheelchair, the blow to the head, and the resulting headache when she awoke. She continued explaining about the French doors, the bursting light bulbs, and the television set incident.

Freeman remained attentive. The interview lasted another half hour. He asked her questions concerning her childhood, her childhood friends, and what kind of games she had played. The whole time, Freeman took notes on his yellow pad of paper.

Finally, he informed her that the interview was over. He picked up the phone on his desk and dialed. "Clara, do me a favor and send Mr. Bailey back to my office. Thanks," then hung up the phone. Two minutes later, Bailey entered the office and sat in the chair next to Alicia.

"Well, Max," Freeman began, "we're all done here."

"Good deal," Bailey responded. "Do you have all the information you need?"

"I think so." Freeman answered, nodding his head. Bailey told Alicia he would call her later and asked her to go home. Alicia was only too happy to comply. She hated that building. The sooner she left, the sooner she would get over her nervousness. She gathered her things and headed for home.

"Can I use your phone?" Bailey asked.

"Absolutely, here you go." Freeman motioned for him to come to his side of the desk, then rose to relinquish his chair.

"I've got to call Gail at the office and tell her to let the judge know that we're finished."

Bailey made his phone call, discussed the case for a short time with Freeman, then left the institute.

# CHAPTER 10

Alicia had just removed a load of hot clothes from the dryer when the phone rang.

"Hello?" Alicia greeted.

"It's me, Max."

"I was beginning to think you forgot about me," Alicia's voice was tense.

Bailey sensed this and softened his voice accordingly. "Sorry, Alicia. I got delayed at the office." Alicia said nothing. After a few seconds which felt like an eternity, he said, "We need to discuss my fee."

"Wait a minute, Max," Alicia cut him off, tension turning to anger. "I already paid you your retainer."

"I know you did."

"Well then, what do you need?"

"Alicia, I have more hours in this case than what you've already paid for. Plus, I had to pay off the bail bondsman so he wouldn't put a lien on your house. So I need to be reimbursed for that, too."

"Oh?" She changed her tone.

"I was thinking, I know that you wiped out your savings with my retainer. So I think we can work out a deal where you sign your house over to me. You know, for collateral. Then, when you get out of the hospital, you can come to work for me. I don't know, maybe filing and typing, or something. That can be worked out later. But anyway, I need the collateral."

Alicia was stunned. This proposal hit her unexpectedly. She thought for a moment.

"I don't know about this, Max, I'll have to think it over."

"I'll just draw up the papers and you can sign them before court begins. That way it'll be taken care of so we won't have to worry."

"I won't be worried."

"I just don't want you to have extra stuff on your mind right now, that's all."

"Sure, sure," Alicia said distractedly, and hung up before remembering to say goodbye.

She sat in her armchair, reflecting on Bailey's proposal. The idea didn't sit well and made her uneasy. She wondered if, or how far, she could really trust him. Strangely, she liked him. He was a handsome man, younger than her by about ten years. Alicia didn't know. She was terrible at guessing ages. His most appealing feature, as far as she was concerned, was his blue eyes. Deep, blue eyes. He was a charmer. Surrounding those blue eyes was an innocent-looking baby face. Alicia took solace in that. He reminded her of a boyfriend she once had in high school. She yawned, and headed for bed.

Thinking about the trial and all its implications was not the only thing making her tired. The weather had turned hot. Just as East Tennessee had experienced a late cold snap, the region was now in the midst of a small heat wave. Unusual weather was something that Alicia had learned to live with. Tennessee was often caught between the cold air masses coming off the Great Lakes and Canada, and the hot, humid air from the Gulf of Mexico. The atmospheric collisions frequently resulted in violent late afternoon or evening thunderstorms. Spectacular lightning displays often accompanied these storms. It was not at all uncommon for these lightning shows, accompanied by high winds, to knock out the power, only to be restored several hours later. Living in the country meant having to wait until the more densely populated towns and cities had their power restored first. But for now, a high pressure ridge dominated the area, resulting in temperatures in the mid-nineties. The humidity was also unusually high, pushing the heat index past the century mark.

The house had a window air conditioner, which didn't do much to cool the drafty old house. The hot weather, with its relentless humidity, made her long for the almost icy temperature of her bedroom, the only room in the house below eighty degrees.

Alicia pulled herself out of the overstuffed armchair. Crossing the threshold into her bedroom was like walking through a wall of invisible ice, raising gooseflesh on her arms. For once, the temperature drop was refreshing. She couldn't wait to lie down on her bed. By the time she undressed and put on her nightclothes, she was quite cold. She slid under the covers, forgetting the summer heat. The weight of the covers on her body temporarily released her mind from the heavy burden of the trial. Her thoughts drifted to S'postu, and how much her life had changed in just a few months. It occurred to her that S'postu had always been her secret, like a pile of dirt swept under the rug. Now the trial was stripping away that rug thread by thread. As she thought back, she realized how much S'postu relieved her loneliness, and how normal that felt to her. Now that he was silenced, she was beginning to see how insane her whole life seemed from the outside. She knew that he was connected to those French doors, and he could only speak to her while the house was complete. As if they were the doorway to where he is now. And yet, she could still feel his presence in the house, like knowing there's a nasty stain on the wall, hidden by a picture. Then it hit her; *since S'postu was asleep, he could only communicate with her when she was asleep! Subconscious to subconscious.*

Each night she faced a dilemma. If she slept in any other room in the house, the heat made it almost impossible for her to sleep, she remembered less, and the dreams were not as vivid or violent, but they were still there. If she slept in her room, the cool air made it easier to sleep, but the dreams were always more intense. Tonight, she opted for the latter, and hoped that sheer exhaustion would get her through the night, her sleep unimpeded. Yet she longed for the communication with S'postu through her dreams, however vague. She hated how empty she felt because of his absence. Finally, she closed her eyes and cried herself to sleep.

"Sarge! Sarge!" Dunlop's excited voice cut through the cold air. Alicia heard the crunch of snow under his feet, no…under their feet. There was definitely more than one person trudging through the snow. The bare branches yielded to his bulk. Dunlop appeared through the bushes. The air was crisp, and Dunlop's breath was visible as he spoke.

"There's two dozen of them damn Yankees on the other side of that ridge," he said, pointing to the hill behind him. "Them bastards was even stupid 'nuff ta light a gall durn fire!" Alicia looked past them. In the distance, she could see a thin line of smoke against the cold, blue sky.

"Must not be a very big fire," she heard herself say in a man's voice.

"Naw, jest a little bitty one. Reese seen it better 'n me."

Reese Fuller appeared from behind Clyde Dunlop. The three of them were in a clearing at the top of a small hill. Thick shoots of bare, thorny bushes surrounded them. She seemed to be crouched down on a large rock above the snow-covered ground. Dunlop emerged from a barely visible path in the thick undergrowth, and squatted in front of her. Reese remained standing, resting his foot on the rock.

"Them northern boys must be used to the cold better 'an us," Reese began, "'cause I don't see how in tarnation that itty bitty fire could keep the fleas off a durn dawg warm."

Alicia laughed under her breath, then stood on the rock. "What's the chance of them Yankee bastards findin' us here?"

"I'd say slim ta none," Dunlop blurted in response. Alicia shaded her eyes from the morning sun. Looking to the east, all she could see was the brown of the bare trees, with the occasional green blot of a pine tree in the distance. The rich green of the pines stood out against the pure white snow. She somehow knew it had snowed suddenly during the night. When the three of them awoke, their bedrolls were covered with the freshly deposited frozen precipitation.

"I say we wait 'til nightfall, then slip into their camp real quiet-like, then slit their throats while they're asleep," Dunlop said, voice low, with an evil crooked smile.

"With just the three of us?" Alicia asked, unsure.

"That's the only fittin' way ta git back at them bastards that bushwhacked us an' took out our whole bloomin' platoon. 'Cept fer us," Dunlop's eyes narrowed with rage. "And not only tha…"

A sudden sound from behind them cut off his words. They spun around. The scene around her suddenly changed. She found herself sitting in a wooden chair in her living room. The sun was streaming in through the open windows. The aroma of a stew cooking filled the air. A strange feeling of deja-vu filled her. Everything seemed so familiar, yet she felt detached from the situation and knew what was about to happen, yet she was locked in a loop of destiny. A strange, surreal sense of seeing the situation both from a third party perspective, and through her own eyes, ebbed through her.

As she suspected, the television and the phone were gone and all the furniture was different. It seemed Victorian, just as it had before. She looked over at the French doors, hanging there as if she had never removed them. Her heart swelled with a powerful sense of beauty as her eyes rested on them. Although she knew what was about to happen, she continued, unable to alter the outcome. She had no choice but to let the events play out, her will succumbing to a familiar, greater force.

Alicia looked down at her legs. As she suspected, there was a large wheel on each side of her chair. Her legs felt strangely numb. She could see a hardwood floor below her feet.

"Supper's ready. Come in here and eat," Daphne's voice boomed from the kitchen.

As she began to roll herself into the dining room, terror gripped her. She wanted to get up and run, but was compelled to continue. She was determined to see who was going to hit her, but couldn't move her head, as if it were locked in a vise. Finally, her head felt free enough to move, but as soon as she began to turn to see, the sound of shattering bone ripped through her head. Unbelievable pain washed over her. Her limp body sailed out of the wheel chair, and crashed against the hardwood floor. As she felt the warm blood soak her short-cropped hair, everything faded to darkness.

She bolted upright in her bed. The dream was so real, so intense that it left her panting. The back of her head throbbed. Her head felt wet, but only at the back. This didn't make sense. Subconsciously, she surmised that sweat would encompass her entire head, not just a one spot. She reached to touch the back of her head, afraid of what she might find. Her stomach tightened. She reached over to turn on the light on the bedside table. Slowly, she brought her hand in front of her eyes, almost too afraid to look. The images and sounds of the dream's final moment repeated themselves again and again in her mind. Would it be blood? She had to know. She breathed a sigh of relief as she saw nothing but the shine of sweat on her fingers. She twisted around to examine her pillow. It was soaked with sweat. Her throat was dry and she realized that she was thirsty. After throwing the covers off, she ambled into the dark kitchen for a drink of water.

Alicia did not turn on the light, but stood at the kitchen sink, letting the water run before filling her glass. She stared through the window into the night sky. A half-moon hung low on the horizon. The grass and trees in the distance were bathed in the eerie, cream-colored glow of moonlight. Alicia could see glowing streaks of green as fireflies flew above the grass behind her house. She could hear the dull chirping of crickets and the occasional croaking of a bullfrog. The water flowing from the faucet sounded like the babbling brook in the background. The night never sleeps, Alicia thought. The human race is just a small piece of the nature's majesty. The earth still turns, the sun still comes up regardless of who lives or dies, or whatever tragedy occurs, by our own definition. Or what any one man or woman is doing at any one time. The proof of that was being played out right here, tonight, in front of her. The insects flew, devouring one another, then another was born to replace the one that was lost. Nature is relentless, and sometimes cruel.

Alicia shook her head in quick little movements to bring her back to the here and now. She was tired. She filled her glass, drank the water, then again stumbled off to bed.

# CHAPTER 11

The elevator doors slid open, and Alicia stepped out into the hallway. It was empty, except for Max Bailey, who was waiting for her on the bench across from the courtroom.

"Max! You're here early."

"Good morning, Alicia." Bailey smiled.

"Well Max," she walked over to him, "I see you have that paperwork you were talking about last Friday."

"Yep. It's all in order, ready for your signature." He half-smiled, half smirked.

Alicia caught his expression and began to feel uncomfortable. *What kind of man is this Max Bailey anyway? S'postu, S'postu, tell me what to do.* She paused a moment, "What if the jury says I have to spend the rest of my life in a padded cell?"

"Remember, it's not up to them. It's up to the judge. And that will happen at the sentencing hearing. That's where the D.A. will recommend the sentence. Most judges go along with what the D.A. recommends."

*This jerk has left a perfect out for himself. I can't turn over my house to this man—but I have no choice. I'm out of money and he's my only hope. My God, what will I do if he won't give me my house back? S'postu, help me!* "But ain't it a little strange? I mean, giving up a house in trade for legal services?" She tried not to let her uncertainty show.

"No, not necessarily."

"Why?"

"Back in the old days, lots of people traded all kinds of stuff for all kinds of services. You know, like horses, saddles, probably even houses."

"Well, I still don't like it."

"Just remember, the plan is that you do six months at Rhinewood. Then, when you get out, you can come to work at my office and you can have your house back."

*This is getting worse by the minute!* "Well, you've got me caught between a rock and a hard place. But, against my better judgment, I'll sign your papers."

"Everything will work out fine, Alicia, you'll see." Bailey felt a twinge of guilt, telling her a lie like that. He had lied to clients plenty of the times in the past to get them to do something that he needed or wanted, and until now, never gave it a second thought.

Alicia took the papers and looked them over quickly. Although she really had no idea what all this legal jargon said, or what exactly she was reading, she at least wanted to give Bailey the appearance that she knew what she was doing. She was not illiterate, by any means. However, she understood very little legal terminology. She looked at the papers for two solid minutes, an eternity for Bailey. From the corner of her eye, she could see a single drop of sweat run from his hairline, along his cheek toward his chin.

"What's wrong, Max?" she asked. *Starting to feel guilty, are we?*

"Nothing," he answered, the lawyer coming out in him. "What could possibly be wrong?"

"If nothing's wrong," Alicia queried, "then why the water works?" Gesturing with the papers to the sweat on his face. "It's not hot in here."

"Don't know, maybe I'm nervous about your defense." Bailey lied again.

*Gotcha! Now that was a damn lie!* Alicia turned her attention back to the papers. *There is nothing I could do or say to change things, so I might as well do it. S'postu, wake up and tell me what to do.* After a few more minutes, Alicia signed them and gave them back to Bailey without a word. He took them and stashed them in his briefcase. The two sat silently, watching people get off the elevator, and waited for the bailiff to open the courtroom doors. She could feel his growing discomfort with each passing moment.

Alicia stared straight at the door without looking at Bailey, thinking about the situation, feeling angry and obviously being taken advantage of. He saw the change on her face, but made no attempt to console her.

The bailiff stepped off the elevator and nodded a greeting to the waiting crowd. As he walked to the door, ready to open it, the Westchesters stepped off. Alicia looked at them with a halfsmile on her face. Nadine looked over at her and smiled ever so subtly. Barely detectable, but a smile, nevertheless. Could she have imagined it? Charles only looked at the floor as they walked past her and into the courtroom. She watched the two of them take their seats. Alicia stood, then went into the courtroom herself. Bailey remained seated on the bench, staring straight ahead, unmoving.

As she passed the Westchesters, she could hear a quiet conversation between them but could not make out what they were saying. After taking her seat at the defense desk, she watched with interest as the court reporter set up her stenography machine. The bailiff sat at his desk, shuffling through a small stack of papers. The rustling of the papers could be heard over the soft murmur of the various conversations taking place throughout the courtroom. She wondered what those papers said. Did they even concern her? Strangely, she did not feel nervous about the upcoming day. Instead, she felt disconnected from it all.

Bailey took his seat next to her with a sheepish look on his face. Alicia felt a little better knowing Bailey felt bad about taking the transfer of title to her house. It made him seem to have a small semblance of conscience. Maybe things would work out the way he had said after all. She hid a self-satisfied smile from him as he looked straight ahead.

The bailiff rose and did his usual routine to address the court. After the formalities, the judge looked at Bailey.

"Mr. Bailey, are you ready to present your defense?"

"Yes, Your Honor." He came to life.

"Then proceed."

"I call to the stand, Patrick Freeman."

Alicia was surprised. She didn't know he was in the room. She guessed that she was too busy feeling disconnected to notice. Patrick Freeman rose and took his seat at the witness stand. After he was sworn in, Bailey began his questioning.

"Please state your name for the record."

"Patrick Freeman. I'm the director at the Rhinewood Mental Institute. I'm also a psychiatrist."

"Dr. Freeman," Bailey cleared his throat, "you had an occasion to speak with my client?"

"Yes."

"For what purpose?"

"As you know, Mr. Bailey, I was contacted by you to evaluate your client to determine, then give testimony regarding, her state of mind during an incident regarding Mr. Charles Westchester."

Henry Walton rose, pushing his seat back with his legs as he stood. "The prosecution stipulates as to the witness's qualifications, your Honor."

"Very well, Mr. Walton," Judge Finney began, "am I to assume that this is the independent psychiatrist?"

"Yes, that would be correct, Your Honor." Walton replied.

"I see." Judge Finney said, turning to Bailey. "Please continue, Mr. Bailey."

Bailey thanked the judge, then turned to Freeman. "What did you determine in your interview with the defendant?"

"Your client claims to have been coerced into hurting Mr. Westchester by a voice in her head."

A quiet murmur rippled through the courtroom. Bailey ignored the audience's response and continued. "Do you feel that my client made this up to avert the consequences of her action?"

"I don't believe so. She actually believed she was talking to, and holding conversations with, an entity."

"What do you mean, entity?"

"She truly believes that this, uh, person has helped her find missing items, taught her songs, and even inflicted pain on her if she disobeyed him."

"Is this like a childhood imaginary friend?"

"No, I don't believe so. Miss Freed truly believes this person, whom she refers to as S'postu, actually exists."

Alicia felt naked. The threads of that rug were unraveling before her eyes. She felt ashamed. As the psychiatrist reiterated her interview, and someone other than herself explained about S'postu, she realized how absurd the situation sounded. Is this what she needed to swing the verdict her way? It was bitter medicine to take.

"So," Bailey continued, "in your expert opinion, was Alicia Freed sane and in control of herself at the time of the attack on Mr. Westchester?"

"I would have to say no," Freeman replied.

"Have you gone so far as to reach a diagnosis, Doctor?"

"Miss Freed is definitely suffering from a mild psychosis which I have determined to be paranoid schizophrenia."

"Will you explain to the court, in laymen's terms, what exactly that is?"

"Certainly. Basically, Miss Freed has lost touch with reality, and has manufactured this fantasy person in order to cope with some tragedy that must have occurred during her childhood."

Alicia was appalled. After a solid hour of questions about the interview with Alicia, his thoughts about her condition based on his past experience and expertise, Bailey was ready to conclude Freeman's testimony.

"Well Doctor," Bailey said, pacing in front of the jury, "I think that's all the questions I have at this time." Bailey walked over to the defendant's desk and took his seat.

"Mr. Walton," Judge Finney commanded, "do you wish to cross?"

"Yes, Your Honor." Walton said, standing.

"Dr. Freeman, are you positive, in your opinion, I mean that the defendant isn't making this all up to avoid prosecution?"

"It would seem sir," Freeman began, "that she didn't avoid prosecution at all."

The judge banged his gavel in an attempt to silence the muffled laughter. His face flushed with anger. "I want order!" he commanded.

"In my opinion, Mr. Walton, I don't think so. Normally, if the story is manufactured or the patient is acting, trying to get out of a situation, the facts are fragmented and inconsistent. But the defendant has a coherent story. No matter from which angle the question is asked, the answer always remains consistent. This, to me, suggests psychosis, or perhaps an alternate reality. Miss Freed switches from reality to reality then meshes the two together. She cannot separate her fantasy from the true reality. I therefore must conclude that, medically speaking, she was suffering, and still is, from a mild psychosis which I have determined to be schizophrenia, which has distorted reality for her."

Henry Walton tried to look sorry he had asked. His question, as answered by Freeman, almost made him look like an incompetent fool. Although he made the deal with Bailey and his losing the case was necessary to fulfil their clandestine plans, being made out like an incompetent fool was not part of the deal. Still, deal or no deal, he hated to lose. He felt sure the jury would find for the defense.

"Thank you, Doctor. That is all I have."

"Do you wish to redirect, Mr. Bailey?" the judge asked.

"No, Your Honor." Bailey said, standing. "In fact, the defense rests."

"Very well, Mr. Bailey," said Judge Finney, turning to Patrick Freeman. "Sir, you may step down." He turned to address the court. "The court will take a ninety minute recess for lunch. After that gentlemen," looking at the two attorneys, "I will hear your summations." He banged his gavel.

Alicia looked up at Bailey. "Is that all?"

"Yep. That's all we need. Well, except for the summations, then it's up to the jury. But I think they'll find in your favor."

"How can you be so sure?"

"When the D.A. asked that question at the end, he practically made my summation for me. Now all I have to do is reinforce that with the jury, and they must, based on Pat's testimony, find you not guilty due to temporary insanity. The rest of the trial is only a formality."

*What a change in you since this morning in the hallway! Oh, now that's very strange! Am I becoming comfortable by this confident, almost arrogant stance?*

"Let's grab a bite," Bailey suggested, breaking her thoughts. "What do you want? My treat. It may be the last time in a while that you get to taste real food."

Alicia hadn't considered that aspect of her situation. She thought for a minute and realized she was hungry.

"Let's have steak." Her request sent a chill down Bailey's spine. The last time he had steak was with Patrick Freeman and Henry Walton. He did not want to be reminded of the conspiracy. Was it possible that Max Bailey was developing a conscience? He suddenly felt terrible for what he was about to do to this woman. Nevertheless, he tried not to let it show.

"That's ok by me." he said, swallowing hard.

"Well Max, you work around here all the time. So, where is a good place to eat?"

"Let's see," Bailey said, thinking out loud. "Oh! I know, there's a little steak house about two blocks over that I heard is real good."

Alicia blinked at him in surprise. "I thought you would know all the great places to eat at around here. You look like a 'let's do lunch' kinda guy to me."

Bailey snorted a laugh as the two headed for the elevator. The courtroom now stood empty.

"Truth is," Bailey informed her, "I usually don't get the chance to eat lunch around here. I usually skip it, or grab a bite at a place near my office."

During their meal, Bailey told Alicia what normally happened when someone is found not guilty by reason of insanity, temporary or not. The defendant is committed to a mental facility. The judge will usually issue a standing order to review the progress of the defendant every six months or so. If, in the opinion of the attending psychiatrist, the defendant has received sufficient treatment for recovery, then a review hearing is conducted and the court orders the defendant's release.

Bailey knew that he explained this to her before, but he wanted to make sure she understood what was about to happen to her, and put her apprehension to rest. At the same time, he made sure he did not imply that these circumstances would occur exactly as he described. He further explained that the judge certainly had a mind of his own, and could make any ruling he thought appropriate for her situation. He did explain that he was reasonably sure that the judge would see things as Bailey described, and rule accordingly.

The two finished their lunch and headed back to the courthouse. They arrived thirty minutes before court began. Since leaving the restaurant, they had not spoken. They stepped out of the elevator, and she sat on the bench opposite the door as usual. Alicia looked on as Bailey walked past her and stood in front of a window overlooking the city, and stared out into the July afternoon. Save for the two of them, the hall was deserted. *What he was thinking? Could he be formulating his summation? Surely, he would have done that by now.* She decided it would be best if she just let him be, and realized that her future resided in those words, so she wasn't about to break his concentration and jeopardize it.

Bailey saw the decorations for the upcoming Fourth of July celebration. He hadn't even realized what month it was, let alone what holiday. A banner stretched across the street below him, advertising a city-sponsored fireworks display at the park. The sight of the decorations made him realize that he had indeed heard about the festivities, advertised on radio or television, but only his subconscious remembered. His mind was preoccupied with the trial, and all the additional factors that this particular trial contained. As he watched two city workers fixing the banner on a telephone pole in front of the Trailways bus station across the street, he realized that the judge would probably want to wrap things up today if possible. For tomorrow was the fourth, and in his past experience with Judge Finney, he knew he liked to tie up loose ends in nice neat packages. Bailey was trying to think of the most efficient way to present his summation. The case was already won. It was only a matter of presenting an open and shut case to the jurors. But he knew that there was nothing he could do to make the jury reach their decision any faster once they began deliberations.

A small crowd of people had formed waiting for the bailiff to reopen the courtroom. Before she knew it, the bailiff had opened the door and people began filtering in. Alicia rose to follow the crowd, took her seat at the defense desk and waited. Bailey was alone again in the hall.

At five minutes before court was set to begin, Alicia began to worry. *Where is he?* She went out into the hall and found him standing at the window, apparently oblivious to the time.

"Max!! It's almost time!"

He jumped and turned quickly to look at her with glazed eyes. "Oh I'm sorry," he replied, rubbing his eyes. "I must have been daydreaming."

"We only have a few minutes 'til court starts again."

"Oh. Right. Yeah, let's go."

As Alicia passed the Westchesters, she noticed Nadine directed a weak smile in her direction. She was surprised at the apparent thaw in Nadine's attitude. Alicia smiled back. Charles nodded his head in response. Alicia and Bailey took their seats once again behind the defense desk.

The court reporter came in and took her seat behind the stenography machine. The bailiff rose and began the proceedings.

"Gentleman," the judge began, "I would like to wrap up this case today if at all possible. Mr. Walton, please begin your summation."

Henry Walton rose and cleared his throat, then walked over to the space in front of the jury. "Ladies and gentlemen, first of all I would like to thank you for your service to this court and to the State of Tennessee. The

State has proven beyond a reasonable doubt that the defendant did indeed commit an assault on Charles Westchester. The only question that you have to answer is whether Alicia Freed was of sound mind when she viciously attacked Mr. Westchester. It's now a question of whether or not you believe the psychiatrist who testified before you this morning. We all know that Alicia Freed did in fact commit this crime. The highlighted map, the knife with the defendant's fingerprints plus the eyewitness testimonies all prove that Alicia Freed is guilty of this horrible crime. The evidence is compelling, and I ask you to grant justice to the Westchesters and return a verdict of guilty. Thank you for your attention." Henry Walton sat in his chair behind the prosecution desk.

"Mr. Bailey," Judge Finney commanded, "your statement, please."

Bailey rose and walked over to the jury, then turned to look at Alicia. "Ladies and gentlemen, take a look at this woman," he began, gesturing toward her. "She's barely five feet three. There is no denying that she attacked Mr. Westchester. Now I am not trying to belittle his pain and suffering, but he's almost a whole foot taller than she is. The question is, was he ever in any mortal danger? I really don't think so. All this evidence is well and good, but it is her sanity that is being questioned here. You heard testimony from Detective Salter and from Charles Westchester himself, how my client reacted by yelling 'S'postu.' Or something about S'postu, whenever Alicia Freed encountered them. I would ask you to ask yourselves if you believe this to be the actions of someone totally in charge of their senses. And then there was the testimony of Patrick Freeman. He is the director of the Rhinewood Mental Institute. He is the independent psychiatrist agreed to by the prosecution. You heard him state in his professional opinion that she needed help. He said that she was not responsible for her own actions at the time of the incident. I'm asking you, on behalf of my client, to please return a verdict of not guilty, but recommend to the court that she be placed in the institute so that she may receive the help that she so desperately needs. Please remember during your deliberations, Charles Westchester will make a full and complete recovery. You people hold the life of my client in your hands. Her future, perhaps even her very life hangs in the balance. Please allow her the treatment she needs to return to society as a productive member. Thank you."

Bailey sat in his chair next to Alicia. The judge poured himself a glass of water from the pitcher and took a drink. He instructed the jury to look only at the facts, then dismissed them to begin their deliberations. Alicia watched them disappear through a door behind the bench.

Her fate was now in the hands of twelve strangers. If Bailey had done his job well, then things would turn out the way he said it would. Otherwise, the unthinkable would occur, and Alicia was not prepared for that.

"What do we do now, Max?"

"We wait. That's all that's left." Bailey stood, taking her by the hand. "C'mon, I'll buy you a cup of coffee."

"What about the jury?" Alicia said, standing to follow him.

"They can get their own coffee."

"No, that's not what I meant!" Alicia said venomously, upset that he would make light of her situation.

"I know what you meant. It's ok, they'll call us when the jury gets in."

She took him up on his offer. As they passed the Westchester's, Alicia stopped to apologize again for the pain she caused Charles.

"Well I can't say it's okay," Nadine began, "because it's not, but I think your lawyer was right when he said Charles will make a full recovery."

"Well I'll tell you what," Charles broke in, "I don't know why you stuck me, really. But if you're sick, I hope you get the treatment you need. And even if my wife won't forgive you, I will. I'm told that it's part of the healing process, forgiving you, I mean."

"We're going to Hawaii in three weeks," Nadine said.

Charles extended his hand to Alicia. "We are leaving the courtroom. Leaving you to your verdict. I wish you well in your life."

Charles took Nadine by the hand, brushed past Alicia and Bailey, and left. Alicia was awestruck. She couldn't believe the compassion of Charles Westchester. Slowly Alicia and Bailey made their way to the cafeteria on the main level of the courthouse.

After sitting at a small table in the cafeteria, Bailey finally spoke. "I don't think I've ever seen that before."

"I was rather surprised by it myself." Alicia confessed.

The two sipped their coffee, and talked about everything else except the trial. Bailey kept asking questions about her house. Alicia countered with questions about the inner workings of his office. She was intrigued at the prospect of working for Bailey, as he had suggested. No matter what Alicia asked about the office, Bailey kept switching the subject back to her house.

She explained that the house was built by her great, great grandfather for her great grandmother as a wedding present. The house passed from generation to generation until the house was willed to Alicia at the time of her mother's death. She was curious about Bailey's constant interest in her house, but didn't think he had an ulterior motive for his interrogation, only perhaps an interest in old houses. At over a century and a half in age, her house was old. After an hour or so of conversation about various current events, the bailiff walked up to the table.

"Mr. Bailey," he said, "the jury is in."

"Wow! That was fast," Bailey commented.

The bailiff turned and walked away. Alicia's mouth was full of coffee. Her eyes widened. She had to fight to keep from spitting the coffee out. She swallowed hard to get the liquid down her throat. A shiver ran down her spine, and she could barely speak.

"Is that bad?" she asked, voice raspy and shaking.

"Well, it could be." he said, drawing a breath.

"This is it, isn't it?" Alicia asked, swallowing hard. Bailey noticed her face turning white. Beads of sweat formed on her brow.

"Look Alicia," Bailey said softly, "it could be good. But we have to go into court and find out." Bailey rose and led her out of the cafeteria.

Alicia felt like she was having one of those "out of body" experiences she had read about. As if she were watching herself from a third party perspective, she found herself sitting in her chair behind the defense desk. She had no memory of getting on or off the elevator, or entering the courtroom. If it weren't for Bailey, she would have never made it back to the courtroom. Several minutes passed, and she found herself standing up. She stared blankly ahead, not realizing that the judge had told her to stand. Yet she was on her feet, Bailey standing at her side. Her mind was a blur, she was barely aware of her surroundings, yet she knew the jury foreman was standing, waiting for the bailiff to return the jury's decision. Slowly, her mind began to clear. What seemed an eternity to Alicia was actually only a second or two.

"Has the jury has reached a verdict?" The judge's words cleared her head.

"We have, your Honor," the jury foreman responded. Alicia sank back inwardly, yet on the outside stood tall and confident. At least, that was the image she was trying to convey. Under the table, her knees shook. She strained desperately to calm them. Her mother always told her to maintain her composure in the face of subjugation. She gripped Bailey's hand tightly, her knuckles turning white. Bailey winced, but managed to maintain his posture.

"What say you?" the judge's voice echoed as if in a great hall, like the voice of God.

"We find the defendant, Alicia Freed…"

Alicia drew a breath, then held it, cringing. The milliseconds seemed to her like hours.

"…Not guilty by reason of insanity."

Alicia let go of her breath.

"We further recommend that the defendant be placed in the state's care for treatment."

"So entered," said the judge.

Tears formed at the corner of Alicia's eyes. She released Bailey's hand, he immediately shook it then rubbed it with his other hand. Alicia tried to wipe the tears from eyes, but they ran down her cheeks like cold rain.

"Sentencing hearing will take place in August," the judge began, looking down at his calendar. "On the first."

Alicia felt great joy at not having to go to jail, and overwhelming sadness at the prospect of living at the institute.

"Thank you," the judge continued, looking at the jury, "you have fulfilled your obligation to the state. The jury is dismissed." The judge banged his gavel, then rose and left the courtroom. As people wandered about in all directions around her, Alicia sat down in her chair. Bailey was busy stuffing papers into his briefcase.

"Max," Alicia asked with a shaking voice, "I don't understand."

"What?" he asked, turning toward her.

"If I was found not guilty, then how come we have to do a sentencing hearing?"

"Alicia," Bailey began softly, compassionately, "I explained this to you before. There's always a sentencing hearing when that particular verdict is reached. As far as the crime itself is concerned, you were found not guilty. But that doesn't do anything with the insanity part. And that is the part that still has to be resolved."

"Yeah but…" Alicia's tears came like someone opened the floodgates.

"It's alright, this is the part where Henry will recommend that you be committed to Rhinewood."

"But I thought that the jury does the sentencing," she stated, wiping the tears again, making a greater effort to control herself.

"Not anymore. They used to. There has been a law passed recently that prohibits the jury from doing the sentencing. They can only recommend. Now all the sentencing takes place in a separate hearing. It's a trial, kinda like this one, except there's no jury."

"Oh?"

"Yeah. See, the prosecution and the defense argue, and the judge decides. It's all pretty simple actually."

"Maybe simple to you. You do this all day long."

"Well, hey! That's why they pay me the big bucks." A grin shot across Bailey's face. Alicia caught a glimpse of the wolf under the sheep's clothing. A cold shiver ran up her sine

"Look," he soothed, placing his hand on her shoulder, sitting down beside her, trying to salvage the moment, "this is what we wanted to happen, remember?"

"I guess, but I'm still scared." She realized she now feared Bailey as much as the sentence.

"I know you are. Things will work out fine, you'll see."

*Maybe for you, you scumbag!*

Bailey closed his briefcase, then stood. "You're still going to have to spend some time in the institute, you know."

Alicia looked at the floor. *So, that's how you'll get rid of me!*

"Alicia," Bailey's tone hardened. "I want you to get your house in order. Once the institute has custody of you, then the ball is in their court. The court system has nothing to do with it, or you anymore. Basically, you are at the mercy of the doctors at the institute."

*You mean your buddy at the institute!*

Bailey jerked the briefcase off the desk, and left without another word. He was obviously upset. Alicia sat, the courtroom was now empty, blankly staring at the spot where Bailey had been standing. Silently, tears rolled down her face. After a short time, she stood and left the courtroom herself, angrier than ever at S'postu. The adrenalin flowing through her veins gave her the strength to make it home.

# CHAPTER 12

The phone rang in Patrick Freeman's office while he was doing evaluation reports, which he hated. Worse yet, he hated to be disturbed while doing them. He tossed his pen at the paper and angrily picked up the receiver.

"Max Bailey on line two," came Clara's gruff voice. Before he could reply, the phone clicked into nothingness. He smashed the button furiously for line two.

"Freeman here."

"Pat, it's Max."

Freeman remained silent, allowing his anger to fade before speaking.

"Returning your call," Bailey said cautiously.

"I called you two hours ago!" Freeman snapped.

"Hey! I was in a meeting with a new client. I do have a job you know," Bailey shouted back.

"I'm sorry." Freeman's voice softened. "I'm in the middle of these damn employee evaluations." His voice became angry again. "Clara is being her usual bitchy self, and you know once you get a civil service job, its damn near takes an act of congress, or even God, to fire you." Bailey laughed as Freeman continued, "God! I'd love to fire that bitch. But you know as soon as you do, then you get slapped with a damn wrongful termination suit, and…"

Bailey laughed even louder. "Hold on. Hold on, maybe I should charge you a shrink fee."

"Sorry," Freeman laughed, "I shouldn't unload on you."

"That's right, I cost too much." Bailey paused. "What's on your mind?"

"Oh yeah, right. I found someone interested in that piece of property you're about to, uh, acquire."

"Oh yeah?"

"Yep. And he's got bucks, too. Big bucks. He'll pay cash!"

"Cash, huh? Sounds like my kind of guy."

"I'll have his people get in touch with your people and arrange a meeting."

"It's gonna have to wait."

"Why? He's ready now."

"We can't do it until the sentencing hearing. You know that."

"Oh. Ok. I forgot. I thought you already had possession."

"Nope. Not yet. Can you stall the guy? I mean, we only have to wait ten days or so, then we can do just about anything we want."

"No problem. I'll make it work. All right Max, I'll talk to you later."

"Ok, bye." The phone clicked in Freeman's ear and he hung it in its cradle. As he stared at the phone on his desk, he felt the anger and hatred of those evaluation reports evaporate. For the first time, he returned to them without dread.

# CHAPTER 13

Alicia sat at the dining room table, sipping a cup of hot tea. She loved tea in the evenings. This particular evening she reflected on the month's events. July drew to a close, and August came like a whisper. Tomorrow was the beginning of her sentencing hearing. She spent the month of July selling anything that anyone would buy. The house was bare except for the dining room table, which had passed through her family for three generations. It belonged to the house, not to her. The few other personal items that were still left in the house were her bed, dresser, and of course, her best clothes. She packed the last remaining suitcase with the last of her clothes, and stowed it in the trunk of the Pontiac. During the sale of her possessions, she had managed to generate some $8,400. She stuffed it into a large envelope, wrapped it in aluminum foil, and hid it under a loose board under the kitchen sink. All of these things took place without Bailey's knowledge. In fact, she barely heard a word from him all month. He only called twice: once on the 11th , to see how she was holding up, and again on the 21st to tell her that she needed to see Patrick Freeman at the institute for two more interviews. Then she heard nothing until earlier that day, to remind her of the sentencing hearing.

The two interviews with Patrick Freeman were very much like the first one. He asked her the same questions. She replied with virtually the same answers. Alicia couldn't see the point of continuing the interviews, but Freeman said they were essential. She showed up under protest.

She decided that she didn't trust Max Bailey after all, which is why she sold almost all of her worldly possessions, and hid the proceeds. She didn't know how long she would be at the institute, and wanted something to fall back on in case Bailey double-crossed her and sold her house without her knowledge. She felt good about the month's ordeal, and could now take time to relax before stepping onto the emotional roller-coaster the hearing was sure to bring.

Alicia picked up her cup of tea and carried it outside. The warm summer night was full of the things she had taken for granted over the years, things she never noticed. Her last night of freedom was sobering. It made her notice the moon, with its pale light washing out the colors of the woods surrounding her house. As she stood on the back porch, she heard the chirping of crickets, and the croaking of bull frogs in the distance. The summer fireflies were almost gone and it was rare sight to see their iridescent green streaks break the velvety air. She sipped the last of her tea, and turned to go back into the house.

# CHAPTER 14

Alicia waited on the bench across the hall from the courtroom. The event was almost routine by now. She had been sitting on the bench for nearly 20 minutes before the court reporter stepped off of the elevator and smiled at her. Alicia returned the gesture. For all the time she had spent with the court reporter, it seemed ironic to her that the two never had spoken. Alicia decided to break the cycle.

"Good morn…" Alicia's voice cracked, dry from not speaking since the day before. She began again, "Good morning." She rose and walked toward the court reporter, extending her hand. The woman took it.

"Good morning, Miss Freed," she said, smiling.

"You know," Alicia began, "I don't believe I have ever gotten your name."

"Selma Hollin," the court reporter said, releasing Alicia's hand. "Glad to meet you."

"Well Selma, how long have you been doing this?" Alicia asked pointing to the metal case at Selma's feet. Selma looked down at her stenography machine.

"Oh, about six years now."

"Do you like it?"

"Yeah, it's great. I can make my own hours, and sometimes the cases I record are very interesting."

"Yeah, I'll bet. Like this one." Alicia suddenly realized this woman probably thought she was crazy, and held back her scowl. "I hope this is my last day," she said, brushing her hair back with her hand, trying not to show her annoyance. "This, all this, is just about more than I can take."

Selma said nothing, she only smiled softly. The door to the elevator slid open again. Both women looked to see who was getting off. Alicia smiled at Selma, and started toward the bench when she recognized Max Bailey. Something was different about him. At first, she did not recognize the change in him. Suddenly, it hit her. Bailey was sporting a beard. She looked hard at his face, and noticed his facial hair was a slightly darker shade of brown than the hair on his head, and was mixed with an occasional strand of grey. Although his beard was distinguished, the overall effect contradicted his baby face. Alicia was slightly impressed knowing from past experience that men with baby faces often found it difficult to grow full beards. Usually, the beards on baby-faced men were sparse at best.

"Wow Max!" Alicia said, enthusiastically, "I like your new look."

Bailey only smiled.

"How do you like it?" Alicia asked.

"Well I'm just getting over the itchy stage, but I like it fine so far."

The two engaged in small talk until the bailiff stepped out of the elevator and unlocked the courtroom door. Alicia had gotten used to having a small audience for the courtroom proceedings. Just before court began she saw only the prosecutor, Bailey, the court reporter Selma, and the bailiff. It seemed there were more people missing than just the judge. She felt as if they were on a trip and had left someone behind.

"All rise," the bailiff's voice boomed. "Court is now in session. The Honorable Judge Thomas J. Finney, presiding." The judge entered the courtroom and seated himself.

"This is a hearing to determine whether or not it is appropriate for Alicia Freed to receive a sentence for a crime for which she was found not guilty by reason of insanity." The gavel crashed.

"Gentlemen, your openings, please," the judge asked.

Henry Walton rose, and stepped toward the bench. "Your Honor," he began, "in light of the testimony given to the court regarding the state of mind of Alicia Freed at the time of the attack, I think justice would be served if she were committed to the Rhinewood Mental Institute." Walton sat.

"Mr. Bailey," the judge commanded, "your statement please."

Bailey rose. "For once," Bailey began, "I concur with my esteemed colleague. It was always the defense's contention during the trial that my client was not responsible for her actions at the time of the attack. My recommendation to the court is also for her to be committed to Rhinewood Mental Institute." Bailey sat.

The judge looked back and forth between the two men. After several minutes of silence, he blew out a breath.

"What do we have here, a mutual admiration society?" The two men remained silent. Judge Finney continued to look back and forth between Bailey and Walton. "This is all well and good. I, however, want to see more testimony regarding the defendant's state of mind. Plus, I want to see evidence supporting this conclusion."

Henry stood. "I have a witness, Your Honor."

"Good, Mr. Walton. When do you suppose we could have a chat with him?"

"He's here, Your Honor."

"Well then, get on with it."

In a loud clear voice, Henry Walton said, "I call Patrick Freeman to the stand."

Freeman rose from the seats beyond the wooden railing and came forward. He took his oath, then seated himself in the witness chair.

"Dr. Freeman," Henry began, "have you had a chance to interview Miss Freed since her trial?"

"Yes."

"Have you learned anything new since your original interview?"

"Only that I'm convinced just as strongly now as I was then that she needs professional help."

"Thank you, Dr. Freeman. That's all I have." Walton sat.

Judge Finney looked at the defense lawyer. "Mr. Bailey, do you wish to cross?"

"Yes, Your Honor," Bailey spoke up, rising to his feet.

"Doctor Freeman," Bailey began, "is there any reason why my client can't receive the treatment she needs on an outpatient basis?"

"Yes."

"What reason?"

"As I stated last month, Miss Freed is suffering from schizophrenia. She has been afflicted with this condition for nearly all her life. There is no evidence to support that she could be cured in a few visits. Like two people working out a troubled marriage, this condition is far more serious, far more entrenched in her psyche. She needs constant attention. There will be a long, slow rehabilitation period, requiring constant monitoring. No psychiatrist or therapist I know would consider anything less."

"I see. Do you have any idea how long this kind of treatment might take?"

"That's a difficult question to answer. I have seen the process take years. As I recall, I had one patient four years ago who made a complete recovery in as little as eight months. But that is a rare occurrence. And that person is undergoing constant therapy sessions to this day."

*Sounds like another quack taking advantage of the situation and milking some poor sap for all he's worth!* Alicia thought.

Bailey raised his eyebrows. "So Doctor, without mincing words, what, in your opinion, would be appropriate treatment for my client to expedite her recovery?"

"As I said earlier, the only way to ensure her recovery, or at least give her the best possible care, is under constant supervision by trained professionals. To that end, the best thing for Alicia Freed is to be placed under my care at Rhinewood Mental Institute."

"Thank you, Doctor."

"Mr. Walton, do you wish to redirect?" Judge Finney asked.

"No, Your Honor."

Judge Finney turned to Patrick Freeman. "You may stand down."

"Your Honor," Walton spoke, "at this time I would like to recommend that Alicia Freed, by order of the court, be committed to Rhinewood Mental Institute until it can be determined she is fit to be released back into society."

"Normally, gentlemen," the judge began, "I would take a matter such as this under advisement. But in this case, with such an overwhelming consensus, in which I am also inclined to agree, I think that your recommendation, Mr. Walton, is appropriate."

The Judge picked up his gavel and banged it once. The sound pierced Alicia's ears like a shot. Life as she knew it was over. Her future was no longer clear.

*Was S'postu real? I can't remember the sound of his voice! Could I have imagined this whole thing?*

She found herself standing and wondered if the judge told her to do so, or if she only stood because everyone around her stood. *Maybe this is just a bad dream and tomorrow morning I'll wake up and everything will be back to normal.* Nausea grew as ringing developed in her ears. It grew louder until it almost drowned out the words now being uttered by the Judge.

"Alicia Freed, You are hereby ordered, on this day, August the first, 1978, to be placed in the custody of Rhinewood Mental Institute. Your release into society will be granted only upon your recovery, as satisfied by the institute. Your release rests solely on the judgement of the institute."

The gavel banged again and something snapped inside her. The world around her became engulfed in a misty haze as two uniformed police officers escorted her out of the courtroom. She barely heard herself ask

Bailey to retrieve her suitcase from her car. The next thing she knew she was being whisked away in the back seat of a patrol car.

Time passed, but she had no idea how much. She could smell the remnants of dried vomit wafting up from the carpet beneath her feet. Cigarette smoke from the head liner. The combined stench made her nausea grow stronger. *Where is Max Bailey? How could he leave me at a time like this?* She watched scenery flash by what appeared to be a car window. Brick buildings turned into telephone poles followed by green and brown shrubs whizzing past. It all seemed vaguely familiar, but she wasn't sure about anything.

"I'll get the door," said a strange voice.

*S'postu is that you? I thought you were asleep.*

Two officers held her by the elbows as they helped her out of the car and gently guided her into the lobby. They stood on either side of her, forcing her to stand there until a woman in an odd-looking gown wheeled in a narrow bed.

*Where am I? Oh, I know. This is where I met that nasty man with the funny ears. Is that alcohol I smell?*

"Please lay down, Miss Freed." It was a soothing female voice this time.

Alicia did as she was told. She felt the bed move and she appeared to move with it. She closed her eyes. The motion stopped and Alicia looked up.

*What's that? White frosted squares, maybe cardboard. No, more fibrous than cardboard, with a thousand tiny holes. Maybe I should count them. Yes, count them like counting sheep. Then I could fall asleep and when I wake up, this horrible nightmare will be over. No, too many to count. Could I touch them?* She reached up but felt nothing. *Maybe that's the ceiling. Yes, yes that must be it.*

"Miss Freed," the soothing voice again drifted to her ears, "I'm going to give you a shot now, honey. Just relax your arm."

Cool fingers took hold of her arm, pulling it gently. Her sense of time had vanished. Alcohol fumes burned her nose. *What's that sound so far away? Sounds like someone yelling.* But the voices were distant and indistinct. Once in a while she could pick out a word or two, but they were detached and without meaning.

Alicia felt a small patch of cold on her skin. *That's right! That lady said she would give me a shot. But why?* She tried to turn her head to ask, but forgot what she was going to say. There was a sudden stinging pressure on the cold patch.

Warmth began to spread out from that tiny point of pain. Alicia tried to lift her head but couldn't, it felt so heavy. The warmth spread from her arm into her shoulders and chest, enveloping her completely. It felt like someone tied bricks to her eyelids. They were too heavy to stay open, despite her efforts to stay awake. She imagined an orange liquid, warm and comforting, surrounding her brain, stifling her thoughts.

*S'postu? Max? Where are you? I'm lost. Lost and so sleepy. I'm going to sleep now. S'postu, tell me what's going on. I know you can hear me 'cause now I'm asleep too.*

Alicia succumbed to the Thorazine with a listless serenity she found quite pleasant.

# PART TWO

# CHAPTER 15

The tires squealed as the 1991 Chevrolet Cavalier rounded a sharp turn.

"Damn nice car," Terry Lambert said, leaning into the turn as he kept his eyes glued to the 1992 Lexus L.S. 400 in front of them.

"And it runs like a striped assed ape!" Shawn Bricker responded. Shawn was riding shotgun. In the back seat sat their wives; Amy, Terry's wife, and Shawn's wife, Bonnie.

The four of them were following Lynn Hooper, a real estate agent they had contacted about a house they wanted to rent. Lynn not only sold real estate, she also managed properties for some of her clients. Terry had called her earlier that day.

Lynn had her cellular phone to her ear. "George?" she asked into the receiver.

"Hey, Lynn. What's up?"

"I'm on my way to the Hartunian house on 61."

"Oh, that's right. You're showing those kids that rental, right?"

"Yep. I'll be there in about ten minutes or so."

"Well, I'm glad you called. The McCarthy's can't make your three o'clock."

"Damn. That's what I called about. I left their number at the office and I wanted you to call them and confirm them for me. But I guess it doesn't matter now."

"Times are tough. Oh! Don't forget the meeting in the morning. It's at eight."

"I'll be there. See ya then. Bye." Lynn hung up.

"That must ride like it's on rails," Shawn began, "Did you see that? She took that turn while she was on the phone!"

Terry nodded, struggling with his underpowered car to keep up with the more powerful Lexus in front of them.

The girls were not interested in cars or horsepower. Bonnie, sitting on the right, had her nose plastered against the glass to get a better view of the late summer countryside going by at 63 miles per hour.

"Isn't it just beautiful out here?" Amy asked, blowing out her breath.

Bonnie did not respond.

Amy waited for a few seconds, then touched Bonnie's shoulder. "Bonnie?"

Bonnie jumped. Amy retracted her hand quickly.

"Sorry. I guess I didn't hear you, what did you say?" Bonnie asked and turned her attention momentarily from the passing countryside.

"I said, isn't it beautiful out here?"

"Oh, yeah, it is nice." After a few more seconds of silence, Bonnie again looked out the window. As they neared the old house, she had become increasingly silent. She had always been prone to receiving premonitions. A light nausea swelled deep in the pit of her stomach. The more they neared the house, the stronger the feeling became. Bonnie found holding a conversation with Amy more and more difficult with each passing moment.

"What's wrong, Bonnie?" Amy asked.

"I'm not sure," she said, "it may be nothing."

Amy had a concerned look on her face. She knew and trusted Bonnie's feelings. After all, they had known each other since grade school.

"I don't know if I have a bad feeling about this house, or a good one," Bonnie explained.

"Then, what's wrong?"

"I don't know. But don't say anything to the guys for now. Let's just wait and see what happens, okay?"

Amy nodded and turned to look out the window.

Terry slowed the Cavalier to follow the Lexus onto a gravel driveway. He stopped the car 10 feet or so behind the Lexus and the engine quivered to a stop.

"Well," Terry began, "the car likes the house. It must have known this might be home because I didn't even have to shut the key off. The motor quit all by itself."

Bonnie didn't like it. "You're not out of gas are you?"

"Nope." Terry eyed the gauge anyway just to be sure.

The driveway ran toward a small white barn behind the house. As it neared the barn, the gravel faded into grass. Terry eyed the structure, wondering whether the barn could be used as a garage in the winter to protect his car. *It needs all the help it could get.*

"I like it already," Shawn smiled as he peered at the large wood frame house with white wooden siding. "Looks like they just painted."

Lynn was now standing on the small porch, fumbling with keys. The four piled out of the Cavalier. The girls headed toward Lynn while Terry and Shawn went around the corner to survey the outside of the house. Terry stopped suddenly to get a closer look at the barn. Shawn, not looking where he was walking, nearly walked into him.

"Hey," Shawn said, "get your brake lights fixed."

"Well, maybe I will," Terry retorted playfully, "but that doesn't excuse you for not watching where you're going."

Beyond the barn, but hidden from view of the driveway, were the remnants of an old outhouse.

"Check this out, Shawn." Terry said, heading for the ancient privy. Shawn followed without a word. Terry reached the outhouse and opened the door to look inside.

"Someone turned this old shithouse into a gardening shed!" Terry laughed. Among the spider webs were the remains of an old rake, the handle long since rotted. Terry backed out of the doorway and Shawn stuck his head in the door.

"Still stinks like shit." Shawn wrinkled his nose, then closed the door.

"I didn't smell anything," Terry said.

Shawn gestured for Terry to continue their survey. As they rounded the corner at the northwest corner of the house, Terry stopped in his tracks. Attached to the house was a rectangular add-on running the entire length of that side. Picture windows made up the wall overlooking a valley in the foreground, followed by successive foothills of the Smokey Mountains. The valley below and the foothills were covered with the deciduous trees indigenous to the area. The two had spent many weekends camping together, and had experienced many such views.

"We gotta get this!" Terry remarked. "I love this view."

Shawn nodded in agreement.

"Let's go show the girls!" Terry said enthusiastically. He stepped through the ankle high grass, laying the tall blades on their sides on his way to the opposite side of the house, Shawn in tow.

Terry bounded up the stairs of the porch adjacent to the cars. As he crossed the threshold, Terry could hear the women's voices echoing off the bare walls of the empty house. As they approached the door leading into the dining room, he and Shawn heard Lynn talking.

"…Yeah, this house was built somewhere in the mid-1800's, I really don't know all the history of the house. I do know that it was owned by a prominent lawyer who sold it to the current owner, a man by the name of Ahmed Hartunian."

"What kind of name is that?" Shawn asked, coming around Terry to stand at the edge of the dining room table.

"It's Pakistani. You know, like in the Middle East. Well, actually Armenian, but the gentleman came from Pakistan," Lynn informed them.

Shawn nodded silently. Terry bent to examine the dusty dining room table with its eight chairs, three on each side, and one on each end. It was the only furniture in the house.

"What's this doing here?" Terry wanted to know.

"Like I was telling your wife, as I understand it, this table goes with the house. It was custom made, I'm told, for this room."

"It's absolutely gorgeous," Amy beamed. She loved woodwork. This table was one of the greatest examples of fine craftsmanship she had ever seen.

The awesome beauty of the house acted like a band-aid that covered the feelings Bonnie had experienced in the car. She loved old houses, and was particularly impressed with this one. She looked up to examine the ceiling and saw a small chandelier hanging over the dining table. It was supported by a dusty chain hanging from a tarnished brass plate mounted on four-inch stained beams. The beams, which intersected at 16-inch intervals, created small dark boxes against the white ceiling. It was beautiful. Even with all the intricate woodwork, the nine-foot high ceiling made the room feel open and airy.

A large built-in hutch ran the entire length of one wall. Above it, at eye level, hung a large, heavy mirror framed with age-darkened wood that complimented the ceiling beams in their dignified beauty.

On the wall opposite the kitchen door stood a wide door frame. Looking at the doorway, Bonnie had the impression that something was missing.

Lynn was explaining to the others about the hutch. Bonnie could hear her, but was lost in her own observations. On the wall opposite the hutch a large opening led into the living room. Bonnie walked over to it and noticed two breaks in an otherwise smooth surface. When she turned to look at the other end of the opening, she found that it was identical. She turned back and examined the two breaks more closely, running her fingers down the wood between the two breaks. Slowly, she realized that she was looking at the end of a door. Her fingers found a metal rocker latch. When she pushed the top half, the bottom popped out. She hooked her finger under the latch and pulled.

"Hey guys, check this out!" The four stopped their conversation and turned to her. The door creaked loudly along its track as it emerged from its alcove. Bonnie pulled the door to its furthermost point, then reached behind her and pulled the other door to meet it.

"How cool!" Amy exclaimed, walking over to examine the slide-out doors. She ran her fingers over the carved woodwork. "This is absolutely beautiful."

Lynn smiled. She did not know the doors were here, but had suspected they might exist because she had seen doors like this in other houses built during the same period. Wanting to get on with the tour, she turned and headed for the large door frame opposite the kitchen door.

"This is my favorite room in the house." Lynn stepped into the room and turned to face everyone. Amy and Bonnie left the slide-out doors closed and followed Lynn through the dining room and the large door frame with Terry and Shawn in tow. The exterior wall was made up of large windows and ran the entire length of the house. Terry walked up to Amy, wrapping his arms around her waist from behind. She looked at him and smiled. Shawn walked up behind Bonnie and draped his hands on her shoulders. Terry recognized the windows as the ones that he and Shawn had seen from the outside as he pushed a dusty curtain aside.

"Breathtaking!" Amy exclaimed. Their footsteps echoed on the hardwood floor as they walked over to the window.

"This room faces west," Lynn informed, "so you'll get spectacular sunsets from here."

"That's where we were outside," Shawn pointed to the footsteps left in the grass.

"There's enough room in here for a couple sets of lawn chairs or something like that…"

"Oh!" Amy cut him off, "I love to watch the sunset." She squeezed his waist. "Isn't it romantic?"

Terry nodded.

"I like to call this room the su…" Lynn began.

"Sunroom," Bonnie finished. A puzzled look appeared on her face. "I don't know how I knew that," Bonnie felt awkward, "but I know it's right. That's the name of this room."

"That's a fitting name for this room," Lynn smiled shakily, her sales instinct rising to the occasion. She decided to smooth things along by continuing the tour of the house. She moved to the opposite end of the sunroom. Along the same wall as the door frame leading into the dining room, at the opposite end, was an identical door frame. Lynn moved through it and into the living room.

The four followed Lynn into the living room.

"And this is the living room, " her voice echoed. With no elaborate ceiling or built-in hutch to dampen the sound, as in the dining room, Lynn sounded as if she were in a cathedral. As Bonnie stepped through the doorway, she stopped to examine the holes in the doorjamb. For an instant, she could see the image of a screwdriver removing screws from a hinge. As the scene flashed across her mind, she had a sense of deja-vu, and felt suddenly sleepy. She shook her head, wiped her eyes, and joined the others at the center of the living room.

"Don't you just love the high ceilings?" Lynn remarked, remembering Bonnie's interest in the dining room ceiling.

"Wow!" Shawn exclaimed, " this room is huge. I bet the stereo would sound great in here." He surveyed the room and suddenly changed directions and walked toward the large fireplace in the center of the exterior wall.

Bonnie walked over to Lynn and stood next to her. "They're all running around like bees, aren't they?"

Lynn laughed softly and nodded her head in agreement. Bonnie looked at her husband who was sticking his head into the fireplace to look up the chimney.

"Shawn Bricker!" Bonnie half yelled, half laughed, "get your head out of that fireplace! God, you're worse than a kid."

The sudden yell from Bonnie startled him. He jerked in response, hitting his forehead on the inside of the chimney. Soot fell from somewhere above his head, spotting his face. He scowled at Bonnie. Bonnie and Lynn laughed loudly.

"Very funny!" Shawn said sarcastically, wiping the soot with his hand.

Amy went to the front door. "Look how wide this door is!" she said as she rubbed her fingers over it. Terry came over to examine the door. Slivers of peeling varnish came loose with Amy's touch. She looked up at her husband.

"Need's refinishing," he said.

Amy wiped her hand on her pants.

Lynn silently looked on, watching these potential clients become excited about the house. Not only did she feel a responsibility to Mr. Hartunian, the owner, but she decided that she liked these young couples and wanted them to have this house. Somehow, they belonged here.

"How long has this house been empty?" Bonnie's voice broke her thoughts.

Amy sniffed the air and realized it was stale, still and musty. She thought Bonnie's question was a good one.

"Um," Lynn began, "the owner, Mr. Hartunian, shortly after purchasing the house 14 years ago, was called back to Pakistan. Apparently his father had taken ill, and Mr. Hartunian, being the eldest son, was obligated to deal with his father's affairs."

"You mean, this place sat empty all that time?" Amy asked.

"Pretty much," Lynn replied. "However, Mr. Hartunian sent money each year to keep up with property taxes, and to cut the grass once a month. I guess you can see it's about time to cut it again," she breathed loudly. "I guess he forgot about the house in any other respect, for a while. Anyway, out of the blue, he called from Pakistan and said he wanted to start renting it out. So I had my maintenance guy, Stan, come over to see what the house needed. We had the outside painted. We had the plumbing and electrical systems checked out, and the roof. To our surprise, everything turned out to be okay. The septic system, too."

"Speaking of septic systems," Shawn spoke up, "we seen an old shi...outhouse out back," pointing his thumb in the direction of the small building beyond the barn.

"Saw, not seen," Bonnie corrected her husband.

Shawn scowled slightly at his wife.

A staircase ran up the wall opposite the sunroom. On the lower landing was a closed door. "What's in there?" Terry asked.

"That's the downstairs bedroom. It has a full bath and a walk-in closet."

"Oh yeah?" Terry said, walking to the door. "I wanna see."

Amy was right on Terry's heels, eager to see the room. Terry opened the door. A blast of cold air hit them in the face as they stepped inside.

"Why is it so damn cold in here?" Terry wanted to know.

"We haven't been able to figure that out," Lynn explained.

"Must not be over fifty degrees in here," Amy said, snuggling up to her husband.

"Sure beats the heat. Don't it, babe?" Terry said softly.

"I kinda like it." Amy squeezed his waist.

Bonnie stepped across the threshold. *There's something wrong here, something terribly wrong. It's cold, so cold—like the cold of death. The terrible empty cold of death.* The first thing she wanted to do was get out of this house and run away as fast as she could. But somewhere beneath the icy cold she felt something familiar. A whisper tugging at her intuition—a dim voice calling to her subconscious, begging for help and demanding that she stay.

"Well I don't!" Bonnie said weakly.

Terry and Amy spun around to see Bonnie standing in the room. Her face was pale.

"This room gives me the creeps. You two can have it." Bonnie quickly left the room.

Amy looked up at Terry. "What's with her?" she asked him quietly.

"I dunno," Terry shrugged his shoulders. The two looked in the closet and into the attached bathroom, nodding and murmuring approval.

"Did you want to take a look in here, Shawn?" Terry asked.

Shawn shook his head. "She doesn't like that room. What would be the point?" he answered, nodding his head toward Bonnie.

"I like the rest of the house. I just don't like that room," Bonnie said defensively. "Is that okay with you?" She was having trouble sorting out what her inner self was telling her and didn't want to confuse her husband and friends, who clearly liked this house.

Lynn continued her speech to break the tension. She drew a breath trying to think of something interesting to say about the house. Then it hit her.

"Originally, the kitchen was another bedroom," Lynn began.

"Oh yeah?" Terry said.

"That's right. When this house was built, they didn't have indoor plumbing. There was not an attached kitchen. In those days, the kitchen was a detached structure. The only bathroom was in the form of an outhouse, which you two saw. The kitchen was remodeled from a bedroom in the early thirties, when Roosevelt started the T.V.A. and electricity was introduced in the area"

"That's really cool!" Amy said.

"I like history," Lynn explained. "So I try to find out things about all the properties I represent. This house, since it's so old, has a rich history. Like I said before, I don't know it all, but if any of you want to find out more, you probably need to go to Knoxville and see the hall of records at the courthouse. Anyway, I don't know for sure, but I would suspect that the plumbing was added shortly after the electricity was."

"Ooh, that's neat," Bonnie said. *But what about the unspoken history? There's a memory calling from the silence of these walls from the distant past.*

Lynn laughed and began climbing the staircase. The four followed. At the top was a hall with windows at both ends. On the left were three doors with another one across from the center door. Lynn opened the first door on the left.

"This is the largest bedroom up here," she informed. "It's about twelve by fourteen." She led them inside.

"What are those two doors for?" Bonnie asked.

"Oh," Lynn explained, "this one," walking over to the door on the left, "is a walk-in closet. The other leads into the bathroom. The middle door in the hall also leads there."

"Pretty slick," Shawn commented.

Lynn led the group out of the bedroom and back into the hall. She headed to the other bedroom, opened the door and stepped inside. As Bonnie passed the smaller door on the right, across from the bathroom, she had a sudden urge to look inside. *What's in there?* She dismissed the thought as she saw the others disappearing into the last bedroom. *It's probably nothing more than a linen closet.* Not wanting to miss any of Lynn's explanations, she hurried to join the others. The second story of the house seemed miles away from that awful lower bedroom, and the layout was more to her liking.

"Well, people," Lynn spoke up as Bonnie entered the room, "what do you think?"

"We'll take it," Amy said with excitement.

"Very good." Lynn turned to Shawn and Bonnie, "Can I show you another house?"

"No, no, you don't understand. We'll ALL take it," Terry said, smiling.

"I'm not sure I understand," Lynn said.

"You see," Bonnie explained, "we want to rent the house together so we can both save up to buy our own houses."

"That's a good idea." Lynn swallowed. She felt as if she were about to drop a bomb on them. "That's okay with me. But you have to understand. This is not just a rental. You have to sign a lease."

The four looked at each other.

"How long is the lease?" Terry asked.

"The lease is for one year intervals. The owner made this very clear to me. Since he's out of the country, he doesn't want to worry about the house. If you default on the lease, you will be liable for the entire year. So, you can't move out early."

"How much is the rent, per month?" Bonnie asked.

"Six hundred."

"Each?" Terry asked.

"No. Total," Lynn smiled. She knew the house was as good as leased.

"Where do we sign?" Terry asked.

"Yeah. Let's do it." Shawn interjected.

"Oh! One more thing—do all of you work? Because I'll have to get your employment records and verify your employment."

"No problem," Shawn said confidently. "We all have jobs,"

"All except me," Bonnie cut in. "My contribution to this arrangement is staying home and keeping the place clean." The idea of actually living in this house was both intriguing and frightening for Bonnie. The rich, historic beauty and nostalgia of the house was at war with its isolation. Yet she was strangely drawn—as if the house needed her. Her mind raced through the preparations that would have to be made before they could move one piece of furniture in. The cleaning and painting would be a daunting challenge to complete before months end, but the hard work would certainly take her mind off the uneasy feelings she had in that lower bedroom.

"Very good. Now if ya'll will follow me to the office, we can get the paperwork started. And if everything checks out, you'll be able to move in this weekend."

"You won't have any problems with the paperwork," Terry assured her, "and we'd like to move in as soon as possible."

"Well," Bonnie said, "I would like to get the keys as soon as possible, because I would like to clean and paint before we move in."

"Well then," Lynn began, "let's go. You may paint the walls on the inside as long as you don't paint any of the woodwork." As she led the way out of the house, she stopped to slide the partition doors back into their alcoves, then proceeded outside. She stepped aside to let the group pass her so she could lock the door.

The two couples piled into the Cavalier. Terry started the engine on the little four door.

"Wait!" Bonnie said, opening her door and jumping out. She ran up to Lynn, who was sliding behind the wheel of her car.

"I forgot to ask you," Bonnie puffed.

"What?"

"I, uh, we have a cat. Is that okay?" *Maybe that's what made me feel so weird in there, I forgot about the cat.*

"I don't think that will be a problem."

"Oh, good," Bonnie breathed a sigh of relief. "I almost forgot about her."

"What's your cat's name?"

"One-night." Bonnie smiled.

"One-night? What kind of a name is that?" Lynn wrinkled her forehead.

"Her momma got out one night and got knocked up by one of the neighbor's Tom cats. Anyway, she had a bunch of kittens. We gave them all away except One-night. A month or so later, a dog killed the momma cat."

"Oh, I'm sorry to hear that," Lynn sympathized. "There won't be a problem with a cat at all. This is a home in the country. As far as I'm concerned, every home in the country needs a cat."

"Oh, thanks!" Bonnie ran back to the Cavalier and jumped inside.

"What was that all about?" Terry asked.

"I had to ask her about One-night," Bonnie explained.

"Oh, that's right, I forgot about your cat," Terry said as he backed out of the driveway.    "God forbid we leave out your cat!" Shawn laughed.

Terry backed the car far enough onto the road to allow Lynn room to maneuver her car onto the street. They followed her to the office.

Bonnie watched the house grow distant through the rear window. *What is it about that house?* She hid her face from the others to conceal her silent tears. Wild, confusing signals like she experienced there created turbulent emotions which almost always resulted in the release of tears.

The house, again, stood alone. But this time, only for a while.

# CHAPTER 16

"Amy! Look at this!" Bonnie called. She had opened the door in the upstairs hall across from the bathroom door expecting to find a linen closet, but instead found a staircase. "Amy!" she called again. *She can't hear me 'cause she's got that radio blasting in her room.*

"Amy!" Bonnie yelled at the top of her voice.

"Did you call?" Amy's reply floated up from the bottom of the stairs, barely heard above the music.

"Look at this," Bonnie repeated. As she looked up the stairs she could see faint images, accompanied by faint sounds. Light came in from somewhere up above. The radio seemed to fade into silence. In its place, she heard the sound of wood being sawed in two with a hand saw. The voices of a man and a woman talking, their tones somehow frantic. She could not make out what was being said, and the images she saw were superimposed over the dust drifting through beams of sunlight. *Is that just dust? Or is it particles of sawdust drifting in the air?* There was no way to tell. She faintly heard the pounding of a hammer as it drove a nail into wood. Bonnie stared, mesmerized.

*Bang, bang, bang.* Bonnie closed her eyes, trying harder to hear the sounds.

*Bang, bang, bang.* She tried harder. The sound changed. Something heavy was being dragged across a wooden floor. The sound changed again, she heard pieces of wood being dragged across the floor.

*Thump, thump, thump, thump.* The hammering sounded different. Then, as quickly as the sounds began, they stopped. Bonnie strained to hear, eyes still closed. Suddenly, something touched her shoulder, and she screamed. The pressure on her shoulder instantly vanished. Bonnie spun around, eyes wide with terror, to see Amy pull back her hand as if she had been burned.

"Sorry," Amy said, "I didn't mean to scare you."

Bonnie clutched her heaving chest. "It's okay," she panted. "I guess I didn't hear you come up the stairs."

Amy noticed the staircase behind the door. "This is cool," she said, placing a foot on the bottom tread. "Let's see what's up here." She began to climb the stairs. "I thought you said this was a linen closet."

"Well, that's what I thought." Bonnie followed her up the small staircase. With each step they could feel the temperature rise. As they approached the top of the stairs, they saw beams of sunlight cascading through a window. Bits of dust glittered in the sunbeams, raised by the disturbance of their movement.

Amy walked to the window and looked out.

"You can see the top of the barn from here."

When Bonnie reached the top of the stairs, she joined Amy at the window, and surveyed the surrounding area like a scout. Beyond the barn, she could see an open field, then the edge of the woods. Bonnie looked down at the driveway in front of the barn, and saw the Cavalier and the front half of Amy and Shawn's El Camino. Her eyes moved back to the barn roof. She noticed something as her eyes passed over the barn before, but had been too preoccupied with looking around first. There was a large gaping hole in the roof of the barn. "The barn leaks."

Amy nodded her head in agreement, "so much for Terry storing the Cavalier in there." She turned her head from the window and looked around the attic. The floor was made of wooden planks nailed to the joists with half-inch gaps between the boards. There was about 20 feet of floor between the stairs and the window, yet the distance from the stairs to the opposite side of the attic seemed much shorter. *There's something strange going on up here.* Amy looked back at the window. *Wait a second! That the staircase is dead center of the second floor.* The windowless gable was out of place.

"Bonnie, does this seem right to you?"

"What?"

"Doesn't it look shorter over there than it does over here?"

Bonnie looked around the attic. Other than themselves, the attic was totally empty. She saw the floorboards stop at the gable with the window, yet they seemed to run underneath the gable that Amy was questioning. "I see what you mean. But see how the floor goes under the wall?"

Amy noticed at the same time Bonnie spoke the words. "Yeah, but...there's something else wrong."

"What?"

"C'mon! If I'm right, you'll see." Amy started down the stairs, Bonnie on her heels. They went down the main staircase and out the front door. Amy walked briskly over the grass.

"Amy?" Bonnie called, "what are you talking about?"

Amy quickened her pace and said nothing.

"Amy?"

When she was about 50 feet or so from the house, she stopped abruptly and turned around. "That," she said, pointing to the gable opposite the driveway side of the house. "See that window?"

"Yeah. So what?"

"It's not in the attic."

*Oh, now it makes sense.* "I know why you can't see that window from the attic."

"Why?" Amy stared at the window.

Bonnie's eyes glazed over.

Amy looked at her friend. "Bonnie?"

"I know why we couldn't see it from the attic," she murmured. "I saw them."

"Who?"

"I saw them. They hid it behind that wall."

"What are you talking about? Hid what? What stuff?"

Bonnie shook her head silently. She had more questions than she had answers. In the distance, they heard what sounded like thunder.

Amy looked up at the cloudless sky. "That sounded like a storm brewing."

Bonnie remained silent, staring at the window in the gable.

As the sound came closer, Amy realized it was the sound of a heavy truck lumbering up the hill. "The guys are coming with our stuff," she said, pulling on Bonnie's shoulder. "Let's go back into the house." She turned and headed for the house with Bonnie following wordlessly.

Their minds snapped back to the tasks at hand. Amy returned to her room to continue preparing for the furniture, while Bonnie returned upstairs to do the same. As she passed the open door leading to the attic, she paused to look up the staircase. No images came to her, so she closed the door.

From the downstairs bedroom, Amy could hear the rented truck's back-up alarm beeping, then silence. One after another the cab doors squeaked opened and closed, followed by footsteps in the gravel.

"Honey, I'm home!" Terry's voice echoed off the walls of the empty house. "Amy?"

"In here, babe," she responded from the downstairs bedroom.

Bonnie came down the stairs. The four met in the center of the living room.

"Well, have you two figured out where you want all this stuff?" Shawn asked.

The girls looked at each other, then broke out in laughter.

"What the hell is so funny?" he asked, placing his hand on his hips.

The girls only laughed louder.

"We forgot about that," Bonnie laughed.

Shawn's eyebrows shot up. "What?"

"We got sidetracked."

"Sidetracked?" Terry joined in. "How?"

Bonnie proceeded to explain to their husbands about the discovery of the attic.

"Well," Shawn began, "we don't have time to fool with that now. We've got to get the truck unloaded and back to the rental yard by six tonight, or we'll have to pay another day on it."

"Shawn and I will unload the truck," Terry explained, "and you two can arrange things. Well, the things you can lift. Otherwise we'll have to do it when we get back."

The rest of the day went as anticipated. The two men unloaded the truck, then Terry followed Shawn in the Cavalier. While the guys were gone, the girls had put away most of the dishes and cooking supplies in the kitchen.

"It's too quiet in here," Amy began. "We need some tunes."

"Sounds like a plan to me."

"Did you see that screwdriver around here, Bonnie?"

"Oh yeah, it's in that end drawer." Bonnie pointed to the kitchen drawer next to the back door.

Amy found the screwdriver. "I'll take care of our audio problem," she said, shaking the screwdriver.

"What are you going to do with that?"

"I'm gonna hook up Terry's pride and joy."

"What's wrong with your little radio?"

"Why should we drive a Pinto when we could be driving a Cadillac?" Amy grinned.

"Terry's gonna kill you if you mess up his stereo."

"I know. I'll be careful. Besides, if he gives me any static about it, I'll get even with him later." Amy headed for the living room. Bonnie followed.

"Do you know how to do that?" Bonnie asked.

"Get even with him? No problem! But the stereo—I'll have to figure it out. Anyway it can't be too difficult, after all, it's only two wires for each speaker. I saw Terry take it apart. And if he can figure it out, so can I."

"You go, girl!"

Amy knelt down and began hooking up the speakers.

Bonnie went back into the kitchen to put up the last of the pots and pans. Minutes later, music came blaring from the living room. Amy returned, beaming.

"What are you gonna do if he gets mad?" Bonnie asked.

"He won't get mad. Well, he better not get mad."

"What if he does?"

"Bonnie, we are both married. What do you do if you want to get even with Shawn?"

"That's mean," Bonnie laughed.

"Maybe so, but that'll teach him not to mess with me."

Bonnie shook her head, "the only problem with that brilliant strategy is that it punishes us as well as it does them."

"Ain't that the truth!"

The girls were working on storing their nice dishes in the built-in hutch when their husbands got home.

The music blared as Terry walked through the kitchen toward Amy. She was taking pieces of china as Bonnie removed them from a box. The girls were so engrossed in their project that they didn't hear the guys pull into the drive. Terry snuck up behind Amy, who had her back to him. Bonnie saw Terry and fought to keep a smile off her face, making sure Amy wasn't holding any china. He wrapped his arms around her waist, pulling her to him. Amy screamed, at first in fright, then in delight.

"You scared me!" Amy looked up at Terry.

He kissed her.

"Sorry."

"No, you're not." Amy eyed her husband, then turned to Shawn, "How come you never scare Bonnie?"

Bonnie smiled. She already knew the answer. Not from any psychic ability, but from experience.

"She always knows when I'm behind her. I've tried. But she always catches me," Shawn explained.

"I see you got the stereo hooked up," Terry changed the subject. "The clock radio wasn't loud enough for ya?"

"No, it wasn't. Besides, it sounded like it was coming from a tin can."

"Well, you got my wires all over the damn place!"

"Yeah I did, and I don't want to hear a word about it, either!" Amy retorted.

"Hey! No problem," Terry laughed. "C'mon Shawn, let's get out of their way."

Shawn bent to kiss his wife. "I missed you, babe." he said softly, wrapping his arms around her.

"I missed you, too," she replied.

Terry pulled Amy by the hand into the living room and began arranging the furniture, allowing the Brickers a private moment.

"Hey Shawn, I could use a hand in here," he called after a few minutes.

"Be right there." He released Bonnie to join him.

A cold front came through in the late afternoon, dropping the temperature and leaving isolated puffy clouds across the sky. The late summer sunset was striking. An orange-red hue lit the bottom of the clouds as the sphere of the sun settled on the horizon, a fiery red sky faded into blue, then blue to black as evening called.

With the bulk of their furnishings put away, they decided to call it the end of a long, tiring day. Bonnie sat in a lawn chair pulled next to Shawn. She laid across the arms of the adjacent chairs to lean on his chest; they dug into her side. They were sitting in the sunroom, watching the sunset. Terry had pulled the couch to the center of the doorway between the living room and the sunroom. He lay on the couch, head propped on a pillow, Amy on his chest, watching the sunset. Everyone was exhausted, and soon all drifted off to sleep.

# CHAPTER 17

"Nathan. Nathan." Her voice touched his ears from behind the closed door. Nathan Powell opened the door to see 72 year old Alicia Freed sitting on her bed, looking out the window at the sunset. He was somewhat surprised she was awake.

Her condition had slowly deteriorated over the years. Countless injections of Thorazine, along with 60 milligrams of Thiothixene each day had resulted in liver problems and bouts of jaundice. Bits and pieces of dreams about the Civil War, S'postu and the house, disconnected and jumbled in her mind forced by the drugs left her nearly catatonic most of the time. Most of the time while she was awake, she was confused. Sometimes, during the time between injections, she would act as though she had swallowed her pills, and hold them in her mouth until she could spit them into the toilet. Her confusion would slowly ebb away as the drugs were flushed from her system. Then Alicia would begin to question her surroundings. Freeman would order another round of injections and she would be out again. Occasionally, Patrick Freeman would hold "therapy sessions" which amounted to nothing more than closed door meetings where he tried to convince her in a most condescending way that her dreams were associated with her condition, and the drugs were necessary to calm her.

"There is no S'postu, he's all in your head." He would say, "just take your medicine and soon you'll be better, and you can go home."

The truth of the matter was that she had no home other than the institute. Her condition was drug induced, and Alicia was powerless to stop him. As the dosages increased, their side effects would manifest themselves as the symptoms most commonly associated with Parkinson's disease. Setting her up for the greater fear she was losing her mind, and Alicia did not want to end up a sad blathering infant in an old woman's body, like her mother. Her new symptoms allowed Freeman to justify moving her to the convalescent wing where her state could be more easily concealed among the patients there.

Nathan knew there was a problem and he often wondered why Alicia remained Freeman's only patient. He was, after all, the director of the facility, and there were plenty of staff doctors. This was one of the reasons he grew so attached to her. But today, something was different.

"Ain't it beautiful, Nathan?"

He noticed that her face under her eyes was wet. "What's all the tears for, Miss 'licia?"

She wiped her eyes with a tissue. He approached her and sat on her bed. She took his hand. "S'postu ain't alone no more."

"Oh. S'postu again, huh?" Concern filled his eyes. Nathan Powell was a convalescent nurse at Rhinewood Mental Institute. During his tenure, he had heard the story of S'postu many times. He had always dismissed it as the rambling of a mind twisted from Parkinson's or Alzheimer's. He paid no attention to the stories. Alicia had become his favorite patient, and he often humored her by listening to her.

"My, Nathan, it sure is a beautiful sunset," she said again, turning to look out the window.

"Hey." Nathan placed his hands on her cheeks to turn her head to look at him. "What's wrong, Miss 'licia?"

"Nothing."

"Then what's with this?" He pulled the crumpled tissue from her hand and shook it gently. "Why the tears?"

The door opened, and a nurse walked in carrying a small paper cup.

"Looks like it's time for your medicine." Nathan rose from the bed and met the nurse halfway. "I'll take care of this Judy. Okay?" The nurse nodded and handed the paper cup to him. Alicia continued to stare out the window. As Nathan came around the bed, he saw something in her eyes. Something he hadn't seen in a long time, and then only rarely. *Was there a glimmer of life in those tired old eyes?* He couldn't tell. Still, there was something different about Alicia Freed.

"Miss 'licia, how are you feeling?"

She turned to face him, drew a deep breath and thought for a moment. "Somehow, I feel...I feel...not lonely anymore." She cocked her head to the side. "Does that make sense?"

"Miss 'licia, you ain't been alone since ya got here. Least not since I come along."

"But that's not what I mean." She leaned forward, and adjusted the pillow behind her. "It's like a part o' me, deep inside; that's the part that ain't alone no more. That's how I know it's S'postu. It's like he's that part. You know what I mean?"

"Not really." *Gibberish again.* He sighed and handed her the small paper cup. Alicia dumped the contents into her mouth. Nathan took the paper cup back and handed her a glass of water. "You drink this all up, now, ya hear?"

She drank the water, washing her Thiothixene pill down. She leaned back against her pillow, smiling at Nathan. He looked at her curiously. On one hand, she was speaking gibberish, yet, on the other, she made sense.

"Miss 'licia. I have not seen you this alert for, God! Must be five years or so."

"Yeah. It's like a part of me is awake. Or, at least not afraid to face the world again. I can't really explain it."

"Now tell me again about your, I mean, this S'postu."

"What do you want to know?"

"How is it he got his name?"

Alicia leaned back against her pillow. After a moment of quiet reflection, she drew a breath. "A long, long time ago. Maybe, it was the first thing I ever remembered, I had this dream. Only, it was so real, it had such an impact on me. Well, it was like the guiding force in my life. It led me down a path I could never change. Still, even after all this time, and all that's happened, I'm still on that path. The only thing is, I don't know where it's gonna take me."

"But what about his name?" *Oh please, don't lapse into more gibberish.*

"Oh, yeah. Sorry. Well I had this dream when I was just a little girl. Maybe I was six or seven. I can't remember. Anyway, in the dream, I woke up one morning. I was in my bedroom. Only, it wasn't my bedroom. Well it was my bedroom, but it didn't have my stuff in it. All the stuff was old. And the house was a little different. Anyway, I got out of my bed, and I was older in my dream than I was in real life. I went into the kitchen. Well, I had to go outside to go into the kitchen. My mom was in the kitchen. Only, it didn't look like my mom. This lady had brown hair and blue eyes. She was really beautiful. My mother's hair was more reddish. Anyway, she had been crying. I asked her what was wrong. She told me that my daddy had been yelling at her. But, she wouldn't tell me why. That made me really mad. I stormed into the living room. My daddy was sitting in a chair. Then it hit me. This man, the person who I knew to be my daddy my whole life, all of a sudden he wasn't familiar to me. Like he was a stranger. I got so mad, I yelled at him. I said, 'Don't yell at my mommy, you're not even sposta be here anyway. My dad's s'postu.' And in my dream I stormed out of the room. When I woke up, that was the first time S'postu ever said anything to me. It was like he was waiting for me to get to a certain age, or something."

Nathan was confused. He still didn't understand how Alicia named S'postu. "But, how did ya name him S'postu?"

Alicia looked at him, narrowing her eyes. "You got rocks in your head?"

"No."

"Well then, what?"

"Did his name just pop into your head, or did he say what it was? I don't understand."

"Oh, I'm sorry. At first, when he spoke, I got scared. Then after a while, I guess I got used to him. Anyway, he said he was the one who was supposed to be in my dream, not that other man. I asked and asked him to tell me his name. Well, he never did. But ever since be began to talk to me, he always said "you're supposed to do this" and "your supposed to do that," and made me do stuff. So I settled on S'postu. That's the only name I ever called him." Alicia yawned, the pills had begun to take effect. She closed her eyes.

"Well, Miss 'licia," Nathan said softly, pulling the covers over her, "you go on to sleep now."

Alicia began to drift off to sleep. But somewhere in the twilight between sleep and wakefulness, she began to speak. "Here kitty, kitty, kitty. Here kitty, kitty, kitt..." Alicia drifted off to sleep.

Nathan looked at her, puzzled, but made no comment. He merely rose and walked out of the room, dismissing the babbling as the effects of her medication. He closed the door quietly behind him.

Several minutes after Nathan left the room, the sunset triggered a memory buried deep in Alicia's mind. Something old. The orange-red sunset burned into her unconscious. The image of the sun grew brighter and brighter and along with it, the image of her house grew, then becoming crystal clear. She tossed in her sleep as she saw herself as a young girl, carrying an oil lamp up the stairs. It was cold; she shivered. For some reason Alicia could not get the old wood stove to light. It was nighttime, and she was in her nightgown. She knew she had to climb the stairs to wake her father. He would know how to light the stove. The lantern cast eerie shadows as she fumbled up the stairs. Suddenly, her foot slipped on a tread. The lantern flew from her hand, shattering on the wooden stairs. Oil ran down the steps, then ignited on contact with the burning wick. Alicia jumped up past the flames. She stood at the top of the stairs, watching the flames crawl up the staircase toward her. She opened her mouth to scream, but nothing came out.

Suddenly, a familiar voice rang out in her head. "Scream child, scream!" the voice commanded. She opened her mouth again. This time she found her voice, and screamed at the top of her lungs. Within seconds, her parents appeared at the top of the stairs. The flames were spreading, now engulfing the staircase, their only means of escape from the second floor.

"My God, Winfred! What will we do?" Her mother shrieked.

Alicia heard S'postu's voice again. "Grab them by the hand, my child, follow me through the arms of hell. I will protect you," he calmly directed. The front door flew open. An icy wind blew up the staircase, parting the flames. Without hesitation, Alicia took the hands of her parents and ran down the stairs, flames licking at their sides. As the three of them ran outside, cold rain began to fall. Her father laughed as he watched the rain extinguish the flames. But Alicia knew better. S'postu put them out. As the images faded into nothing, Alicia relaxed and fell deeper into sleep.

# CHAPTER 18

Bonnie woke with a start, thinking of One-night. Funny, she hadn't given her cat a second thought all day. She straightened up in the lawn chair. Her side ached where the arm of the lawn chair had dug in. It was dark outside, and the house was pitch black. She could hear the slow breathing of Terry and Amy asleep in the living room. As her eyes adjusted slowly to the dark she could see the faint silhouette of Shawn, his head back, mouth open, snoring away. *How can you sleep like that?* Slowly, she rose from the lawn chair. It creaked as she shifted her weight. Her muscles ached after the toil of moving, and the contorted position in which she had slept.

She moved through the darkness with her arms stretched out in front of her, hoping to grope her way noiselessly to the kitchen. Somehow she found the wall separating the dining room from the kitchen. Her eyes almost completely adjusted to the dark. Bonnie ran her hand along the wall until she found the door to the kitchen. She found the light switch and flicked it upward. Light poured into Bonnie's eyes. They hurt and she covered them until the pain to subsided. Bonnie walked to the back door and called for One-night. "Here, kitty, kitty, kitty."

After several attempts, the medium-sized calico romped in from somewhere out in the nearby woods. One-night curled around her ankle, meowing.

"Come here, Baby," Bonnie cooed, picking up the cat, "where have you been today? I forgot all about you until...." Bonnie dropped the cat. She suddenly remembered what woke her. It was the faint sound of a woman's voice. She stared hard into the night, trying to remember what the voice said.

"What's wrong, Bonnie?" Amy's voice broke her thoughts. Bonnie spun around to see Amy standing in the doorway between the kitchen and the dining room, rubbing her eyes.

"Nothing," Bonnie lied.

"Are you hungry?" Amy asked.

"Damn straight," Shawn's voice called from the sunroom. "Let's go get a pizza or something. I could eat the northern end of a southbound skunk!"

"How gross!" Bonnie exclaimed. "That's disgusting!"

"Maybe so," he said, coming into the light of the kitchen, "but I know you love me just the same."

Bonnie did not respond. She went into the utility room off the kitchen and poured some dry cat food into a bowl.

Terry appeared in the doorway. "Pizza sounds like a good idea to me."

"Who has money?" Bonnie asked, picking her purse from the back of a chair in the breakfast nook area of the kitchen. "I'm not sure how much I have." She found a single five-dollar bill. "All I got is five bucks." Bonnie replaced the wallet in her purse and slung the strap over her shoulder. Terry pulled his wallet from his jeans.

"I think..." he opened his wallet. "Yeah, I have a twenty left."

"Good," Amy said, gathering her purse, "let's go." They piled into Terry's Cavalier and headed into town to find a pizzeria.

On the way, Bonnie sat in silence. She pressed her nose against the window, watching the shadows of the trees as the car sped past. They reminded her of the shadowy dream that woke her. The dream disturbed her and she did not know why. That was probably more disturbing to her than the dream itself.

# CHAPTER 19

Sunlight cut through the cold air, warming it only where the beams cascaded through the curtainless windows. Amy opened her eyes and looked around her bedroom. She saw the bright sunshine light up her room, and smiled. The morning light brought out its timeless beauty. Terry was still asleep, his snoring breaking the morning silence. She huddled next to him. He stirred, but did not wake.

The building pressures in her bladder encouraged her to brave the sharp transition from the warmth of their bed to the crisp air. She shivered as the cold air drifted up beneath her thin tee-shirt. As she placed her feet on the floor, she expected it to feel icy, but to her surprise, the floor was warmer than the air. For a moment, Amy thought she had stepped in a pan of warm water, and looked down to make sure her feet were on the floor. They were. *That's odd!* She touched the headboard. It was warmer too! She suddenly remembered why she had gotten out of bed and half ran, half walked into the bathroom. The bathroom air was as warm as the floor and the headboard. *How weird! What is it about that room?*

The cold air woke Terry because Amy had left the blankets off. He sat upright.

"Amy?" He called.

"In here," her voice drifted in from the attached bathroom. "Terry?"

"Yeah?"

"Are you cold?"

"Now that's a stupid question!" His tone was indignant. "You left the covers off me, Remember?"

"Sorry."

"Aren't you cold, honey?"

"Yeah. But listen. The air around you is cold, right?"

"Yeah. Freezing. But you're the snow bunny. You know I don't like the cold as much as you do."

"I know. I know. Just shut up a minute." Silence followed for several seconds. *Uh oh, I forgot how crabby he gets when someone wakes him up.* "I—uh—."

"What am I listening for?" Terry broke in. His tone said it all.

"Nothing. Do me a favor and put your feet on the floor."

"Without my slippers? Wait a minute, where are my slippers?"

"I don't know. I promise you won't freeze your tootsies off."

Terry reluctantly placed his feet on the floor. The cold air surrounded his naked legs, sending shivers up his spine. As soon as his feet made contact with the floor, he understood his wife's anxiety. The bottoms of his feet were warm, yet the biting coldness of the air seemed more intense on top of his feet. He was puzzled. *What the hell?* "What's going on?" he called into the bathroom.

The toilet flushed and Amy appeared in the door way. "I don't know. Maybe we should ask Bonnie." The moment she stepped through the doorway, she again felt the blast of cold air.

Terry watched her long blonde hair blow back away from her face, as if a slight puff of wind came from the bedroom. "Stop!" he said suddenly. Amy froze in her tracks. "Go back in the bathroom for a second."

Amy did as she was told. "Why?"

"Now come back into the room." Terry ignored her question. Amy walked across the threshold and into the bedroom. Her hair puffed back as before. *What the hell?* "Did you feel that, Amy?"

"The cold? Yeah. Why?"

"No, not the cold. The wind."

"Wind? What wind?"

"When you came through the door, did you feel the wind?"

"No. Just the cold."

"Do it again."

*What is going on here?* Amy became interested in Terry's observations. She backed through the door into the bathroom, and felt the skin on her back warm as she stepped through the doorway. *That's really weird!* Once Amy was well inside the bathroom, she began to move forward.

"Wait!" Amy froze as Terry jumped out of bed. He came over to the doorway and looked at her intently. "Come on."

Amy closed her eyes and moved forward slowly, feeling every feeling. As she passed over the threshold slowly, the warm air suddenly gave way to a wall of ice. Beginning at the tip of her nose then moving to the rest of her face and body. When the wall of cold air neared her hairline, she tried to feel each strand of hair as it moved, but felt only cold.

Terry moved to within inches of her hair at her temples and watched it move backward as she came into the bedroom. "Did you feel the wind?"

"No." She opened her eyes. "But I tried. Isn't it strange how the air is cold, but everything else in the room is the same temperature as the rest of the house?"

"It is?" He wrinkled his nose with disbelief.

"Yeah, try it."

Terry stood at the doorway and passed his hand through the door-jamb repeatedly, feeling the change in air temperature. Then he touched the wall, then the dresser, then every object in the room. "This is so weird!" He turned to his wife.

Amy sat on the bed with a bounce. Her breasts bouncing beneath the thin shirt, nipples hard from the cold. Terry's eyes locked on her chest. "What are you looking at?" she asked, looking down at her chest.

"What do you think?" He smiled, walking toward her. Terry became more and more aroused.

Amy stared at his groin, and noticed the change. "Is that a pickle in your pocket, or are you just glad to see me?"she asked with the most seductive bedroom eyes she could muster.

"This ain't no pickle," he grinned, and began to remove his shorts. In his desire for her, he forgot the cold for a moment.

"Well, what is it then?" She cocked her head and gave him a crooked smile.

"This is a heat-seeking moisture missile!"

"Oh, yeah?" she laughed.

"Yeah," he wrapped his arms around her, "and it's locked on target, dead ahead."

He kissed her, his tongue exploring the inside of her mouth as it had done a million times before, but this time the cold air added an additional sensual element that enhanced their excitement. Her tongue played with his. They stopped only for a breath. He removed her shirt and threw it on the floor. She removed his remaining clothing, and it wound up on top of hers in a heap. He kissed down the length of her body, leaving patches of wet skin that made Amy shiver with delight. In the cold air they made love as passionately as on their wedding night. The fire of desire warmed them from their core as the morning beams of sunlight kissed their skin.

The sudden pressure on his chest woke Shawn with a start. He opened his eyes to find two large yellow eyeballs with vertical pupils staring him in the face.

"What do you want, One-night?" he said softly. The cat meowed a reply. He stroked her calico fur. One-night kneaded his chest, poking her sharp claws through the covers to prick his skin, then dropped to her belly and began to purr. With One-night on his chest, Shawn propped up his pillow against the headboard and pulled himself into a half-sitting position. Bonnie stirred with the movement of the bed. Shawn looked at his wife. He reached over to run his fingers through her hair. As he fondled her auburn locks, he noticed her head was soaked with sweat. Puzzled, he touched her pillow to find it soaked through and through. Bonnie stirred.

"Hey babe," he said softly, "what's wrong?" Bonnie turned toward his voice and opened her eyes, slowly at first, then suddenly thrust them open in a panic. For an instant, she remembered her dream. But as she tried to focus her thoughts, the memory evaporated.

"Huh?" came the reply. "What did you say?"

"I said, what's wrong?"

"I—I dunno."

"Did you have a bad dream?"

"Yeah. Yeah, I think so. But I can't remember." She pulled herself against the headboard, and raked her wet hair back across the top of her head with her fingers. Rubbing her eyes, she looked down at One-night perched on Shawn's chest, purring away. "It's a shame you don't like cats."

"Yep. A damn shame." he said, stroking the animal's fur. One-night arched her back with each stroke.

"And I can see that she hates you just as much!" Bonnie said playfully.

Suddenly her face turned serious. She flung the covers off her and swung her feet to the floor, sitting on the edge of the bed, with her back to Shawn. A glimmer of the dream that had disturbed her sleep flashed across her mind. She closed her eyes, trying hard to remember.

"Bonnie?"

She did not reply, fearing that speech would cause her to lose her train of thought.

"What's wrong, babe?" Concern saturated Shawn's voice. Bonnie put her hand in the air, gesturing for him to stop. She saw bits and pieces but no coherent image.

The aroma of cooking bacon wafted up the staircase. Shawn was standing in the bathroom wiping the steam from the mirror with his towel. Bonnie was still in the shower with the water as hot as she could stand it. The mirror soon steamed up again. Shawn gave up trying to comb his hair, still wet from the shower, and stepped out into the hall. His mouth began to water from the smell of bacon, and he realized that he was hungry. Hurrying into the bedroom, he threw on a shirt, fluffed up his hair with his fingers and headed for the staircase. As he passed the bathroom he heard the shower turn off and stuck his head in the bathroom.

"I think Amy's cookin' breakfast."

"What?" Bonnie said, rubbing her head with a towel, "I couldn't hear you. I had water in my ear."

"Take a sniff."

Bonnie paused, then drew a deep breath through her nose, immediately smelling the bacon. "I think Amy's cookin' breakfast," she said.

Shawn rolled his eyes. "That's what I just said."

"It is?"

Shawn shook his head, playfully annoyed. "I'll see you downstairs," and started toward the stairs.

"Jeez, what's wrong with you?" She watched as he disappeared without a reply, then heard only the sound of his feet on the stairs. "Grump!" she called after him.

When Bonnie came down for breakfast, enough time had passed that she completely forgot her disturbing nightmare. Terry was sitting on the couch, petting One-night.

"Where's Shawn?" she asked Terry.

"He's in the kitchen."

As Bonnie headed for the kitchen, she could hear One-night purring. "She purrs almost as loud for you as she does for Shawn."

"Just proves that she's not so dumb after all. Plus, not to mention her excellent taste in men." He looked down at the cat. "Ain't that right, baby?"

Bonnie laughed and moved toward the wonderfully dense aroma of bacon coming from the kitchen. She was close enough to hear its sizzle, when halfway through the dining room she felt something crunch under her foot. She bent down to find a curved piece of thin glass. Bonnie suddenly felt queasy. *We all walked past this spot maybe a hundred times yesterday, and no one stepped on any glass. What broke?*

Holding the shards delicately in her hand, she took the pieces into the kitchen. Amy was busy at the stove, cooking bacon. Shawn was leaning against the counter behind her, happily munching.

"Did you break something, Shawn?" She handed the piece of glass to her husband.

He took the piece and examined it. "Innocent this time." He tried to hand it back.

"Wait." Bonnie said as she stepped over to the trash can, "I gotta get the rest of this glass off my hand." She carefully brushed the shards into the can, took the glass from Shawn and showed it to Amy.

"Do you recognize this?"

Amy took the piece of glass and turned it over. "Yep. It looks like a piece of light bulb." As she started to hand the jagged glass back to Bonnie, her hands greasy from the bacon, the thin glass rotated in her grip. She tried to catch it and dropped the spatula from her other hand. It hit the floor, sending hot grease flying onto her bare legs. Amy winced in pain, and squeezed her hands together in reflex. The jagged edges cut deeply into her palm. She cried out in pain and dropped the glass. Blood flowed from the wound and ran down her arm.

"Terry!" Bonnie called in panic, "Amy needs some disinfectant NOW!"

Sensing the distress in her voice, Terry jumped up immediately, still holding One-night. "What happened?" he yelled back to the kitchen.

"Amy cut her hand," Shawn's voice boomed. "Bring a bandage or something."

Terry ran toward his room, still holding the cat. As he approached the doorway, One-night began to fidget in his arms. The cold air enveloped them. He looked down at One-night in time to see her fur ripple as they crossed the threshold. The cat wriggled violently hissing and showing her teeth. One-night dug her claws deep into his chest, fighting to be released from his grip. She lunged from his arms, and landed on the opposite side of the doorway. *What the hell is wrong with you, One-night?* He hurried into the bathroom and dug through an open box and found a bottle of disinfectant and a roll of gauze. As he approached the door he could see One-night crouched down, her fur standing on end, hissing. Terry did not pay attention to the cat. He was worried about his wife.

"What happened to you?" Bonnie gasped as Terry ran into the kitchen.

"What?" Terry hurried to the sink where Amy was running water over her hand. As he set the supplies on the counter next to the sink, Terry suddenly realized that his chest hurt. He pulled on his shirt and looked down to see his white tee shirt soaked with blood. Bonnie went to the sink to help wrap Amy's hand.

"What happened?" Amy asked, concerned.

"I'm not really sure," Terry said, still examining his shirt. "I carried One-night with me when I walked into our room to get that stuff, when she went ape-shit."

"There's something wrong with that room." Bonnie's tone was serious.

"Well there's one damn thing," Terry began, "One-night sure feels the same way. She scratched the shit out of me to get out of there."

"Let's see just how bad she wants to get out of there." Shawn turned and headed for the living room. Terry was right behind him.

One-night was sitting in the center of the living room. She acted jumpy when Shawn bent to pick her up. "Well, you furry little pussy," Shawn began as he grabbed the animal, "Let's see what's up with you." As he neared the doorway, he could feel cat's muscles tense. "Wow. She really is afraid," he said, looking at Terry.

Terry nodded his head in agreement. Standing away from the doorway, Shawn tossed the cat into the lower bedroom. Her eyes widened in panic. The moment her feet touched the floor, One-night darted out of the room and ran up the stairs.

"Shawn Michael Bricker!" Bonnie's stern voice filled the room. "You leave that poor cat alone!"

Shawn grinned at Terry. Terry did not return the expression.

"There's something wrong with that room," Bonnie said sullenly. "And I don't like it."

"Well it's too late now," Terry said, "we signed a one year lease."

Bonnie looked at the floor, blankly. "I know." She looked at Shawn, "You're not gonna find One-night in that room. Animals can sense things. And I can feel it too. One-night is scared to death of that room, and I understand it. So please, don't throw her in there, again. Ok?"

"Sorry honey."

"Don't 'sorry honey' me. Go tell One-night."

Shawn only looked up the stairs. It was obvious to Bonnie he was ashamed of what he had done.

"How's your hand?" Terry asked Amy, looking at her bandaged hand. *Maybe this would be a good time to change the subject.*

Amy narrowed her eyes at him. "You guys are so mean to that cat." She glanced at her hand, "I'll live." Then stomped into the kitchen. "C'mon Bonnie. Your breakfast is getting cold."

Bonnie followed silently.

The two men were left in the living room alone and after several moments, Terry broke the awkward, silent tension. "You know Shawn," Terry walked over to his stereo, "Amy didn't do such a bad job with this. But what do you think about running the wires underneath the house so we can't see them?"

"Not bad. The only problem is, we need to make sure those two women know what they want as far as how this room is arranged. Because once we drill holes in the floor, there won't be too much rearranging."

"True. Let's find out what they think." Terry turned toward the kitchen and called for his wife. Seconds later, Amy appeared in the doorway, Bonnie right behind her, munching bacon.

"Shawn and I were discussing the possibility of running the speaker wires to the stereo under the house. What do you two think?"

Amy turned to Bonnie. Bonnie, her mouth still full of bacon, shrugged her shoulders. Amy turned back to Terry. "Sounds okay. But you ain't gonna get me under this house. I hate bugs. And I'm sure there are plenty of them under there."

"We'll put a drop of silicone in the holes to seal them up," Shawn informed.

"And," Bonnie said, with her mouth half-full, then swallowing, "I'm claustrophobic so you can count me out of crawling underneath. Besides, that's a guy thing anyway."

Amy laughed and turned to go back into the kitchen.

"Wait!" Shawn yelled after them. He glanced over to Terry, who rolled his eyes. Seconds later the girls reappeared. "Is this how you two want this room?"

Amy looked at Bonnie. "Why?" Amy wrinkled her forehead.

"Because. Once we drill holes in the floor, that's it. The furniture stays where it is. No changing around."

"I don't know if I like that," Amy said.

"Why?" Terry wanted to know.

"Because," Bonnie began, placing her hands on her hips, "it's a woman's prerogative to change her mind. That's why."

"Well, excuse me!" Shawn retorted, "but that's why we want to know if this is the way you want this room."

"Alright. Alright. Why don't you two go round up your tools, since I know you're just dying to drill a hole in something." Bonnie laughed.

The guys went on a great quest for tools.

Minutes later, Shawn came back into the room with a power drill, which he dropped on the floor. Terry was right behind him with an extension cord looped around his shoulder.

"Have you two made up your minds about the furniture?" Terry asked.

Bonnie looked at Amy and broke into laughter. *It would serve you two right to make you move this heavy stuff around 5 or 6 times after you threw poor One-night into that room.*

"What's with the two of you?" Shawn demanded, then glanced at Terry, who shrugged his shoulders.

"Bonnie, what do you think? Should we cut them some slack?"

"Even though it's not McDonalds, and I'm not sure they deserve a break today, yeah. I think I can live with the arrangement."

"Well, be still my beating heart," Terry said, rolling his eyes, "it's probably the first time in the history of mankind that a woman is happy with the living room arrangement the first time out!"

"Well amen to that! Shawn agreed.

"You know, you two," Amy said crossly, placing her hands on her hips, "we could have made the two of you rearrange this room five or six times before you finally made us happy. But, it looks like you got lucky today!"

"I remember getting lucky…" Terry grinned.

Amy shot him a smile, then walked over to kiss him. "Someone has to give you a hard time around here. I know it's a thankless job, but someone has to do it!" Amy laughed and gestured for Bonnie to follow her into the kitchen.

Shawn knelt behind one of the four large speakers and began to drill a hole through the floor. The drill bit twisted its way into the century-and-a-half year old floor.

"The acoustics in this room are gonna make these old MK4's sound like a concert hall." Terry said proudly.

"Any room sounds great with these babies." Shawn grunted as the drill bit hung in the wood, stalling the drill motor. He wrenched it free and resumed drilling. "Why don't you go find a flashlight." Shawn said as he finished with the first hole.

"Me?" Terry said, pointing a thumb at his own chest.

"Yeah, you. You were the plumbers assistant. You're the one who crawls under houses. It's your stereo. And besides, I'm drillin' all the holes."

"Big deal." Terry shook his head and turned on his heel to head for his bedroom. As he crossed the threshold of his bedroom he immediately felt the sudden change in air temperature. He tried to feel his hair blow back like he had seen Amy's do earlier and, like her, he couldn't.

Terry rummaged around in the top drawer of his dresser, found the old two cell light and switched it on. Nothing happened. He walked over to the doorway and stuck his head into the living room.

"Amy!" he called, trying to overcome the sound of the drill. "Do you know where the batteries are?"

"I think they're in the bathroom vanity."

Terry lingered, half in, half out of the door savoring the strange sensation of his head feeling warmer than his body. *Oh yeah, that's where I saw them.* Abruptly, he turned to cross his bedroom toward the bathroom. He twisted off the bottom of the flashlight and replaced the batteries with the batteries he found in the drawer.

Terry switched on the flashlight and pointed it toward the opposite wall of his bedroom. The darkness in the bedroom seemed to swallow the beam, leaving a dim circle of light on the wall. *Now that is weird as hell. I hope these batteries aren't too old.* As Terry crossed the threshold into his bedroom, the light ceased to shine. Puzzled, he turned the light to his face and hit the case gently while turning the switch on and off. Nothing happened. *Oh, what's the matter with this damn thing? Must've blew the bulb.* Disgusted, Terry walked into the living room.

"Shawn, do you have any bulbs? This one has had it."

"No." Shawn looked up. "Why? That one works fine."

Terry looked at the lens, perplexed. The lamp was indeed glowing. He walked back into his bedroom to get his jump suit that he used when he worked as a plumber's assistant. Without turning off the light, it went dark again. He walked back into the living room, watching the light. As he crossed the threshold, the light glowed brightly again. *Now what the hell is this? This is too weird!*

"Shawn! Check this out." Shawn looked up from his work to see Terry standing at the threshold of his bedroom, just inside the living room. He was holding the flashlight so Shawn could see the lens with his hand well away from the switch. He began to pass the light through the doorway. Shawn's jaw dropped in amazement. When the light was in the bedroom, it was off. When it was brought back into the living room, it came on again. Terry repeated the maneuver three more times, and each time, the light acted exactly as it had the first time.

Shawn raised his eyebrows. *Bonnie is right about this room.*

Terry stowed a staple gun in the back pocket of his coveralls, then knelt at the access door that lead underneath the house. Like the house itself, the panel was made of wood, and very old, but he guessed that it was only about half the age of the rest of the house. In his experience as a plumber's assistant, he knew that most houses of this age did not have foundations, only piers to hold up the wooden girders, and usually a metal underpinning around the perimeter to keep out small animals.

The access door was made up of three one-by-ten pieces of wood, nailed together at two cross pieces. A small wooden frame had been set into the stone-and-mortar foundation. The door was held in place by two large nails pounded into the frame about half way, bent over to it against the frame. Terry reached over and turned the nails to remove the access door. The nails were turned, yet the access door was held fast. Upon further examination, Terry noticed a bead of paint holding the door in place. There was a small gap between the top of the door and the bottom of the frame. He squeezed two fingers in the gap and pulled hard. The door made a cracking sound as it pulled free of the wooden frame. Terry laid the door on the grass next to the access opening.

The access opening was in the center of the exterior wall facing the barn and old outhouse. Terry laid on his belly and switched on the flashlight. Adorned in his jump suit, he felt only marginally better about crawling under the hundred-plus-year-old structure. He shined the beam of light around. At the opening, the space at the upper corners were heavily laden with spider webs. Normally, spiders gave Terry the creeps. But for some reason, they did not have that effect on him today. He reached for a small twig lying on the ground next to him, and began twisting the spider webs around the stick. When the opening was clear, he slid through.

The air under the house was stale and stagnant, and felt heavy in Terry's lungs. The beam of light sparkled with particles of dust raised by his intrusion. He saw piles of dirt along the sewage pipes, and he recognized them as having been made by a plumber when the water system was added to the house. He knew the system was old, since the sewer lines were three-inch cast iron pipe, and the water supply lines were three-quarter-inch threaded galvanized pipe. Terry knew that was an old set up because when he was installing supply line, he always used copper tubing, which he had to sweat-solder together. He smiled when he thought of the first time he ever used a propane torch under a house to connect some copper tubing. There wasn't much space in the crawl area and the joint happened to be next to a floor joist. He accidentally caught the joist on fire with the flame. He threw some dirt on the smoldering piece of wood. When he told his boss about the fire, the man only laughed and said that it happened quite often.

Terry had to contort his body over a sewer pipe running parallel to the foundation wall so he could get completely under the house. He could see the house had been added on to. There were piles of wood chips and sawdust under each place where a pipe went up through the floor. Clearly, the plumbing had been installed long after the house was built. He suddenly realized why the air was so stale. There were no foundation vents. The substructure was totally dark; no sunlight came in except through the access opening. He looked over at the center of the house. His eyes were now adjusted to the darkness, although he still needed the flashlight to see by. He pulled himself toward the center of the house, and realized that he could now get up on all fours and crawl on his hands and knees. He no longer had to pull himself along on his belly.

Terry could now see five small beams of light cascading down from the floor above his head. He realized that those little beams were his destination. He crawled toward them. Suddenly, he felt a wall of cold air. The sudden change made the hair on the back of his neck stand up. He felt anxious, and realized he was under his bedroom. He thought more about the words that Bonnie had spoken about this room. *There is definitely something wrong here.*

He focused on the beams of light coming through the holes in the floor. The space around him seemed darker. Only the light beam penetrated the darkness, which swallowed up the reflected light from the flashlight. Only the main beam was visible. As Terry moved his leg to advance his position, he suddenly hit something hard with a thud. Pain shot up his leg. He cried out, clutching his knee. He shined the light to see what caused his agony. There was a large pile of dirt with a halfburied rock protruding from the pile. He had slammed his knee squarely on the rock. He looked around for the source of the pile. Suddenly curious, he noticed a pipe going into the ground and dismissed the pipe as the source of the pile, realizing that some poor fool had to get under this house and dig to install the pipes. *Oh man, I'm glad I wasn't the one who had to do this—what a bitch!*

Terry hurried over to the beams of light to pull the speaker wires. Each time he moved, he was reminded of the dirt pile by the pain in his knee. Shawn fed the wires down through the hole so Terry could grab them and quickly pulled them through, then crawled to the single larger hole near the stereo stand. As he moved, dust stirred in the confined area, filling his nostrils with fine particles of dirt. Shawn took the wire, pulling it through the larger hole at the stereo stand. When Shawn was sure he had enough wire, Terry stapled it to a floor joist. Each staple barely penetrated the age-hardened wood just enough to hold the wire in place.

When he was finished, he crawled quickly to the access door. He emerged to see Bonnie standing at the opening.

"Are you okay?" she asked anxiously.

"Yeah. I'm fine."

"Is your knee okay?"

Terry stood, his hurt knee shaking. He eyed her curiously. "How'd you know my knee hurts?"

"We all heard you yell. But I just knew you banged your knee. What happened?"

"There is a huge pile of dirt under there." Terry pointed to his bedroom, under which the pile of dirt was located. "I guess I just slammed my knee into it. It hurts like hell."

"How big is this pile of dirt?"

"What is it with you and this dirt pile? If you want to know bad enough, then you go under and check it out yourself. You can even use my coveralls."

Bonnie reared back. "No way. I don't do well in enclosed spaces. You get to describe it for me."

Terry's knee began to throb even more now that he was standing. "Let's go inside. I gotta get these grubby's off."

Terry turned and limped to the door facing the driveway, Bonnie following closely behind.

"Terry, how big is that pile. I need to know."

"Why?"

"Because—I don't know, I just need to. Are you gonna tell me or what?"

Terry stopped abruptly and turned to face her, wincing in pain. "Okay. It was—maybe a foot and a half high, and about, mmmm, maybe six or seven feet long and probably three or four feet wide. It just looked like a pile of dirt to me."

"How do you think it got there?"

"There was a pipe next to it, so I figured it was left over from that plumber, or whoever put the pipes in. I guess they were just too damn lazy to take the dirt out from under the house. It's a simple deal really. Why does it eat at you like this?"

"I don't know. I can't really put my finger on it."

Terry shook his head in amazement and went into the house. Bonnie stood in the driveway and a cold chill suddenly ran up her spine. She tried to shake off the feeling, but it remained strong. She turned back toward the house, still feeling uneasy. *What have we gotten ourselves into?*

Shawn was waiting for her at the back door, "it's your mom," he said, handing her the phone.

*Something's wrong.* Bonnie placed the phone to her ear and went pale. "Shawn we have to go to Chattanooga."

"What happened?"

"We have to go to Erlanger now," Bonnie sobbed.

"What happened?"

"My dad had a heart attack—he's in the hospital."

# CHAPTER 20

The lights from the Christmas tree reflected off the glass, superimposed on the December night sky. Shawn stood looking out the window at the silently falling snow. It was an unexpected surprise, and he beamed with pleasure. Nothing could have made Christmas better. It had been the first white Christmas he had seen in Tennessee since he could remember. The trees silhouetted in the distance bent with each gust of wind, snow swirling in looplets with an occasional whirlwind.

With a fire roaring in the fireplace, he felt more than a special closeness with his wife. More than just being married. Shawn loved the holiday season. When Terry and Amy announced they were going to visit their families in Nashville for the holidays, Shawn couldn't have been happier. Although he loved the Lambert's dearly, he needed to spend some time in the house alone with Bonnie, especially after the death of her dad the day after they moved in. He thought that he could somehow make her feel more comfortable in the house if they were alone. Her mother had gone to Oklahoma to celebrate Christmas with her older sister. It had been a difficult three months for Bonnie. Shawn had the sense to give her space when he thought she needed it.

The Christmas tree in the corner near the sunroom was beautiful, with Terry and Amy's gifts underneath. They would exchange gifts with them when they returned home in two days. The house was laden with torn wrapping paper, a pleasant reminder of the day with Shawn's family gathered in the old house. But finally, the activity had stopped and he and Bonnie were alone.

Bonnie knelt in front of the brick hearth stoking the fire. He could see its reflection in her eyes, her auburn hair red with the firelight. Her face glowed. She was beautiful. Although he seldom told her so, he always felt that way. The spirit of the holidays always seemed to bring out the deep feelings he had for her. He knew she was his soul mate. He looked at her, smiling. She stared straight into the fire, unblinking, not noticing his stare.

"I love you, too, Shawn," she said suddenly, not removing her gaze from the fire.

"How did you know what I was thinking?" He walked over and knelt beside her.

"You always do this at Christmas time," she said tenderly, yet with an odd detachment.

*Are you thinking of your dad? And all the Christmases you spent with him and your mom before we got married?* "Ain't it neat to have the house all to ourselves for a while?"

Bonnie nodded without a word, her eyes still locked on the flames.

Each time a gust of wind came up, she felt icy air swirl around her seeping in from around the old front door. She turned to look at the door to the lower bedroom to be sure the air wasn't coming from that horrid room. It was secure, just as Amy had left it.

A piece of wood burned in two, its falling halves sending sparks up the flue. She turned quickly to see. There was something familiar about the way the pieces had fallen. She looked harder into the flames. Shawn was talking to her, but his words were distant and without meaning. The roar of the fire grew louder in her ears, drowning out his voice.

The house loomed through the flames, a black shape against the orange-yellow light. *The house is on fire!* She heard distant screams, faint in her ears. Images of a man, a woman and a small child—a girl, running from the house. *That's our House! Yet it's different—as if from a different time.* Suddenly she felt great anguish and loss, as if she had lost everything she owned. Bonnie fell backwards as the scene played out in her mind. She barely caught herself, when she felt her husband's strong hands on her shoulders.

"Bonnie? Are you alright?" he asked tenderly. She looked at him, blinking. Her body shook, her hazel eyes clouded with tears. "Babe, what's wrong?" Concern grew in his voice. Tears began to run down her cheeks, he wiped them away softly with his hand. "Now Bonnie, what's the matter?"

"Oh Shawn!" she cried. Tears were streaming down her face. "I saw it all. I saw the whole thing go up in flames."

"What went up in flames, something in the fireplace?" She nodded. "You mean the logs?" She shook her head no. "Well, what then?"

"Our house."

"Are you saying that you think this house is gonna catch fire?"

"No."

Shawn looked at her, puzzled. "I don't understand."

"It was this house. But it wasn't us in it when it burned. It happened a long time ago. It was an accident."

"What was? The fire?"

"Yes." The word caught in her throat.

Shawn just held her close. It was the only thing he could think of.

It was the only thing she needed. She felt safe in his strong embrace, and breathed a sigh of relief.

The past few months in the house had been stressful. Though she tried to hide it from the others, Shawn knew. He knew his wife. A bond that only comes from your soul mate. But Shawn was a patient man. He normally would wait until she told him what was wrong. He knew not to push her, and simply be there for her until she was ready to discuss what was bothering her. But this silence had gone on far too long.

"What's wrong, babe?" he asked tenderly.

She looked at him with tears in her eyes. He delicately wiped her tears with a finger. She broke from his embrace and led him to the couch. The two sat, his hands surrounding hers.

"I haven't been sleeping too well."

"I know. Most of the time when you wake up, your head is all sweaty."

Bonnie said nothing. She only blinked at him. She did not realize he knew about the dreams.

"What are the nightmares about?"

"I really don't know. When I wake up, I can't remember what I dreamed about. Only that I dreamed. But lately, I've been sleeping pretty good."

"Since when?"

"Well, ever since Terry and Amy left for Nashville, I guess."

Shawn pulled her close. She closed her eyes and nestled her head on his chest. As she relaxed into his embrace, the vision of the house fire faded in her mind. The two sat in front of the fireplace, holding each other. Its warmth was only surpassed by the burning love they felt for each other. It was the perfect end to a holiday.

# CHAPTER 21

The snow fell through the night and all the next day until thirteen inches had fallen around the old house. Bonnie, when she could tear her husband away from the televised football games, had him help her prepare the house for Terry and Amy's homecoming. Other than the sound of a snowplow heaping the snow into high rows along the roadway, everything was quiet.

The next morning Bonnie awoke, after yet another restful sleep, to the sound of a car running. She jumped out of bed and rushed to the window. Shawn stirred in his sleep but did not wake. The clouds from the previous day had cleared, revealing a bright blue sky against the pure white snowcovered ground. She could see Terry's Cavalier at the mouth of the driveway, the driver side door open, steam rising into the clear sky from the exhaust. Terry was bending down at the front of the car. She could hear muffled profanity. The little car tried to plow through the mound of snow left by yesterday's snowplow. As Terry attempted to drive into the driveway, the snow stopped the car from advancing as the front wheels lost traction. Bonnie turned to her sleeping husband.

"Shawn! Wake up! Shawn! They're here!"

He lifted his head and rubbed his eyes. "What time is it?"

"I don't know."

"Well, where are they?"

"They're stuck in the snow at the front of the driveway."

Shawn squinted at his wife. "Huh?"

"It looks like they tried to use their car as a snowplow. I can hear Terry cussing from here." Bonnie laughed as she threw on her clothes.

"I gotta see this!" He threw the covers off and went to the window. He could see Terry shoveling the pile of snow with his bare hands. Shawn grinned. "I'd better go and help him," he said as he grabbed his jeans from the back of a chair.

Bonnie heard a car door slam, and looked out to see Amy trudging toward the house, her breath visible in the cold air.

Amy walked into the living room and removed her coat. She smiled as she smelled the smoky residue from the fireplace. "Bonnie? Shawn?" Amy called up the stairs.

"Hang on a minute. We'll be down in a second." Bonnie's voice drifted downstairs.

Amy hung her coat on the coat tree next to the front door. She turned as Shawn thumped down the stairs.

He smiled as he went passed her. "Welcome home. I'll be out yonder, helping Terry with the car," he said without breaking stride.

Amy watched him disappear through the dining room then looked up the stairs. Bonnie appeared at the top.

"Hey girlfriend!" Bonnie said, beaming, "glad you're back home." She ran to greet her best friend.

"It's good to be back home—oh, Bonnie! You should have seen it. The first white Christmas in Nashville since 1968. It was fabulous."

"We had our own right here. Plus, we had a fire and everything," Bonnie smiled faintly.

"I see that." Amy walked to the couch where One-night lay sleeping, curled in a ball. She bent to pet her. One-night stirred, then arched her back with each stroke and purred. The calico stretched her front legs, exposing her claws, and yawned. After a few moments of awkward silence, Amy stopped petting the cat and looked at Bonnie. "Are you okay?" she asked, noticing Bonnie's distant stare.

Bonnie forced a smile and nodded.

"I was kinda worried about you. I know you're not really that comfortable with this house, especially after your father died. But I really couldn't cancel going out to my Mom's because my older brother Carl was there."

"I thought he was on some ship in the Persian Gulf."

"He was. But he came home on leave. He was stationed on the *USS Ranger*. And, guess what—he brought his new wife!"

"Oh yeah, where's she from? What's her name? What's she like?"

"She's nice. Her name's Elise and she's from San Francisco. He met her before the war and she waited until his ship came back to port in Alameda. Then they got married. My stupid brother didn't even let anyone know."

"I guess he wanted it to be a surprise."

"Well, yeah, but you'd think he would've let us know so we could've gone to the wedding. But I've been worried about you. Have you been able to remember any of your dreams?"

"Actually, I slept pretty good while ya'll were away. No dreams at all."

"I wonder if it's because nobody was in my room." Amy said, gesturing toward her bedroom door.

"I hadn't thought of that." Bonnie sat on the couch next to One-night. "Yeah, that makes a lot of sense."

Amy turned and walked toward her room. One-night suddenly reared her head and looked intently at the bedroom door. As Amy pushed the door open, One-night sprang to her feet.

Bonnie placed her hand on the cat's back. She could feel the animal trembling.

Amy felt a slight resistance as she tried to open the door, as if the room were pressurized. Bonnie studied the cat. *Oh no, it's starting again.*

Bonnie watched Amy's hair blow back at her temples as she crossed the threshold. One-night hissed. Her stomach began to tighten, and a shiver went up her spine. *But this time, it's worse.* Amy disappeared from view. Bonnie saw light as Amy flipped on the switch in the bathroom.

Amy appeared in the doorway. "Is there some meat that went bad?" she asked, wrinkling her nose.

"What? No." Bonnie thought for a moment, then restated, "no."

"Oh!" Amy's expression cleared. "Never mind. I thought I smelled some bad meat or something. But, it's gone now." Amy wondered if she had really smelled anything in the first place, and disappeared back into her room. Bonnie continued trying to calm One-night. *I know baby, I can feel it, too.*

"Hey, Terry!" Shawn yelled. "Hang on. I'll help you. Just let me get a shovel."

Terry had moved most of the snow with his bare hands, now numb with cold. As he watched Shawn trudge through the snow toward the barn, Terry unzipped his jacket halfway, and placed his hands under his armpits. He imagined he was a frozen vampire with his arms crossed over his chest.

Bonnie's eyes widened with terror as she threw One-night from her lap. "Oh my God!" she screamed. "Amy! C'mon!"

Shawn reached up to slide open the barn door. It was a large wooden slab with wheels bolted to the top that hung in a metal track. The door hung freely from the top. He grabbed the frozen strap with both hands and pulled hard. The bottom swung out a little, but the door refused to slide. Shawn could hear snow crunching as Terry came up behind him.

"What's wrong?" Terry asked.

"Oh, this damn thing is frozen shut. It rained out here first, then turned to snow. So, the track that this stupid door slides in probably filled up with water, then froze."

"Well, will the door swing out enough at the bottom for one of us to squeeze underneath?"

"No, I don't think so. I don't want to risk popping the door off the track. We ain't got a ladder big enough to put the door back. Plus, this looks like one heavy soma bitch!"

"Can we rock it back and forth to break up the ice?"

"Let's see."

Terry grabbed the end of the door opposite the strap, while Shawn pulled on the strap itself. The door rocked up, trying to come up out of its track. Chips of ice fell from the top, but the door would not move.

"How about shaking the door? You know, maybe twisting a little, like an ice cube tray."

"I'm game." Shawn said. He released the strap, then bent to grip the edge of the large door. He looked over at Terry at the opposite end, nodding his readiness to proceed. Terry nodded. The two began shaking the door, first in unison, then alternating in order to twist the door. Suddenly they felt a single, deep, forceful reverberation.

They heard wood splintering, and Terry's eyes grew wide. He wasn't sure what was happening, but he was sure that whatever it was, wasn't good. Stale air billowed out from under the door. Terry panicked. He released it to run just as Shawn did the same.

The bottom of the door began to swing up toward them. The ground shook as something extremely heavy hit the ground inside the barn. The door gained speed as it swung upward, scooping snow out of its path. It hit both men in the lower legs with such force that they were thrown back. The door continued to swing up, its rollers breaking free of the track, then started to come down. Both men rolled away as the door fell. The thick layer of snow made their movements appear to be in slow motion. The concussion was deafening as the door landed between them. They both sat in the snow, looking at each other, rubbing their lower legs. Eyes wide, hearts pumping, they were too shaken to speak.

The back door burst open as Bonnie ran from the house, Amy on her heels. She was angry at herself for not recognizing her feelings sooner.

She knew her husband was in mortal danger. The girls reached their husbands, and helped them to their feet.

"What the hell happened?" Terry finally spoke.

"Are you all right?" Bonnie asked, regaining her breath.

"Yeah, I think so." Shawn whispered, bending to brush the snow from his pants. He was pale. They turned to see the gaping hole in the barn where the door had been. The door lay face up in the snow between them. Terry looked at Shawn.

"That was damn close!"

"Too close!"

"What happened?" Amy asked.

"I don't know," Terry said, "but let's find out."

They approached the opening cautiously. The barn had been closed for the past 14 years except when they put away the gardening tools the day they moved in. The air was stale and smelled of decaying wood and hay. Beams of sunlight cascaded through a large hole in the roof, and glimmered with dust and bits of hay suspended in the air.

Amy looked at the gaping hole. "I bet I know what happened," she spoke suddenly.

"What?" Bonnie asked, then looked at Shawn. Shawn made no reply.

"I'll bet," Amy began confidently, "snow came in through that hole in the roof, and the weight was too much for the second floor—"

"The loft," Terry cut in.

"Yeah, the loft," Amy continued, eyeing Terry, "It, ah, collapsed."

"Not bad," Shawn said with approval.

"Okay Sherlock," Bonnie said, pointing to the large pile of snow in the center of the barn, "what's that?"

"What's what?" Terry asked in a serious tone.

"That. Over there, the square things." Bonnie pointed to the faint outline of four rectangles under the mixture of snow and hay, fanned out like playing cards. The loft was still attached to the inside wall at the far end. The contents of the loft had slid to the ground after the near end collapsed.

"The little bit that we shook the barn," Shawn began, "when we tried to free the door was all it took to shift the weight. The supports probably deteriorated after all the years of that roof leaking."

Bonnie walked cautiously over to the rectangles under the snow. She began to brush the snow and hay away. A putrid odor filled the air, like rotten vegetables.

Terry nodded in agreement. "That's what that smell is—those supports are rotten."

Amy knew the smell. She sniffed the air, wrinkling her nose.

"Bonnie."

"What?" Bonnie stopped to turn and look at her friend.

"This reminds me of that smell I noticed when I first got home. Remember? I asked you if there was some bad meat."

"Yeah, I do. But this smells different than bad meat."

"I know," Amy answered, "but maybe it was my turn to have a premonition."

Bonnie turned toward Amy "I hadn't thought of that. Maybe so." Bonnie turned back to the rectangles. She caught sight of a dull black surface. "It looks like an old trash bag."

Terry and Shawn came over to help. Amy stood back, hands on her hips, watching. Shawn dug his hands underneath the top rectangle to lift it and take it into the house.

"Wait a sec," Terry grabbed a shovel, "we oughta finish what we started first."

Shawn set it down and followed Terry to the Cavalier. The engine was still running, the driver's side door wide open. Terry shoveled furiously as Shawn slid behind the steering wheel. The little car lurched forward, then began to spin its front tires in the snow.

The girls were examining their find, debating among themselves as to whether or not to tear open the plastic and see what treasures awaited them. Bonnie looked at Amy and smiled. *I feel like a kid at Christmastime and I'm home alone and I get the urge to open my presents to see what they are, then re-wrap them before my parents get home.*

"What?" Amy smiled.

"Nothing," Bonnie grinned.

"No way, I know that look."

The sound of the Cavalier's engine racing and tires spinning in the snow floated in from outside. They turned simultaneously to see Terry motioning for them to help. Amy looked at Bonnie, shrugged, then trudged through the snow toward the car. Bonnie followed.

Terry sat on the hood of the car, over the left fender and gestured for Amy to do the same on the right fender. "We need weight on the front end."

Amy slid onto the hood. "Are you making a crack about my weight?" Amy barked playfully.

"Only when your clothes are on." Terry grinned. He turned to Bonnie. "You need to get on the hood in the middle. Put your feet on the bumper and lean over and grab the windshield wipers."

Bonnie silently climbed onto the car. Terry turned to Shawn, then motioned for him to proceed. The tires gripped then spun, gripped then spun as the car moved forward slowly. Amy laughed with delight. Shawn saw Bonnie's eyes widen with exhilaration mixed with fear through the windshield. The front cowl under the bumper pushed snow like a tiny snow plow. When Shawn finally positioned the car in the driveway, he headed toward the barn. The three slid off the hood and followed. Shawn grabbed the first package from the barn, balanced it on his shoulder and brought it into the house.

"Ten to one says these are French doors," Bonnie blurted out when they were all in the house. The plastic was held in place by masking tape, now hard and brittle. In places where the plastic had worn through, Bonnie could see tattered cloth beneath. She carefully tore the plastic off. Shawn helped her by lifting, then twisting when necessary, to remove the plastic. The blanket, now exposed, cracked and popped when Bonnie unwrapped it. It was indeed, a French door. Bonnie sat on the couch, felling ill as she watched the others unwrap the other doors. *Why do I get the feeling that something bad is about to happen?*

"Miss 'licia? Miss 'licia?" His voice was distant and barely discernable from the distorted images and garbled sounds Alicia heard in her drug-induced psychosis.

Over the past few months, she had become resistant to the dosage of Thorazine originally prescribed by Dr. Freeman. Only the day before, Alicia had become more mentally alert, and began to question her surroundings. Nathan mistook Alicia's alertness for delirium and reported his observations to Patrick Freeman, who promptly upped the dosage, while praising Nathan for his discretion when he learned that Nathan had spoken to no one else.

"Now Miss 'licia, I'll be right back."

She tried to turn her head to the sound of the voice in the distance, but her head felt like an anchor tied to a bowl of jelly, impossible to move. At the sound of Nathan's voice, Alicia's mind fought to keep out the strange, surreal images that flashed through her mind and tried to concentrate on the sound of his voice. Jumbled memories flooded in and blended with current reality. She opened her mouth to speak. In her mind, her response was clear and concise, despite the images.

Nathan only heard garbled tones. "Gotta go to the little boys room," he said softly. "I'll be right back."

Somehow, she understood what he said. But the understanding was slow in coming. His face disappeared from view. Her eyes focused on something slightly farther away. *What is that? Stars? In boxes? Black stars against a white background. In boxes. Aren't stars white against a black background? Yes. Yes, they are! Well then, what is that?* She looked hard at the black stars. Slowly, she realized they weren't stars. *Oh, those are dots. Dots! Of course they're dots. Could I count them?* The thought was distantly familiar.

The air filled with a strange, sweet smell. It was perfume. *Strange perfume.* A warm hand cradled the back of her neck, pulling her into a sitting position. The fields of black dots moved to a smooth green field. *Was that grass? No, not grass.* She recognized the field of green now. *Oh, it's only the wall in my room.* A face moved into view. *Who are you? Blue eyes. Overdone mascara. Too much rouge.* She did not recognize the woman's face. Blonde hair fell in ringlets at her cheek bones. Something hard and bitter was pushed between Alicia's lips. *What are you doing?* Her head was tilted back. The dots were in view again. Cool liquid filled her mouth. She could feel the hard, bitter thing float off her tongue. Involuntary muscles took over, making her swallow. The hard bitter thing was gone. Her head was again resting on the pillow. Time passed. *Nathan, where are you? S'postu?* She turned her attention back to the dots. Her eyes slowly became heavy. The surreal images in her mind, the bright colors, faded into black. She felt her energy draining. *Am I dying?* She fought hard to think. *No, I can't die! I still have too much to do. But how?* Her eyes closed despite her effort to keep them open. This sleep was not normal. It was heavy. Deeper. Her energy gone, she let the hard sleep come. Alicia slipped into a coma.

Nathan Powell stepped out into the hall in time to see a young blonde woman coming out of Alicia's room. His heart pounded in his throat. He felt as if he were watching a small child step in front of a speeding car, but was too far away to stop the inevitable.

"Hey! You!" Nathan yelled across the hall. "What were you doing in that room?"

The woman stopped in her tracks. Her eyes wide, mouth open. "Me?" she mouthed in response.

He ran toward her. "What were you doing in that room?" he demanded forcefully, glaring at her. "What's your name anyway?"

The woman gulped. "Teresa. I—I gave Miss Freed her medicine."

Nathan looked as if he had been shot. "You what?!!"

"I gave Miss Freed her prescription–I."

"Oh NO!" Nathan cut her off as he ran to her room. He felt his stomach drop as he caught sight of Alicia motionless on her bed and realized she was not merely sleeping.

"Oh! Miss 'licia." He bent to touch her face but she made no response. His hopes sank even deeper. "What has she done to ya?" Teresa appeared in the doorway, tears in her eyes. Nathan turned to glare at her. "Dr. Freeman changed her injections to a higher dosage."

"I didn't know," She cried.

"Can't you read a chart?" he growled venomously. "Well don't just stand there, girl! Call Dr. Freeman–STAT!"

The words hit Teresa like a freight train and she sprang to life. Nathan saw her disappear from the doorway, her footsteps trailing off as she ran down the hall. He stroked Alicia's grey hair and noticed it was no longer greying brown, as he remembered. All traces of the brunette color were gone and he watched his chocolate skin against her silver hair. *Where had the years gone?*

"Oh Miss 'licia," he spoke softly, "I'm so sorry–I know Teresa's new, and she probably meant well. She didn't know the Doc changed your shots. She didn't know you weren't supposed to take your pills anymore. It's all my fault," he sobbed. "I should have never left you. Please wake up–." His words trailed off to silent tears.

Patrick Freeman placed the last of his late breakfast in his mouth when the phone rang. His wife Sara rose from the table to get the phone. *It's probably for her, no one ever calls me anyway.* He looked up to see his wife's face lose its color, holding the phone receiver out to him, her hand covering the mouthpiece.

"It's for you. There's an emergency down at the institute."

Patrick swallowed hard, his food only partially chewed. *So much for that theory.* He quickly rose to take the phone.

"Dr. Freeman?" The female voice was frantic.

"Yes. What's wrong?"

"I'm sorry. I'm sorry. I didn't know. I gave Miss Freed her pills–I, er."

"Oh no!" he cut her off. "What's her status?"

"I don't know–Nathan's with her."

"All right. Just stay calm."

"I didn't know–I think she's asleep. OH NO! I'm sorry–."

"Get a grip on yourself. What's your name?"

"Teresa Perry."

"Take it easy Teresa. Tell Nathan I'm on my way." The phone clicked in his ear. *Didn't anyone ever say goodbye anymore?* He handed the phone back to Sara to hang up. "Gotta go in. I think Alicia Freed is in a coma."

Sara put her hand over her mouth in horror.

Freeman rounded the corner into Alicia's room. As expected, Nathan Powell was at her side. Over the years, Nathan had become Alicia's best advocate, executor of her best interests. He would question Freeman's orders on occasion, but he did so with tact and subtlety. Freeman was actually somewhat jealous of his superior bedside manner. Nathan turned to watch Freeman enter the room. He was looking for something in the doctor's face. Something that would give away the guilt he was sure was there. But he saw only concern. Shallow concern, but concern nevertheless. Nathan wondered if Freeman knew that he himself had almost finished medical school before his money ran out. In Nathan's mind, he was more qualified to care for Alicia than Dr. Freeman. For years, he had become suspicious of Freeman. Why, he did not know. He only knew that after he informed the doctor of Alicia's resistance to the Thorazine (he had later realized was the problem, not delirium), Freeman did not remove the standing order for Thiothixene from her chart, but merely gave everyone a verbal order. For a fleeting instant, Nathan thought that perhaps Freeman merely forgot, but then he real-ized no one could be capable of that kind of incompetence. The truth was, Freeman indeed was capable, and forgot. Nathan examined Alicia's chart. The standing order for Thiothixene was still on the chart. He handed the chart to Freeman.

"Why didn't you remove the order for the pills?" Nathan's voice was harsh.

"I can't believe I forgot," Freeman moaned.

"That poor nurse. She thought it was her fault. I yelled at her thinking she didn't read the chart. But when I checked, I found out what really happened."

Freeman looked at the floor in disgrace. "I'm sorry Nathan."

"Don't tell me. Tell her. She's the one in the coma because of your incompetence. This will not go unnoticed. Tomorrow I'll report this to the AMA."

Freeman's eyes narrowed into steel gray slits. "Do you really think the AMA will listen to you? A nurse who couldn't complete med. school? An argumentative nigger who questioned me, a hospital administrator, at almost every turn? Ha! We'll see who they believe," Freeman snarled.

Nathan looked around the room for a witness, but they were alone. Except for Alicia, who would do him no good at all in her current state.

"Oh there'll be an investigation all right. When they find out that you never assigned her another doctor when you became senior administrator." Nathan rose, standing face to face with Patrick Freeman. "When they see the careless doses of Thorazine you prescribed to this woman, then the Thiothixene on top of that, almost insuring that she would never recover, God only knows, they won't be questioning me at all. No sir, they will be looking right at you." He poked Freeman in the chest. "And you can bet your bottom dollar, I'll be helping them as much as I can. I've always felt you've been doing this lady dirty. Maybe now we'll find out the real truth."

Confronted with unequivocal truth, Freeman took a frightful step back.

Nathan returned to Alicia's side. Freeman, even in his anger, could see the bond between one of his nurses and his only patient. Like the love that exists between two people who've been married for a half century. He watched in silence as Nathan lovingly stroked her hair.

"Look Nathan, I'm sorry," Freeman squeaked. "No more injections. Okay? No more pills. Let's just wait and let her come out of this on her own."

Nathan glared at him. "She really needs to be in a hospital."

"This is a hospital."

"No. A real hospital. Under a real doctor's care." Freeman winced, but let the insult pass.

*Do I really want to take on Freeman? If I could change things for Alicia without turning Rhinewood upside down, that would be just as well, wouldn't it?* "Okay doctor," he said, feeling as if he were stepping onto a ledge above a deep chasm, unsure of his footing. "We'll try it your way. But here's how it's gonna be, if you start giving her more injections, I'll nail your ass to the wall. Do you understand? And if you ever call me 'nigger' again, I'll knock your teeth down your throat." Nathan swallowed hard after his outburst.

Freeman had the presence of mind to appear shame-faced, but looked around to see if anyone was watching. "All right, Nathan, you win. But I want her monitored twenty-four hours a day. I think it would be better if she just comes out of her coma naturally."

"I know. That way you can still keep your dirty little secret. I'll probably hate myself later, but fine. Okay, I'll agree, but I'm staying with her." He felt a real sense of satisfaction.

"Fine. Just keep me informed." Before Nathan could respond, Freeman turned and left the room.

# CHAPTER 22

"They're absolutely beautiful." Amy sat next to Bonnie on the couch looking at the French doors laid out against the wall. They needed to be refinished, and two of them had some broken panes of glass.

"We can stop by the lumber yard on the way home tomorrow, and get the stuff we need to fix 'em up," Shawn said as he bent to measure the glass.

"Could you also see about getting a new front door?" Bonnie asked, remembering the gaps around it.

Shawn went to the front door to check its width, and for the first time realized how wide the front door actually was. It was almost wider than he could reach. His eyebrows shot up as he read the measurement. "This door is 66 inches wide!"

"It is?" Terry said, coming over to see. Everyone knew it was wider than the front doors on most houses, but he never expected the door to be five and a half feet wide.

Amy went into the utility room and opened her husband's red toolbox. She selected two flatblade screwdrivers, one small and one large for prying, went to the French doors and began to work on the quarter-round molding that secured the broken panes of glass. She worked loose the quarter-round with the small screwdriver, then used the larger one to remove the piece.

Shawn continued to examine the front door, noticing for the first time, the workmanship that went into it. He ran his fingers over the woodwork, sending loose shards of shellac onto the floor. True, the door was warped, but if worse came to worse and they could not find a replacement, he thought he could repair it and then refinish it.

Terry heard the sound of wood popping as Amy worked on the French doors, and went to investigate. "Hey babe, you want me to do that?"

"No. I got it." Amy pulled the piece of wood from the door to show him her accomplishment. "But what about these nails?" She held the thin rusted shafts between her thumb and forefinger, showing Terry that they were almost rusted through.

"I don't think we oughta re-use them. Let's get new ones."

Amy nodded and continued working. Terry left the room without a word, then returned a few minutes later with a pair of pliers and began working the nails out.

Bonnie sat quietly on the couch watching her husband and friends work, and began to feel a strange fear lurking behind those beautiful doors. Anxiety swirled in the pit of her stomach. After a while she closed her eyes, trying to force the fear from its cloak, but only became frustrated. *What was it about this house? Something is here, nagging me like we are all sitting on a time bomb waiting to explode.* The tension was mounting and she had to fight the growing irritability inside her. She shifted on the couch to get comfortable, but only fidgeted in discomfort.

Shawn pulled his El Camino into the parking lot of the lumber yard, its headlights shining on the remaining snow. A high pressure ridge had entered the area earlier that morning, dissipating the clouds and allowing the bright sunshine to melt most of the snow. The streets were still wet and the temperature was expected to fall below freezing during the night. Shawn was in a hurry to get into the store before it closed at six, and they had about 15 minutes to do their shopping.

Amy and Terry pushed the door open. Shawn, who was the tallest of the three, scanned the aisles for employees, but the store was nearly deserted. "I wonder where everyone is?"

Amy shrugged her shoulders. "Terry, let's go find someone to cut the glass for us. Shawn, why don't you see someone about the door?"

"What door?"

"The front door." Amy rolled her eyes. "Do you have the measurements for the glass?"

"Yep. Right here." Shawn reached into his jacket pocket and handed her the crumpled piece of paper. She straightened it out.

"When we're finished we'll meet you at the check-out counter," Terry said.

"I guess I won't have too hard a time finding you two in this huge crowd." Shawn replied dryly.

Terry took Amy's hand and led her down the aisle to the window section of the store.

Shawn saw an older, heavy-set man in overalls and an orange employees apron thumbing through the display of doors as if looking for something. He smiled when he saw Shawn.

"What can I do for you, Sir?" the man said in a thick southern accent.

Shawn noticed his name tag: Clive. He smiled. His uncle's name was Clive. He was Shawn's favorite uncle until his death from an automobile accident when Shawn was 9 years old.

"I need a front door."

"Well, ya come to the right place. What kind didj'a have in mind? What kind of house?"

"The house is real old. I don't really know what type it is. I guess maybe like an old farm house." Clive nodded, encouraging him to continue his description. "The door is really wide."

"Really? How wide?" Clive became interested.

"Ah. I have it right here…" Shawn pulled a piece of paper from his pocket. "Sixty-six inches." The old man's eyebrows shot up. He took the piece of paper from Shawn and looked at it.

"How old did you say this house was?"

"Well, I'm not sure, I think the lady said it was built right around the Civil War."

"Where is this house at?"

"Out on 61. North of here."

"Sixty-one! Is it a white frame house, two story?"

"Sure is."

"I know that house. My older brother went to school with a girl who lived there. I can't remember her name though. It was 50 years ago or more." He looked off in the distance trying to remember.

"What about my door?" Shawn broke his concentration.

"Oh. Sorry. We don't have anything like that in stock. They quit making doors like that back in the '30s. I suppose I could have one custom made for ya. But it'd cost a shiny penny."

Shawn smiled at the misuse of the expression.

"Why is that door so wide anyway," Shawn asked.

Clive's face lit up. He loved history, especially local history. "See, back in the old days, when someone died, it was traditional to have the wake at the house. So, the front doors were made real wide so they could get the casket and pall bearers through the door."

Shawn was fascinated, but eager to get home. "So, what do you suggest about my front door?"

"What's wrong with it?"

"It's warped and doesn't seal too good around the edges."

"I don't think you're gonna find a replacement without having something made up custom. And that will cost ya pretty good. Why not try some new weatherstripping, that might be enough to seal the gaps."

"Well, thanks for your time. I'll try that."

"Sorry I couldn't help ya with that door. If you need anything else, come back."

Shawn smiled as a courtesy and grabbed a roll of weatherstripping. Terry and Amy were waiting for him at the check-out counter. They paid for the glass panes and weatherstripping, then headed for home. On the way to the house, Shawn told Terry and Amy about Clive.

Bonnie was just taking the last plate into the dining room when she heard the El Camino pull into the driveway. Dinner was sitting on the table when the three trooped in. As usual, Bonnie's timing was perfect. Terry carried in the sack of glass and set it down next to the French doors in the living room. One-night lay on the couch, watching lazily.

Amy walked past the dining table. "Bonnie, that meatloaf smells wonderful. You're such a good cook, and I'm so hungry. But first, I need to hang up my jacket."

Bonnie followed her to the threshold between the dining room and living room and stopped to watch One-night track Amy to her room. Bonnie was intrigued. When Amy opened the door, One-night jumped up, and hissed at the doorway. Her fur stood as she growled deeply.

Bonnie rushed over to pick her up. "It's okay, baby." Bonnie soothed, feeling the cat's tense muscles under the calico fur, "I don't like that room either." The cat jumped from her arms and ran into the kitchen.

Terry watched the scene in amazement. "Wow. That cat really hates that room."

Bonnie stared at the door, nodding her head.

Seconds later, the back door slammed and Shawn walked in through the kitchen. "What the hell's wrong with that damn cat? The stupid thing nearly took my leg off running out the door."

Bonnie looked at her husband. "I'm not sure." she lied. "By the way," she said, changing the subject, "where is my new door? I thought that was why you drove that gas guzzlin' El Camino to work today."

"Yeah, well, they don't have any, and you can forget it. They don't make doors like that anymore. We're gonna hafta try this weatherstripping. If that don't work, maybe fix it or something."

After dinner, the girls watched as their husbands lit the fire in the fireplace, then set out to replace the broken glass in the French doors. After gathering drills, bits and screws, Bonnie sat on the couch and watched Shawn hold each door in place, while Amy handed Terry a nail or screw, whatever was needed, while Terry secured it in place. After the glass had been replaced in the doors, Terry and Shawn moved into the dining room to install those doors first. Bonnie stayed on the couch in the living room staring into the fire. Amy assumed her supervisory position while Terry screwed the hinges to the door jamb. After the doors were hung in the dining room, Amy called Bonnie in to examine their work. Bonnie stood at the head of the dining table, just inside the room. The French doors were beautiful.

"You know," Bonnie said, "they really set this room off. It makes this room complete somehow."

Amy smiled. The guys picked up their tools and moved into the living room. Bonnie again sat on the couch, but she was beginning to feel nauseous. As she watched the others settle into the same routine to install the doors, she began to get dizzy. She laid her head on the arm of the couch and wondered what was wrong with her. *Am I getting sick? I'm not pregnant.*

Amy handed Terry the final screw. He placed it against the doorjamb in the center of the hole in the hinge. With a phillips bit in the drill, the screw easily twisted its way into the wood. The instant the head of the screw made contact with the hinge, a blue flash came from the point where the Phillips bit touched the screw. Terry pulled the drill away and looked at it. He pulled the trigger repeatedly, but the drill wouldn't work.

"Did you see that spark?" he asked Shawn, "My drill bit the big one."

Before Shawn could answer, the glass in the doors began to vibrate. Bonnie bolted upright. Suddenly, Terry and Amy's bedroom door slammed shut. An icy wind rushed from the room, blowing out the fire as it passed, sending glowing coals onto the hearth and the floor. As the icy wind rushed past Bonnie toward the French doors, she screamed. The instant Terry felt the cold air, every light bulb in the house exploded in a moment of blinding brilliance. The house shook as if from an earthquake. Hot shards of glass flew in all directions from every light bulb. All they could see were the glowing embers on the floor.

Alicia bolted upright in bed.

"He's awake!" she screamed.

Nathan had been snoozing in a chair next to Alicia's bed. Her sudden outburst brought him from his slumber. He rushed to her side. "What's wrong, Miss 'licia?"

Her eyes were wide with panic. He put his arms around her. She pulled him close. "He's awake—S'postu is awake!" she cried on his shoulder.

# CHAPTER 23

"What the hell happened?!" Terry exclaimed.

"Beats the shit out of me." Shawn responded, as he began to grope in the dark, looking for Bonnie.

"Amy?"

"Right here." Her voice was shaking, "What happened?"

"Well I'm not sure, you understand, but I think Bob Vila here just screwed that last screw into some electrical wiring."

"Now wait just a damn minute," Terry retorted, "that's not fair. Besides, there ain't no power in this wall. You said so yourself. Anyway," his voice lower, more serious, "that seemed more like a power surge. Maybe lightning hit a transformer or something."

"No!" Bonnie's voice came from the darkness, sounding weak and frail, "It was something else."

Shawn moved toward her voice. He knew she was sitting on the couch. As he neared her, he felt something crunch under his foot. "What was that?"

"What?" Her voice served to guide him closer. He reached out and felt a wet cheek.

"Why have you been crying?" he asked tenderly.

"Shawn, I'm scared–" She reached up and pulled him close, sobbing on his shoulder.

"What are we gonna do about the lights?" Amy's voice penetrated the darkness.

"I don't know." Terry said as he walked carefully past Shawn and Bonnie. "I'll get a flashlight. We can start from there."

Bonnie gasped as she felt the sofa cushions rise and fall as Amy sat. Pale moonlight streamed in through the windows. In the time since the lights went out, everyone's eyes adjusted to the dim blue light. Bonnie could see a dark figure passing the fireplace, heading in the direction of the lower bedroom.

"Terry?" Bonnie called.

The figure stopped. "Yeah?"

"Be careful, okay?"

"All I'm doing is gettin' a flashlight, not skydiving. Everything is okay." Terry continued toward the door.

"Personally," Bonnie said in a low voice, "I'm convinced skydiving is safer."

Shawn snorted a laugh.

Amy rose from the couch. "No use just sittin' here." She took the clean-out shovel and began scooping up cooled embers, threw them into the fireplace, wadded up a sheet of newspaper, then tossed it with a small log into the fireplace. She leaned over to blow on the embers. As she inhaled in preparation to blow, the fire suddenly flared.

"Nice going, Amy." Shawn said. The room filled with the soft glow of firelight, adding an orange tint to everything.

Bonnie looked over to Amy. She could see puzzlement on Amy's face. "What's wrong?"

Amy turned to her. "Nothing."

"You can't lie to me, Amy I know that look. What's wrong?"

"The fire started all by itself," Amy whispered, stunned.

Shawn began to laugh. "Don't worry about it, girls. It can do that. Those coals are so hot, that paper will ignite just by being close to them."

"Check this out." Terry appeared in the doorway of his room. He shook the flashlight he was holding in his hand.

"Sounds like a box of rocks," Shawn smiled. "What'd you do, drop it?"

"Nope. This is the way I found it." He went into the kitchen, found a candle and lit it, then he searched through the drawers for spare light bulbs. He found the cardboard square containing four 60-watt bulbs, and slid open the package. Broken glass fell out into his hand, glinting in the flicker of the candlelight. He noticed that the inside of the box was blackened, as if exposed to high heat.

"Shawn, come here."

Shawn released his wife. The tone of Terry's request troubled him. He looked at Bonnie, and after giving her a squeeze of confidence, went into the kitchen.

"Look at this." Terry handed Shawn the box. The color drained from his face.

"We need new light bulbs." Shawn said finally.

"Well, let's see how many we need, and I'll go to the store. You stay with the girls, Okay?"

Shawn nodded in agreement. Terry went around the house and counted the bulbs.

Shawn returned to the living room and knelt in front of Bonnie, her moist cheeks reflected the firelight. "You gonna be okay?" He asked her tenderly.

She nodded. "I need to clean up this glass."

"I'll stay with her." Amy volunteered.

Upon investigation, it was determined that every light bulb in the house burst whether it was in a light socket or not, whether the light fixture was plugged in or not. Indeed, no power surge could have caused all of this. Shawn cleaned up the broken glass. Terry went to the store by himself. Before he arrived home, Bonnie and Shawn went to bed. Amy tended to the fire while she waited for him.

When Terry arrived home, he and Amy went to bed. Amy was sure that their room was colder tonight than it had ever been.

Bonnie clung to Shawn throughout the entire night, too afraid to sleep.

# CHAPTER 24

The shrill bell broke the silence of the early morning darkness. It rang again. This time, Patrick Freeman stirred to consciousness. Groggily, he reached for the phone.

"Yeah."

"Doctor Freeman?" He didn't recognize the deep, gruff southern voice.

"This better be good." He squinted at the alarm clock. "It's 3:15 in the morning."

"Alicia Freed is having convulsions. Come right away."

The phone clicked in his ear. Freeman looked at the mouthpiece of the phone as if to see the person who spoke to him.

"Damn, I hate that! Doesn't anyone know how to say good bye anymore?"

Sara sat up. "What's wrong, honey?"

"Alicia Freed is having convulsions. I hafta go in."

"But you just came from there."

"I know. I know." Freeman swung his feet to the floor then hung up the phone. "God. I'm really tired." He rubbed his eyes.

"Well, it's no wonder. You only got to bed a couple of hours ago." Sara cocked her head to the right to think. The habit annoyed Freeman. But he had learned to live with it during the 24 years of their marriage. Freeman was a man of little patience, and a great many things annoyed him.

"Isn't she the one who just came out of the coma?"

"Yeah, but I wasn't expecting this. Well, I better get dressed and get down there so I can find out what the hell is going on."

"Who called? Was it Nathan?"

"I'm not sure. I didn't recognize his voice."

Sara turned on her side to return to sleep. Freeman dressed quickly and left the house.

He drove around the corner from Alpine drive onto Highway 61. The rear-end of his Buick fish-tailed fiercely, sending a shiver up his spine. *Oh, shit!* He turned into the skid to keep from sliding off the road. He pulled his car carefully off onto the shoulder and waited for the adrenalin to drain from his body. *Please God, no!* He did not move his car until his heart stopped pounding in his chest. *Think, damn it, think. Ok, the day before had been the first day the temperatures had been above freezing since the snowfall, so some of the snow melted. The night temperatures fell below freezing, causing the streets which were still wet from the melting snow to freeze over. I have got to be careful.* Freeman exhaled loudly to help dissipate his lessening fear. *Actually, I think this is good in a way, because as tired as I am, I need the effort of concentration to stay awake.* Satisfied with his assessment of the icy roads, he continued toward the institute. The yellow lines on the road were mesmerizing, and he kept shaking his head to keep his heavy eyelids from closing. Yet, no matter how hard he tried to concentrate on his driving, his mind drifted to Alicia.

Earlier that evening she had woken suddenly from her coma, screaming. Nathan had called from the hospital as soon as Freeman walked through the door. After a quick dinner, he had gone back to Rhinewood. When he arrived, he found Alicia sobbing, saying something incoherent about S'postu. Freeman was puzzled at her abrupt awakening, and lied to everyone about understanding what was going on. Being the hospital administrator, he felt he had to present an image of complete understanding, of absolute control. However, Freeman was very insecure. As he checked on Alicia, he felt Nathan

Powell's penetrating eyes, and was terrified that he knew. Nathan, indeed, saw through his facade.

As he swung around a corner, his headlights illuminated something on the road in front of him. At first he thought it was a deer, but panicked as he realized he saw the figure of a man in a grey suit standing in the roadway. Instantly, without thinking about the road conditions, he slammed on the brakes. His tires locked up instantly and the car began to slide uncontrollably. His eyes were fixed on the man. *Why didn't he run? Surely, he could see the danger in staying on the road. Was he mesmerized by the lights on the car like an animal?* The car began to slowly rotate to the right. Paralyzed by fear, Freeman could only watch the car slide toward the man. Time moved like mud. The car was now sliding down the icy road sideways. Even though the headlights were no longer trained on the man, he seemed to glow in the darkness. The car was almost on top of him and Freeman could see the grey suit, the many gold buttons, the blue stripes. *That suit looks familiar. Where have I seen it before?* The car plowed into the man. Freeman expected to see his body fly through the air, away from the car like a rag doll, but he remained in the same place as the car door passed *through* him! Freeman could not believe his eyes. He was almost on top of the man himself. He saw a head of red hair, long, almost shoulder length, glowing green eyes, and a red beard. Their faces were inches apart. The man smiled. Freeman smelled a repugnant odor. *Is that his breath?* He reared back to avoid contact but it was no use. Inevitably Patrick Freeman began to pass through the man. His skin crawled as they made contact. It was cold, too cold to stand and he shook with fear. *What is that? High voltage electricity? But it's so cold! Cold electricity? Is there such a thing?* Words forced themselves in from the outside, cleared the jumble of thoughts coursing through his mind.

"This is to avenge Alicia."

*Where have I heard that voice before?* As quickly as it began, the shaking was over, the electricity gone. The memory of those words left him empty. The car continued to rotate as it slid down the road. *I actually passed through that man?* The car was now traveling backwards at 50 miles per hour toward a curve in the road. Freeman could see him, still standing but growing more distant as the car slid away. Thunderous laughter filled his mind. Freeman was lost in thought as the car flew off the road. The laughter grew in intensity, drowning out the sound of the tree limb crashing through the rear window. He only realized what was happening in the last instant of his life, when the tree limb made contact with the back of his head. *Oh, Lord! That was the man who called on the phone. Alicia was telling the truth! My God, she isn't crazy!* The limb penetrated through his skull, continuing out his mouth, then through the windshield.

Freeman was found two hours later by a volunteer firefighter who had slid off the road near the place where Freeman had. He later described to police how he found the silver Buick suspended nine feet above the ground, its engine still running, rear wheels spinning and red craters melted in the snow under the car made by warm, dripping blood.

# CHAPTER 25

Bonnie gazed in awe at the pre-dawn light. Nothing could have been more beautiful. Not for the golden hue bathing the partially snow-covered landscape, but for the relief from the long night. Bonnie was grateful for the sound of the alarm clock. She reached over Shawn to silence it. Shawn stirred, but did not wake. Bonnie shook him to consciousness. He protested, knowing he had to go to work, but she persisted. Not for her undying sense of responsibility, but for his company before he had to leave for the day. For his touch, and the reassurance of his love, which would give her the strength to go on through the day in his absence. He finally rose and headed off to the bathroom for his morning shower.

"What do you want for breakfast?" she called over the running water.

"What?" He stuck his head out from behind the plastic shower curtain.

"I said, what do you want for breakfast?" Bonnie repeated.

Shawn looked hard at his wife. He noticed the solemn look, her forced attempt to look normal and most of all, her red swollen eyes. "What's wrong, honey?" he asked tenderly.

She turned away and bit her lip. She didn't want to tell him that she suddenly feared the night and felt as if she were being stalked. As if some carnivore had escaped from its cage to prey upon her.

"Hey," Shawn began, firmly, but still tenderly, "What's wrong? You look like you've been awake all night."

She turned to face him again. "It's okay," she lied. "I just didn't sleep too good, that's all." A tear ran down her cheek.

Shawn reached out with a wet hand to wipe it away, but only succeeded in making her face more wet. She smiled with his touch. Happy at his willingness not to push her into an explanation, satisfied with his ability to make almost any situation better, even if he didn't know why.

"I love you," he said, pulling himself back under the running water. "Eggs sound good to me," he called over the shower.

As Bonnie came down the staircase, she could see light coming from the crack under the door of the lower bedroom. She knew that her house mates were awake. As she passed the door to the bedroom crossing the landing, a shiver went up her spine. She hurried to get away from the door. Just before crossing the threshold into the dining room, Bonnie suddenly stopped and looked at the French doors. *Those doors are really beautiful. We woke something up when we put them up.* She wanted to break the glass in the doors, but knew that if she did, whatever was asleep would come after her. *That's why I feel like I'm being stalked.* None of this made sense to her, but things that bothered her often didn't make sense.

In the kitchen, Bonnie began to make breakfast. Not only for Shawn, but for Amy and Terry as well. She was by no means obligated, but when any of the four started to prepare a meal, enough was always prepared for the four of them. As Bonnie reached into the freezer to pull out some frozen hash browns, Amy appeared in the doorway.

"Mornin' Bonnie." Amy smiled. "Thanks for starting breakfast. I would have been out here earlier, but Terry had me rubbing his back."

"No problem." Bonnie responded, "Why don't you put the ketchup and the jelly out and set the table?"

"You got it." Amy grabbed four plates from the cupboard and while balancing them in one hand, opened the refrigerator to get the strawberry jelly, then the bottle of ketchup. She placed the glass containers on the plates and walked carefully into the dining room. As she tried to turn on the dining room light with her elbow, the jar of jelly slid off the plates and spattered across the floor.

"Damn!"

Bonnie appeared in the doorway and wordlessly handed Amy a wet sponge and several paper towels. Amy bent to clean up the mess.

"Yuck!" Terry said, coming into the dining room, "What happened?"

"Oh nothing," Amy said, looking up at her husband, "I just took out the strawberry."

"Do we have any more?"

"Only grape." Bonnie's voice boomed from the kitchen."

"Well, I guess it's better than dry toast." Terry said, seating himself at the table. Shawn joined him and they talked about cutting firewood for that evening after work when Bonnie brought in breakfast. Shawn watched Bonnie play with her food more than eat it, but said nothing to the others. Terry and Amy waited for Shawn in the Cavalier while he and Bonnie exchanged hugs and kisses.

"Now babe," Shawn said during the embrace, "if you have any problems, just call me at work and I'll come right home and take care of you."

"Oh Shawn, I love you so much!" she squeezed his waist. The thought was nice, but she knew that since the three of them car-pooled together, all would have to come home early if one did, so unless it was a real emergency, she would never call him. They broke their embrace and Shawn headed for the car.

"Tell Terry to watch it on Highway 61," She suddenly called after him, her breath visible in the cold air. "I got a bad feeling about that road, okay?"

Shawn waved his hand in response. Bonnie watched as her husband got in the car, then watched it back out of the driveway and pull away in the distance. Shivering from the cold, Bonnie went inside. She suddenly felt better. *That's odd. Maybe there's something wrong with highway 61.* It was a morning like any other morning, and logically, there should be no difference in the road today as yesterday. *Must be. After all, when I warned Shawn, I felt a lot better.*

Exhaustion overwhelmed her, and she decided to forgo doing the dishes for now in favor of taking a nap. The sun had risen, and Bonnie took comfort in its warming rays. As she went up to her room, she felt a sense of deja-vu. Yet she couldn't remember ever having gone to bed in the morning after staying awake all night. Bonnie slipped into bed and as soon as her head touched the pillow, she drifted off to sleep.

Deep sleep succumbed to the image of the late summer woods. The late afternoon sun shimmered through the leaves on the trees. In the distance, she could see a figure crouching behind a thick bush, as if surveying someone covertly. She seemed to drift toward the figure noiselessly. By now she could make out features on the person, a man, perhaps in his mid twenties, she could only see his back, but his red hair was clear. He was wearing a grey suit. *No, not a suit, a uniform. But what kind? I know I have seen it somewhere before. If only I could remember.* Shots echoed in the distance. Wailing of the injured was heard. She drifted toward the man again, coming up right behind him. The man reached up and moved a branch from his view. The reason for his stealth became clear. He seemed to be spying on two men in blue. It suddenly dawned on her that these were Civil War uniforms. The man in the grey uniform leaned forward, presumably to get a better view of the two men. He shifted his weight from one foot to another, the snap of a twig filled the air. The two men in blue uniforms tuned quickly toward the direction of the sound. Right at him. One of them raised his hand.

"There he is!" he yelled, pointing a finger. The man in the grey uniform rose and began to turn toward Bonnie. One of the blue-clad men raised a rifle in her direction. The face of the man in grey became clear. A full red beard framed his face. He began to run toward Bonnie, fear filling his green eyes. A shot rang out. His face twisted in agony, his hand went behind his back. He was almost on top of her. He fell through her, as if she were mere vapor. Blood flowed from the wound in his lower back. The woods rustled with the sound of foot steps coming from somewhere behind her. Two men appeared in grey uniforms and picked up the shot man. The two in blue uniforms ran away. The scene faded into the dull thud of something soft hitting the floor, then the sound of sticks, or something wooden on the hardwood floor.

Bonnie sat up quickly in her bed. *Were those last sounds real, or part of that dream?* She couldn't tell. Her heart pounded in her chest. She was instantly awake. *Maybe the guys are home early.* She looked over to the alarm clock. It was only 1:30 in the afternoon.

"Shawn!" She yelled as loud as she could. After listening intently and hearing nothing, she decided to go downstairs and do the breakfast dishes. *Maybe work will take my mind off that disturbing dream.* She dressed and went down the stairs, heart pounding, and caught some movement in the corner of her eye. She turned her head quickly to see the curtain beside the fireplace move. She froze in her tracks. Everything remained still and she realized she was alone in the house. She swallowed and continued down the stairs. She breathed a sigh of relief. *The wind probably blew the curtains through the leaks in those old windows.* Her mind drifted back to her dream. She was lost in thought as she crossed into the dining room when something on the floor caught her eye. It was red. She knelt down to examine the small puddle on the floor. She touched it with her fingers, looking at the red, thick liquid while rubbing with her thumb to check the consistency. *Surely, Amy had cleaned up the strawberry jam on the floor. She couldn't possibly have missed a spot this large. And there's no way it could be what it looks like.* Bonnie sniffed the substance; It had no odor whatsoever. *It sure looks like blood.* She got up and went into the kitchen. The towel Amy cleaned up the jelly with earlier was floating in the sink. Bonnie washed her hands then took a sponge and cleaned up the puddle on the dining room floor.

She washed the dishes and did the laundry. The work, as she had hoped, took her mind from her nightmare. As she stood at the open clothes dryer, pulling out warm shirts, she felt a chill run up her spine. Even with the warmth of the dryer washing over her, the icy feeling remained. *Oh no, not now when I'm all alone in this awful house!* She turned toward the kitchen, and was compelled toward the dining room. The instant she crossed into the dining room, she heard the sound of panes rattling on the French doors. Her heart pounded fiercely. She swallowed hard. The sound seemed to come from the set in the living room. She crept toward the living room, almost too afraid to look, but something beckoned her into the next room. Her eyes caught something moving into the lower bedroom. Her eyes locked on the door. A sort of blur, whitish grey mainly, with reddish brown at the top. The sound of a door slamming filled the room, echoing off the walls like an empty room. The sound was barely audible to her above the sound of her own heartbeat. The door to the lower bedroom never moved. She could barely keep her thoughts coherent. *Oh God! Shawn! Where are you? I need you. Why did I agree to be here all alone in this awful place?* She grabbed her coat off the coat tree and ran outside. The air was still and cold, but it felt better than the air in the house. That air made her feel cold *inside.* Bonnie took refuge in the El Camino, and locked the doors in panic. Only then, could she breathe easily.

# CHAPTER 26

Nathan stood at the door of Patrick Freeman's office, waiting to be summoned inside, wondering why he had been called. Was he to be formally disciplined for his outburst to Freeman the afternoon before? He didn't know. Anticipation filled him and he became more nervous the longer he waited, his thoughts wandering to the possibility of losing his job.

His nostrils filled with a sweet smell. The instant he recognized the smell as that of the perfume that Teresa Perry wore, the door opened. Teresa stepped into the hall, her eyes red from crying.

"He wants to see you now," she said, brushing back her blonde hair.

Nathan swallowed hard. What could that jerk Freeman have said to her to invoke such a reaction? He smiled at her wordlessly, then pushed the door open to go inside. To his surprise, Patrick Freeman did not occupy the office. A short, stocky man with dark hair rose from behind the desk, his mustached face smiling profusely at him.

"Nathan Powell?"

Nathan nodded, wondering what was going on.

The man thrust a hand toward him. "I'm Corey Brennan."

Nathan shook his hand.

"Sit down, Mr. Powell."

Nathan did as was requested. Brennan gestured to an older man, hair and mustache mostly grey dressed in a County Sheriff's uniform.

"This is Sheriff Salter."

The Sheriff smiled and nodded in response.

"I am the new administrator here at Rhinewood," Brennan continued.

Nathan was dumbfounded. "I don't know what to say," he said finally.

"Well, you could start with hello."

Nathan blushed, then shook the Sheriff's hand. "What is this all about, Mr. Brennan?"

"The Sheriff has a few questions for you."

Nathan turned to face the uniformed man. *What the hell is going on?* "Am I in some kind of trouble?"

The policeman did not answer.

"Where is Doctor Freeman?" Nathan asked.

Sheriff Salter and Corey Brennan exchanged a quick glance.

"Mr. Powell," the Sheriff said finally, "Patrick Freeman is dead."

Nathan's jaw dropped. "I don't understand," he said slowly.

"What's not to understand?" Salter asked suspiciously. "Death is a fairly simple concept. Where were you last night around three in the morning?"

Nathan glanced to Brennan, who remained stone faced.

"I was here. At Alicia Freed's side."

Something in Sheriff Salter's face changed, as if he remembered something.

"Did you make any phone calls?"

"No sir."

"Do you know of anyone who might have called Dr. Freeman last night?"

"Yes."

"Who, and when?"

"Teresa Perry. She just left this office. I told her to call Dr. Freeman around six."

Brennan nodded his head as if he already knew the answer.

*He knows that.* "What is this all about?" Nathan asked again, his confidence returning.

"I understand you and Dr. Freeman had an altercation Sunday morning," Brennan suddenly blurted out.

"Well, I don't know if I would call it an altercation." Nathan suddenly understood the meaning of the interrogation. Obviously, there were some questionable circumstances surrounding Freeman's death.

"What would you call it, then?" Salter demanded.

"Just an argument, I guess." *Do they suspect me? Surely not!* The expression on the Sheriff's face softened. His mouth curved to a half-smile.

"How old is Alicia Freed?"

"Seventy-two," Nathan answered. "I have a question." He looked at Brennan, who gestured for him to continue. "Why is it that Alicia was Dr. Freeman's only patient?"

"Now that *is* a good question!" Salter remarked, sitting next to Nathan. "Why do you think?"

"I don't know for sure. But I suspect–"

"Suspect what?" Brennan asked.

"There was a dirty deal, I know it. I never did trust that S.O.B. He was shootin' her up with 50 milligrams of Thorazine, three times a day. And on top of that, gave her those damn Thiothixene pills too. She was out of it constantly. Drug induced psychosis, I'm sure of it. That's why I stuck by her so closely. But he was the boss. There was no one else I could go to."

"Her chart says that she only got 25 milligrams of Thorazine. But it's incomplete. Do you know where the rest of her chart is?"

"That isn't it?" Nathan referred to a manila folder on the desk, the chart he had seen for years.

"No. It's missing the court orders, personal history of the patient, and so forth. Everyone here at the hospital knows who she is, but no one seems to know why she's here."

"I ain't seen it. What happened to the doctor?"

"He had an automobile accident early this morning," the Sheriff answered. "Do you know when she was committed here?"

"About 14 or 15 years ago, I guess. Look," Nathan said, "Alicia and I have a special sort of relationship. I want to help her. But I don't know anything about the doctor. About his death, I mean. Why don't you ask his wife?"

"We already have," Salter looked Nathan over. *I don't need to justify my investigation to this man. Nor do I owe him an explanation. He has, however taken excellent care of Alicia Freed. That alone deserves a little latitude. Because, he's right, there was a dirty deal, and that poor woman got the shaft. Nathan was man enough not only to recognize it, but to act on it. I guess it won't hurt to let him in on a bit of what's going on.* "She says someone called from the hospital, saying Alicia Freed was having convulsions, which of course we know is not true."

"I honestly don't know who might have called, but I'll help you in any way I can."

"I appreciate your cooperation. I will contact you later if I need any further assistance. Thank you, Mr. Powell."

*That was quite a change in the Sheriff.* Wordlessly, Nathan left the room.

Sheriff Salter looked directly at Corey Brennan. "He's right, there damn sure is something going on here."

Brennan nodded in agreement.

"You need to find out where Freeman's records are for Alicia Freed. Call me when you do. Also, I don't want to tell you your business, but I suggest you assign a doctor to her."

"Already taken care of. In fact, he should be with her right now."

Salter nodded approvingly, shook Brennan's hand and left the building.

# CHAPTER 27

As Terry pulled into the driveway and the headlights swung around to illuminate the El Camino, he could see movement in the car. The door opened and Bonnie emerged, rubbing her eyes. Terry parked the car then he and Shawn and Amy walked over to where Bonnie was standing and stretching.

"What are you doing out here, babe?" Shawn asked.

"I'm not going in that house until you make sure there's no one in it. I saw someone go into Terry and Amy's room."

"What?"

"You and Terry need to check it."

Amy stood next to Bonnie. "I'll bet you were scared."

Bonnie nodded. "That's why I came out here and locked myself in the car. If I hadn't left my keys in the house, I woulda drove into town."

Shawn led Terry into the house. The girls watched different windows light up, then go dark as the two checked each room.

"What did he look like?" Amy suddenly became curious.

"I really didn't get a very good look at him. I know he had red hair."

"How weird. Do you think it's one of these local farmers?"

"I don't know. I don't think so. I just saw someone run into your room."

"I locked it this morning. I know you hate that room, and sometimes the latch doesn't catch just right."

Bonnie's eyes widened and her stomach tightened, though Amy couldn't see it in the dark. The back porch light came on, getting the girls' attention. The back door opened, and they could see Terry's silhouette motioning for them to come inside. In the company of the others, Bonnie's apprehension seemed to dissipate and she found herself wanting to go inside and out of the cold.

During dinner, Bonnie asked Amy if she could remember missing some of the strawberry jelly that fell to the floor that morning.

"Of course not, Bonnie!" Amy almost sneered, annoyed at her accusation, "I'm not totally inept, you know." Terry was surprised at his wife's sudden outburst.

"That's not what I meant." Bonnie apologized. "But after ya 'll left for work, I found a puddle of red stuff on the floor in the same spot. But it was hours after it spilled. Doesn't jelly get thicker and gloppier when it dries out?"

"Usually, yeah." Amy became interested.

"This stuff was more runny. And smooth, you know, it looked like thick blood."

"Oh, how gross!" Amy made a face that made the men laugh. "Well, I hope you at least cleaned it up." Amy looked on the floor, only to find it looking normal.

Bonnie lay next to Shawn thinking about how Shawn and Terry tried to make it seem as if nothing unusual happened during the day. She dreaded staying awake all night again and trying to force herself to sleep only heaped more anxiety upon her. Shawn and Terry came up with what they thought was a logical explanation for everything that happened. Except, of course, for the light bulbs bursting in their box. That, they claimed, was nothing but an anomaly that could be explained with the discovery of some future unknown facts. Besides, she was now beginning to remember her dreams. *That was good, wasn't it?* She snuggled next to Shawn and forced her eyes closed.

Bonnie fidgeted in her sleep. The darkness of deep sleep gradually brightened to a snow-covered landscape. She recognized it as the field behind the house near a thicket of woods. She heard Shawn's laughter as a snowball hit her in the back. She turned laughing, scooping up a handful to sling at her husband. Shawn ducked and the snowball sailed past him and hit Amy in the leg, who was stalking Terry with a snowball of her own. Suddenly, the three of them attacked her all at once. She tried to shield herself from the incoming barrage of snowballs. Inundated, she attempted to fight back with some frozen ammunition of her own, but couldn't get off a shot. Finally, she ran for the woods, hoping the trees would protect her from the relentless onslaught. The snowballs stopped suddenly. Bonnie turned to tease her attackers, but there was no one in sight. She was only a few feet into the woods, yet for as far as she could see, there were only trees. Panic raced through her. Frantically, she ran in the direction she came from. Strangely, for as long as she ran she did not become tired. Dodging trees and moving saplings out of her way, she came upon a clearing at the top of a small hill. She thought she was lost but then heard men's voices. Smiling playfully, she scooped up a large handful of snow to get even with Shawn and Terry. As Bonnie approached the clearing, she saw three figures. Two in the clearing, and one in the brush. The smile ran away from her face when she realized she was looking at three strange men dressed in grey uniforms. One of the soldiers, a red-headed man, was squatting on a large rock, elevated from the deep snow. Bonnie dropped her snowball and crept closer. *That guy on the rock, where have I seen him before? I know I don't know him, yet he seems so familiar.* Two men were talking to him. She cocked her head to listen.

"There's two dozen of them damn Yankees on the other side of that ridge," the one in front of the man with the red hair said, pointing to a hill behind him. Bonnie could see a thin line of smoke rising against the clear blue sky. "Them bastards was even stupid 'nuff ta light a gall durn fire!" *The air must be cold because I can see their breath when they talk. But, I'm not cold. This is weird!*

"Must not be a very big fire," commented the man on the rock. *Obviously, he's in charge.*

"Naw, jest a little bitty one. Reese seen it better 'an me." He squatted down. The man in the brush stepped forward and rested his foot on the rock. *That must be Reese.*

"Them northern boys must be used to the cold, better 'an us." Reese began, "'cause I don't see how in tarnation that itty bitty fire could keep the fleas offin' a durn dawg warm." The red-haired man laughed under his breath, then stood on the rock.

"What's the chance of them Yankee bastards findin' us here?"

"I'd say slim ta none," the man still squatting blurted out. The red-haired man standing on the rock shaded his eyes from the sun.

"I say we slip in their camp real quiet-like," the man squatting said, voice low, with an evil, crooked smile, "then slit their throats while they sleep."

"With just the three of us?" the red-haired man asked, as if unsure.

Bonnie leaned forward in the bare, thorny shoots to hear better.

"That's the only fittin' way to git back at them bastards that bush-whacked us an' took out our whole bloomin' platoon. 'Cept fer us." The squatting man's eyes narrowed with rage. "And not only tha—"

Suddenly, the bush Bonnie was leaning against, snapped with her pressing weight. The three men spun around in her direction. *Oh, God what will they do if they see me?* But the men seemed to look right past her. She turned, curious to see what they saw. Something in the snow caught her attention, or rather the lack of something. She saw no footprints in the snow from the direction she came. *What the hell?* She looked down at her feet. Now she was looking at a hardwood floor. Looking up, she saw that she was now standing in her living room. All the things she knew to be in her home weren't there. The furniture seemed Victorian, and she was not in the room alone. *Now what?* The red-headed man with the beard was with her, sitting on an old wooden wheelchair, oblivious to her presence.

The man in the wheelchair looked around the room, as if looking for something. His green eyes, looking sad at first, seemed to lock on the French doors. A smile appeared on his face. Bonnie noticed the homey aroma of stew cooking.

"Supper's ready." A woman's voice rang out from the kitchen. The man jumped in his wheelchair, obviously startled. He turned his head in the direction of the voice.

"Come in here and eat," the voice continued, sounding cold and callous. He spun the wheelchair and wheeled it slowly in the direction of the dining room. Horrible anticipation gripped her. *Oh no, I know something bad is about to happen, but there's nothing I can do to stop it.* The man was now crossing into the dining room. To her horror, Bonnie saw the arm of another man, who was hiding behind the wall, swing a hammer at the back of the red headed man's head. *Oh God, no!* A loud crack shattered the silence of the still air as the hammer made contact with his skull. The force of the impact sent him sailing out of the wheelchair. He lay on the floor beside the dining room table, blood flowing from the wound, creating a puddle on the floor, his body quivering. It was in the exact shape and location as the mysterious puddle she found the afternoon before. She looked into the mirror to see the reflection of the killer. To her horror, she saw two reflections of herself, one standing in the doorway, and the other standing behind the wall, holding the hammer.

Bonnie bolted upright screaming. Shawn jumped, turned on the bedside light and silently held her tightly in his arms while she wept on his shoulder.

# CHAPTER 28

Something brought Amy out of her sleep. Was it a sound? She didn't know. Glancing over at the clock radio, she noticed the time: 1:17 a.m. Terry rolled over onto his side, his back now towards her. The sound of a car coming up the road was muffled through the glass. Looking out the window next to the bed, she could see headlights. As the car neared the house, its headlights lit up the bedroom. She turned to snuggle against Terry's back. From the corner of her eye she saw the outline of a man standing at the foot of the bed. She opened her mouth to scream, but no sound came out. The car passed, the light, now gone. She fumbled for the light on the bedside table. Amy found her voice as the light flooded the room, her scream breaking the silence of the night. Amy cut her scream off suddenly, seeing no one else in the room. Terry bolted upright.

"What's wrong?"

"There was someone in the room with us!"

"Where?"

"Standing at the foot of our bed." Amy started to cry.

"It's all right, babe." Terry soothed, holding her close.

"Check the bathroom," she breathed.

Braving the frigid air, he threw the covers off to investigate the bathroom. *It never ceases to amaze me how the air in this room could be so cold, yet the floor and all the furniture is the same temperature as the rest of the house.* He hurried into the bathroom to check for possible intruders.

Amy sat in the bed, holding the covers tightly to her, not for the warmth, but for the implied protection.

*That's what I thought, there's no one in here at all.* He re-entered the room, he strode over to the closet, flung open the door to mock a raid. *Let's see if we can lighten up the situation.* "Oh my God!" He said, with pretentious surprise in his voice.

"What? What's wrong? Terry?!" Amy cried, genuinely frightened.

Terry emerged from the closet holding her black negligee, grinning. "This is empty."

"Oh! You Pud!" Amy said, disgusted, "You scared the absolute shit out of me!"

"Oh, come on now, there's no one here, but us," he shot back sarcastically.

"If you think I'm going to put that on and play French Whore for you, you got another thing coming. You don't even care what I just went through, do you?" She began to cry.

Terry dropped the garment on the floor, and climbed on the bed to console her.

"I'm sorry. I thought you had a bad dream or something. I didn't think you were really serious about seeing someone in here."

"Well I was," she sniffed.

"I figured you had a nightmare because of what Bonnie said when we got home. Plus, it was dark in here–Wait-a-minute! How could you have seen anyone in the dark?"

"A car came up the road. I saw him in the headlights."

"Okay. Now I understand," Terry laughed softly. "Listen Babe, this house was built over a hundred years ago."

"So?"

"Just listen. The windows were made at a time when...they didn't make them then like they do now."

"Okay?"

"The glass is flat on one side, and the other side is wavy. The point is, light coming in through the window is likely to bounce in all directions. Plus, you just woke up. Maybe you just thought you saw someone."

"Well, he was gone when I turned on the light."

"There, you see. The light was playing tricks with your eyes. Anyway there's no way that someone could run out of the room without you hearing them is there?"

"No, I guess not." Satisfied with Terry's explanation, Amy snuggled next to him.

A knock sounded on the door. Both Terry and Amy turned to see the door open, and Bonnie sticking her head in, looking like she was wincing in pain. Her hair blew back at the temples, as Terry had seen Amy's a hundred times before.

"Are you okay?" Bonnie asked.

Amy smiled and nodded.

"Do you want some hot chocolate?"

"Ooh, that sounds good," Amy replied, sliding out of Terry's arms and out of bed.

Bonnie's head pulled back from view. Amy grabbed her bathrobe and joined her. Terry sighed and grabbed his bathrobe as well. He was disappointed, he wanted to make love to his wife. But, for now, hot chocolate would have to do.

The women walked side by side wordlessly in the dark. A few feet into the dining room, Amy made a high-pitched squeak as her bare foot stepped in something on the floor. Bonnie quickly snapped on the light. Amy stood, holding her foot above the floor. Both girls gasped in unison as they saw red liquid dripping from her foot. Bonnie's eyes rolled in her head, and she began to crumple. Terry came up from behind, managing to catch her. He carried her to a chair. Meanwhile Amy stood motionless, with her foot in the air.

"What did you step in?" Terry said as he went into the kitchen for a towel. He wet it in the sink, then knelt in front of his wife, avoiding the puddle.

"Just get it off," Amy said frantically.

He wiped the thick, red liquid from her foot. Terry looked up at his wife. "I thought that cute little squeak was only for me?" He teased.

Amy's face flushed, and she turned away to the ceiling and laughed in embarrassment. Chuckling, they turned to Bonnie. She sat at the table, expressionless. With Amy's foot now clean, she sat beside Bonnie, and put her arm around her. Terry cleaned up the puddle on the floor. The toilet flushed upstairs and seconds later, Shawn thumped down the stairs. The instant he saw his wife, he rushed to her side.

Amy released her. Terry returned to the kitchen to start the tea kettle for their hot chocolate.

"What happened?" Shawn asked.

Bonnie only stared blankly ahead.

Shawn turned to Amy. "What happened?"

"I stepped in a puddle of blood on the floor." Bonnie turned to Amy, her eyes glazed.

"I saw the whole thing." Bonnie said slowly.

"Is that what you dreamed about?" Shawn asked tenderly.

Bonnie nodded, then yawned and rubbed her eyes. Shawn was mildly relieved and sat in the chair next to her. Amy joined her husband in the kitchen and returned with Terry a few minutes later with mugs of hot chocolate. The four of them sat at the table, sipping hot chocolate, while Bonnie told them about her dream.

It was difficult for Terry and Amy to get back to sleep after hearing about Bonnie's dream. They discussed it until, finally, Terry nodded off and Amy soon followed.

Both regretted it when the alarm went off at six. For their normal routine, they would select their clothes from the closet, then bring them into the bathroom to get dressed there to avoid being exposed to the cold air of their room while still wet after their morning shower.

The bathroom seemed rather small with the two of them stumbling over each other. The thick air from the shower made Terry want to dress quickly. Amy usually protested when Terry goaded her into hurrying. This morning, however, Terry was moving slower than usual, so they finished at the same time. He opened the door to enter their room, Amy at his heels, both bracing themselves for the transition from the hot, steamy air of the bathroom to the frigid air of their room. Suddenly, Terry stopped dead in his tracks. Amy bumped into him.

"Hey? What's the big idea—" Amy's words trailed off as she saw why her husband stopped. In the center of their room, a man appeared to be standing on the floor of their bedroom, through the center of their bed, as if the bed wasn't there. Terry was stunned, both caught off guard and frightened. Amy was only frightened. They stared in horror at the spectacle before them. The man's head was striking. Red hair, green eyes, and a reddish-brown beard framed his face. His eyes were piercing, yet reflected pain. Terry recognized his Confederate uniform instantly. His upper body and head seemed as solid as anything else in the room, but his lower body and legs seemed to become more transparent as they neared the bed. His lower jaw moved as if to speak, but there were no sounds. Terry advanced toward the figure, his fear fading into curiosity, and attempted to communicate. Slowly the figure began to fade until he was no longer visible. Just before the figure disappeared totally, they smelled a faint odor of rancid meat that ebbed into nothingness along with the apparition. At first, Terry thought he imagined the odor, but after turning to look at his wife wrinkling her nose, he realized it was not his imagination.

Bonnie tossed in a twilight sleep. Somewhere between the consciousness of reality and the retreat of slumber, she could hear the shower running through the wall, though it sounded detached. Amidst the reality of the lulling sound of the shower, two faces came into view.

At first she did not recognize them, then slowly, they became recogniz-able. They were slightly distorted, as though looking through hazy glass, but she recognized them as Terry and Amy. Terry was in front of Amy. Somehow, Bonnie could make out the fact that their hair was wet. The look of sheer terror was apparent on Amy's face. Terry took a step toward her. His mouth was moving to speak but Bonnie couldn't hear him.

"Help me." A man's voice boomed in her head. "Help me. Find my child." *I know that voice! Where have I heard it before? It's almost like it was in a different life. Detached and far away.* The faces of Terry and Amy faded, and Bonnie woke to the sound of the shower shutting off. She remembered the dream so clearly, so vividly, it was as if she lived it and not dreamt it.

Shawn came into the room. Bonnie looked at her husband blankly. She suddenly realized who that voice belonged to.

"That was the voice of the man that died in my dream!"

"What?" Shawn asked, puzzled.

Bonnie said nothing as she threw the covers off her and hurried downstairs. As she reached the landing at the bottom of the stairs, Terry and Amy burst out of their bedroom. They looked exactly as they did in Bonnie's dream. She looked at the two of them, obviously in shock.

"What's wrong Bonnie?" Amy asked. Concern for her friend distracted her from her own fear.

"I saw you two in my dream. You were looking at me, and you were scared."

"When did you have this dream?" Terry asked.

"Just now. It woke me up."

Terry looked at Amy. The color seemed to drain from their faces.

"What's wrong?" Panic was clear in Bonnie's voice.

"We–" Amy began, then paused to look at Terry, as if unsure how to continue, "just saw something in our room…"

"What? What did you see?"

"Ah—I'm not really sure."

"I think we saw a man." Terry broke in, "He was standing through our bed."

"What?" Bonnie was shocked.

"Just like the bed wasn't there."

"What did he look like?"

"Well, he had red hair and these really piercing green eyes, and a red beard. He had on a Confederate army uniform."

"A what?"

"A Confederate army uniform. You know, from the Civil War."

"That's the man I saw in my dream. He–" Suddenly a dull crack like someone snapped a dry twig wrapped in a cloth cut off Bonnie's words. The three moved toward the direction of the sound. They stood at the threshold between the living room and dining room and heard the sound of something heavy and soft hitting the floor as the chair at the end of the dining table moved forward slightly. *As if something fell on the floor, hitting the chair at its legs, causing it to slide forward.* In the cold grey light filtering through the windows, a dark puddle appeared, growing to the same size and shape, and in the same location as the last two puddles of blood.

Bonnie's ears started to ring. She gasped as a sweet sickening feeling came over her. The ringing became louder and louder, drowning out the morning silence. The expanding puddle on the floor washed out to whiteness, then suddenly turned black.

Terry glanced over to Bonnie in time to see her eyes roll in her head. He moved to catch her as she crumpled and carried her over to the couch in the living room. Shawn was half way down the stairs when he saw Terry lay his wife on the couch. He ran to her side.

"What happened?" His voice was frantic.

"She fainted when we saw the blood on the floor." Terry answered. He suddenly remembered his own wife, and went to her. Amy was still standing at the threshold, staring at the puddle, her eyes glazed. She yelped when Terry touched her shoulder. It was just too much for her to cope with so soon, and helpless tears rolled down her cheeks. Terry held her while she cried on his shoulder.

Bonnie opened her eyes. She saw the faces of her husband, Terry and Amy. Her mouth felt dry, she licked her lips and swallowed.

"Please—I need a drink." Both guys turned to Amy. Shawn gestured his head toward the kitchen.

Amy's eyes widened. "Not a chance!" Amy half-screamed, her voice dry, "Not me! I'm not going near that puddle!"

Bonnie jolted upright at her words.

"I'll go." Terry said, as he turned to the kitchen.

"Are you all right, babe?" Shawn asked tenderly. Bonnie looked deep into his eyes, she saw real caring, real concern. She nodded her head in response, as she swung her legs over the edge of the couch to sit. Terry returned and handed her the glass.

After drinking the water, Bonnie looked hard at the three of them. "There's no way any of you are leaving me here in this house alone."

Something odd clicked in Amy Lambert. Even after seeing the figure standing in her bedroom and the puddle form on the dining room floor, she was not petrified with fear. She was more intrigued than afraid, even respectful. It was like hearing Terry and Shawn talk about one of their power tools. "Bonnie's right," Amy suddenly spoke up, "we can't leave her. We need to find a way to be off for a few days while we figure out what's going on here."

Terry looked at his wife, somewhat astonished. He was surprised at her sudden curiosity, especially after their episode in the bedroom. She had always been adventurous, but he never thought that when confronted, she would actually instigate a search for the truth. He felt proud.

"No way!" Bonnie said, still a note of panic in her voice, "We gotta find a way to get out of this house. Especially if I have to stay here all by myself."

Wordlessly, Terry took her glass and went back into the kitchen for a wet towel to clean up the puddle on the dining room floor. Shawn turned to watch Terry walk out of the room, then faced his wife.

"I'll call Lynn Hooper after I call work," he said to Bonnie softly.

When Amy heard Shawn she filled with anger. *What are you saying? That we just walk away from this mystery? No way!* Her face flushed, and she trembled with anger. Pursing her lips together, she rose and stomped out of the room to help Terry.

Bonnie watched Amy in utter amazement. She buried her head in Shawn's arms and wept.

"Hey, babe," Shawn consoled her, "it's all right. I'll go talk to them."

"Don't they even care what I feel?" Bonnie sobbed, "How this is affecting me? Don't they know that I haven't had a decent night's sleep since we moved here?"

Shawn only held her close.

Terry returned with another glass of water and a pill.

"Here Bonnie, take this, it will make you sleep."

"What is it?"

"Just a muscle relaxer. The doctor gave them to me when I sprained my shoulder last year. It'll knock you out. It always did me."

Bonnie took the pill, then handed the glass back to Terry. He disappeared into the kitchen. Bonnie could hear the sound of a towel being dipped into a bowl of water, wrung out, then the sound of rubbing on the floor. In her mind, she could picture every step as Amy cleaned up the puddle.

Bonnie settled back on Shawn's chest, nestling in his arms. She felt safe and warm. Leaning her head back, she closed her eyes and allowed the drug to take effect. She slipped into a deep, dream free sleep while the drug was active. Shawn laid her head on a pillow and joined the others in the dining room. As the drugs' potency diminished, a familiar subliminal feeling came over her body, causing her to fidget in her sleep.

Slowly, the inside of a horse drawn carriage became clear. She was sitting on purple velvet cushions, looking out the window at the passing countryside. The cloppety-clop of horse hooves on the ground was clearly heard over the sound of the metal rimmed wheels over the terrain. Trees passed by the window as they went through the woods. The trees gave way to a clearing. In the center of the clearing sat the house, looking new and peaceful. Trees again. The cloppety clop sound of the horse's hooves changed slowly into the sound of rubber tires crunching over gravel. Puzzled, Bonnie stuck her head out the stagecoach door. The coach was now being pulled by a large blue car. She recognized it as an old Pontiac like the one her father had in the early seventies. She turned to look again at the passing countryside. They passed a subdivision with modern houses made of brick and vinyl siding. All but one of the houses were blurry. The clear one had white Roman or Greek style columns and black shutters. There was a walkway running from the road to the porch with neat rows of shrubs on each side. The clearing gave way to the woods again, a short time later another clearing came into view. This one held a courthouse. Oddly, it sat by itself. Woods again. In the next clearing, a large one-story brick structure stood, surrounded by a chain link fence. It looked to Bonnie like a hospital or a jail, she couldn't tell which. The stagecoach driver whipped the reins to the sound of leather slapping metal. The coach lurched forward as they went up a hill. The woods disappeared behind her. Looking out the rear window, she saw only solid woods. The coach came to rest in the center of a dusty old town in front of a train depot.

A man and a woman holding the hand of a young boy came out of the station building and boarded the coach. The little boy sat next to Bonnie. The man and woman sat on the seat across from her. The man smiled at Bonnie. The stagecoach suddenly lurched forward.

"How do, ma'am?" The man said, tipping his hat.

Bonnie smiled in return.

"This here's my wife Nelda."

The woman nodded.

Bonnie smiled again in return.

"...My son, Bobby."

Bonnie turned and smiled at the little boy.

"And my name's Lester. Lester Howe."

"Pleased to meet ya 'll," Bonnie said.

The coach slowed to a stop.

The coach had stopped in front of a beautiful plantation house. "This is where we git off." Lester announced, leading his family off.

Strangely, the coach did not move, and Bonnie watched through the window as Lester and Nelda went into the house. She saw Bobby, whom she judged to be five or six years old, sit upon the edge of a brick well. He began to carve on a stick with a pocket knife. Although the well seemed to be one hundred or so feet from her, Bonnie could see each action the little boy made as if she were a few feet away. Bobby set the stick on the edge of the well. He began to rub the knife on a brick as if to sharpen it, and in doing so, knocked the stick into the well. Bonnie gasped in horror as she watched him grab for the stick, then fell in behind it. Bonnie screamed and tried to open the door. But it was stuck. Time passed. Bonnie could hear Bobby crying loudly in her ears. She yelled to the house, but it was as if she was not there. Finally, Nelda came out of the house carrying a bucket. Relief cautiously came to Bonnie as she watched Nelda walk toward the well. Surely, she would hear the cries of her son. He sounded uninjured, something in his cries told Bonnie that he was only frightened.

Nelda dropped the bucket when she saw her son's prized knife laying on the ground next to the well. She screamed loudly for her husband. Seconds later, Lester burst from the house. They searched frantically for their son. Bonnie beat the inside of the coach violently with her fists, yelling for the two of them. They acted as if Bonnie were a thousand miles away. She watched Lester and Nelda check the buildings around the yard in vain, frustrated with not being able to communicate the whereabouts of their son to them. More time passed. Exasperated with her search, Nelda returned to the well, hooked the bucket on the hook, and lowered it into the well. Suddenly the rope vibrated as if a heavy weight unexpectedly encumbered it.

"Lester! Lester! He's here! He's here in the well!" Nelda yelled. Bonnie felt relief wash over her as Lester cranked up the bucket. Minutes later their son appeared. He was wet, cold, and frightened, but otherwise uninjured. The little boy hugged his parents.

"I knew that if I yelled loud enough, and waited long enough you would find me." Bobby hugged his father. Lester picked up his son and carried him toward the house. For some reason, Lester carried Bobby past the stage coach. As they passed by the window, Lester turned and looked directly at Bonnie. His eyes were bright green like emeralds.

"Find my child," he said, carrying the odor of rotting meat. As he faded away, his face morphed into the face of the Confederate soldier. Bonnie's nausea grew in direct proportion.

Bonnie opened her eyes. She breathed heavily with lingering nausea and the memory of her dream. The mid morning light filtered in through the curtains. She gradually became aware of the voices of her husband, Terry and Amy talking softly in the dining room.

"I'm sorry, Shawn," Terry's voice was sympathetic, but firm, "I just got off the phone with Lynn, and she said we are locked into this house for a year–."

"Well, what about Bonnie?" Shawn's voice sounded panicked, "she can't keep going through this. She's scared shitless."

The remark caused Bonnie to take stock of her feelings. *Am I as frightened as all that?* Somehow the memory of that last dream changed her attitude, giving her an almost obsessive urge to investigate. She rose and found herself standing on the threshold between the living room and the dining room.

"Ya 'll," she announced, "I think we need to stay."

The three of them stopped and looked at her in amazement.

"I think we need to find out what's going on in this house." Bonnie sat at the table next to Shawn and described her dream to them. After her story, all three agreed with Bonnie's conclusion. They would stay and investigate the history of the house. It almost sounded like fun.

# PART THREE

# CHAPTER 29

Water splashed from the pothole as the right front tire of the Sheriff's car pushed through. Milton Salter rounded the corner into the Rhinewood Mental Institute's parking lot. It was partially empty, due to some of the staff being off during the time between Christmas and New Year's eve, making it easy to locate a parking place. He went inside the building eager to get to Corey Brennan's office. Brennan had called earlier in the day with new information and he wanted to get on with the case of Patrick Freeman's death. All his external leads led him nowhere, so he was forced to wait until Brennan contacted him. There were several questions raised by Freeman's untimely demise. His gut reaction and police instinct told him there was a connection between Patrick Freeman's death and Alicia Freed. Although he had no idea what.

He walked up to the reception window. The small office beyond the window was as vacant as a ghost town. Salter thought how typical this institution was, from the attitude of most government employees milking their time until their pension kicks in, to the building itself, an old one story brick affair probably built in the 1950's, down to the furniture in the lobby, with its gaudy orange vinyl seats. He leaned over the small counter that made up the lower ledge of the receptionist's window hoping to find someone, perhaps using a copy machine or something. When he saw the little office deserted, he resorted to ringing the bell on the counter.

Less than two minutes passed when a thin, young looking black man wearing surgical greens walked around the corner into the little office. Salter had to keep from laughing when he saw that the young man had blue fibrous paper coverings over his shoes. They looked to Salter like shower caps retained by elastic around his ankles. He looked away to hide his smile. For reasons he could not identify, had always found those shoe coverings comical.

"Yes sir, may I help you?" The young man smiled.

"I'm here to see Corey Brennan. He's expecting me."

The young man picked up the phone and dialed. "Mr. Brennan? Darby. There's a Sheriff–here to see you." The young man swung the mouthpiece to his neck, looking at Salter as if asking a question.

"Salter."

"He says his name is Salter." He paused, "Yessir." Darby hung up the phone.

"Sir, please go through that door," pointing to a grey metal door. "His office is two doors down on the left. He said for you to go right in."

Salter nodded and proceeded into Brennan's office. Brennan rose to greet him.

"You have something for me?" Salter asked authoritatively.

"Yes. You asked me to contact you if I found something that had to do with Pat's death."

"And?"

"Well, I found a doozy!"

"How so? What did you find?"

"Sit down, Sheriff." Salter pulled a chair close to the desk and sat. Brennan bent to pick something off the floor.

"I couldn't open this drawer all the way. At first I thought it was busted. But when I pulled–well, actually forced it out of the desk–I found this." He placed a small metal box on the desk, the lid bent. "It was taped to the underside of the desk top, and this metal box was preventing the drawer from opening all the way."

"Does it have the file for Alicia Freed?"

"Well, sort of. It has a different file. I found the official file. It was misfiled, I think intentionally. But there are several discrepancies in the official file, plus the other stuff in this box, that made me take a real close look at what Dr. Freeman was up to."

"I'm not sure I understand." Salter removed a small pad of paper and began to write.

"I'm sorry. Let me start from the beginning. The day I took over I happened to look at some of the accounts receivable books, and something caught my eye. That day, we received a voucher from the government for $576,375.00. That's the amount of our monthly budget. As a matter of habit, I always check the amount of the check against the number of patients. We currently have 259 inmates. That should have worked out to $571,958.33. That is a discrepancy of $4416.67 per month. I can't stand it if the books aren't right. It drives me crazy. Now, I…"

"Wait a minute, you're talking too fast. Slow down so I can write this down," Salter cut him off.

"Oh, sorry. Anyway, I happen to know that we get $26,500 for each inmate per year. It didn't take a genius to figure out that's a difference of two inmates, on a monthly basis. It seems that Freeman had the payee vouchers come through his office for approval. Plus, I kept seeing repeated payee vouchers to a company called Baywalfree Supply Company."

"Baywalfree? I'll have to check that out."

"You don't have to. There is no Baywalfree Supply Company, I checked."

"Did you want to drive my squad car, too?" Salter looked up at Brennan with a raised eyebrow.

"What?"

"Generally, I do the investigating in my investigations. I mean, you really have this thing all figured out, don't you?"

"Well, when I was in the Marines, they taught me to always have an answer when I came up with a problem or a question."

"Well then, carry on, Marine!"

"Yes sir." Brennan cleared his throat. "In looking at Alicia Freed's file, the prosecuting attorney was a man named Henry Walton, her defense attorney was Elroy Sneed. With testimony from Patrick Freeman. But in the file I found in the metal box, everything was the same except the defense attorney was Max Bailey. There was also another file in the metal box. One for someone named Jake Streator. But the funny thing is, we don't have a patient here by the name Jake Streator. There is a duplicate set of books in the metal box. In that book, it lists everyone that we have here, plus Jake Streator, and a Jack Stratton. We do have a Jack Stratton. Neither of those two names are listed in the books that we work from. We usually get audited once a year, so Freeman must have been switching the book from the box for the auditors. When I went through Jack Stratton's file, I found Jake Streator's mixed in. Since the auditors never actually count the patients, Freeman could get away with it as long as he remained in charge."

"So, how was he getting the extra money?"

"That's the good part. Also, in the box, I found a bunch of canceled checks from the institute to Baywalfree Supply company. And get this, they either had Patrick Freeman's, Max Bailey's, or Henry Walton's signature as the endorsee." Brennan paused for a moment, with a puzzled frown on his face. "But for the past five years or so, the only endorsee on the checks has been Freeman."

"That's a pretty clever scheme. Ha! Baywalfree! I'll bet that's a conglomeration of the names of those three." Salter paused a moment. The name Jake Streator struck a chord with him, but for now the memory eluded him. "But who is this Jake Streator? How does he fit into all this?"

"I checked the books for the past twenty or so years. And it seems that when Alicia Freed came to us, the discrepancies increased by one inmate. So these guys have been in cahoots for quite a long time." Brennan handed Salter the metal box.

"Thanks, I'll take this evidence and start an investigation on Walton and Bailey. By the way, how is Alicia Freed anyway?" Salter couldn't help asking.

"I assigned Jerry Adcox to her case. He completely took her off all medication. She seems to be doing one hundred percent better. But I still have to do some psych evaluations to satisfy the terms of her sentence."

"Are you going to release her?"

"I'm not planning on that. She lost fourteen years. You can't just throw someone who has basically been asleep for fourteen years back into society and expect them to go on as if nothing ever happened. No, there's lots of work that has to be done with her before anything like that happens."

"You never did answer my question about Jake Streator."

"Oh, right. I'm sorry. He was a patient here from–let me see–." He opened a drawer in the desk and dug until he found a pad of paper. "I thought you might ask, so I wrote this down. Ah, here it is, from December 1973 until January 1976. Evidently, he hanged himself with a telephone wire."

Suddenly, Salter's memory jogged. "Seems to me I remember reading something about that. It happened right after I joined the Knoxville police force."

"There are some other dubious correlations between the Streator case and the Freed case."

"Like what?"

"Well, for instance, Max Bailey was his defense attorney, Hank Walton was the prosecuting attorney, and guess who was just made director of this facility?"

"None other than the illustrious Patrick Freeman," Salter guessed.

"Bingo. These guys have been running some kind of racket for close to twenty years. There are only six or seven staff members who have been here since the time of Jake Streator, one of them being Nathan Powell."

"Well, Brennan, you sure gave me plenty of food for thought. I think it's time I checked into the affairs of two very prominent attorneys."

"I will help you in any way I can."

"I appreciate that, but first I need to ask Alicia Freed some questions. Can you arrange that?"

"No problem. I'll page Nathan and he can help you."

He rounded the corner at the intersection of two long halls and stopped at the nurses station to wait for Nathan Powell, as they had arranged. Age brought to Milton Salter the gift of patience. As a young man, he had always wanted things done yesterday, with no regard for letting things occur naturally. As a result, he typically found himself in a difficult situation. It usually took his quick thinking, and a generous portion of good fortune to get him out of whatever his impatience got him into. But now that he was older, he had become more reserved. Which, to his amazement, seemed to get things done just as quickly as when he constantly tried to force the situation. This realization came to him eight years before, when he decided to leave the fast pace of Knoxville city law enforcement and run for the office of Knox County Sheriff.

"Sheriff Salter?" Nathan Powell extended his hand to greet him. "You wanted to see Alicia?"

"Yes I do. But first, I want to ask you some questions about someone else."

"Who?"

"Do you remember a man named Jake Streator?"

"Jake Streator? I haven't heard that name spoken around here for nigh on twenty years! Yep, I remember him."

"What happened to him?"

"It was quite a deal. He committed suicide."

"Is that all?"

"As far as Jake himself is concerned, yes. But there is something else. It seems to me that around that time is when Freeman and I started having conflicts. At first, I thought it was a racial thing. But later, well I used to question Pat on the Thorazine he had constantly pumped into that man. Freeman didn't like that at all. He hated it when anyone questioned his authority. He thought I wanted his job, I guess. Of course that couldn't have been further from the truth. Anyway, one day Pat left a folder in Jake's room. And being as nosey as I am, I took a look. There was a whole bunch of receipts for medical supplies from a company with a weird name. Geez, I can't remember the name. It was something like Baywatch, or Bogfree, or somethi–. "

"How about Baywalfree?" Salter helped.

"That's it! Baywalfree. But we deal with a company called Fairmont Medical. I know. I was the one who helped unload the truck. I would have known about another supply company. So, like a fool, I asked Pat about it. Boy, was that a mistake! He told me that if I ever looked into anyone's file again, he would have me buried. So from then on I walked around him in big circles. He had me transferred over here to the convalescent wing, and I've been here ever since."

"So, is there a connection between Jake Streator and Alicia Freed?"

"I can't be sure. But I have this feeling that there is, because Pat was kinda acting the way he did when I worked the loony wing, when Jake Streator was here. So I kinda took up for Miss 'licia."

"I see. Where is she?"

"Right this way." Nathan led Salter into a large dining room. Alicia was sitting in a chair at a round table, looking out the window. Her walker was next to her chair.

"Is she a cripple?" he asked softly.

"No," Nathan whispered, "she's suffering from atrophy in her legs. See, she has been bed ridden for such a long time, she has to work real hard just to be able to walk. Doc Adcox thinks she'll make a complete recovery."

"My ears work fine, Sheriff." Alicia suddenly spoke without taking her eyes from the window. Salter was surprised since he and Nathan were some twenty feet from her.

"I told her you were coming." Nathan informed Salter. Both he and Nathan pulled up a chair and sat at the table. Alicia looked at Salter. Her eyes lit up as she suddenly recognized him.

"You! You're the young man who came to get me at my house!"

"Yes, ma'am."

"But, weren't you in a suit?"

"Yes, ma'am, I left the force about eight years ago and got elected Sheriff."

Alicia nodded in acknowledgment. Anguish washed over her face as she looked down at the floor. "My house," she breathed, barely audible.

"What about your house?"

"Well, it ain't mine no more."

"What do you mean?"

Nathan leaned back in his chair, anger flushed across his face. "I know what she means." Salter looked at Nathan.

"She means some no account, back room, city slick lawyer snaked her out of her house. But he got his due, didn't he Miss 'licia?"

Alicia nodded her head.

Salter looked back and forth between the two, puzzled. "What are you two talking about?"

"Her lawyer, that two timin' snake, that's who." Nathan responded.

"You mean Max Bailey?"

"Yep. That's the one." Alicia replied.

Salter was perplexed. "What? What happened to Max Bailey?" He felt like his case was slipping through his fingers,

·   "He died back about five years ago." Nathan said.

"Died? How?"

"He got shot by one of his clients who he was doin' dirty. Shot him right in his office." Nathan's eyes narrowed at Salter. "Don't you read none?"

Salter's jaw dropped. "Well, I came to ask you about Bailey. To see if you could remember anything. Anything that could connect him with Patrick Freeman. But I can see now, that would be pointless."

Alicia straightened in her chair, eyed Salter, then leaned toward him. "Listen, Sheriff," she began, "that no account son-of-a-bitch lied to me. He and that jerk Freeman had me put here. I have been in a fog for fourteen years. That bastard tried to make me a damn junkie…"

Nathan was impressed. *Good goin' girl. I'm so glad you are coming out of that drug-induced stupor. It does my heart good to see you with your faculties again.*

"He told me that if I did six months here," Alicia continued, "he would put me to work in his office. Once I had his legal fees worked off, he was supposed to give me my house back. But that quack Freeman kept me pumped up with dope."

"I kept by her side when I found out that Alicia was Freeman's only patient." Nathan interjected, "I knew she was found not guilty by reason of insanity, so when a year passed and they were still giving her the needle, and no type of rehabilitation, I thought I better stick by her. The whole thing reeked of Jake Streator all over again. But I have a conscience, so I couldn't let Miss 'licia go and kill herself. I found out as many details of her case as I could. If I ran across a newspaper article that pertained to her, or anyone connected with her case, I kept it. I figured that they couldn't keep her down forever."

"Sheriff?" Alicia broke in, her voice sounded frail, as if the sudden burst of energy drained her, "will you find out about my house?"

"Sure. What do you want to know?"

"I want to find out who is living there. I gotta tell them."

"Tell them what?"

"Well," Alicia looked away, "I just want to talk to them."

Salter smiled. He was pleased she was getting better. To him it was obvious she had told him everything she knew about Max Bailey. Salter said his good bye, and left the building.

"Miss 'licia?" Nathan asked after Salter left, "Do you think he will find out who is living in your house for you?"

"I think so. He seems like a nice man. But if he don't, I have a feeling they will find me." Nathan looked at her, puzzled. *What do you know?*

Alicia turned to look out the window, tears in her eyes. "Nathan, I want to be alone for a little while."

Wordlessly, Nathan rose and left the table.

The weight of the words she spoke to Sheriff Salter washed over her. The knowledge of her house belonging to someone else, and her life forever altered seemed somehow detached to her until she actually spoke the words. That house had been in her family since its construction, an estate originally with eight thousand acres whittled down to four hundred when she signed it over to Bailey. Now that it was hers no longer, sadness overwhelmed her. As she pondered these thoughts, tears ran down her cheeks. The rays of the mid morning sun streamed in through the window, lending a golden hue to each teardrop.

# CHAPTER 30

"All right Bonnie," Shawn said, "if that's the way you want it, then that's fine with me, we'll find out what's going on here."

"That's fine with us, too." Terry added. Amy nodded in agreement. Bonnie took a seat next to her husband at the dining table. Terry rose from the table and returned a few minutes later with a pad of paper.

"Okay, let's see what we got." Amy began, with authority in her voice, "Terry, take a note!"

"What?!" he said with playful indignance.

"Oh, c'mon Terry, you're the one with the really nice writing." Amy cocked her head to the side and began to bat her eyelashes.

"Well, since you put it like that, okay. But it'll cost ya later."

Shawn looked at Bonnie, mindful of her somewhat fragile state. *Why do they always have to joke like that? Don't they know how serious this is to Bonnie?*

Bonnie glared at Terry and Amy and narrowed her eyes. She stood up suddenly, pushing her chair over with her legs as she stood, and slammed her hand down on the table top. The other three jumped in their seats.

"Do you think this is some kind of joke?!" She yelled, leaning over the table. "This stuff is really happening."

Amy's eyes widened as she reared back. With her mouth open, she looked over to Terry. "You know about my dreams. They—they're so real–I've never had dreams like this before. And what about the blood on the floor? You know there's something real going on here!"

Shawn stood, bent over to set Bonnie's chair upright, then placed his hands on her shoulders, applying gentle downward pressure. Bonnie sat, tears streaming down her face.

"I'm sorry, Bonnie." Amy apologized, "I promise I wasn't trying to patronize you. I was just playing with Terry."

Bonnie hung her head, "It's okay, it's just–well, this whole thing has been pretty stressful for me."

Terry slid the pad in front of him and began writing, hoping to salvage the moment. "Okay, we know someone died in this room, right?" He glanced up to Bonnie.

She nodded in response.

"He was in the Civil War, right?"

"Yep." Bonnie said, wiping the tears from her face. "And these French doors have something to do with it, too. But I don't know how."

"Bonnie," Shawn began, "in your dreams, do you get the feeling somebody is trying to tell you something?"

"Yes."

"But what?" Amy asked. Almost as soon as she spoke, it hit her. "The attic!"

"What about the attic?" Terry asked.

*That's right! I had forgotten about that vision I had in the attic the day we moved in. But there was something else wrong with the attic, what was it?* "Yeah, that's it. We never told the guys about that, did we?"

Shawn looked over to Terry, "Did we miss a staff meeting or something?"

Terry rolled his eyes and nodded. "We do that a lot, don't we?"

Amy looked at Terry, lightly hitting his shoulder. "Oh, stop it you two," she retorted.

"What was it that was wrong with the attic, Amy?" Bonnie tried to remember.

"The size was wrong."

"That was it."

"How could the size be wrong?" Shawn asked with a laugh.

"C'mon, I'll show you." Amy rose, taking Terry by the hand and led him to the attic, with Shawn closely behind. She showed them the discrepancy they had discovered with the size of the attic in relation to the upper floor. Terry stood on the top step, Shawn stood on the next tread down while Amy explained about the gable window, the only one in the attic, yet two visible on the outside.

"Well, that's obviously a false wall," Shawn stated.

"I think," Terry eyed the wall, "that sucker needs to come down."

Shawn thumped down the stairs to get his tools, with Terry at his heels while Amy joined Bonnie at the dining room table.

Bonnie sat, holding her head in her hands fighting her growing nausea. "I don't know if I like this, Amy," she said in a whisper barely above the noise their husbands were making as they rummaged through their tool boxes in the utility room.

"Whaddya mean?"

"Shouldn't we find out whose house this was? I mean, maybe they're still around, and we could get some answers. We probably should think about some kind of permission, too. After all, this ain't like drillin' holes in the floor, it's more like remodeling."

"You know," Terry called from the other room, "it ain't like people go into the attic all the time. I bet if we take the wall down, no one will even know we did it. So, I really don't think we need to get permission, or even say anything to anybody, and who will be the wiser?"

"Do you think Lynn knows who the old owner is, or was?" Amy asked.

"No, I don't think so. Didn't she say something about the hall of records at the county building, or something like that?"

Amy's eyes widened with remembrance. "Yeah, I think you're right."

Terry and Shawn filed through the dining room on their way to the attic, each with an arm load of tools.

"Hey ya'll!" Amy said. They stopped in their tracks and faced the two girls.

"Let's not do that right now, okay?"

"Why?" Terry wrinkled his forehead. "I thought we discussed this already."

"Bonnie and I think we should go into town and find out who this house used to belong to before you two do your Bob Vila impression."

"Why?" Shawn asked, sounding as if someone had just taken away his favorite toy.

"Remember what happened the last time you guys did something to this house? I mean I found some more pieces of light bulb glass only yesterday."

"Amy, that wasn't their fault," Bonnie interjected.

Amy wrinkled her forehead at her friend. *Stop that, Bonnie. You're supposed to be on my side, remember? You're not allowed to steal any of my thunder while I'm busy barking orders at Shawn and Terry.* "Whaddya mean by that?" Amy snorted.

"They didn't do that, he did."

"He who?"

"You know damn well who—" Bonnie's temper was beginning to escalate, "that guy in my dream. That guy who was standing in your room. I think that when we put the French doors up—well I think we woke him up or something."

"Well, all this is well and good, honey," Shawn started, "but we ain't got all year, in fact, we were only able to arrange to extend our vacations until next Monday. So, whatever we do, we gotta do it within the rest of this week."

"I understand what you're saying, but I don't think we ought to go tearing up this house without finding out who it used to belong to."

"Why?"

"I can't explain it, I just know that's what we gotta do."

"Well, given your track record on your premonitions, let's go where we need to go to satisfy your uneasy feelings. You know what they say; if momma ain't happy, ain't nobody happy."

Bonnie smiled. Terry and Shawn placed their tools on the table.

The four piled into Terry's Cavalier. Bonnie was glad to get away from the house for a while. Whenever she was inside the house, she had the continuing and nagging feeling of a headache at the back of her head coming on. Lately however, she had begun to feel a strange attachment to the house. This made her uneasy since she had come to almost fear it. One feeling fought the other.

Terry turned the little four-door onto Highway 331 from Highway 61. Bonnie could hear Terry and Shawn talk about tearing down the false wall in the attic, but their words were detached as her thoughts were drifting toward the dream she'd had earlier about the snowball fight.

Terry turned onto Washington Road on their way to Interstate 40, but she was lost in thought. The memory of the three men talking in the clearing burned in her mind. Amy was quietly watching the scenery go past.

"Look, Bonnie!" Amy suddenly broke the silence in the back seat. "Look at that church. Isn't it beautiful?"

Bonnie looked up. Amy was pointing at a church building visible from Bonnie's window. Without looking at the building, or even acknowledging Amy, Bonnie's eyes widened as she spotted an old cemetery outside Amy's window.

"Stop! Stop the car!" Bonnie pounded on the passenger seat back. "Terry, stop the car."

Shawn turned around, angry at first with his wife for pounding his seat back, until he saw the look on her face.

"All right, all right," Terry responded. "Keep your shirt on." Terry pulled into the center of the old cemetery on a small driveway made of ruts in the dirt from countless previous vehicles, and stopped beside a small leafless tree. Bonnie flung open the door and began to walk through it as if she were looking for something. Shawn followed his wife. The cemetery had a mixture of gravestones, both old and new. Bonnie walked quickly, her actions now appearing to Shawn more focused. She stopped at a small group of gravestones in the northeast corner. They were so weathered, they appeared to be slabs of ordinary granite instead of grave markers. The engravings had diminished with the passage of time. Bonnie stood before the markers, tears in her eyes. Shawn walked up and stood beside his wife.

"These are the Dunlops," She sobbed, pointing to a group of five stones. "And those," she pointed to another group of weathered stones, ten or so feet away from the Dunlop stones, "over there, belong to the Fuller family." Shawn bent to examine the stones, but could see no markings. Turning to his wife, Shawn looked puzzled.

"How can you know that? There are absolutely no marks on these tombstones."

"I just know, that's all. It just came to me. And somehow, this is connected to whatever is happening at the house. But the strongest feelings I get come from here." She touched the gravestone next to her. Shawn leaned close to see. He touched the stone, barely able to make out the faint, weather-worn engraving.

"Lester Howe," Shawn read, "born August 14, 1818. Died November 6, 1871. It says 'loving husband' across the top. I guess these people had money since these gravestones are so much bigger than those other ones you were talking about." Shawn moved to the adjacent stone. "Nelda Ann Howe, born October 12, 1821. Died January 4, 1872. This one says 'loving wife.'"

"Shawn, I don't know how I know this, but, I know there is some-one missing."

"Who?"

"I don't know, but it's giving me an empty feeling in my gut." She looked into his eyes as if searching for the answers to her questions, or perhaps comfort, she didn't know which. "Let's get out of here," she continued, "this place is starting to give me the creeps."

Shawn held his wife as the two walked back to the car. Again, they were off to Knoxville to continue their search.

# CHAPTER 31

Terry pulled the Cavalier into a vacant parking place adjacent a digital parking meter on Main Street. As Bonnie got out of the car, she caught sight of the old brick building next to the City-County Building. Terry and Amy headed for the front door that housed the City and County offices.

"What's that?" Bonnie asked, pointing to the old brick building.

"That's the old Knox County Courthouse," Shawn answered. "Why?"

"It seems like I've been in it before."

"Well, I don't know when that would have been. I thought you've never been here in downtown Knoxville before. Or, at least, in this section before."

"I haven't. It just seems familiar. Maybe I came here a long time ago and just don't remember."

The four entered the revolving front door and walked down the long hallway to the elevator. On the second floor, they proceeded to the west end of the building, to the Registrar of Deeds Office.

"May I help you?" asked a pleasant looking middle aged woman.

"Yes, " Bonnie answered. "How can we find out who the previous owner is of the house that we're renting?"

"Well, that information is on the deed. You'll have to get it from the current owner."

"I don't think that's possible. He's...out of the country." Bonnie felt her hopes fading.

"Is there a real estate agent or someone handling the property in his absence?"

"Yes!" Bonnie became somewhat excited.

"Well, I need you to have that person contact me here at the registrar's office."

Bonnie forced a smile. She was somewhat upset with the woman and certainly upset with these stupid rules. Without saying a word, she turned to walk out of the office. The other three looked at each other. Terry smiled. He was amused at Bonnie's volatile behavior. They followed her to the elevator, out the front door, and stopped at a pay phone.

"Terry, call Lynn. She has to help us."

Terry dug in his pants pocket for a quarter.

Amy leaned over to Terry's ear."Want me to help you with that?" she asked seductively. Bonnie glared at her. Amy shrank back a bit at first, then retorted with her own anger.

"Sorry! Jeez, we are married, you know! Bonnie, I don't know what's the matter with you, but this has got to stop. There is no reason for you act this way at all. We're all on the same side. This thing with the house is affecting all of us, not just you. You may be more sensitive to it than the rest of us, but we are just as scared as you."

Bonnie began to cry, and took solace in Shawn's arms. She felt bad for hollering at Amy, yet at the same time, angry for being called out, knowing she was wrong. Shawn held her tenderly. He knew his wife needed only silent support, but he had no idea what to say to the Lamberts to explain his wife's bizarre behavior even though he was becoming irritated as well.

"Sorry," she said, looking at the ground, "I guess I got carried away."

"Maybe somebody ought to carry you to the mental hospital. At the rate you're going, you're gonna drive us all crazy!" Terry laughed, trying to break the tension.

Bonnie only blinked at him as a strange feeling of familiarity swept over her. *Mental Institute? Mental Institute? Now that reminds me of something. But what?* She was barely aware of hearing Terry call Lynn Hooper on the pay phone. *Oh my God! It was that dream I had. That's where I saw that old courthouse!* Butterflies twitched in her stomach. *And that large one story building, that was a mental hospital! But there's something else.*

"Shawn!" She burst with the look of someone who just found a lost item.

"What?"

"Those gravestones! They belong to the people in my dream."

"Which dream?"

"The one with the little boy. You know, in the well."

"Which gravestones?"

"You know, the ones we saw when we came up here. The Howe's. But I don't know how it's all connected."

Terry walked back to the three standing near a concrete bench. "Lynn says the name of the previous owner was a man by the name of Max Bailey. She said she'll call the registrar's office and talk to that woman."

"When?" Shawn asked.

"I guess now."

"You two go in and see who this Max Bailey got the house from. I'll stay with Bonnie out here." Terry and Amy disappeared into the building.

"Shawn?" Bonnie said in a low voice and leaned her head against his chest.

"What babe?"

"We need to find out the history of that house. The last few owners is a good start, but I need to have a complete understanding of that house. There's something going on deeper than what we're seeing now. Something terrible happened in that dining room, and we've got to find out why it happened and who the person is that died. I won't get any rest until we do."

Shawn took Bonnie's hand as they sat on the concrete bench. "Okay, honey. Look, I need to talk to you while Terry and Amy are inside that building. I know you have a problem with this house. And you've been having trouble sleeping."

"I know Shawn, I'm sorry."

"Wait a minute, let me finish."

"Sorry."

"And you know I have a lot of patience with you when it comes to your premonitions and dreams. But honey, this weird behavior is driving me crazy."

Bonnie's eyes narrowed at him, "Have you and Terry been talking about me behind my back?"

"No, of course not! As far as he and Amy are concerned—well, I don't know what they think, but I do care because we have to live with them. I have not discussed anything with Terry about this because even though we live with them we still have to keep some parts of our marriage private."

Bonnie held him close. "Shawn, do you remember what happened on the day we met?"

"Sure, I wanted to either kick your ass, or have you arrested."

Bonnie smiled. "Yep, that's right. And do you know why."

"Because I caught you letting the air out of the tires on my El Camino. I didn't even know who you were and here I was coming through the school parking lot when I spotted this cute redhead messin' with my car."

"That was the day Tommy Logsdon died, wasn't it?"

Shawn remembered. "We were going up the street to race and I was in a hurry 'cause Michael Cooper, Tommy and I were going to have a three-way race."

"Shawn, I know I told you this before, but I may not have told you quite all of the story. You know I had a crush on you ever since I saw you in English class. I knew that we would be married. I just knew it. Every time I saw that day I saw flames all around your head, and I knew that you would be dead. I didn't know why, but I had to find a way to disable your car."

"Tommy and Michael hit that fuel truck during the race."

"That truck driver and Tommy died, and Michael lost his legs in the crash. And who knew what would have happened to me that day?"

"I knew, Shawn. I saved your life. And I don't have all the answers but I feel as strong about finding out what is going on with this house as I did about stopping you that day in high school.

"I love you." Shawn kissed her and held her close. "Well, maybe something will turn up. If Terry and Amy can come up with another name, maybe we can go to the library and look up...I don't know! I don't even know what we're looking for. Do you?"

"No. But I'll know it when I see it."

"Maybe the police can help, or at least give us some direction."

Bonnie pulled away from her husband's embrace. He sat on the concrete bench and watched her walk in front of the old courthouse.

She looked at it intently, studying every brick, every pillar. It was indeed the same building she saw in her dream. A sickening feeling came over her, as if she had suffered a terrible injustice within its walls and yet the feeling was detached. She knew she had never set foot through the door. Yet the building seemed familiar. She closed her eyes, and could almost see a corridor, running the length of one side of the building with a window at the end. The window must have been on an upper floor, for she could see a park, or a grassy area below. The faint whispers of an elevator door opening, then the sound of a gavel crash in an empty hall, like a shot, echoing in her mind. She opened her eyes suddenly, trying to diffuse the hazy vision in her mind, but only caught the revolving door of the City-County Building as Terry and Amy emerged and walk over to Shawn. She joined them.

"We got names of the past owners," Amy informed.

Bonnie could only smile meekly, still feeling the effects of her vision.

"Let's go home," Shawn suggested. Bonnie looked tired. Wordlessly, the four piled into the Cavalier for the drive home. Strangely, all were silent. Bonnie didn't ask about the names because she assumed Terry or Amy would be so excited about the information, they would begin discussing them immediately, but that was not the case. Shawn shifted in the front passenger seat, adjusting himself to lean his head against the glass. He thought of that race where he surely would have died. *Bonnie was right, she did save my life.*

Bonnie looked over at Amy. She was looking out the window, picking her teeth with her fingernail. Bonnie reached over to touch her on the shoulder.

"Amy?" she asked quietly.

"What?"

"Who used to own the house before that lawyer, what was his name?"

"Max Bailey."

"Yeah. Was it a woman?"

Amy's eyes widened in surprise. "How did you know? Never mind. You had a feeling, right?"

Bonnie nodded. "What was her name?"

"Alicia Freed. Evidently, the house had been in her family for a long time. She inherited it from her mother, who had probably inherited it from her parents. But I don't really know because the records don't seem to go back that far."

"I wonder how we can find this woman."

They passed the small cemetery. In looking at the stones from the car, Bonnie thought of death certificates, or some other record indicating lineage. "Amy, how can we find out about where the original owners are buried?"

"I don't know."

A feeling of utter helplessness swept over her. A rising need to find the history of the people who owned the house swelled in her. Maybe then, some light would be shed on why things were happening there. Frustrated, Bonnie leaned her head against the window and closed her eyes.

As the house came into view, Terry noticed something out of place. He reached over and lightly slapped Shawn on the shoulder to wake him.

Shawn bolted upright.

"Where did you get that?" Terry asked, pointing to a Knox County Sheriff's car sitting in the driveway.

"Don't look at me, I was asleep." Shawn rubbed his eyes.

"Sounds like a likely alibi."

"What do you suppose he wants?" Amy asked.

Bonnie looked up suddenly to see what was going on. Terry pulled in behind the police car, effectively blocking it. The uniformed man was walking from the back porch to the car when he stopped to watch Terry pull up. Terry exited and walked up to the officer.

"Can I help you Officer?"

"Are you the one renting this house?"

"Well, me, my wife and our friends. What can I do for you, sir?"

"Salter. Can we sit down and talk?"

Amy walked past her husband, fumbling with her house keys. "Right this way," she said. When Amy reached the house, she picked up the business card the Sheriff had stuck between the door and the doorjamb, then unlocked the door. They filed into the house.

As Amy walked through the kitchen toward the dining room, she caught sight of a dark puddle on the dining room floor. She stopped in her tracks and let out a squeak. Bonnie, as if in a trance, immediately ran the water in the sink to wet a towel, then began to clean up the puddle. Amy grabbed another towel to help.

"What is that?" Salter questioned, as he bent down to touch the liquid. He rubbed it between his fingers, feeling the smooth, thick constancy. Bringing it to his nose, he sniffed, but could smell nothing. "What is this?" he demanded. "What's going on here?"

"You better sit down, Sheriff," Terry said, seating himself. Bonnie handed Salter a damp towel.

"It looks like blood, but it has absolutely no smell," he said as he wiped his hands, wrinkling his nose as if smelling a repulsive odor, then took a seat to watch the girls clean up the puddle on the floor.

"We don't know what it is," Amy said as she sat on the sofa, "but it happens every now and then."

"Why are you here, Sheriff?" Shawn asked.

"The previous owner asked me to look in on the place."

"Max Bailey?" Bonnie asked.

The Sheriff eyed her suspiciously. "Do you know any of the history of this house?"

Bonnie's hopes were starting to rise.

"Do you know Max Bailey?" Salter asked.

"Well, no. Actually, we only found out a couple of hours ago that he used to own this house," Terry offered.

"Sheriff, what is the name of the person who asked you to look in on the house?" Amy asked.

"Her name is Alicia Freed. This house had been in her family since before the Civil War."

"Why did she sell it?"

"She didn't really, she was sort of swindled out of it."

"How?"

A glazed look appeared on Bonnie's face. Her eyes became fixed straight ahead.

Shawn noticed her expression. "What's wrong honey?" He placed his hand on her shoulder.

She turned to face him. A profound look of sadness came over her. "It had something to do with that old courthouse we saw today. The old Knox County Courthouse."

"What?" Shawn, Terry and Amy asked in unison.

"She's right," Salter explained. "You see, back in 1978, I arrested Ms. Freed for stabbing a man who lives in Knoxville, on the other side of town. At that time I worked for the city force. She hired Max Bailey to defend her. Evidently, Alicia had some sort of financial difficulties because she signed over the house in trade for his legal services. Anyway, she got off on an insanity plea and was sentenced to Rhinewood Mental Institute for evaluation. I guess she got swallowed up by the system or something, because she's still there." He felt the truth would only confuse them.

"Is that the one on Highway 61 in Union County?" Terry asked.

Salter nodded.

Bonnie smiled. "Thank you, Sheriff. You just gave us some answers to questions we didn't even know how to ask."

"Well, I've taken up enough of ya'll's time." Salter rose, and left.

A few moments later, Terry rose suddenly, eyes wide. "I got to move the car!" Just then, the horn sounded from the Sheriff's patrol car. Terry ran out of the house.

"I wonder if that can get him arrested for obstructing justice?" Shawn laughed.

# CHAPTER 32

Bonnie jerked open the door leading to the attic stairs. As she looked up, she could see the beams of sunlight coming through the gable window, particles of airborne dust glinting with the sudden disturbance of air. She led the others up the stairs, and began to feel growing anticipation, as if she were about to find the answers to a century's worth of questions.

The girls stood back and watched the men pry on the wall boards with their crowbars. The air filled with the sound of wood creaking as it broke, followed by screams from the nails as they were forced from the wood against their will. Finally, the wall succumbed to the greater force to yield its secret.

"There's another room in here!" Terry said excitedly, tearing the hole larger to accommodate his frame.

"What's in there?" Bonnie took a step toward the hole in the false wall, then stopped, afraid of what she might see. "Terry, what's in there?"

"Hang on, we gotta make the hole bigger. You two stay over there. Shawn, help me with this stud, then we can swing this whole section over to the side."

Shawn responded wordlessly, prying at the top of a two-by-four. Bonnie looked at Amy for comfort. After a grunt from Shawn followed by a mighty creak, they swung a section of the wall to the right. Dust filled the stale air. Bonnie could hear her own heart pound in her chest as she waited for the dust to settle. Light streamed in from the newly revealed window. A single rectangular shape appeared among the settling dust.

"That's all?!" Bonnie exclaimed, obvious disappointment in her voice.

"What, Bonnie?" Amy said indignantly, "Were you expecting a body? A pile of old bones?"

Bonnie looked at her friend in disbelief, jaw open.

In the center of the room stood a single trunk. Terry and Shawn each grabbed a thick leather strap to carry the medium size trunk downstairs.

"It's pretty heavy," Shawn informed, "but I don't think there's any body in here, it's not quite big enough."

"I can't believe you even said that to me," Bonnie said to Amy's back as they went down the stairs.

Amy stopped suddenly and turned around, glaring upward at her. "Well, what the hell do you expect?" she almost shouted. "You have been acting crazy lately." She paused. Suddenly the expression on her face changed as she remembered their exchange at the courthouse. "But I bet we find a good many clues about this house in that trunk." Amy lowered her voice as she pondered the thought of delving deeper into this mystery. "Let's go find out what's in that thing." She turned and bounced down the stairs.

Bonnie stood alone for a moment, watching Amy disappear from view. *I guess I've been putting them all through hell with my damn mood swings. And it really should be Amy having the roughest time, after all, she and Terry stay in the most affected room.*

When Bonnie entered the dining room, the table had been cleared and the trunk sat on the floor where the puddle of blood always formed. Shawn knelt in front of it, fumbling with the latch. Terry and Amy hovered over his back, watching expectantly to see what was inside. Bonnie sat at the table in her usual location, staring at the wall directly in front of her trying to sort out her feelings.

"Do you want me to do it?" Terry asked impatiently. Shawn immediately stopped his work to glare at him.

"I think I'm capable of figuring this out. You just step back and hang on."

"No problem."

The latch popped open. Shawn looked at Terry, grinning.

"Smart ass."

"What's in it?" Bonnie asked, eyes still fixed on the wall.

The hinges creaked in protest as Shawn opened the lid, as if resisting to reveal its secrets. He leaned back so Terry and Amy could pour over the open box.

A thin layer of fine dust covered the contents.

"It just looks like a bunch of old papers." Amy reported.

"Pieces." Bonnie said, barely above a whisper.

Shawn looked over at his wife, then rose to sit by her.

"What do you mean, babe?"

"They're pieces, but not the whole puzzle."

Amy carefully dug through the century old trunk. Terry, recognizing her superior dexterity, wisely stepped back so only one person had access to the trunk, so as not to damage anything inside.

"There are some old letters in here. The paper is really thin and yellow and the writing is barely visible." Amy blew off the dust covering the letter, a single piece of paper folded in half.

"I can't make out the date and most of it is really hard to read."

"Amy. Just read the letter!" Bonnie said impatiently.

"Okay, here goes: 'I hope this writing finds you well. Unfortunately this letter must bring with it some sad news. Robert was sent to Atlanta for an operation at the expense of the military to rectify his war injury. It was in his hopes to be able to walk again. How could we have known of the terrible tragedy following the march of the Union Army.'"

"What was that all about?" Terry asked.

"You know," Amy said, putting the paper aside, "this doesn't look finished. There's no signature, it almost looks like notes, or a rough draft to a later letter or a collection of incomplete thoughts."

"You know what I feel after hearing that?" Bonnie offered.

"What?"

"I feel dirty. Like company is coming over and all we just did was sweep the dirt under the rug. What else is in there?"

"Well, here is—I guess, it's a marriage certificate. It's all hand written. It says: 'Witnesseth hereto on this tenth day of January in the year of our lord, eighteen hundred and sixty-five by the Reverend Henry Trenton Gibson, the matrimony of David Allen Westchester to Daphne Beatrice Nelson on this day'. There is no official seal or anything like that, it's just written on a plain piece of paper."

"That makes me feel even dirtier. Even slimy."

"We need a picture or a chart or something on who all these people were," Shawn added.

"Maybe we can visit that lady that sent the Sheriff over here to check on us," Terry wondered aloud.

Bonnie's eyes opened wide. "Now that's a good idea."

"Not today," Terry said, "It's going on four o'clock. And since we didn't get any lunch, I'm getting hungry. So by the time we get lunch or early supper or whatever, it'll be way too late to see anyone at any kind of government facility."

"Eatin' sounds good to me," Shawn offered, turning to the women. "What ya'll gonna make?"

Bonnie looked at Amy and laughed.

# CHAPTER 33

Evening fell and Alicia fought sleep watching the sunset through the dining room windows. She almost felt as if she were sitting in the sun-room at her old house. She eased back in the easy chair Nathan had positioned in front of the windows after dinner. Laying her head back against the chair, she could no longer fight the drowsiness.

Gradually, she found herself standing at the front door at her old house. She knocked. Somehow, she could hear the echo bounce throughout the house. Soon, Nathan answered the door.

"May I help you?"

"Yes. I'm here to see S'postu."

"I'm sorry. He's…shall I say…incapacitated, at the moment."

"Oh, I know he'll see me. I'm his…I'm his…" Her word suddenly eluded her. It seemed so clear only a moment ago. Now, it was as if she never knew.

"I'm sorry, you'll have to come back later." Nathan slammed the door in her face. Alicia turned around, angry. Standing directly behind her were four young people. A tall blonde man standing with a young lady with hazel eyes and auburn hair. Another man, slightly shorter than the other with dark hair and chestnut brown eyes, standing with a young woman with blonde hair and blue eyes. Standing behind them was Sheriff Salter. Alicia turned back toward the front door. She was now standing in front of old wooden storm doors leading to the basement under the house. She turned around again to find herself standing alone. She bent to open the storm doors. They creaked open, the light illuminating a staircase going under the house. But this couldn't be her old house, it didn't have a basement. Where was she? Fear enveloped her as she descended the staircase, yet she was compelled to go on. She walked on the dirt floor past an old wooden wheelchair covered with cobwebs. The chair looked so familiar, she should have known who it belonged to, but her memory was blank. As she moved forward, the walls of the basement gradually narrowed into a hallway. On the old rock walls a picture hung. She walked over to see. It looked like a photograph, blown up and framed. It was a car, its silver surface reflecting the color of the dawning sun, supported by the limb of a huge tree. The limb passed through the back window and out the front. The landscape around the car was patchy snow with the colors of the sunrise glistening on its shiny surface.

Alicia found herself walking down the narrow hallway, the walls seeming to get closer together with each step she took. The hall ended at an old wooden door. There was no doorknob, yet she felt compelled to open the door. Looking around, she spotted an old rusted sword leaning against the rock wall. She picked up the sword, using it as a pry bar and forced open the old wooden door. It seemed to be nailed in place, as it yielded very slowly, creaking with every inch as Alicia pried on the door with all her might. Suddenly, the door flew open, the sudden release in pressure snapping the sword blade in half, causing her to lose her balance. She tumbled forward into the open doorway, but stopped suddenly as she came in contact with a wall of dirt. The earthen wall came loose as her head slammed into it, collapsing on her. Dirt, rock and debris covered her. Alicia struggled to free herself, but the avalanche was relentless and began squeezing her breath out of her.

Alicia woke with a start. A blanket had been placed over her. Somehow, it managed to creep up on top of her during her sleep until it covered her face. After flinging the blanket to the floor, she looked around the room, her eyes straining to adjust. It was now dark outside, and the light from the nearby houses and street lights lit the night like stars in the distant sky. She found herself alone in the room.

Cory Brennan had lifted her status, so she had freedom to roam the convalescent wing at will. She rose from the easy chair, wiping the beads of sweat from her brow, and ambled off to her room to go to bed.

# CHAPTER 34

Bonnie sat in bed waiting for Shawn. He was in the bathroom, and with the door closed, the light from inside the bathroom peeked out casting eerie shadows in the bedroom. Bonnie sat, holding the covers close to her breast, listening to the sounds of the house late at night, longing for the comfort of her husband.

A southerly warm front had come through the area, bringing with it gusty winds. The sounds the house made as the wind battered its side and rattled the window panes terrified her. Bonnie breathed a sigh of relief when the bathroom door opened. Shawn's silhouette was backlit by the moonlight coming in from the bathroom window. Suddenly the bed shook softly. Bonnie could hear Shawn's footsteps as he neared the bed. *What the hell?* Her heart pounded. The bed quivered again with something depressing the covers between her legs. Bonnie screamed, then stopped suddenly when she heard the familiar sound of a purring cat.

"One-night! You absolutely scared the shit out of me!" Bonnie gasped.

Shawn slid into bed next to her. "Why are you so jumpy tonight?"

She faced him knowing he could not see her face in the darkness. *You know damn well why I'm so jumpy, it's this house!*

"Never mind. Sorry I even said it," he said before she could answer, then leaned over, kissed her, and snuggled under the covers. Bonnie, satisfied with his response, snuggled against him. He swung his arm around her so she could nestle against his chest, feeling safe in his arms. One-night kneaded the covers at the foot of the bed then curled into a ball. Shawn was soon asleep, and once again, Bonnie was left alone with the sounds of the night.

Gradually, the sound of voices coming from downstairs drifted to her. They were unfamiliar, one deep and gruff, the other mid-pitched and dry. She slid out of bed to investigate. It was hard to make out what was being said, yet they were clear. Strangely, she was not cold. She knew it was still winter, and very cold outside. The sound of Shawn sleeping faded quickly behind her as she descended the staircase. Upon reaching the landing at the bottom, she found herself at the end of a great hall, seeming to stretch into infinity, with doors, some open, some closed, lining the hall. It was paneled in deep, rich hardwood, framed by fancy molding at the ceiling and the floor and around the endless door frames. The voices were louder now and becoming clear.

"Lester, I know what we said when the young-uns were born, but they're growed up now an' Daphne, well, she's becoming quite stately in her opinions. She ain't takin' too kindly to Robert at all."

"Does she know about the house?"

Bonnie peeked around an open door, seeing two men, dressed in coats, sitting in two chairs, talking to one another with their backs to a window.

"Naw. I got it bein' built on the other side of the plantation. She don't never go there."

"Robert can't think of nothin' else. He's real sweet on Daphne."

From the corner of her eye, Bonnie saw movement just outside the window. She turned to see, and realized a man was eavesdropping on the conversation as well. She recognized the man outside, the green eyes, the red hair, it was the same man she had seen countless times in her dreams. His hair was shorter and he was clean shaven, but she was sure it was him.

"But your son sure knows where it is. My carpenter told me he been over there a half a dozen times tellin' them he wants a room facin' west with French doors so he can watch the sunset."

"That's his momma comin' out in him, she always liked that kinda stuff."

"Well, my boys finally gave in, but it's gonna cost about five hundred dollars more."

"That's a whole helluva lot a money just fer one room."

"It's that or he don't git his sittin' room. Besides, it's them doors that's so expensive."

"Okay, I'll send a boy up here with the money tomorrow."

Bonnie heard a cracking of wood behind her, and turned toward the sound. She was now standing in the woods behind an old barn. Bonnie saw a young woman with her arms around the shoulders of a man, who somehow, she knew was a hired hand for the young woman's father. They faced each other, his hands around her slender waist. Her pale green dress fluttered in the gentle breeze. He pulled her closer to him and kissed her. Bonnie could see movement in the shadows of the barn. A man began to emerge. But, upon seeing the couple kissing, pulled back into shadows. A sickening feeling of rage and jealousy swept over Bonnie, jealousy directed toward the man kissing the woman, and the rage directed toward the woman. She recognized the man in the barn as the same one who'd been watching the two men talking inside.

"Daphne!" The man came from the barn, carrying a plowshare, "You traitorous bitch!" He ran toward them, wielding the implement. "And you! You take your hands off her or I'll run you through where you stand."

The man released the woman. She ran toward the man with the plowshare.

"Robert! No!" she pleaded.

Robert threw her to the ground. Bonnie could actually feel his jealous rage, almost on the verge of uncontrollable, murderous actions. He stepped toward the other man, then stopped himself, dropping the plowshare to the ground. He turned back to Daphne, bending to help her stand.

"Daphne, I love you. I love you with all of me there is. I can't stand to see you with anyone else." He turned to the other man and narrowed his eyes. "David, if you ever touch my woman again, I will kill you where you stand. Have I made my meanin' clear?"

"Yes, sir." David looked to the ground.

"Go!" Robert ordered.

David turned and walked away.

Robert turned to Daphne. She looked at him strangely, sort of half smiling. A feeling crept over Bonnie as if she could feel Daphne looking at Robert in a different light. Perhaps it was the sight of a man, fighting another, over her. It excited her, and Bonnie could see evil delight flash across her face.

"He made me kiss him," Daphne lied. *She lied! Why couldn't Robert see that? Maybe love is truly blind, and ignorant as well.* Robert only held Daphne close to him. She returned the embrace, her face toward Bonnie, smiling. Bonnie felt sick to her stomach.

Light poured in from the bathroom as Shawn switched on the light, bringing Bonnie to consciousness. She sat up in bed, rubbing her eyes. Glancing over to the clock on the bedside table, she noticed the time: 2:45.

"Shawn?" she called.

"What?"

"Would you ever fight over me?"

"What the hell is that supposed to mean?"

"I mean, would you fight another guy if he made a pass at me?"

"Why are you asking me a question like that?" The toilet flushed, the light went off, Bonnie felt Shawn crawl back in next to her. "Has someone been coming on to you? Was it Terry?"

"No!" her tone was indignant, and she was surprised at his response. "No, nothing like that."

"Well, who then?"

"No one. I just want to know what would you do if you saw someone coming on to me."

"I suppose it depends on what he did."

The moonlight cascaded through the window from the clear night. Now that Bonnie's eyes had adjusted to the pale light. She could see him looking directly at her.

"What if he grabbed me around the waist, pulled me close to him, then tried to kiss me."

"I would hit the son of a bitch so hard, he wouldn't be able to kiss anyone for a month." Bonnie felt strangely excited. The thought of Shawn hitting some other guy to defend her honor left her aroused. The more she thought about it, the more aroused she became. She threw the covers off then straddled his pelvis, grinding against him. Shawn groaned in delight.

"What brought this on?" he asked, becoming excited himself.

Bonnie crossed her arms, grabbing her nightgown at the waist, then pulling it over her head. She bent to kiss him. He could feel her hard nipples brush against his chest through his thin tee shirt. Bonnie ground her pelvis into his and kissed him with passion she hadn't felt in years. She dismounted him and removed his clothing. He could hear her pant as she kissed him again. Bonnie again straddled her husband to make love to him with an uncontrollable desire.

# CHAPTER 35

The gentle morning sun beamed in through the uncovered window, warming Amy's face. She stirred to the sun's warmth and the sound of One-night growling outside the bedroom door. She sat up suddenly in bed, straining to hear the cat hiss and growl. Apprehension and fear swept over her as she slid out of bed, the cold air in the room hitting her like a freight train. Slowly, she walked toward the door to investigate the noise in the living room. After grasping the doorknob, she turned it slowly to open the door. The doorknob was ice cold. Nevertheless, Amy cracked the door open. The sound of jingling keys echoed in the quiet house. The cat hissed again. The door suddenly slammed shut, pulling her forcibly against it. She pulled hard on the doorknob and flung the door open. Sticking her head into the living room, Amy caught the metallic glint of something in or near the dining room. Suddenly, her curiosity overrode her fear, and she crept in to find out what was going on. The cat hissed and growled again, then ran into the sunroom as if being chased. More metallic movement caught her eye, followed by the sound of a set of keys hitting a padded hard surface. Amy charged toward the dining room to investigate when she was stopped short of the threshold between the living room and dining room by the sound of a muffled crack, followed by the sound of something heavy and soft hitting the floor at the end of the dining table. The chair at the end of the table moved forward slightly, and a puddle of blood began to form on the floor around the old chest. The blood did not touch the trunk. It instead, encircled it leaving a space around the trunk, by half an inch, where the floor was perfectly dry. Suddenly, papers, envelopes and dust flew out as if propelled by a blast of compressed air, landing on the dining room table in obvious piles followed by a stream of blood landing in droplets on one of the piles of papers on the table. Amy could not believe her eyes. She opened her mouth to scream, but could not force out a sound. The room began to spin. Loud ringing developed in her ears, accompanied by a white wash out of the room. The louder the ringing in her ears became, the more the room washed out to white then, as quickly as it started, the room went black.

Amy felt as if she were floating on a cloud. A cloud of euphoria, with the wind whistling softly by. Distantly, she heard the sound of a voice. A familiar voice, calling her name. It was Terry! She tried to respond, but the wind was drowning her out. The voice of her husband seemed to be getting louder, and sounding more concerned, but she could still not understand what he was saying to her. The clouds began to dissipate, and Terry's face gradually became clear.

"Amy! Amy! Are you all right?"

"Huh?" She murmured as Terry's face became clear. He was standing over her.

"What happened?" he asked tenderly.

"What happened to the clouds?"

"What?" Terry asked in confusion.

"What happened, Terry?"

"That's what I just asked you."

"I don't know."

"I came out when I heard you hit the floor. Are you okay?"

Amy thought for a minute. After deciding that she felt no unusual pain, she began to stand.

"Now take it easy, honey," Terry instructed. Amy looked at her husband and smiled. She suddenly asked herself if he would say those words to her in the same tender way if she were pregnant, and had just told him. She almost longed to be, just to hear the words.

"What?"

"I said, take it easy, babe. It looks like you took a nasty fall. Are you okay?"

He said it again! She suddenly felt this overpowering love for him. She always loved him before, but never with this intensity. It was almost hypnotic, and artificial. She grabbed his head and pulled his face to hers, kissing him passionately and tenderly.

"Yeah, I'm fine, now."

Bonnie and Shawn appeared behind Terry. "Are you all right, Amy?" she asked, obvious concern in her voice.

Shawn walked into the dining room. "Did you put these papers into piles, Amy? I thought we were all going to do it together."

"No."

"He did it." Bonnie said. Everyone knew who she referred to.

"Look at this blood on these letters," Shawn said, picking the top envelope off the blood stained pile. "Check this out, it's even on the letters and papers under the top one." He began to sort through the letters and papers.

"It shot out of the trunk after the papers flew out and separated into piles." Amy explained.

"Look at how the puddle on the floor goes around the trunk, but doesn't touch it." Bonnie said.

"How is that possible?" Terry asked.

"Terry," Bonnie began, "how could you ask a question like that after all the things that have gone on in this house? You can't possibly think there's a logical explanation for this, do you?" She raised her eyebrows in anticipation of his answer.

"Not hardly. But I think it's a simple one."

"Okay, Einstein," Amy cut in, indignant, "what have you concluded?"

"We have a ghost," Terry replied, somewhat sheepishly.

"Oh that's just brilliant!" Amy said, then looking at Bonnie, then back to Terry. "I'm glad you're here to tell us these things. Now, how about some new information?"

Bonnie laughed.

"Like what?"

"Like who, what, and when, for starters."

"Let's do what we started to do last night," Bonnie began, "Write all the information we have to date, then we'll take it to that lady the Sheriff told us about. I know she can shed some light on what's going on. Or at least, she can help."

"The only papers that have this blood on them seem to be correspondence between this David Westchester and Daphne Nelson," Shawn said, "Plus, that marriage letter, or whatever that thing was that we read yesterday."

The names Shawn mentioned made Bonnie think of her dream from the previous night. It was as if she saw someone from her past, recognized them, but could not remember their names. She strained to remember, but it was no use.

"Look at this!" Shawn exclaimed. The three crowded around him. Shawn pulled an old news paper article from the bottom of the blood stained pile. The paper was yellow with age and very fragile, the drops of blood made the faded print difficult to read.

"Local hero lost in Atlanta fire," Shawn read the headline. "According to his wife, Robert Howe of Knox County was lost in the fire set by General Sherman. Apparently en-route for an Atlanta hospital for back surgery, Sergeant Howe returned from the war only a month previously, after taking a bullet in his lower back. It was in hopes, according to Daphne Howe, the surgery would restore her husband from his crippled state. Exact details, however, are unclear."

"Well, I can see that newspapers told you more back then than they do now."

Bonnie felt her blood pressure shooting up. She became angry with what she heard Shawn read. After stomping into the kitchen to retrieve a damp towel, she proceeded to clean up the puddle surrounding the trunk. Shawn looked at Amy and Terry with a puzzled look on his face.

"What's with her?" He said quietly to the others. Amy shrugged.

"That article is a load of crap!" Bonnie snapped.

"What do you mean?" Shawn asked.

"I mean it's a load of crap. It's a lie."

"Why?"

"Because he never went to Atlanta, that's why."

"How do you know?" Amy asked.

"I want to talk to Alicia Freed first." Bonnie said, looking up at her as she mopped up the last of the puddle. "We should get going 'cause I want to see her."

Bonnie gathered the different piles from the table, placing each one in a separate paper bag, then stashed the small bags in a cloth bag. After a quick breakfast and shower, Shawn and Bonnie, being the quicker of the two couples, waited in the living room for Terry and Amy. The door to the lower bedroom opened and Amy appeared in the doorway, then sat in the easy chair waiting for her husband.

"I thought men were supposed to be the ones waiting for women," Amy said, after several minutes, and turning to Shawn and Bonnie. "What could be taking him so long? He was almost ready to go when I came out of the room."

Terry appeared in the doorway with a puzzled look on his face. "Have you seen my car keys?" he asked. "They were right here on the dresser last night." Amy suddenly remembered seeing the metallic glint before the blood volcano earlier that morning.

"Check the trunk." Amy said.

"How can I check the trunk without my keys. The trunk is locked."

"Not the trunk on the car, the one in the dining room." Amy laughed.

"Why? Did you put them in there?"

"No," Bonnie answered for Amy, her tone very serious. "He did. Robert."

Terry turned wordlessly and walked into the dining room. He didn't know what to say, so he said nothing. The remaining three rose to follow him. Terry bent to pick his keys up from the trunk, then retracted his hand quickly as if a snake were coiled in the bottom, ready to strike.

"Oh my lord! Look at this!" Terry exclaimed.

At the bottom of the trunk sat Terry's car keys. The inside and bottom of the trunk was covered in blood, yet there was not even as much as a drop on the keys. Bonnie bent to retrieve them.

"He's trying to tell us something," Bonnie said, handing them to Terry.

"But what?" Amy asked.

"I think he wants us to go and see Alicia Freed."

"Well," said Shawn, "let's not keep her, or him, or whoever waiting."

Soon the two couples were on the road, heading for Rhinewood.

# CHAPTER 36

Terry walked up to the little window in the lobby of the Rhinewood Mental Institute. The rest of them stood behind him. A short time after he rang the bell, a young black man dressed in surgical greens appeared.

"May I help you?"

The young man's words almost angered Amy. He sounded so robotic and smarmy. *What's wrong with this guy? Are we such an imposition on his life that he has to treat us like we crawled in from under the door? What a jerk!*

"Yes, we would like to see Alicia Freed," Terry stated.

The man looked as if Terry had just asked to borrow his car. "Just a minute sir, I will have to check with the hospital administrator. We normally don't allow any unannounced visitors to the patients."

"What was that all about?" Shawn asked. "He acts like this is Fort Knox."

The young man turned and disappeared from view without a word. The two couples took seats in the lobby. After several minutes the grey metal door opened and a short, stocky man with dark hair and mustache came into the lobby.

"I'm Corey Brennan, the hospital administrator. What can I do for you?"

Terry and Shawn stood. "We would like to see Alicia Freed," Shawn asked.

"Are you relatives?"

"No sir," Terry answered.

"What is this regarding?"

Bonnie rose and walked to Brennan. "Please, we really need to see her."

"Why?" Brennan folded his arms across his chest.

"We moved into a house that used to be hers. There's been some strange things going on there. We think she can help us."

"What sort of things?" Brennan became interested.

Bonnie felt him softening. "We found some papers in an old trunk. We think she needs to see them, maybe she could help shed some light on who they belong to."

Brennan stood in silence for a moment, sizing up the situation. *These kids seem harmless enough. I'm not sure what this young woman was talking about, but visitors might do Alicia some good. There certainly are enough strange things going on here at the hospital. What with the death of Patrick Freeman, and all its bizarre circumstances, the diversion may do us all some good.*

"If you'll wait here," he said after a short time, "I'll check with her doctor. If he says she can see you, then I'll go along with that. But you have to understand, normally we only allow immediate family visitation to our patients. But since she's in our convalescent wing, and in consideration of our other patients there, I can only allow you a short visit. Maybe an hour, maximum."

The four sat in the lobby in silence as if waiting for a courtroom verdict. After what seemed an eternity, but in reality, only several minutes, an older black man opened the grey metal door.

"Hello. Are you four the ones to see Alicia Freed?" the man asked.

The four rose almost in unison.

"Yes." Terry stated.

"My name is Nathan Powell. I help to take care of her. If ya'll will follow me, I'll take ya to her." Nathan turned, holding the door half open until Shawn reached it and opened the door the rest of the way. Nathan silently led the two couples down a hallway, past the open doors of some offices.

As they walked by the closed door of Corey Brennan's office, Bonnie could see the engraved plastic sign on the door. They headed for a set of metal double doors with bars mounted over the windows, that said: "Secure Area–Authorized Personnel Only" in bold red letters. Just before the security doors, they made a right turn at the intersection of a perpendicular hallway, their footsteps echoing off the white, square tile floor. When they reached the end of the long hall, Nathan stopped at a nurse's station to talk to the woman sitting in a chair behind the station. Amy was thinking how this part of the institution looked like any other convalescent hospital.

"Is Alicia still in the dining room?" he asked the nurse.

The nurse nodded. "She's been in there since breakfast."

"This way ya'll," Nathan said, turning to the group, then led them into a large room at the end of another intersecting corridor. Several tables and chairs were scattered throughout the huge room in no discernable pattern. At a table next to a large picture window overlooking a large expanse of grass before a view of rolling hills, sat the sole inhabitant of the large room; an elderly woman. Nathan stopped at the door, gesturing for the group to enter. They filed past him. Nathan smiled at Amy, the last to enter the dining room, then left. The two couples approached her from behind as Alicia looked out the window.

"Stop!" she commanded. Her tone was gentle, but firm. "Stop where you are."

Silently, the two couples complied, but looked at each other, puzzled.

"Is there a young lady among you with auburn hair and hazel eyes?" Alicia asked without turning to see.

"Yes." Bonnie replied as the color drained from her face and the hair on the nape of her neck stood up.

"Do you have a boyfriend or husband who's tall, with blonde hair?"

"Yes, my husband." Bonnie's voice was dry, and she could barely get the words out. She swallowed hard. The four looked at each other. *How could this woman know what we look like? Could Sheriff Salter have described us to her?* Bonnie's fear and trepidation began to give way to a faint understanding as she remembered how she felt the first time one of her premonitions came true. How unsettling it was to see visions, or flashes, then try to interpret the images into something that made sense, with only her intuition to temper her judgment.

Alicia exhaled and trembled. Meeting someone whom she had seen in a dream was a new experience. Half of her wanted to tell the young people to go away and leave her alone, and the other half felt determined to go on. Her heart beat furiously in her chest.

"Is there another couple with you, child?" Alicia's voice was audibly shaking.

"Yes."

"Does he have dark hair and brown eyes?"

"Yes."

"And her. Does she have blonde hair and blue eyes?"

"Yes."

"Oh, lord!" Alicia placed a trembling hand over her mouth. "Come here, please."

Bonnie walked as carefully as if she were walking on eggshells into Alicia's view. Alicia sat with her eyes closed as if too afraid to see.

Slowly, she opened them, instantly recognizing Bonnie as the young woman in her dream. "What is your name?"

"Bonnie. Bonnie Bricker."

"And your husband?"

"Shawn."

"Who are your friends?"

"Terry and Amy Lambert. The four of us are renting your house." The four took seats around the table at which Alicia sat.

"I'm sure you all know who I am. I'm Alicia. The house that you live in was built by my family, just before the Civil War."

"That's what we want to talk to you about," Terry offered.

"Oh no, honey!" Alicia let out a laugh. She felt better about the situation the more she talked to these obviously nice young people. "You're not here about the house at all. No, you're here about S'postu."

Bonnie felt a chill go up her spine. Amy got goose bumps. Shawn looked at Terry with his mouth open. Terry didn't know what to think.

Alicia leaned back in her chair waiting for someone to say something.

"S'postu?" Bonnie asked after the shock had passed.

"Yes," Alicia smiled. She was elated that after all these years, there was someone to talk to about S'postu besides Nathan or some shrink, patronizing her.

Bonnie became more and more comfortable with Alicia with each passing second. It was as if the two shared an unspoken bond.

"I feel like I know you, Miss Freed," Bonnie stated.

"Call me Alicia. And yes, I get the same feeling."

Amy leaned forward from across the table. "Alicia?"

She turned to her, raising her eyebrows, urging her to continue.

"I was wondering…"

"Yes."

"Why are you here?"

Alicia looked down at the table with sad eyes. "I hurt someone." After a short pause, Alicia narrowed her eyes at Amy. "That sure was an abrupt question, young lady. What made you ask such a thing right off the bat?" She wasn't angry with her question, just curious.

"I–I don't know. It doesn't seem right, I mean you're such a nice person and all, you know, to be stuck in here." Amy stumbled over her words, realizing what a crass question she had asked.

"How do you know that I'm so nice?"

"I can tell, that's all," Amy tried to redeem herself.

"Oh yeah?" Alicia laughed softly. "Ask Charles Westchester how nice a person I am."

Bonnie's eyes grew wide, the color drained from her face.

"What's wrong, honey?" Alicia said, half laughing, "Did you just see a ghost?" She had no idea why she felt so giddy.

Bonnie shook her head.

"Who is Charles Westchester?" Terry asked.

"It's really a long story. Maybe I'll tell it to you. But not now, I'm not ready for that just yet. I think we should start with ya'll. What brought you to me?"

"We rented the house in September," Terry explained, "and ever since we did, Bonnie has been having dreams, well, at first she couldn't remember them. But then we found the French doors in the loft…"

"You found them? So you are the ones who woke up S'postu. Well, it actually makes perfect sense. I suppose I owe you for it. When did you put them up?"

"Last Sunday night," Amy answered.

"The week before last?"

"Yep," Shawn answered. He had to say something.

"And that's the night I woke up, too. And the night Patrick Freeman died. How interesting. Sorry, I didn't mean to interrupt you. Please go on."

"Well," Bonnie explained, "ever since then I have been able to remember my dreams, and my headaches went away. There has really been some weird stuff going on at the house."

"Like what?"

"Like a puddle of blood that forms right next to the dining room table."

Alicia went pale. The mention of the blood brought back vivid memories of the dreams with her dying in the wheelchair.

"What were the dreams you remembered?" Alicia's voice was dry.

Bonnie went on to describe in graphic detail the dreams about Robert at the clearing, then in the living room and dining room. Alicia described her dreams. They concluded that both Alicia and Bonnie were having different perspectives on the same event, obviously a murder that took place long ago.

"Oh!" Bonnie said, suddenly remembering the old trunk. "We found an old trunk behind a false wall in the attic. It had a bunch of papers in it. We were hoping you could tell us more about who these people in the letters were."

"Bonnie," Alicia began, "I don't mean to change the subject, but are you trying to say that S'postu is this Robert?

"It sounds to me like he is," Amy added.

Alicia looked at the rest of the group, who nodded their heads in agreement. "But the question is, who is Robert? And how do I fit into this?"

"That's what we need to find out," Bonnie said, placing the cloth sack on the table, removing the paper bags to set them on the table. "And if you can tell us something about the people in these letters, maybe we can find out." Bonnie opened the bag with the blood stained papers to hand them to Alicia.

"What happened to them?" Alicia asked, noticing the stains.

"You don't want to know," Amy said firmly.

Alicia smiled and opened the letter on the top of the pile. Where ever her fingers touched the paper, the bloodstains disappeared.

Alicia read: "'Witnesseth hereto on this tenth day of January in the year of our lord, Eighteen hundred and sixty-five by the Reverend Henry Trenton Gibson, the matrimony of David Allen Westchester to Daphne Beatrice Nelson on this day.'"

"My God," Alicia gasped, "Charles Westchester must be my kin! What have I done? What has S'postu made me do?" Alicia began to cry.

Bonnie went around the table and held her against her shoulder. The other three looked on, not knowing what to say, only feeling awkward. Alicia stopped crying and Bonnie wiped away Alicia's tears with a gentle stroke of her finger.

"Who is Charles Westchester?" Bonnie asked softly.

"He is a nice man who I stabbed. S'postu made me do it. He sort of took over my body. I stabbed him on his front porch."

"Did you kill him?"

"Oh no! Thank God and all the angels in heaven. No, I only wounded him, which was bad enough."

"So," Amy asked, "who is S'postu?"

"His name is Robert Howe," Bonnie answered. "I'm sure of that. And I'm also certain that Charles Westchester ain't kin to you."

"Okay, then," Amy said. "Who is Robert Howe?"

"He's the guy in both mine and Alicia's dreams. Which means this David Allen Westchester is someone else, and not S'postu. We just gotta find out how."

"Have you noticed," Shawn suddenly spoke up, "that the only letters and papers that are bloodstained by Amy's volcano, are the ones that David's name is mentioned in?"

A surprised look, like 'why didn't I think of that?' appeared on Alicia's face. To test the theory, she opened another letter. It was one that hadn't been opened by anyone sitting at the table, and it was also the one with the most blood on it. Alicia read:

"'My Dearest David, I am writing this to you in great haste as Robert has announced to me his intention to fight in the war. To my surprise, I am not upset at the thought of him not returning. My thoughts are only of you. I cannot wait to be in your arms again and without the cloak of darkness to conceal our love. He said he would be leaving on Monday next. Then I will be rid of him. You may come to the house then. I am looking forward to your arrival. All my love, Daphne.'"

"Hearing that makes me sick to my stomach!" Bonnie announced. Alicia thumbed through the rest of the small stack. All of them were letters between David and Daphne.

"Well," Amy asked, "then what happened to Robert Howe?" Alicia and Bonnie's eyes widened at the same time.

"We know," they said in unison.

"Well. What?"

"Does this have anything to do with the blood that keeps forming on the dining room floor?" Terry asked.

"Yes, blood. You mentioned blood before. Tell me about it." Alicia said.

"Well," Terry began, with a chuckle, "Amy found it first, with her foot." Amy shot him the death look.

"What happens," Terry continued, his tone turning serious, "is first we hear a muffled sort of a cracking sound, then it sounds like something soft and heavy hits the floor at the end of the dining room table. Then the end chair slides forward a little bit. And after that, that's when this puddle forms. It happens a lot."

"We keep runnin' out of clean towels," Shawn added.

"Worst of all, it happened right in front of that Sheriff."

Alicia put her hand to her mouth and turned pale.

"Oh my God!" she gasped. "I dreamed that! And I was the one killed."

"I dreamed it too," Bonnie said. "But I watched it happen."

"But when it happened to me," Alicia continued, "I was in a wheelchair."

"I don't understand," Amy questioned.

"Look," Bonnie began, "Robert went to the war. I saw it in my dream. But he was shot in the back by two guys in the Union Army. The next thing I saw, was him gettin' hit in the back of the head in the dining room, so hard it sent him flying out of that old wooden wheelchair."

"That's right," Alicia added.

"But who did it?" Amy asked.

"It's pretty obvious, isn't it?" Shawn said. "David did it." The five of them sat in silence, pondering what was just said. Alicia realized for the first time that her grandmother's mother had a hand in someone's murder. The two biggest questions in her mind were, who was the murdered man, and how did all of this connect with her?

"Do you think Charles Westchester could be kin to this David Westchester?" Terry asked.

Alicia suddenly went pale. It made sense to her somehow. She closed her eyes, trying to remember. Something in Terry's question reminded her of her old blue Pontiac. But what? Her mind drifted back some fourteen years ago as she sat on the side of the road, before completing the journey to Charles Westchester's house.

"Remember what I felt from his blood," she suddenly said aloud, reaching to touch her hand to the back of her head.

"What?" Bonnie asked.

"That's what S'postu said to me when he made me hurt that man. I didn't want to do it. I didn't even know him. His name just popped into my head, then I felt this overwhelming urge to find him and kill him. But after a while, I realized I was feeling S'postu's feelings. Anyway, what he said to me makes sense, now."

"But, where is Robert Howe?" Amy asked. "I mean what did they do with him?"

"Do you think they sent him to Atlanta?" Shawn asked.

"I told you before, Shawn," Bonnie shot back, "that article was a load of crap. I'll bet Daphne told that to the paper, so no one would look for Robert. And so Daphne and David could get married and live in the house that was built for her and Robert. You know the families would have wanted to know where he was. "

"What do you mean?" Alicia wrinkled her forehead.

"I had a dream that I saw Robert's father and Daphne's father talking about the construction of the house. And Daphne's father was saying something about how Daphne didn't really like Robert that much. And from what I saw, Daphne's father was going to make her marry Robert. The house was like a wedding present. You know, a dowry."

"I'll bet," Terry spoke up, "that they threw Robert down a well."

"What?" Bonnie asked.

"Remember you told us a couple of days ago about the dream you had where the little boy that fell down the well?"

"Yeah, so?"

"You said it was Robert, didn't you?"

"Yeah."

"Well, I bet they threw him down a well. And the dream you had was trying to tell you where he is."

"I don't know. Somehow that doesen't seem right."

"Well, it makes perfect sense to me," Shawn added.

"As I recall, there is an old well behind the out house," Alicia said.

Bonnie eyed her husband. "I don't think these two need any encouragement to go climbing down some old well. Once these two start cave climbing, or something like that, that's all we hear about for weeks. And you know how I hate dirty, slimy caves."

Shawn shot her a Cheshire cat grin.

Nathan Powell walked over to the table. No one at the table knew how long he might have been standing there silently listening to the conversation, or if he had just walked into the room.

"Folks," he began, "ya'll are gonna have to leave now. It's fixin' to be lunch time and we need this room for the patients. Besides, Mr. Brennan says that ya'll gotta leave now. If Miss 'licia feels okay tomorrow, ya'll can see her some more then."

Alicia looked up at Nathan. "So soon?"

"I'm afraid so, Miss 'licia."

The four young people stood, said their goodbyes, and followed Nathan to the lobby.

# CHAPTER 37

"What a nice 'ol lady," Amy said as she slid into the back seat of the Cavalier.

"We'll need to come back tomorrow, to talk to her some more," Bonnie said.

On the trip back to the house, Terry and Shawn were unusually quiet. Bonnie knew they were planning something. She could feel the tension as they tried to conceal their excitement over whatever it was they were scheming; something she was sure she wouldn't like.

"Do we have enough rope?" Bonnie heard Shawn ask Terry in a whisper, barely audible above the road noise in the moving car. Terry nodded almost undetectably. Bonnie narrowed her eyes at the two men in the front seat.

"You need to find a tall tree, too," Bonnie said angrily.

Shawn turned around to face her. "What?"

"You know damn well what! I'll use that rope you're talking about to string the two of you up with."

"What do you mean?" Shawn asked as sheepishly as he could muster.

"Don't you lie to me Shawn Michael Bricker. Have you forgotten that I can tell when you're lying? And I can tell–you're lying."

Shawn knew she was right.

"We gotta see if he's down there," Terry said.

"So the two of you have decided that you're going rock climbing down a well?"

"It seems like the thing to do, doesn't it?"

"No."

"Oh, let them try," Amy said.

Bonnie glared at her friend. "I suppose you want to go, too!"

"Not necessarily. That's a guy thing. I'll do what I do best."

"And what is that?"

"What you do best—straw boss!"

Terry and Shawn burst out in laughter. Then, when Amy could no longer keep a straight face, she began to laugh. Finally Bonnie laughed too.

"Well," Bonnie began, still chuckling, "I guess if you're real careful."

"Maybe he'll be down there." Amy said solemnly.

Bonnie turned her head to look out the window at the passing countryside. They were passing through a stand of trees. Her feelings were mixed between the excitement of finding Alicia's "S'postu" and sadness over the thought of him being murdered.

"Maybe. But I don't think so," she said quietly to herself. They completed the trip back to the house in silence.

"I think this is it," Shawn yelled to Terry. He was pointing to a sunken section of ground some twenty yards behind the old outhouse. Terry went over to see.

"See how the ground is sunken in a circle?"

The grass over the sunken section was thicker within the circle, indicating a higher moisture content of the immediate area. Terry handed Shawn a shovel, and the two began to dig. After a short while, Shawn dug the point of his shovel into something perhaps two feet down.

"We found something!" Terry yelled back to the house. Shawn bent to smooth away the dirt with his gloved hand. The footsteps of Bonnie and Amy could be heard as they ran across the dry, winter grass, crunching under their feet.

"What is it, Shawn?" Terry asked.

"I think it's wood," Shawn looked up at his friend. Terry's eyes grew wide.

"Get off!" he yelled. Without thinking, Shawn jumped out of the shallow hole.

"Why?"

"So you don't fall in, that's why," Bonnie panted as she reached her husband.

"That's wood, buried in the ground," Terry explained. "Termites could have made an early lunch out of those boards, and once we got the dirt from off the top of them, you might fall through. And there's no tellin' how deep this well is."

"What about the dirt that's on top of the wood? Why doesn't it fall through if those boards have been munched?" Shawn asked.

Terry laid on his belly, on the ground, hanging his head and upper torso over the edge to examine the old planks more closely. "Oh," he explained, "it looks like these boards have been soaked in creosote."

Shawn gingerly slid back into the hole, and continued to clear off the wooden planks with his shovel until he reached the ends of each board. The perimeter of the hole grew to eight feet or so in diameter. The two men cleared the remaining dirt off the boards. Both laid on their bellies on the ground above to grab one of the four-inch thick boards and lifted it out of the hole, revealing a large hole underneath lined with bricks. After removing the rest of the wooden planks, they could see four steel I-beams resting on top of the bricks to hold them up.

"How deep do you think it is?" Amy asked, handing her husband a flashlight.

"No tellin'," he answered, as he switched on the light to illuminate the well.

Terry, Shawn, and Amy bent to peer inside. Bonnie only stood staring off at the horizon with her arms folded across her chest. Terry stood, removed his right glove, and dug in his pants pocket to produce a quarter.

"We'll flip, to see who gets lowered in." Shawn stood.

"I call heads," Shawn said.

Bonnie looked at Amy, rolling her eyes in her head. "Men!"

Terry flipped the coin. It tumbled in the air as if in slow motion. It hit the ground, landing heads up. "Best two out of three," he said, bending to pick the coin up from the ground.

"No way. What's fair is fair. I get to go in. You get to pull me out."

"Isn't that just like a couple of guys? Arguing to see who gets to go down a hole in the ground!" Bonnie said indignantly.

"Hey," Shawn began, "this isn't just any hole–this one is ours!"

"I have a question." Bonnie announced. Both men looked at her but remained silent. "How are you going to lower him in? By yourself?"

"What do you mean?"

"I mean, how are you going to lower him in the well? Your not strong enough to do it by yourself. And if you drop him there'll be two ghosts around this house."

Terry looked at Shawn. *Oh shit! Now that's a good point.* Suddenly, Terry's eyes grew wide.

"Shawn, why don't you back the El Camino over here. We can tie the rope to the trailer hitch, then a loop at the other end. You can put your foot in the loop, after we hang the rope over the side, then Bonnie or Amy can back up, lowering you into the well. When you want to come up, all she's gotta do is drive forward, and you get a free ride to the top," Terry smiled, "Brilliant, huh?"

Shawn smiled. He liked the idea. Amy thought it was okay.

"On one condition," Bonnie said. "Terry, you gotta be the one to lower him in with the car."

"Me? Why me? I think I should direct."

"You're not Steven Spielberg. You're more like, I don't know, maybe Richard Petty. You drive."

"You better do it, Terry," Shawn chimed in, "or she'll have a screamin' duck fit."

Terry looked at his wife.

"Don't look at me, Terry!" Amy said, "I'm sittin' this one out. I'm not really sure what a screaming duck fit is, but whatever it is, it's probably not good. So, you're on your own."

"Trust me," Shawn informed, "it ain't a pretty sight."

"It ain't," Bonnie added, smiling.

Shawn tied a loop at the end of the half-inch diameter rope, large enough for his foot to comfortably fit. He fished in his pants pocket for his car keys, then threw them to Terry. Terry jogged over to the El Camino, and backed it near the well. The girls stood by, watching the men.

"Do you sense if Shawn is in any danger?" Amy asked Bonnie.

"No. I don't think so."

"Do you think there is a body down there?"

"I doubt it."

"Then why are you letting Shawn go down there without a fight?"

"Because everyone else seems to think he's down there, and everyone won't be happy until the well is checked out, so why not?"

Terry got out of the car and tied the rope to the trailer hitch. Then he slid behind the wheel of the El Camino to pull it forward, taking up the slack in the rope. Shawn threw the other end over the edge of the well, knelt on the edge to fit his right foot through the loop, then stood, allowing the rope to bear his weight. He steadied himself on the edge. He looked up at Bonnie, and nodded for her to direct Terry to back up. She motioned for Terry to reverse. Amy looked on, then handed Shawn the flashlight. Shawn began to descend slowly into the old well, he leaned into the rope, wrapping it around his left arm. With his right, he switched on the flashlight. His head was now below ground level. Stale, musty air filled his nostrils. The sound of the exhaust pipes of the El Camino faded to the sound of gently running water. As he was lowered further down, bits of brick and dirt fell past him, hitting the water below. The sound echoed off the cylindrical walls. About ten feet down, the brick walls gave way to hard mud, or plaster, Shawn couldn't tell which. He pointed the beam of the flashlight below him. Fifteen feet below, on an outcropping of rock just above the tiny stream of flowing water, several dingy brown bones reflected in the beam of light.

"Stop!" he yelled. His voice sounded detached and amplified at the same time as it echoed off the sheer walls of the well. Bonnie instantly motioned for Terry. The rope jerked to a sudden halt.

"What?" Bonnie shouted down the well. Her voice, likewise, echoed off the walls. "What is it? What do you see?"

Shawn looked up. He could see the two silhouettes of his wife and Amy as they peered down into the well.

"There's some bones down here," Shawn called back.

"I knew it!" Amy exclaimed.

Bonnie looked at her friend and began to question her own senses. Were Amy and the rest of them right about Robert being hidden in the well? Could that be why it was covered up and not in use?

"I hate to disappoint you, Amy, but I…bring me a little lower, I can't see too well."

Bonnie motioned for Terry to back up. Shawn again began his slow descent.

"Stop!" he yelled when he was five feet above the outcropping.

The sound of running water almost completely dominated his hearing. The rope jerked to a stop again. He examined the bones more closely, and began to recognize the shape.

"What is it, Shawn?" Bonnie yelled.

Shawn was surprised at how, just a few feet further down the well shaft, Bonnie's voice was obscured under the sound of the running water. He could barely understand her.

"I think it's a deer," Shawn yelled up the shaft. "Bring me up. There's nothing down here but water."

Bonnie shot Amy the "see, I told you so" look, then motioned for Terry to pull the El Camino forward.

The rope lurched, and Shawn found himself slowly ascending to the top of the well.

# CHAPTER 38

Doctor Jerry Adcox stood next to Alicia's bed after having finished his examination. She had her face turned away from his as she looked at the orange, late afternoon sun filtering in through her bedroom window.

"I said, why do you think you have gotten so much better, so quickly?"

Alicia heard her new doctor, but wasn't really paying attention to what he was saying. She thought of the sunroom in her old house. The view from her window served as a constant reminder. Her mind was on her newfound friends. And, of course, S'postu.

"What?" she turned to him.

"Why do you think you have gotten so much better, so quickly?" Adcox repeated a third time.

"Why are you asking me?" Alicia's eyes widened. "You're the doctor."

"Yes I know, but I want to find out what you think about this—this—unusual occurrence."

Alicia looked him squarely in the eye. "Isn't it obvious? I am no longer being pumped full of dope, and my head is beginning to clear. And my new friends, the Bricker's and the Lambert's; they're so young and full of life, it almost makes me feel like a kid again."

"And that's why you think you've made such a fast recovery?" Alicia only turned away to gaze out her bedroom window. She was mildly upset with him and felt he was patronizing her, something she loathed. "I think they're coming back tomorrow," she said suddenly. "You need to let me see them. There's some unfinished business that they're help-ing me with."

"What kind of unfinished business?"

"It's personal."

"I'm not sure I can authorize for you to have visitors unless I know the nature of the visit."

"Why?"

"I wouldn't want these people to say something that might cause a relapse."

"Don't worry about that. It concerns my kin, and the man I hurt—the reason that I'm in here in the first place. So don't give me any of your—oh, what do you call it? Oh yes, psychobabble!"

Adcox laughed. "I just want to see what your perspective is on all this, that's all."

"Doctor?"

"Yes?"

"Will you send Nathan in here with my dinner? I don't want to eat in the dining room. I think I need to be alone for a spell."

Adcox looked at his patient. He couldn't see any reason to deny her request. "Okay, Alicia. I'll send him in." He rose and left Alicia alone.

The late afternoon sun backlit scattered puffy clouds dotting the sky, their edges bathed in fiery red, framing their darker centers. Alicia sighed at the sight.

Corey Brennan was pouring over employee records when a rap sounded at the door. "Come in," he called.

The door opened and Jerry Adcox appeared. "Do you have a minute?"

"Sure. Sit down."

Adcox sat in a chair next to the door across Brennan's desk, then leaned over to swing the door shut.

"What can I do for you, doctor?" Brennan asked.

"I just wanted to give you a report on Alicia Freed before you left this evening."

Brennan looked at his watch. He hadn't realized it was so late. "What's up with her?"

"She genuinely seems to be doing well. I have never seen anyone make such a recovery after the amount of time she has been bedridden. It's almost as if it never happened. Do you know that she can walk normally now, without the aid of her walker at all?"

"Wow!"

"But there's something else…"

"What?"

"Her mind is ticking away at something. I think it's those kids that came to see her earlier today. They got her involved in something…but I can't get her to tell me what. She has an incredible will. Anyway, whatever it is, it seems to be helping her. So, I think she should be allowed to have those people visit her. The interaction will do her good." Adcox paused for a moment. "You know, if this keeps up, I can actually see her being released in the not too distant future."

"That's amazing!" Brennan's eyebrows shot up. He was pleased with the news.

"I just thought you'd like to know."

"Thank you. It actually does my heart good to see that this woman, who has been getting the shaft all these years, might make it after all." Brennan extended his hand. The two men shook, then Jerry Adcox left the office.

"That was wonderful, Nathan." Alicia wiped her mouth with the paper napkin.

"I'm glad you enjoyed your dinner, Miss `licia. Now tell me what's going on with your new friends."

"I think we're about to find out who S'postu is."

"I thought you already knew who he is."

"I *think* he's kin to me. Remember I told you about my dream where I was shot in the Civil War?"

"Yeah."

"And then I was killed in my dining room?"

"Yeah?"

"Well, I think I was living his memories. And Bonnie, that's one of the young ladies who was here today, she had the same dream. Only in her dream, she saw it all happen as if she was watchin' a movie."

"That's a queer thing!"

"I think S'postu can somehow talk to her, she's real sensitive to that sort of thing even though she's not kin. See, that's why I think he talks to me. He's got to be kin to me. And something else, he was done dirty like I was. But, and I hate to say this, but I think my great grandmother had a hand in killin' him. I'm not for sure, but I think it."

Nathan listened to what she was saying with interest. *Well, she's not under the influence of Thorazine, and she's coherent. She must be telling me the truth—at least the truth as she sees it. I haven't seen any evidence to support what she is saying, but as long she believes it and is happy, who am I to burst her bubble?*

Terry and Amy watched their friends ascend the staircase on their way to bed from the sofa.

"Wait here, babe," Terry said softly. He rose from the sofa, heading for their bedroom. Upon crossing the threshold, he felt the now familiar drop in temperature. He turned on the light on Amy's bedside table and exited the bedroom, leaving the door cracked open, then turned off all the lights in the downstairs of the house. Amy watched silently as he knelt before the fireplace to start a fire. With the firelight flickering dancing shadows on the living room wall, he turned the stereo on low and rejoined his wife on the sofa.

"Are you feeling frisky tonight?" Amy giggled softly. Terry nuzzled his wife's neck, sending electric shivers up her spine.

"It's just been a long time since we sat in the dark and listened to music."

"Is that all you wanna do is listen to music?" Amy whispered in his ear, then gently bit his lobe.

Terry laughed softly. "What do you think?"

"Ooh, I like it already." They kissed. The music played softly in the background. The room glowed from the firelight. Then, without warning, what sounded like someone pounding on the front door broke their mood.

"What the hell was that?" Amy demanded. Her heart pounded in her chest. The last thing she expected was a knock at the front door. She was both afraid and angry.

"I don't know, I'll see." Terry went over to see what was going on. As he opened the door, the cold mid-winter air whipped around his legs, making him shiver. He looked out on the front porch but could see no one. After closing and locking the door, he walked back to the sofa with a puzzled look on his face. "There's no one out there."

"What was that noise, then?"

"I don't know."

"I'm sorry, Terry," Amy said sadly, "but my mood has evaporated."

"I can believe that. So did mine." Terry turned off the stereo. "C'mon babe, lets go to bed."

Amy rose and followed him into the bedroom.

Shawn lay awake next to Bonnie as she fidgeted in her sleep. He was still keyed up after his trip down the well. Just thinking about it sent adrenalin rushing through his body. The anxiety he felt when he first spotted the deer bones left him with a whole new perspective *What would I have done if there actually was a body in there? Would I have been scared? Yeah, I'd probably have been scared.* He looked at his wife. *What could she be dreaming about now?* She had such a desperate look on her face. Shawn suddenly became angry. Sleep was supposed to be restful, even an escape from reality, from the pressures of life, not to be forced to endure the pain of another. Yet, he felt, that is what was happening to Bonnie. He snuggled next to his wife, wrapping his arms around her hoping to calm her. It seemed to work. He felt a sudden sense of relief as her fidgeting quieted. He lay with his head touching hers to try to feel what she was feeling, to see what she was seeing, but the only thing that came to Shawn Bricker was sleep.

The voices of Amy and Terry faded as Bonnie peered over the edge of the well watching Shawn descend. Suddenly, she was in the well, looking up at the other three. Yet she was going lower and lower. Who was backing the El Camino? It didn't matter. The opening of the well was far above her now, and the silhouettes of her husband and friends were mere dots against the blue sky. Her feet came to rest on muddy ground. Bonnie stepped out of the loop in the rope. It was dark at the bottom of the well, yet she could see. The things around her were like the shadows in a dimly lit room. She stood at the muddy edge of an underground creek in a vast cave. Above her, at eye level, she could hear a sort of clicking sound; like the sound of two pieces of dry wood striking each other. Looking up, she could see the bones of a deer assembling themselves before her eyes. Bonnie reared back in fear and amazement. The skeletal outline jumped from the outcropping. She tried to scream, but nothing came from her mouth. The skeleton bent it's head as if to drink from the creek, then jumped across the creek and ran out of sight. She turned around to get to the rope, and ran into someone. Strong hands grasped her shoulders, pushing her away from him, yet his grip retained her, holding her at arms length.

"You found my child. Tell her who I am." It was Robert. He was pleading. With each word he spoke came a rush of putrid odor. Bonnie turned away, to avoid the foul breath. Her shoulders were released. She turned back, and found herself standing alone. Bonnie threaded a muddy foot into the loop at the end of the rope, and found herself ascending the well shaft. As she neared the top, she could no longer see the sky. It had been replaced with wooden girders supporting planks. It looked to Bonnie like the underside of a floor. The rope seemed to be passing through the floor as if it weren't there. Her head was almost in contact with the boards. She pounded the planks with her fists.

"Let me out! Let me out!" she yelled. The rope pulled her up against the wooden structure, crushing her against it.

Bonnie bolted upright in bed. Shawn sat up to turn on the bedside light. Bonnie looked at her husband with tears in her eyes.

"Are you okay?" he asked tenderly, reaching to embrace her.

"It was awful." Shawn released her, looking for some relief on her face. Bonnie suddenly realized how thirsty she was, and threw the covers off to get a drink. As she stepped onto the floor, her foot slipped. She landed on the floor and looked at her feet. They were covered with mud!

"Oh my God!" Shawn exclaimed. "There's mud all over the bed where your feet were!" Shawn slid out of bed, threw his arm around her, and helped her downstairs.

Amy and Terry awoke to their bed jumping up and down. The sound of forceful pounding under the floor caused the bed to bounce off the floor. They jumped out of bed and ran into the living room.

"What the hell was that?!!" Amy shrieked. Terry turned on the light. Shawn and Bonnie thumped down the stairs.

"I don't know. But whatever it was, it scared the living shit out of me!" Terry exclaimed.

"She had a bad dream." Shawn said, as he and Bonnie reached the bottom of the stairs. Amy looked down at Bonnie's feet.

"What's all over your feet?"

"It's mud, at least that's what it looks like," Shawn answered.

"What was she doing outside? Terry asked.

"I thought I slipped on something on the floor."

"That mud was on the sheets," Shawn said.

Bonnie looked at Amy. "Why are you two up?"

Amy looked at her friend in surprise. She had almost forgotten what woke her and Terry. "It was the weirdest thing. It was like there was someone pounding under our floor so hard it made our bed jump."

Shawn looked in their bedroom. "It doesn't look like it's jumping now."

"Very funny Shawn, you know damn well we're not lying," Amy snapped.

Bonnie walked over to the sofa and sat down. Little balls of dried mud left a trail where she walked. "I just had a dream about–well that it was me who was lowered into the well," Bonnie began, "and when I was brought back up, it was like someone had built a floor over the top and I couldn't get out. I pounded on the underside for someone to let me out."

"How many times?" Terry asked.

"What?"

"How many times did you pound?"

"Twice."

Amy looked at Terry. "That's how many times our bed jumped." Amy was shocked at first, but then, after considering all that had gone on in the last few months, she realized she should have expected it.

Terry looked at the trail of dried mud on the floor.

"When I woke up from that dream, my feet were covered with it."

"Yeah," Shawn interjected, "it's all in between the sheets where her feet were."

Amy shivered as she turned to Terry. "I'm not sleeping in that room tonight. I'm scared," pointing to the downstairs bedroom.

"I can understand that," Terry nodded his head. "But do you want to just stay up? It's 2:35, and that's a long way till morning."

"I don't think I can stay awake the rest of the night, then expect to be worth a damn tomorrow." Amy sat at the end of the sofa and leaned against its arm. Terry sat between Bonnie and Amy, leaning on his wife, resting his head on her side.

Bonnie rose from the sofa and walked into the dark sunroom, pausing first to touch the French doors. She remembered so clearly the night they had re-installed them. How everything seemed to start the moment they were again part of the house. She entered the sunroom and sat on a small sofa facing the window. Shawn stepped up behind her.

"Do you wanna go back to bed?" he asked tenderly, rubbing her shoulders.

"No. I can't. Nothing like that has ever happened before. In all the time that stuff has happened around here, nothing has ever happened to us. Only around us. It's scary. I just want to be in here for now. I have always felt a little peace in this room. It's like the eye of the storm."

"We gotta go to bed sometime."

"Yeah. But not now."

Shawn sat beside her. Bonnie leaned her head against his chest, and closed her eyes.

# CHAPTER 39

Alicia tossed in her bed. Restful sleep gave way to the dining room of her home. She wheeled the wheelchair across the hardwood floor into a bedroom off the dining room where the kitchen should be. Somehow, she knew the house was configured this way before a major renovation in the 1920's. She wheeled over to a window to look at some activity near the barn. Moving the flimsy curtain out of the way, she saw a woman with long, straight brown hair, obviously in the last term of pregnancy, talking to a man. She realized the woman was Daphne, and the man, David. Her dream seemed to incorporate facts from the letters she had read, and people as Bonnie had described to her. The woman was laughing and touching the man on the shoulder. Alicia felt jealousy and rage building up inside of her. She couldn't bear to watch, yet couldn't take her eyes off of what was happening outside the window. A shadow moved in the half lit interior of the barn, then the figure of a young boy, perhaps five or six years old, stepped into the sunlight.

"It's just grand!" the young boy said. "That colt will be a fine horse."

"I knew you would want to see it. That's why I brung ya," David said.

Daphne reached over to stroke the blonde locks on the little boy's head. Alicia was now feverish with rage. She flung the curtain back over the window, and turned around quickly with the wheelchair. She knew she couldn't go far, but she knew she couldn't stay and watch Daphne touch HIM! She just had to go where she couldn't see David, or the boy.

Daphne must have caught the movement of the curtains, because the moment Alicia crossed the threshold into the living room, Daphne appeared at the front door. Anger shrouded her face.

"Were ya spyin' on me?" Daphne sneered.

"How could you act like that around him with my child in your belly?"

"Can you be a father? Can you show it how to ride a horse? Load a saddle? No! You're useless. I didn't tell you to go get shot up by them Yankees. That was your own stupidity."

"Who's the boy?" Alicia heard herself ask forcefully in a man's voice.

Daphne paused for a moment. "That's Scotty," she sighed. "David's son. His momma died birthin' him six years ago."

"I ain't never laid eyes on him no way."

"He's been around. Helpin' me when you were away." Daphne crossed her arms across her chest. "The two of them been helpin' me keep this place goin.'" Her face contorted with anger. "I need him now more than ever since you come back—no account," she sneered in a low voice.

Alicia looked to the floor feeling hurt and useless.

"I need a man around here, and around me," Daphne's voice escalated to a shout, "not a no account cripple!" She stomped out of the house.

Alicia sat up in bed, tears streaming down her face.

# CHAPTER 40

The dawn light filtered in through the sunroom windows. Bonnie stirred awake. She had fallen asleep lying on Shawn's chest and was now sore from the contorted position. Shawn's head rested on the back of the sofa, as if looking at the ceiling, with his mouth wide open. Bonnie began to laugh. Shawn opened his eyes and slowly tilted his head forward.

"Oh! I got a stiff neck," he said, rubbing the back of his neck.

"Well it's no wonder, the way you were sleeping," Bonnie chuckled. "I'm surprised you didn't already get breakfast."

"What are you talking about?" Shawn wrinkled his forehead.

"Your mouth was wide open, so you could have had a spider omelette, or maybe a fly waffle." Bonnie broke out in laughter.

"Oh, that's completely disgusting!" Shawn scowled as he rose shakily from the sofa and walked into the living room, holding his hand on his lower back. "God, I feel like I'm 95 years old."

Bonnie followed. The living room was empty, with no sign of Terry or Amy. The only one on the sofa was the sleeping cat.

"Do you think they went back to bed?" Bonnie suggested. Shawn turned to face his wife.

"That's probably what we shoulda done," he replied, rubbing his neck.

The door to the lower bedroom was cracked open, letting in bright shafts of light that sliced through the dim living room. Bonnie thought the bedroom light was on until she knocked, and getting no answer, pushed the door open. She felt the sudden drop in temperature as she stuck her head into the room and looked around as the cold air waved across her face to the back of her head. When the line of cold air reached her temples, she could feel her hair blow back slightly, sending a chill down her spine. The room was empty, save for the furnishings. One-night rose up, hissing. Her calico fur stood on end. She ran into the kitchen as if being chased. Shawn looked at the floor where the little balls of mud had been the night before. The floor was as clean as if the incident never happened.

"Amy must been in one of her famous rare cleaning moods." Shawn announced.

Bonnie pulled her head back into the living room to face her husband. "Why do you say that?"

"The mud is all gone." Shawn headed for the staircase, contemplating the unlikelihood of Amy cleaning up the mud so early in the morning since she was not a morning person. "I wonder–."

"You wonder what?" Bonnie queried as she watched him disappear at the top of the staircase.

"The mud is all gone in the bed!" Shawn called from upstairs.

*Well, I know damn well she didn't clean the mud out of my bed.* She went into the kitchen only to find it empty with the exception of One-night cowering by the back door. Bonnie walked over to the door to let the cat outside and found it unlocked. Shawn appeared at the threshold between the kitchen and the dining room.

"I think they left." Bonnie said. Shawn turned on the light in the dining room, then sat at the table.

"I wonder where they went?"

"I don't know," Bonnie said. "What do you want for breakfast?"

"You mean besides spider omelettes and fly waffles?"

"Yeah," Bonnie laughed.

They heard the familiar whine of the Cavalier as it pulled into the driveway. Bonnie looked out the kitchen window to see Terry and Amy getting out of the car with an armload of white paper bags.

"They're here," Bonnie announced. She opened the back door for Amy and Terry.

"Where were you two?" Bonnie asked.

"We went out for breakfast. Are ya'll hungry?" Terry replied.

"We brought Waffle House," Amy said, placing the bags on the dining room table. "I didn't feel like cooking this morning."

"Amy, did you clean up the mud on the living room floor and my bed?"

"No," Amy replied, as she removed the Styrofoam boxes from the bags to distribute them. "Do you really think I would do such a thing before breakfast? You know I'm not a morning person."

"Not a chance," Terry replied.

They discussed the previous night over breakfast.

# CHAPTER 41

"No, Nathan," Alicia argued, "I don't want to go nowhere today. I wanna stay here."

"But why?" Nathan asked. He wanted to get her out with some of the other patients, thinking the company of others her own age would do her good.

"No. I'm waiting for Bonnie to come by."

"How do you know she will even come?"

"I know she will. She has to. There's still so much to figure out. Besides, I want to find out what happened in the well."

"What well?

"The well out back of my old house. I think that's where he is."

"S'postu?"

Alicia looked at Nathan and smiled. He had finally admitted the presence of S'postu. She knew he couldn't deny it. "So, you finally admit he's real?"

"Well, what choice do I have? It's not only comin' from you, but them younguns too. The way I see it, there's gotta be somethin', even if Doc Adcox don't think so."

"He don't know everything. These shrinks get a theory going in their fool heads and think it's got to be that way. Like it's gospel or something. You know there are things in this world that plain and simple,

286

don't got no explanation. You just gotta believe, that's all. It's just the way it is."

"Sounds to me like you're describing faith."

"You call it whatever you want." Alicia paused for a moment, drew a breath, then narrowed her eyes at him. "Let's do this more–lawyerly. I have described S'postu to you for years. I know you didn't believe me at the time because of all the dope that Dr. Freeman had me on, but you have to see now the evidence brought to us by Bonnie, Shawn and the other two. I ain't never laid eyes on them before. They came to me. You know that's true. You been by my side this whole time, and you know I ain't got no access to the outside. That has got to prove to you I ain't makin' all this up. They didn't know about S'postu until they put up the French doors. Now I know I told you about them French doors."

"Yes, you did."

"Good. Then you can see that there has to be something to what all of us are sayin'. Don't you think those younguns got better things to do than chase around after an old woman like me?"

"Ok, Miss `licia, I can see your point." Nathan looked down at his watch. "Do ya want lunch, or not?"

"Can ya bring it to me? Please?"

Nathan smiled, shook his head and left the room. Alicia knew he would bring it to her. He was only playing hard to get, and she enjoyed the game.

As Nathan passed by the nurse's station on his way to bring Alicia her lunch, Teresa Perry stopped him. "Nathan!"

He stopped to look at her. She was holding a phone receiver, covering the mouthpiece with her palm.

"What?"

"Those young people are here to see Alicia Freed again."

Nathan looked at the tray of food he held. "Okay. Tell `em to wait in the lobby. I'll fetch `em in a bit."

"It's not like they got a lotta choice."

"Huh?"

"Waiting in the lobby, I mean."

"Oh, yeah," Nathan responded with a laugh. As he rounded the corner into Alicia's room, he saw her sitting on the edge of her bed, looking out the window. He paused for a moment in the doorway to watch her. *I wonder what she sees out that window. Is it just the snow outside? Or maybe she's re-living that old Civil War dream she's told me about so many times. It's so hard to tell. All this time, dealing with that voice in her head, which nobody, not even me thought was true. And now it seems like it's true after all, especially when she talks with them younguns.* Over the years, he appeased and humored her, thinking she was influenced by the drugs, or perhaps suffering from psychosis, yet somewhere deep inside he knew she was telling the truth. But logic and common sense had to cover up the unthinkable possibility that a voice from generations past could communicate with the present, so Nathan forced himself to put it out of his mind.

"How long have you been standing there, Nathan?" Alicia asked in a quiet voice without taking her eyes off the window.

Nathan was taken aback. "How did you know I was here?"

"I don't know, I guess I just knew you were watchin' me."

"How?"

"Even when I was in my deepest fog, you know, while Dr. Freeman had me on that dope. I could tell you were there. It's like you were giving me some of your strength to help me through. S'postu couldn't, he was asleep, so it was you."

"Oh. Miss 'licia, what is it you see when you look out that window, anyway?"

Alicia turned to him, her eyes red. It was evident she had been crying. Tears again, welled up in her eyes. "My freedom. I should have been out there long ago. The years I lost are irreplaceable." She hung her head to cry.

Nathan set the tray on her bedside table, then sat next to her on the bed to comfort her. "There, there—," he held her tenderly, "those younguns are here to see you. Do you want them to see you like this?"

"No," she breathed.

"Do ya want me to fetch `em for ya?"

Alicia pulled away and nodded.

"Well, you better dry your tears," Nathan stood, "and eat your lunch, and I'll go git em."

Alicia wiped her eyes, went over to the armchair next to the bedside table, sat down and began to eat. "Thank you, Nathan," she said as she watched him leave the room.

Nathan appeared at the door with the Lamberts and Brickers in tow.

"I'm so glad you came!" Alicia's face brightened. "How's everything at the house?"

They saw how much it meant to Alicia that they'd come back to see her, and were encouraged that they had done the right thing.

Bonnie sat down next to Alicia. "Well, everything has been crazy at the house—but how are you feeling?"

"I guess that makes sense, 'cause I've been having some troubling dreams." Alicia was relieved to say this to someone who really understood what it was like.

"Me, too," Bonnie said, and the two women began to describe in detail for each other their dreams of the night before.

Amy sat in the arm chair swinging her leg and listening, becoming increasingly bored. The two men sat quietly watching and talking among themselves, knowing they needed to be patient while Bonnie and Alicia sorted through all of it.

"Alicia?" Amy interrupted, "I thought there were supposed to be two people in this room."

"Why do you say that?"

"I don't know, it just looks like there should be two beds in here."

"I guess about two months ago, I can't really remember, I was all doped up, the lady that used to be in the bed where your two handsome men are sitting, died. Nathan moved the old bed out and fixed it so I could have my own room."

Alicia and Bonnie continued their conversation. Amy had heard Bonnie's dream earlier in the day and since that was what they were now talking about, she was now totally bored. She began to look around the room for something to do. How could those two men just sit there talking and watching without being bored out of their skulls? Her eyes settled on two newspaper articles that had been cut out of the *Knoxville News Sentinel* and thumbtacked onto the wall opposite the foot of Alicia's bed. Amy, suddenly curious, walked over to delicately remove the thumbtacks, taking the articles from the wall, leaving darker spots where the paint had not faded. Amy guessed the papers had been there, exposed to the evening sun for quite a while, since the edges of the paper were yellowed.

"Let me see that," Terry said, noticing what she was doing.

"Better yet," Shawn said, scooting Amy's armchair next to their's, "why don't you read them to us. That way we can all hear them at the same time."

Bonnie paused from her conversation with Alicia.

"Go ahead, dear," Alicia said.

"'Prominent attorney found dead in office,'" Amy read. "'Knoxville attorney Max Bailey was found shot dead in his office yesterday. Bailey is been noted for his high profile cases, the most recent being the allegations regarding City Councilman Reed Alexander's involvement with the Family Mutual Savings and Loan scandal. There was no connections between the Family Mutual scandal and Bailey's murder, police said. Bailey is survived by his wife, Gloria. They had no children. Funeral services will be held Thursday at the Avondale Baptist Church. All inquires regarding the funeral services should be directed there.'"

"Why do you have this on your wall, Alicia?" Terry asked.

"Read the other one," Alicia said.

"'District Attorney dies in pile-up,'" Amy began. "The early morning fog was blamed for the unusual circumstances surrounding a four-car pile-up on Interstate 40 yesterday morning, police said. Witnesses said a car owned by Deputy District Attorney, Henry Walton suffered mechanical difficulties and stalled under the Main Street bridge and was hit by three other cars as it remained hidden in the fog. Walton was killed instantly according to the coroner's office. The names of the other victims in the crash are being withheld pending notification of the next of kin. Walton is survived by his wife, Melanie, and two sons, Raymond, 18 and Leon, 22. Funeral services will be held at the Knoxville Church of Christ on Tuesday at 10 am.'"

"Those two men," Alicia explained, "are the reason I've been here so long. They swindled my house away from me. I don't normally wish folks dead, but these two, and Patrick Freeman, are the ones who kept me in this place. Max, he was my lawyer, told me he needed my house in trade for his legal services. And like a nitwit, I took the deal. Then he said he worked out a deal with Henry Walton, the prosecutor, and I would only have to spend six months in here as a formality. Then he said when I got out I could work in his office until I worked off my legal fees and I could have my house back. Well, he sure worked out a deal. Those two bastards double-crossed me and sold my house out from under me. And that jerk Freeman kept me doped up in here."

"You mentioned Patrick Freeman before, who was he?" Amy asked.

"He used to be the hospital administrator. But now he's pushin' up daises. In fact, Nathan gave me an article to put up on the wall about him too, but I just ain't put it up yet. I been thinkin' 'bout puttin' them all in a frame together. I think that would be a fittin' tribute to those three shysters."

Terry silently took the papers from Amy to replace them on the wall. As he walked past the end of the bed, he caught his knee on the metal bed frame. He cried out in agony, his leg buckling under the pain. Bonnie whirled around to see Terry grimace.

"Are you alright?" she asked.

Amy rushed to her husband and helped him sit on the edge of the bed as he rubbed his knee. Shawn's attention was not on his friend, but on his wife. Bonnie's eyes grew wide. Shawn could sense that she was putting something together in her mind and smiled in anticipation.

*What does that remind me of? That's so familiar, but what was it? Something Amy did, or was involved in. No, it reminds me of music. Oh my God! The stereo! That was the same knee Terry hit when he was under the house threading the wires. Under that lower bedroom, which is always cold. Why was it cold? What was it he hit his knee on, under there? A rock? No! It was a lump of dirt. Large enough to hide–.* Bonnie's face lit up.

Alicia realized Bonnie knew something. She touched her shoulder, and Bonnie jumped.

"I don't know what you're thinking, child," Alicia whispered, "but I get the feeling that all of a sudden, you know where S'postu is. So go find him. And when you do, look under the kitchen sink. When you find it, you'll know what to do."

Bonnie looked at Alicia with a puzzled look on her face.

"Children," Alicia announced, somewhat sternly, "go on home now. I'm tired."

Shawn had been watching the interaction between Bonnie and Alicia, and knew Alicia's announcement was just something to say to get them to leave.

"I gotta go home…" Bonnie said.

Shawn rose from his chair and helped Terry stand up. They said hurried good-bye's, and left.

A short time after the four left, Nathan stood at the doorway watching Alicia look out the window. Her face was turned away from his. Suddenly, she brought her left hand before her face, and began clenching and unclenching her fist. She turned toward him suddenly, in obvious agony. The color began to drain from her face. She clutched at her chest. It was obvious she had trouble breathing. Her eyes began to roll upward. Nathan ran to her side, grabbing the phone on her bedside table.

"Emergency in Alicia Freed's room! Emergency! Stat!" He yelled into the mouthpiece.

The sound of running footsteps soon echoed off the hall, Nathan could hear the emergency team getting closer to Alicia's room. As the team entered the room, Nathan turned to them helplessly.

"She's in cardiac arrest! Don't let her die..." His words trailed off as he slumped into the chair Shawn had sat in only minutes before. Nathan watched the team work on Alicia, and wept.

# CHAPTER 42

Shawn pulled the Cavalier into the driveway. Terry sat in the passenger side of the front seat, still rubbing his smarting knee. Amy helped Terry into the house, as Shawn followed. About halfway to the back door, he suddenly stopped and turned toward the car. Bonnie still sat inside. Shawn went back, opened the passenger side rear door, where his wife still sat.

"Are you okay?" he asked tenderly. She looked up at him, forced a feeble smile and nodded her head.

"You didn't say one word on the way back. Are you mad about something?"

"No, but I wanna be alone for just a little while. I'll be in there in a minute, okay?"

Shawn kissed her tenderly on the forehead, turned and went into the house. Bonnie watched him disappear inside. After several minutes, she went into the house as well.

Amy was at the sink doing the dinner dishes from the night before when Bonnie walked in. The football game on T.V. could barely be heard over the running water. Bonnie stopped at the sink.

"Are you okay?" Amy asked, turning to look at her.

"Yeah," Bonnie sighed. "I think I know where Robert is..." Her voice sounded to Amy as if she were depressed.

"What's wrong? That should be good news."

"I know. But ever since we left the hospital, I got a feeling that something ain't right."

"Whatdaya mean?"

"I'm not sure, exactly. I kinda feel sick, but it's not like I'm the one who's sick. I hope Alicia is okay."

"Well, she was fine when we left."

"I know.

"Tell me what you mean about where Robert is? Which is where, by the way?"

Bonnie's eyes lit up. "I wanna tell you and the guys together." She turned and headed for the living room.

Amy followed her and shut off the T.V., to the protest of her husband and Shawn.

"I think I know where he's buried," Bonnie began, instantly gaining the men's attention.

"Where?" Shawn asked, eyebrows raised.

"I was thinking, it suddenly hit me at the hospital. When Terry hit his knee on the bed. It kinda makes sense."

"What does?" Terry said, rubbing his knee.

"Why is your room always cold? There has to be a reason. No other room in the house is that cold. According to Alicia, that room was cold back when she owned this house. It has been empty until we got here, but I think it has been cold all this time. The cat will not go in there. Why? I think Robert is buried under that room. Underneath that lump of dirt you hit your knee on when you were under the house wiring up the stereo."

Shawn looked over at Terry. Both men rose from the sofa simultaneously. The look on Shawn's face suggested to Bonnie her theory was well received. After donning their coats, they went outside to investigate. Bonnie went into the dining room and sat at the table.

"Aren't you coming to see?" Amy asked, heading outside herself.

"No. I don't want to see. I'll just wait here."

Amy shrugged and went outside. Going around the corner to the side of the house where her bedroom was, she could see Terry's legs as he disappeared under the house.

"Amy!" Terry's muffled voice wafted from the access door. "Hand me that trowel." Amy bent to pick up the trowel from the ground. Placing it in Terry's protruding hand, she then squatted to try to peer into the blackness under the house. It looked dark and forbidding, sending shivers up her spine.

The darkness absorbed the beam from Shawn's flashlight. He shivered from the intense cold seeping from underneath the downstairs bedroom.

"See how all but the main beam from the flashlight is swallowed up under here?" Terry breathed as he pulled up alongside Shawn.

"It's creepy. You know, I really didn't believe you much after you came out from under here the last time. It kinda has my stomach in knots."

"Kinda?" The two slid themselves to the large mound of earth directly under the center of Terry's room. Terry reached out a gloved hand and began scooping the dirt away.

Bonnie rose from the dining room table and walked to the kitchen phone. Directly under the phone, on the counter, lay the business card of Sheriff Milton Salter. Bonnie picked it up and dialed the number.

With the dirt moved away from a corner of the mound, a hard, dingy white material now lay exposed.

"Is that concrete?" Shawn asked.

"No, I don't think so," Terry answered. "It looks like plaster or something. Besides, I don't think they had concrete back then."

"Sheriff Salter?" Bonnie's voice echoed off the walls of the kitchen, sounding detached and foreign to her.

"Yes."

"This is Bonnie Bricker. I live at Alicia Freed's old house. Do you remember me?"

"Of course."

"I think you need to come over here."

"What's wrong?"

"Please come. Come right now. We've found something...some*one* under the house." Bonnie hung up without saying goodbye and began removing the contents from under the kitchen sink. She spotted the loose board and pulled it up. Bonnie smiled as she pulled out the dusty foil package.

Terry brought the trowel down hard a second time on the hard plaster. This time, the ancient paste cracked. Shawn grabbed the corner and began wrenching it from side to side. Terry stuck the pointed end of the trowel into the crack and began prying, separating the corner from the mass. Slowly, the corner came loose, exposing a skeletal hand.

Alicia sat up in her bed, shaking off the effects of the sedative the emergency team had given her. Seeing her movement from the corner of his eye, Nathan put down his newspaper and went to her side.

"Well now, Miss 'licia, you gave us quite a scare. How do you feel?"

"What happened? Where are the kids?"

"You had a mild heart attack. Doc Adcox says it was probably from stress. He says you should be up..."

"Nathan! Someone touched my hand. That's what woke me up." She brought her right hand to her chest. "It was icy cold..."

Nathan could only look on in surprise, not knowing what to say.

Blue and red beams of light swung around from the sheriffs car, reflecting off the white sides of the house and barn. The Knox County coroner pulled up and removed a heavy black bag from the rear of the station wagon. He took the bag to the back of the house at the access panel, where two deputies were finishing the excavation of the body.

Successive blue and red flashes of light lit up the kitchen from the window overlooking the driveway, giving an eerie backdrop for the four, sitting with Salter at the dining room table.

"Who did you say that is, buried under the house?"

"I said," Bonnie explained, "his name is Robert Howe. He was in the Civil War. He came home a few months later after being shot in the lower back by the Union Army. He was sent home in a wheelchair, and his wife was having an affair with some guy named David. I think it was David who killed him."

"How?"

"He hit him in the back of the head with a hammer or something. Do you remember the last time you came here and saw the blood on the floor?"

"Do I? That was all I could think about for the rest of that day and all of the next."

"Robert was sitting in the living room when he was called into the dining room for supper. David was evidently hiding behind the wall inside the dining room, and as Robert came in this room, David let him have it. He went flying out of the wheelchair and landed here on the floor at the end of the table, leaving a puddle of blood."

Salter swallowed hard; the hair on the back of his neck stood on end.

"Anyway," Bonnie continued, "David and Daphne told everyone, even the newspaper, that Robert had gone to Atlanta for an operation to cure his back. But now it's obvious they buried him under the house. Daphne must have gotten pregnant with Robert's child, conceived the night before he left to go fight in the war. Somehow Alicia's grandmother, who never saw Robert, knew that David was not her father."

"How do you know that?" Salter asked, a bit confused.

"We've been talking to Alicia for a couple of days. We talked about the dreams we've been having, all the weird stuff going on in the house. Basically, we compared notes. She would get some information in a dream, and I would get some other pieces and some of it would be the same. Anyway, David had a son named Scotty from a previous marriage, whose mother died during childbirth. Alicia's grandmother broke all ties with Scotty. And when Daphne died, the house was willed to Alicia's grandmother, who passed it down to Alicia's mother, who passed it on to her. We can't figure out what happened to David though. I guess it doesn't matter about him any way. We found some stuff that helped us piece together this puzzle."

"What? Where?"

"We found this stuff behind a false wall in the attic," Amy interjected and handed the Sheriff the stack of papers from the trunk.

He began to thumb through them. The color drained from his face when he got to the marriage certificate of Daphne and David Westchester.

"What's wrong Sheriff?"

"Westchester! That's the name of the man Alicia stabbed!"

"Alicia told us," Bonnie explained, "that this S'postu person, who we now know was Robert, made her stab Charles Westchester in revenge for what "his kin" did, at least, that's what she said."

"We all thought she was crazy, at her trial, I mean," Salter was characteristically thinking out loud. " I'll never forget what she said at her trial. How S'postu made her head hurt and then what she yelled at Westchester just before she attacked him. "Your blood for his–this is to avenge S'postu." It was really Robert Howe getting his revenge for his own death. It still sounds crazy."

"Crazy or not," Shawn interjected, "it's what happened."

"The biggest question I have is why did this Robert Howe wait this long to get even with Westchester?"

"That's fairly obvious, isn't it Sheriff?" Shawn chimed in.

"Why do you say that?"

"Alicia is the last of Robert Howe's descendants. She was his last chance for revenge, and ultimately, peace."

The back door opened and the coroner appeared in the doorway.

"Sheriff, may I have a word with you?"

"You may speak freely. Go ahead, tell me what you got."

"Okay. The victim was a male, about, well it's hard to tell…the lye in the plaster really bleached those bones. And the time that has passed, well, my best guess for now, without running any tests, is the victim was in his early thirties, or maybe late twenties. Major trauma to the back of the head. We found a one-inch hole in the back of the skull."

"Any guess as to the murder weapon?"

"No guess. We've found it. A ball-pein hammer, buried with the body. And bits and pieces of what looks like an old wheelchair. I'd say the body had been there for over a century."

"Thanks," Salter could barely speak. "I need that report ASAP."

The coroner nodded, and left the house.

Salter eyed Bonnie. "How did you find all this out?"

"Robert told me. Through my dreams."

# CHAPTER 43

It had been hours since the Sheriff, his deputies, and the coroner left the house. Bonnie was leaning against Shawn on the sofa, Terry and Amy occupied the two chairs facing them. They were talking about the day's events. Bonnie felt totally drained. She looked over to One-night curled up in a ball, sleeping at the end of the couch.

"She looks a little bit more relaxed, but I think she's still on pins and needles."

"I wonder if our room is still cold," Terry said, rising to investigate. He walked over to the bedroom, stuck his head in through the doorway. Upon opening the door, One-night quickly looked over to the lower bedroom, and hissed at the open door. No one paid any attention to the frightened cat.

"I didn't even think about our room," Amy said.

"It's still as cold as a meat locker," Terry said with a disgusted look on his face.

"Of course it is," Bonnie said. "There's still one thing left to do."

"What?" Shawn asked.

"We have to have a funeral," Bonnie answered. "And now we can afford to give him the funeral he deserves."

"He was in the war, right?" Amy asked.

"Yep." Bonnie answered as she went into the kitchen.

"Well how about a—what do they call it when they shoot guns at someone's funeral?"

"A twenty-one gun salute," Shawn answered.

"Well I think we need one of those," Amy said.

Bonnie returned and set the dusty foil package on the table. "This is Robert's funeral money."

For the first time since moving into the house almost a half a year before, Bonnie slept the entire night without any disturbing dreams.

The workday grind seemed even more boring to Shawn, Terry and Amy since the body of Robert Howe was discovered under the house six days before. Shawn was glad when it was time for Terry to pick him up from work. The little four-door pulled up to the curb. Shawn, noticing the front passenger seat was occupied by Amy, opened the passenger rear door and slid in.

"You have any trouble getting off for the funeral tomorrow?" Terry asked.

"No. You?"

"My boss tried to give me a little static," Amy said. "But I managed to straighten him out."

"Terry?" Shawn asked.

"No problemo."

"I wonder how Bonnie is holding up, you know with the funeral being tomorrow and all," Amy queried.

"I called her during both breaks and at lunch. She seems to be doing okay," Shawn responded.

"I guess you're right," Amy said. "It seems to be all she talks about these past few days. The funeral, I mean."

Shawn looked over at Amy. "Don't I know it!" He blew out a breath. "It seems like she almost doesn't know what to do since all this stuff is over."

"Oh," Amy began, tilting her head back, grabbing the back of her neck. "I feel so drained myself. I can only imagine how she feels."

"She doesn't want to talk about it right now. So when we get home, don't say anything about her personal feelings. You can talk about Robert, or S'postu, or whatever you want to call him, all you want, or even Alicia, but don't say anything to Bonnie about herself."

"Why?" Terry asked, as they pulled into their driveway.

"Because she says that this whole thing wasn't about her. It was about him and Alicia, not about us or her. You know how she is."

Terry turned off the engine. "Do you know what we're having for supper?" he asked, trying to change to a less tense subject.

"God, Terry!" Amy exclaimed. "You always think with your stomach, don't you?"

They laughed nervously as they went into the house, each trying to act as if there was nothing wrong. Yet strangely, all felt apprehensive about the next day's events.

# CHAPTER 44

"Good mornin' Miss 'licia," Nathan's cheery voice brought Alicia out of sleep. She opened her eyes to see his silhouette backlit by the flourescent lights in the hall. Nathan walked over to her bed to help her sit up. Over the past few days, it had been getting increasingly difficult for her to move. The doctor had attributed her deteriorating condition to her mild heart attack a week before, but Alicia knew better. Since the discovery of S'postu under the house, and the subsequent removal of his remains, she felt as if his spirit had left her, leaving only a frail shell behind.

"The funeral is in two hours. I know how much this means to you. And even though Doc Adcox wants you to stay here, confined to your bed, I got a plan going to get you out of here so you can go."

Alicia's face lit up as the thought gave her a sudden burst of strength. She smiled as she swung her legs over the edge of the bed. Nathan moved quickly to close the door. After a quick sponge bath, Nathan helped her put on a black dress he had stashed in her closet the day before. After she was dressed, he slipped on her bathrobe over her clothes. She sat in a wheelchair, Nathan draping a blanket over her lap to dangle low enough to cover her shoes, then wheeled her into the hall on his way to the dining room. Beads of sweat appeared on his forehead. He looked around to see if any of the nursing staff had noticed. To his amazement, no one gave them a second look. It was perfectly normal for a nurse, dressed in surgical greens, to be wheeling a patient through the halls. He wheeled her into the empty dining room, stopping at the swinging doors leading into the kitchen. Leaving her alone for a second, Nathan checked to make sure the kitchen was empty. He was delighted that his plan was coming together. Earlier that morning, he had posted a sign for the office staff to have a meeting at 9:00 a.m. in the employee lounge. There, of course, was no official meeting, but the disinformation strategy worked well enough to have the kitchen abandoned long enough for him to pull off what was, in effect, a jail break.

"The coast is clear," Nathan whispered as he helped her out of the chair, shuffling her through the deserted kitchen and out the delivery door. It was the only other door except the front door at the facility not monitored by guards. He helped her into his car waiting at the loading dock, and soon Alicia saw the outside of the building for the first time in fourteen years. She watched the building get smaller as they drove away, and was reminded of the time she watched her house grow more and more distant the day she was arrested. And how she got the feeling she would never see home again. She turned quickly to face the road, realizing that she had come to feel the institute was indeed home.

They turned on Highway 331 and headed south, stopping at a small church with a cemetery across the road. Nathan pulled into the small church parking lot and parked next to a small white car. Nathan helped Alicia out of the car and across the street to a small group of people waiting in the cemetery next to an open grave. She immediately recognized her four young friends. A minister stood behind them along with seven people dressed in Civil War uniforms, bearing Civil War era rifles. The group waited in silence for Alicia to join them. Alicia felt increasingly weak with each step she took toward the grave site. Nathan held her firmly on her left, but she could feel him fatigue under the extra strain. Suddenly, she felt the pressure of another strong arm helping her along.

"I got you, too," came the gentle voice of Sheriff Salter. "I should be arresting you and Nathan both, since they've issued an A.P.B. on you two."

"What?" Nathan asked. He knew what he had done was wrong, but never really considered the ramifications of his actions if they were caught.

"Don't worry," Salter said, "there has already been enough injustice where Alicia is concerned. And history won't repeat itself this time. But after this funeral you get her back to that institute fast. Do you understand?"

"Yessir," Nathan answered.

As if on cue, the minister began, "My friends, we are gathered here today to lay to rest a man named Robert Howe. Son of Lester and Nelda Howe, Robert died over one hundred and fifty years ago at the hands of another. Surviving is his only known relative, Alicia Freed. We grieve for Robert not only for his death, or the time when he was forgotten kin, but for the century he endured before he could be laid to rest. Although none of us knew him personally, we have records of his courageous contribution to the history of this great nation. Robert, we commit you to the ground on this day with the honors of a hero…"

The minister's words grew faint in Alicia's ears. Mild nausea swept over her. She could feel her skin grow cold and clammy. A familiar voice masked that of the minister. She could still hear the eulogy, but only in the background, like the gentle breeze that rustled the leafless trees around her.

"Thank you, my child," S'postu's voice echoed softly in her ears. She bent her head, covering her face with trembling hands. She hoped everyone else would think she was crying.

"S'postu, are we right? Are you Robert Howe?" Her voice reflected back off of her hands, sounding strange in her ears.

"I am."

"You are my great-grandfather."

"Yes. You have unlocked me from my prison. I have you and the others to thank for my peace. Bad blood was set right by good blood."

"S'postu? Why did you leave me all those years?"

"I must go now, my child."

"Where?"

"To where I should have gone long ago. Good-bye, my child."

"S'postu," Alicia took her hands from her face. "S'postu!" she said louder. "I can't lose you again." It was as if the blood suddenly rushed from her head, leaving her feeling woozy. A thin trail of blood trickled from her nose. Nathan, seeing this, took a handkerchief from his hip pocket and wiped her face. The casket was lowered into the grave.

"Ashes to ashes, dust to dust. We lay Robert to his final resting place, next to his parents." The minister's voice was clear again in her head. Alicia was now very weak, as if her age suddenly caught up with her. She started to collapse. Nathan reached over to catch her.

"We need to get you back." Nathan and Sheriff Salter helped her across the street to Nathan's car.

"I'll take her back now, Sheriff."

"Okay. I'll follow you."

As the minister threw a shovel full of dirt onto the casket, now sitting at the bottom of the grave, Bonnie turned to see Nathan's car, followed by Sheriff Salter's, pull out of the church parking lot and head in the direction of the institute. Bonnie jumped at the sound of seven rifles, fired in unison. A bugle blew taps. A second volley of shots was fired, the echo ricocheting off the surrounding hillsides. As taps was concluding, a third and final volley of shots was fired by the men in Civil War uniforms. Bonnie noticed for the first time, that the man who played the bugle wore a Union army uniform. The men who fired the salute wore alternating Confederate and Union army uniforms. Four each. Wordlessly, Bonnie and Shawn, followed by Amy and Terry, walked across the street to the Cavalier in the church parking lot.

Nathan pulled up next to the front door of the institute. Salter stopped his car right behind Nathan's.

All during the trip back, Alicia felt herself slipping into a state much like that of her first trip to this building. She felt out of place, with no sense of belonging, utterly alone. The Sheriff opened the car door. Feebly, she swung her legs over the edge of the seat to rest her feet on the ground. She attempted to stand but didn't have the strength. Salter, joined by Nathan, helped her out of the car. With Nathan on the right, and Salter on the left, they made their way to the front door. Alicia found each step more difficult than the last. Suddenly, she clutched at her chest. The pain was overwhelming, and she could not breathe.

"Alicia, what's wrong?!!" Nathan screamed. "Call the E.M.T.'s!"

She began to collapse on the threshold of the door. She lay on the ground looking at Nathan and Sheriff Salter kneeling beside her. She could hear the footsteps of the E.M.T.'s as they ran toward her. The daylight began to fade into darkness. The sounds faded into silence. The life drained out of Alicia Freed.

"No..." Nathan cried. "Don't die..." He began C.P.R.

"It's too late," Salter said. "She's gone."

"I'm glad it's finally over," Amy said as she opened the back door of the house. She stopped to look at Bonnie. "It is over, isn't it?"

As Bonnie entered the kitchen she felt peace in the house for the first time, along with a strange emptiness. They all followed her into the living room. Bonnie noticed the bedroom door standing open. She could see One-night lay sleeping on Terry and Amy's bed. She walked to the room, and crossed the threshold, expecting to feel the traditional cold blast of air, but instead found the air as warm as the rest of the house. She smiled as she picked up the purring cat off the bed. Carrying her into the living room, she held the cat close to her chest. Before she could answer Amy, a knock sounded at the back door.

"Who could that be?" Terry asked.

"It's your mom," Shawn answered as he opened the door.

"I have been trying to call you all morning."

"What's wrong, Mom?" Bonnie asked as they sat at the dining room table. "Why are you here?"

"Oh, Bonnie. I need to talk to you alone."

"Okay, we can talk in my room." Bonnie led her upstairs.

Bonnie's mom wiped her eyes. "I had to show you—I had to tell you how much your dad loved me—how much he loved you."

"Of course he did, Mom."

"No, no, you don't understand." she handed her a folded piece of paper. "I found this in an old trunk in the attic."

"It looks like an itemized statement from the hospital." Bonnie said.

"Yes, but look at what he had done!" Bonnie's Mom sobbed.

"He had a vasectomy," Bonnie read.

"Yes, but look at the date."

Bonnie went pale. "This is dated three years before I was born!"

"I can't keep this a secret any longer. Before we got married we used to argue about kids. He didn't want any. Then shortly after we got married, your dad and I almost divorced. He used to drink. He'd drink and get violent but he loved me so much and I couldn't see it back then. He used to travel as a salesman for days at a time and I thought he was seeing other women. So, to get back at him I had an affair with my boss."

"What?"

"Let me finish or I'll never be able to get it out. The man I was seeing committed suicide when his wife found out. That was after I'd already broken up with him. Your dad never did have an affair and I never knew about his operation. Don't you see how much your dad loved you? He raised you as his own flesh and blood all along knowing what I had done and never said a word. You brought such joy to his life."

"What is my real father's name?" Bonnie could barely ask.

"Charles Westchester Jr."